WRAITH KNIGHT

THREE WORLDS
I

C.T. PHIPPS

RAGNAROK
PUBLICATIONS
CRESTVIEW HILLS, KENTUCKY

WRAITH KNIGHT
Ragnarok Publications | www.ragnarokpub.com
Editor In Chief: Tim Marquitz | Publisher: J.M. Martin
Wraith Knight is copyright © 2016 by C.T. Phipps.
All rights reserved.

Published by Ragnarok Publications, LLC
206 College Park Drive, Ste. 1
Crestview Hills, KY 41017

ISBN-13: 9781941987780
Worldwide Rights
Created in the United States of America

Editor: Tim Marquitz
Associate Publisher: Melanie R. Meadors
Publishers Assistant: Gwendolyn Nix
Cover Illustration: Alex Raspad
Graphic Design Coordinator: Shawn T. King

CHAPTER 1

Snowflakes fell as I stood surrounded by frozen stone on the peak of a mountain. My body stretched outward, hunched over the hilt of a sword blade. Snow heaped up to my calves. I had no notion of how I'd gotten there, where in the World Between I was, or what my purpose here could be.

Indeed, I had no real conscious thought at all, only memories and feelings.

I remembered life.

My absent mother. My cruel sire.

An unhappy parting. Training in the Grand Temple.

I remembered love.

A woman's face with black eyes and skin the color of chestnuts. I remembered her touch and the forbidden joys we'd found together in each other's arms. Her name. *Jassa.*

I remembered sunlight. The brilliant, gentle rays of it against my face.

Knighthood. The hammering of the forge. Battle.

Blood and screams of pain, metal on metal, metal on meat, crashing, maiming, Formor battling sidhe, the deathless hounding the living, Lightborn and Shadowkind on two sides of a great melee. I remembered using the magic sword I'd enchanted with the divine sorcery I'd learned as a Temple Knight to shatter the blade of a deathless shade. I remembered ending that creature and challenging its master.

Then pain, followed by darkness.

Immense, immeasurable, unendurable darkness.

Was I dead?

If so, why was I not in the World Above? I'd followed the Path all my life, even dedicating myself to the Grand Temple at Warmaster Kalian's behest. I believed in the Lawgiver, the Peace-Weavers who were his son and daughter, and the Great Mother amongst the other Gods Above. Yet, for all my vivid recollection of dying, I was most certainly not in the City of Light nor the endless gardens promised to the faithful.

It was…painful.

Slowly, the memories and images formed a coherent pattern. I knew who I was, possessed most of my memories, and had a sense of reason. There were large holes in my identity, though, like a mosaic missing a quarter of its tiles. I shook away those thoughts, deciding I was not dead since I was moving around the top of a mountain.

I struggled to remember more but the blackness formed an impenetrable wall. After a few minutes more of trying and failing to recall anything beyond that battle, I decided to take a moment and think about my situation. Despite being on top of a mountain, I did not feel in the slightest bit cold, but that told me nothing. There were many spells which could guard against the winter's chill.

Looking down, I saw my hands covered in studded black gloves made of a peculiar sort of material I'd never yet seen before. A heavy cloak mantled my shoulders. A hood shrouded my face. I wore boots designed more to stamp than to stride and coarse robes covering all the rest of me, belted in battered leather.

My right hand still clutched the grip of a curved black demonsteel sword, almost beautiful for all that its edges were notched and toothy. Frost runes of immense power were engraved across its sides, beautiful in their terribleness. The blade shimmered in the moonlight of the Peace-Weavers above and possessed an eerie pale blue aura of witchfire. I forced my hand to open and the blade stood erect in the snow in spite of the wind and its curved shape. I'd seen weapons like it before but only once or twice in my lifetime.

The memories cut deep into my recollection, even in my current state of confusion.

Oh no.

I reached up to touch my face, worried I'd gouge myself with the studded gloves.

But I had no face.

And I knew why.

I was a Wraith Knight, one of the four Dark Lords of the King Below.

Shit.

How is one supposed to react to the discovery you're a monster out of children's story? For the past thousand years, the King Below and the Dark Lords had been a curse on the Southern Kingdoms. Over and over again, they'd risen to devastate the land with their armies. Usually, they'd been beaten back with great cost to all the races of men but not always.

Always had the Wraith Knights been the King Below's chosen four, their names each burned into the minds of children and shared over fires at campsites. I had become one, perhaps because I was one of the few to have laid one low. A monster I had met on the fields of battle only to cast him down.

Kurag Shadowweaver.

I'd killed him.

Or so I thought.

Glancing over at the sword beside me, I saw it to be identical to the one wielded by that terrible creature. I'd shattered Kurag's sword, what poets called Chill's Fury, and the creature had withered away into nothingness. I had awoken with that very sword held in my hand as naturally as though it were mine own.

Had I somehow *become* Kurag?

"*No*," I said, my voice sounding like an echo from beyond the grave. "*I am Jacob Riverson, Knight Paramount of the Shadowguard.*"

But was I?

Jacob the Fisherman's son, the bastard slave turned warlord, seemed like a dream now. I remembered how my sire had sold me to Kailin as a slave, how my master had freed me as part of his religious conversion, and how I'd ended up in the Grand Temple's service.

I recalled my stolen time with Jassa in the hidden nooks of that courtyard between the Temple Guard Barracks and the Priestesses Chambers. All the years before my disgrace and atonement as one of the Shadowguard.

The memories came hot and thick now, threatening to drown me. There were gaps after that. Long ones. Flashes of important people, meetings, general strategy, politics, and nothingness.

Then death. Sudden death on the same fields I'd slain Kurag.

Killed by the King Below himself.

Gods Above and Below.

The memory of the King Below's giant hellish sword piercing my chest threatened to overwhelm me. The God of Evil had been a warrior, nine-feet-tall, made of living darkness and armed in icy black armor harder than adamant. I'd been a fool, trying to fight the invincible, but it had been to protect the fallen form of Edorta Tremor, Warlord of the Southern League. It was a choice which had resulted in my death.

What a jest this was. After achieving a victory against one of the great evils of our history, I'd fallen in battle only to be raised up again as his replacement. Wraith Knights weren't invincible. Several times, they'd been reported killed, only for these same beings to rise again. How *humorous* humanity had assumed they were all immortal when it was merely their evil master replacing them with whatever soldier had killed them. The Trickster had been having a joke on us this entire time. After all, one hooded ghost looks the same as another.

"I must destroy myself," I whispered.

I'd witnessed the King Below's power over the dead. He'd called forth the souls of those who fell in battle to aid him. If I was free from his control, it was only a matter of time before he resumed it. I did not know whether I would go to the World Above or Below but either was better than preying on the living.

Walking over to the place Kurag's sword still stood, I grabbed it by the hand and placed its hilt on the ground while aiming the blade where my heart should be. As a ghost, it didn't technically matter where I struck, but I figured I'd go with the traditional suicide method for a disgraced soldier.

"Courage, honor, duty," I whispered the words of the Shadowguard. I steeled myself against all fear with the thought of Jassa, struggling to believe this honored her whether she was alive or dead. Though we were never married—such things forbidden by our vows—I held her to be my wife. I tried to throw myself on my blade but, no matter how hard I willed it, my body did not move an inch. No matter how hard I tried.

"Bastards and hellspawn!" I cursed, knocking Chill's Fury aside. *"You are a coward and a fool."*

A voice from the shadows spoke, "As cowardly as any man who wants to live."

I turned around and stared at the figure which greeted me. He seemed a lad with not above twenty years to his name, impish in feature and wearing something too wicked to be a smile under eyes which gave the lie to the youth he pretended. He was clad in sage-green and sable clothing, motley like a court jester from the bells of his collar to the points of his shoes.

I stared at him, wondering where such a comical figure had come from. "Gods Below, are you?"

"Asked and answered, Wraith Knight," the figure said. "But do you not recognize your master?"

I did.

I snapped up Chill's Fury and turned it upon him. "Back to the shadows, fou—"

The figure snapped his fingers and my sword became a bouquet of withered black roses. I tossed the useless item aside. It turned back to its original form in the snow, if it had ever turned in the first place outside of my head.

"*You are the Trickster*," I growled, staring at him. "*The form the King Below takes when he wishes to sew mischief and lead men's souls astray.*"

The Trickster grinned. "As if men have ever needed me to lead them astray! I play out my part in the universe for the young races, as does Old Man Law, my brother. You should thank me, Fisherman's bastard, for I provide mortals the opportunity to strive against something wicked. I provide the contrast which allows men to speak of good and evil, honor and dishonor, order and chaos."

"*Release me from this cursed torment, fiend. I will not be your puppet.*"

"You have been my puppet for two hundred and fifty-two years, six months and three days. Two Ages and a half, roughly."

I stared at him, a second wave of dawning horror passing over my body in as many minutes. "*No.*"

"Oh Yes."

"*Jassa—*"

"Is dust and memory, I imagine. If it's any consolation she undoubtedly mourned, moved on, and had many fat little brats who

went on to do the same. Mortal love tends to go like that. They forget. It requires a truly immortal being to carry a torch for their loved ones across the ages as you have."

I fell to the ground, wishing I could weep.

"Oh don't be like that. I'd not have unleashed you if I had known it would lead to such maudlin *sentiment*."

"*You freed me?*" I asked, confused and appalled at once.

"I retreated to my black throne after casting down Emperor Edorta during the Fourth Great Shadow War." The Trickster paused, looking to the sky. "I rebuilt my armies, planned and plotted until it seemed mortals had forgotten their gods needed devotion, then I launched my fifth invasion. This time, you won."

"*We...won?*" I was too put off by the Trickster's causal manner to respond.

"Yes, I'm dead. At least the King Below is dead," the Trickster said, giving a short clap and something almost a smile. "My brother sent a vision of a holy sword and a cup, or perchance it was a cauldron, I forget, and a band of ruffians called the Nine Heroes claimed them. The Dark Lords were defeated, save yourself, and I was struck down. My evil was ended and armies scattered. There was a bit with some gryphons and a crowning. It was all very beautiful and poetic."

I pointed at him, paused to take in that rush of recollection, then looked at him sideways. "*Uhm...*"

"You mean, how can I still stand before you in spirit?"
"*Yes.*"

"I, of course, am eternal." The Trickster shrugged then gestured to the sky. "But King Below had become a tired jest. It's hard to embody cruelty and tyranny, no matter how many victories you have to your name, when you must *always* be driven back. I am laying said identity to rest. I shall craft a new one when time permits me and mankind needs some new villain to blame for their problems. That is, after all, my purpose. You mortals would destroy yourselves if not sufficiently distracted."

I was disgusted by his blasphemous claim. "I refuse to believe the last thousand years and ten Ages have been a *farce* put on by you and the Lawgiver!" I was surprised to find my voice sounded almost normal.

Everything seemed crisper and sharper.

And colder.

I edged my gloves up to discover I had a face again.

The Trickster looked as amused as ever. "I'm pleased to see you remember how to put on a human semblance, even if it's only because you're too angry to go without substance enough to strike me."

I was too confused to respond. I felt my face, stunned by its sudden appearance. The spikes in my gloves hurt but even that feeling was welcome.

"You need to get the blood pumping, so to speak." The Trickster put his hands on his hips. "As for a farce, you should try and imagine it from my perspective. What else could mortal lives be *but* a joke?"

I picked up Chill's Fury off the ground and sheathed it. "I will no longer listen to this nonsense."

"You speak as if you have a choice. Your willfulness is an indulgence I am offering you because of recent inconveniences. Take no great comfort from your new form either," the Trickster said, pulling out a pan pipe and giving it a whistle. "Blood is the only path to something akin to life and you will need to shed it copiously to enjoy much by way of mortal pleasures. Not that you ever had a problem with such in life."

"What game do you play, spirit?" I asked, wishing he'd send me off to the World Above or Below rather than toy with me.

The Trickster stared with cold sapphire eyes. *"Humanity is ruining my demise."*

"Such a tragedy," I said, daring sarcasm to the God of Evil.

"All of the Fir-Bolg, giants, men, and sidhe were united against me. Even Trow and Spiderfolk joined the alliance to upset me. Only the Formor remained entirely loyal, which was touching albeit pathetic. It was the perfect end to my reign." The Trickster wrinkled his nose.

"The epilogue leaves something to be desired, however. Victory hasn't ushered in an age of peace and cooperation but rather petty ambitions. I want you, Wraith Knight, to be the instrument which brings the Nine Heroes to ruin and take my place as mankind's bane."

This was ludicrous. "Forgive me if I do not accept such an honor."

"What if I offered to raise you back to manhood and turn your lover's memory into substance? I'm *quite good* at offering temptations be they kingdoms, consorts, gold, or glory. Nefras, the Dark Lord of Lusts could tell you such stories had oblivion not swallowed her up."

"Leave now, demon, and trouble me no more."

The Trickster shrugged. "Methinks you'll change your mind soon enough. One man's villain is another man's hero. In the meantime, this discourse bores me. It needs more ... fire."

That was when I heard the shrieking roar of a dragon. Turning around, I saw a brown beast twenty feet wide in the wings, with a body half as long set between them.

It was a Lesser Brown, what the people of my village called a Goateater. It had a head too small to swallow a goat whole, but a belly big enough to eat a whole herd at a sitting. Upon its back, I saw a knight swaddled with leather and decked out with silver clasping a golden goad-spear. Right before the creature under them opened up its mouth as if to breathe out a great fury of flame down upon me.

CHAPTER 2

Much to my surprise, I saw the brown dragon turn its head and fire a column of roaring flame at a *second* dragon coming up behind it.

The second dragon was a Great Blue, what the Grand Temple termed a Storm Dragon. It was easily twice the size of its quarry, showing exactly why any dragon could be referred to as 'lesser.'

A Goateater was an impressive creature on its own but compared to the forty-foot monstrosity behind it, it might have as well have been a child. I was surprised to see a trio of men riding on the Storm Dragon's back, wearing golden armor in contrast to their quarry's rider's silver. Much to my surprise, I discovered my vision was able to narrow in on them as if I was looking through a spyglass.

It seemed being dead had its advantages, because I could make out every little detail of their gilded, gaudy armor. I blinked when I saw the painted symbol of the Shadowguard on their shoulders. Normally, the sacred compass and serpent was drawn in the plainest of fashion but this was surrounded with flowers and griffons. The symbol was unmistakable, however. To see it used as decor for such silly ornamental armor was revolting.

The Shadowguard were a humble order of poor knights and yeoman who guarded the Southern Kingdoms against the horrors from the Northern Wasteland. We hunted Formor, trow, spiderfolk, ghosts, ghouls, demons, and other cursed creatures. We sported no heraldry, flew black banners, wore black hooded cloaks, and plain steel armor. Who were these shining peacocks? Surely, they were not my brothers in this time.

Looking to the rider of the Lesser Brown, who was maneuvering the creature with effortless grace, I tried to get a glimpse of their identity. Much to my surprise, I saw she was a woman with a mane of silver-white hair flowing from underneath her helmet. Female warriors were not unknown in my time, mostly amongst the sidhe or Fir-Bolg, but I'd only known a few in the Shadowguard.

"Much has changed since you fell for the first time." The Trickster leaned in over my shoulder, causing me to recoil. "I think you'll find her...interesting."

"She is probably a criminal." I reassured myself. I didn't want to become involved without knowing all the facts and the Trickster's goads weren't helping.

"Crime is determined by the King and Queen. Who may be good or evil, depending on your perspective."

"The King is law," I countered.

"And yet *I* am a King."

I did not have a response for that as the Lesser Brown was struck by flames which set its lower half alight before the Great Blue moved its claws to rip its wings away, denying the mystically flying creature its ability to navigate.

As a final stroke, the Great Blue grabbed its neck in its jaws and clamped down hard. I had seen only a few dragon-fights in my time and they were uniformly vicious cruel things. I felt sorry for the woman on the Lesser Brown for there was nothing I could do for her now.

"Or so you tell yourself," the Trickster said, lifting up a small black iron ring. It was shaped like a circle of rose stems, thorny and unfeeling. He flicked it like a coin at me. "Your symbol of office."

I instinctively caught the item and slipped it on my left middle finger. I wouldn't normally have done this but did so without thinking.

The Trickster pointed at my chest. "It will open the way to the Tower of Everfrost and there you shall find the Crown of Weeping Gods. If you wish to follow my path, Dark Lord, that way is open. If you ever choose to opt out, well, you just have to muster enough courage to fall on your sword."

"Leave me be!"

The Trickster faded away, leaving only shadows and ice around me. Right before the Lesser Brown flew over my head and collapsed with a titanic thud against the side of the mountain. The entire mountain shook as if reacting to the passing of such a magnificent beast.

Dragons were unintelligent, ones possessed by the King Below's demons aside, but they were the greatest of the Lawgiver's creatures. Dragon-taming had been a new art during my time, begun by Gladys Stonebrooke, so it was doubly disconcerting to see Shadowguard so causally wasting the beings who had helped turn the tide against the King Below.

Looking down at the dead or dying beast below, I was stunned to see the rider crawling up from over its side. Unlike the other group, her silver armor was dented and showed signs of being repaired multiple times. The armor's too-bright nature offended me but it at least had the look of a warrior's armor, however decorated.

The woman was in her mid-twenties, horribly injured, and likely suffering several cracked ribs. Something about my senses could tell she was close to the edge of death. It was said the Dark Lords could sense when a person was close to death and derive power from it, I did not know of such things but I could tell she was not long for this world unless she received healing magic. I knew such spells but would they work in my present state? I didn't know.

The woman spotted me, at least to the point she waved to me. "Arcus Maeharl!"

The words shook me to the core.

Old Terralan for *Shadow Aid, My Brother*.

It was a plea from one Shadowguardsman to another. I did not know how she knew me to be one or whether she simply mistook my attire in the snowy landscape for that of our orders' cloak, but it was the most sacred plea of our kind. Each and every Shadowguardsman was bound to honor such an oath.

Yet, I was an undead monster and these were dressed as Shadowguardsmen.

Did my oath apply to aid in such a case?

Did my oaths even *matter* anymore?

I looked to the sky and saw the Great Blue was coming around for another pass to finish off the woman and her dragon.

I made my decision in that moment. Drawing Chill's Fury, I lifted it into the air and shouted, "Arcus Maeharl!"

I felt my human semblance fall away and be replaced once more with the black visage of a Wraith Knight. A terrible black power grew within my breast as I decided to kill the Great Blue and its riders. It was as if there was a hungry evil within that desired to lives of the living and I had gained its attention at last.

A whirlwind in the back of my mind was filled with every dark spell, curse, and incantation I'd learned across two centuries of service. I instinctively knew this form had experienced war like no living man, practiced on the living of every nation. Holding my blade, I remembered being trained in its use by the other Dark Lords, beings only slightly less terrible than the King Below. They had also taught me secrets of Dark and Twilight magic which would put the greatest of fallen wizards to shame.

I would use that power for good.

Feeling the terrible energy within, a single word crystalized in my head, one which gathered all of the magic within my body. Aiming my sword at the Great Blue's chest, I spoke the word with a raspy hiss. It was Demonspeak and the very sound of it warped the fabric of the universe, twisting it and defacing it into something unrecognizable.

Still, I spoke it.

A terrible power left me, surging forward as a bolt of black reality-tearing lightning and striking the blue dragon in the chest. Yet, I was the first one to feel pain rather than the dragon. I felt like my newly-created skin was being ripped from my body. I was diminished, weaker, less substantial, and it was in that moment I realized there was a terrible price for the Wraith Knights' famous powers. The Dark Lords were ghosts. Beings composed of stolen life and magic, so when they unleashed their strength, they lost some of it. One who used too much would fade away to nothingness. I would have been happy to do so if not for the fact I was needed.

"*Stay alive, for whatever that's worth,*" I whispered to myself. "*For now at least.*"

My curse, meanwhile, had struck home.

The Great Blue roared backwards, the black lightning moving up and down its body like sparks on a burning log. The dragon twisted and thrashed, throwing one of its riders down past the side of the mountaintops to the valleys far below. The creature did not die, however, but belched forth flame and fire in every direction.

A glob of flaming phlegm landed beside me and created a brilliant white-gold pyre. The flames caused me to jump backward as they seemed to seek out my cloak and clothing, driving away the magic which kept me alive. Fire was one of the few ways to destroy a solid ghost, I'd used it often enough as a member of the Shadowguard, so it stood to reason a Wraith Knight would be vulnerable too.

I moved away from the flames, once more cursing myself for my refusal to die. Raising my left hand, I concentrated and a composite bow formed of shadows appeared in my hands. Conjuring a shaft of deepest midnight, I aimed at the dragon's swinging head and fired.

The bolt homed in despite its rapid movement and pierced the size of its scales. It let out another roar while its riders struggled to regain control. I put three more shafts of the cursed black arrows into the snout of the beast. It was terrifying, really, watching the creature's pain.

I'd taken a Wraith Knight's arrow once during battle and spent the next month feverish and delusional, gripped by a madness which only the ancient arts of the sidhe had been able to keep me from succumbing to. I couldn't help but wonder as I continued to pepper the creature, how many innocents I'd killed on behalf of the King Below.

One was too many.

My thoughts were interrupted by the dragon throwing off the control of its riders and bearing down directly at me. The Great Blue stretched out its claws and threw up its tail, opening its arrow-filled mouth as if to swallow me whole. The two remaining riders struggled to hold on as it rushed at me.

"Bastards and hellspawn," I muttered, leaping over the side of the peak and down the snowy sides.

The Great Blue smashed into the peak, causing it to explode behind me in a shower of ice and rock. Flames exploded from the dragon's mouth, dribbling down and setting fire to what was otherwise snowy-filled rock. Steam clouds burst everywhere as the creature lifted its head to shoot forth a column of flame at me.

That was when I ran up at it, leapt in the air, landed on its snout and plunged my blade into its left eye, driving it forward to the handle. As the weapon buried itself in the dragon's brain, I felt its life-force pass unto me.

Oh gods, *the power*!

If I had a hundred years and the tongue of a poet, I could not describe for you the sense of rapturous bliss which was the dragon's energy. The sense of fading away passed and my spectral frame grew solid again. It was an insidious trap the King Below had given his servants.

Kill to live.

Live and kill.

Gods Above, I could *taste* the air and wind.

That was when I heard the words, "Blasphemous creature! Pit spawn! I shall send your unholy spirit to your master!"

The accent was heavy and while we spoke the same language, it was a bit hard to follow. The language of the Anessian Empire seemed to have changed in the past two centuries. I turned to face the two surviving dragon riders who were rising from the back of their now-slain mount.

My initial impression of them as shining peacocks by their heavily styled hair, face-paint, and gold earrings. The last person, man or woman, I'd seen dolled up like that had been Gariss the Gallant and he'd had the decency to wear proper Shadowguard attire. That was when my new senses saw something invisible to the naked eye, woven into their armor. They glowed with an eerie red aura, radiating magic which drained away my power as they approached.

Blood runes.

The very sight of them nauseated me and made me wonder if this was all some sort of illusion or dream because such was preferable to the truth. Blood runes were magic forbidden across almost the whole of the Southern Kingdoms and practiced only by the heathen magicians of Natariss. Each rune required a human sacrifice to create, their life-force captured at death and woven into the symbol. Natariss mages preferred to use the innocent as they believed it made the magic holier. Prince Eric the Unsteady had wielded a sword called Hopebringer, a blade created from the sacrifice of children.

And I saw a *dozen* such runes on their armor.

"For the Lawgiver!" the first of them said, drawing his blade and then coating it in a glowing white sheet of fire. He had called upon a spell spoken with the mind called *Saint Roland's Flame*. Such a spell made weapons far deadlier to creatures of shadows. The man behind him did the same.

"You dare speak the Lawgiver's name wearing such foulness!?" my voice sounded like the wailing of the damned. *"I send thee to the World Below!"*

I stepped forward and our swords met with sparks flying from dark magic meeting light. They both moved forward to double-team me and it was to their credit both men fought like Masters. Only the fact I'd been trained for centuries and men like Warmaster Kailin had taught me tricks for keeping warriors off balance kept me from being overwhelmed at once.

Even so, their skill only increased my irritation for they did not fight like men accustomed to battling Shadowkind. No, their training and skill was in fighting men with swords. I wondered who the guard had been fighting these past centuries or whether they'd joined later on. Either way, I knew the best response to being outnumbered in a duel: reduce their number.

I kicked one in the stomach, grabbed him by the neck and slit his throat with Chill's Fury. The sight horrified his companion, who did not take advantage of the situation to run us both through. I then tossed the bleeding frame of his compatriot into him. The other man instinctively caught him. So I charged and knocked them both over the side of the cliff face. The pair fell forty-feet off the side and landed on an outcropping below. If the pair weren't already dead, they soon would be. It was a callous way to win a victory, but victory nonetheless.

A victory over three of my fellow Shadowguard and their dragon.

What had I done?

CHAPTER 3

Walking away from the dead Great Blue, I tried to put into context what just happened. I had killed three Shadowguards and a dragon. I wasn't sure which was the more shocking. Too much had happened in the past hour for me to comprehend. My memory was still weak and absorbing the dragon's life force made a series of images flash across my mind like walking down a hall of portraits.

I saw Prince Eric, wielding Hopebringer above his head, and causing those who looked upon it to be enthralled.

I saw the Royal Dragons unleash flame and doom onto the slums of the Imperial City, purging them of rioters.

I saw Jassa no longer clad in the holy vestments of a Great Mother priestess but the royal robes of a Great Wizard.

I saw that madman and prophet, Valance the Red, preaching of the sinfulness of the Anessian Empire and its need to be purged with fire.

I saw two brutally-stabbed young girls, angelic in appearance with dark hair and skin like the High Men of Old, lying in a sacrificial circle in the basement of the Grand Temple.

A glowing white hand, radiating cold like the heart of a blizzard, reaching out to grab my throat.

I saw...

I saw...

Blackness.

I fell once more to my knees and stumbled against the snow, trying to make sense of what my conscious mind refused to remember. My history was a foggy battlefield and I was being forced to march through it. I focused on what I did know: I'd joined with the Shadowguard to do battle with the King Below's armies, slew Kurag, died at the King Below's hands, been raised as a Wraith Knight, and it was now two-and-a half centuries later. The King Below was dead, or so he claimed as strange as that was, and individuals called the Nine Heroes had done the deed. I should have been comforted by the fact that the God of Evil was defeated but the Trickster taunted me with its continuing existence. I supposed one could not defeat a being like the King Below forever. Darkness like that was beyond any mortal to defeat.

None of this told me what was going on, what I was supposed to do, or how to do it. I needed more details, more knowledge of what had come to pass. The best place to start was with the person I just rescued.

Rising to my feet, I continued to walk forward to the fallen form of the Lesser Brown. The female warrior rose to her feet and held a broken sword toward me. Once, the weapon might have contained magic, but it was long past. Her helmet was to one side and her long flowed in the snowy winds.

The woman was surpassingly lovely with perfect teeth, elfin features, marble-like skin, almost iridescent catlike green eyes, and hair which shown like strands of silver. The only quality which marred her otherwise perfect features was the fact her nose had been broken a number of times.

It was an admirable quality, like the damage her armor possessed, showing she'd actually put herself to use in the Shadowguard's service. The woman was favoring her right side and I could tell she was bleeding badly from a wound there. My unnatural senses could tell she also had cracked ribs as well as a sprained ankle.

I admired her scars and practiced fighting stance more than her beauty because it was the attractiveness of an elfblooded. The sidhe had long lived beside humanity, immortal and perfect, but condescending. Too often, humanity raised these children up as if demigods, treating their unnatural attractiveness and longevity as if a blessing from the gods. In short, I'd always found them to be *too* pretty to be attractive.

"Begone, Dark Lord, or I will strike you down!" The woman said, waving her broken blade. "The retching stench of your necromancy befouls the air I breathe."

I stared at her, my voice closer to my original but deeper and throatier. "In my day, we spoke with less insolence to our rescuers."

"I need no help from a creature of—" The woman collapsed to one knee, her injuries getting to her. "Ugh. I mean to say I did not recognize you as a creature of the King Below when I called out to you. I had thought your kind ended with the passing of your master. I cannot defeat you in my present shape but know I will wound you if I may." The woman ended her speech in a wracking series of cough.

"You've been stabbed well. You will not survive long. I am sorry."

"I will not die. I have a purpose I must fulfill," the woman said between coughs.

The fact she'd managed to fly a dragon despite this amazed me. Only sheer determination and willpower must have kept her going after the fight she'd been in. A practiced healer might be able to save her life but it would be months in recovery and I was inclined to believe light magic was beyond me now.

Searching my fragmented memories, I sought some way to save her life. I'd already called upon the powers of darkness to defeat the dragon and his riders, so it seemed foolish to hesitate now. Still, I couldn't help but wonder why I was so easy to pursue such an option. Did my current state dull or perhaps remove my conscience? I couldn't say.

Yes, go ahead, blame my influence. Everyone else does. I could hear the Trickster laughing in the back of my head.

Curse him.

Searching my disjointed fragmented memories, I found a spell which could heal her but it was like all medicinal magic of the King Below: painful and bloody.

So be it.

"No, you will not die," I said. Opening my hand, I closed it into a fist and spoke the healing magic's words.

The woman screamed. It was terrible to watch her bones knit, her wounds seal, and her body to produce new blood as the stolen life essence moved through her body.

But it worked.

The woman blinked, looking up. Recognition of what I'd done passed across her face. "You healed me?"

"Yes."

"*Why?*"

"Why not?"

"Because you're a Wraith Knight and likely eat infants for supper?"

"I sincerely hope that is not the case."

The woman stood up and said, "I am Regina Whitetremor. Knight-Captain of the Shadowguard. I am sworn to destroy your kind but I will hold off on doing so out of gratitude for the next thirty minutes or so if you wish to flee."

"How generous of you. Your sword is broken."

"It's supposed to be broken."

"This must be a new form of combat I'm unfamiliar with."

Regina raised an eyebrow. "For a Dark Lord, you're unusually snotty."

"I confess, that was my flaw when I was Knight Paramount." I tried to return my visage to its previous form. I felt a normal human appearance return and lowered my hood to show it. "My name is Jacob Riverson."

Regina nodded, then blinked. "Wait, you're claiming to be *the* Jacob Riverson? The Knight Paramount during the last war against the King Below? Jacob the Bastard?"

I stared at her, annoyed. "*That* is what they decided to remember me by? The fact my sire put a child in the widow down the road?"

"No," Regina said, her attitude changing immediately. She raised her hands as if reassuring a horse. "You're a legend. A cursed legend it seemed, but a legend. Stories are told all over the Southern Kingdoms. How you took a priestesses' virginity, were a notorious drunkard, slept with every whore—"

I stared at her.

Regina raised her hands. "No, I mean, it's part of your roguish allure! I mean, you still helped Eric the Great and Saint Jassamine the Deliverer slay Kurag Shadowweaver and drive the King Below's armies away."

"Eric...the Great." The words had a foul taste upon my lips.

Regina nodded and produced her broken sword. "This is his holy blade, Hopebringer. Well, part of it. The sword given to him by the Lawgiver himself. The Heroes of the Nine used it to smote the King Below and banish him from this world."

I stared at the weapon created by murdering children and bought with a king's ransom. Eric had been a coward who stuck to the back of the ranks for much of the war. I'd only been at his side for much of the war at Jassa's insistence as his patronage made the Shadowguard's movements easier. "That's not how I remember the story."

"Well, legend says you died sacrificing yourself so he'd be able to drive back the King Below."

"I see."

This was a particularly cruel jest by the Gods Above. I had only ever been with one woman in my life, did not drink anything but light wines, and the only priestess I'd ever been with was Jassa. How she'd gone from being a disgraced sorceress to a saint while I was somehow played the lecherous drunk bothered me less than Eric having hidden his cruelties. There'd been rumors he'd had his younger sisters murdered lest he be passed over.

I knew the truth.

Wait, did I?

It seemed like I should but the memory was lost to me, like a raindrop in a pool of water.

Argh! Curse this foul state!

I needed to focus on the present. "Putting aside the appalling state of history in this Age, I need to know why you are carrying a sacred relic of your time and why you are fleeing from your fellow Shadowguard." I struggled not to retch at the idea of anyone thinking Eric was a great anything. Instead, I took comfort from the fact Jassa was remembered fondly.

"Swear to me by your dark master you mean me no ill." Regina waved the broken sword in front of her.

"I will swear I mean you no ill by the Lawgiver and every god *but* the King Below for he is none of mine," I said, placing my hand over my chest. "I know as little as you. Less even. I awoke on this mountaintop and have found myself transformed into this thing. If I was cursed by the King Below, it was centuries ago and against my will. I am a man again, though, and seek to give no evil to any being."

Yet you leave the part out about me meeting with you, the Trickster said in my head. *How shameful. Less than an hour awake and already an oathbreaker.*

I have broken no oaths, I thought at him. *I am simply not sharing a detail. I must protect this woman and her distrust in me would put her danger.*

What a wonderful lie to tell yourself! The Trickster laughed. *Splendid!*

There's a reason you were always my favorite.

Regina, thankfully, could not hear the God of Evil's taunts. "Those were no true men of the Shadowguard but assassins sent after me by the False Empress Morwen and her steward, Jon Bloodthorn. Those two so-called heroes gave orders to take my life. They have already slain my kin."

"You'll have to assume I have no idea who these two are or why they hunt you." I suspected referring to this Empress Morwen as a usurper might have something to do with it.

Regina nodded. "After the Nine Usurpers defeated the King Below, they had the whole world's armies behind them and decided they should rule rather than the old monarchies. They divided the Southern Kingdoms like a cake. Morwen took the greatest slice, setting herself up as ruler of the Anessian Empire."

I thought of Emperor Edorta who sent his armies to seize the Petty Kingdoms and force their armies into his so they were capable of avenging the Imperial City's sacking. While I was a man of honor, I had no illusions a king was a ruler as long as he had the strength to defend their crown. If these Nine Usurpers destroyed the King Below, even just the form he used to invade the Southern Kingdoms with then maybe they deserved to title themselves monarchs.

I wasn't about to tell her such, though.

"And why do they seek your death?"

Regina looked over the horizon. "A stupid reason. House Whitetremor is descended from Eric the Great's paternal line through Mathew Elf-Friend."

"So if the main house is extinguished, you have a claim to the throne."

"Half of Anessia's nobles have Eric's blood through their veins. I'm seventy-fifth in line for the throne at best. No, this was more about what my family represents. King Eric's legacy and the honor he brought to the realm."

I grimaced at that thought. As noble as his father's deeds were, Eric had been a varlet. "Yet, you're elfblooded and I suppose your relatives are as well. The sidhe do not care much for humans but when they do support our kind, they tend to do those mortals who most obviously have their blood. Any revolt would do best to have their strength."

The sidhe came, originally, from another world and still had many moongates to other planets where man had evolved differently into species like them or otherwise. A few legends, particularly those of the ancient Terralan, spoke of us all hailing from the same world originally but having been divided by great epochs of time. Some blasphemous souls even claimed the Lawgiver and King Below were nothing more than beings from a world with exceptionally powerful knowledge. I was not so foolhardy, even if I often wondered what world or worlds my ancestors originally hailed from.

"I'd rather have the friendship of a race which didn't consider my blood a mixture of wine and sewage." Regina curled her lip in disdain.

I smiled at her summation. "I take it you are not fond of your relatives?"

"The only thing my ancestors have ever received from the sidhe were headaches and broken beds. I do not revere them the way my family does. I can see why the Empress would fear us, though." Regina smiled at that notion. "It is all the more reason I have to get this blade to one of the Great Houses. It will serve as a rallying cry to the oppressed peoples of the land."

I neglected the fact that the weapon was created with blood magic and murdered children to compensate for Eric's abyssal fighting ability. "You think people will rally around a broken sword?"

"A symbol of a broken house which can be re-forged." Regina held it tightly. "It will show the Empire's true heirs resist her."

"Which are?"

Regina frowned. "That's a matter of some dispute. There's multiple candidates, though, all who are uniquely qualified to—"

"How did you get this blade?" I doubted the Empress would part with such an important relic.

"I took it." Regina looked abashed. "The Empress entrusted Hopebringer's broken pieces to the Shadowguard. I had already joined by the time I heard my family had been destroyed by Steward Bloodthorn's armies. That was when I seized it and rode my dragon to this place. We are in the Storm Giant Mountains and I hope to meet the Lord of the Lake beyond."

"So you robbed the Shadowguard and they sent dragonriders after you." I was starting to regret my involment.

Regina looked to one side, grimacing. "Mayhaps."

"I will not help you foment a brothers' war."

Regina looked at her now-dead dragon then back to me, clearly guessing her chances of getting off this mountaintop were slim. "You must. The Nine Usurpers are tyrants and if you are cursed, then surely this is the Lawgiver's way of allowing you to atone."

"I am beginning to wonder about both the Lawgiver and King Below's interest in morality, to be honest."

Regina sheathed Hopebringer and pressed her hands together. "In the name of Saint Jassamine, I beg of you. Help me."

Regina had no way of knowing that was my weakness. "In Jassa's name then, I suppose. I will take you from this place."

I hoped this wasn't a mistake.

I suspected it was a vain hope.

CHAPTER 4

Y ou'll help?" Regina said, surprised.

"You asked in the name of someone I cared for very deeply," I said, placing my hand over my unbeating heart.

Killing the Great Blue had given me solid form, but I was still dead. Oddly, despite this, I felt inappropriate urges when looking at her. I had only loved—*would only love*—Jassa but I had always appreciated other women's beauty. I looked away to avoid thinking about such things. My situation reminded of the Gael scare stories of women who bore children sired by ghostly spouses and spectral seductresses who drained the life-force of men. It made me wonder if those stories were true and if there was no end to the depravities the King Below practiced.

No, the Trickster said. *There is not.*

"You are a member of the Shadowguard," I added, trying to think of something else. Ours is the order which has three rules: stand fast against the darkness, give up everything to the cause, and sacrifice all for your brothers."

"We say siblings now," Regina corrected me.

"My mistake, sister."

Regina looked over to the fallen form of the Great Blue. "I suppose it must have been a stronger order in your time. It is mostly a ceremonial group now, a place for houses to stick unwanted second or third sons and daughters. The ones you killed were amongst the few who still knew how to fight. As for giving up all for your brothers, those three just tried to kill me so one could say the family is divided."

"They don't keep men and women sharp by sending them out to fight monsters anymore?"

"Outside the Nothern Wasteland's ice deserts and tomb kingdoms, there's not many monsters left. Even the once-proud Shadow Races are reduced to scattered tribes, broken and defeated."

I turned back at her. "Truly?"

"Have an order of professional monster slayers working on killing Shadowkind for a thousand years and you'll see an effect, however delayed."

I supposed that was true. Still, I couldn't help but feel like my purpose was gone. "Then who rallied to the King Below's side this last time?"

"The Formor, as always, and he had his undead but he was defeated within a year's time. No human nations allied themselves with him this time. The Fifth Great Shadow War was the shortest of them all. It was like the King Below wasn't even trying."

I wasn't, the Trickster said. *Strange how the Nine Heroes were able to get such a fantastic alliance together against me, though. Someone was cheating!*

"A short but victorious war is to be commended," I said, still too surprised at this turn of events. I'd been prepared for just about anything but victory was not one of them.

"Except for the aftermath," Regina said, sighing. "Blood runs from the Western to East seas in rivers. The Anessian Empire, Ashlands, Borderlands, Eternal Isles, Fireforge, Gael, Natariss, Riverfords, Rolant, Tyrash, and Winterholme are all ruled by the usurpers or their puppets. Lakeland has remained neutral but is surrounded and will capitulate unless a resistance within the Empire can be formed with Indras and G'Tay's support. The Southern Kingdoms are wholly under the Usurper's sway."

"So you have said," I said, checking the Lesser Brown. The dragon had passed during our conversation and would never fly again. I had no idea how I'd gotten up on this mountaintop but I was more concerned with how we were going to get down. I was dead, so I didn't fear falling but my living companion was another story. That's assuming we didn't freeze or starve to death.

I, at least, knew where we were by her invocation she was traveling to Lakeland. We were in the Storm Giant mountains, named after that now-extinct sub-race. They had sought to resist the encroachment of the King Below during the Second Shadow War only for them to be finished off by Empress Anessia who chose to claim the mountain passes for herself.

"I'm not lying. They're tyrants," Regina said, holding her hands together as her frosty breathes became somewhat labored. "Murderers, thieves, and religious fanatics who have perverted the Lawgiver's—"

"I believe you." I looked over at the dead Great Blue. It was our best chance of getting out here. "I hate to ask you this, but how do you feel about dark magic?"

"Poorly."

"That's unfortunate," I said, walking over to the dragon and seeking the words in the back of my mind. What I was about to do was a blasphemy against all the Gods Above. I had made a promise to her, however, and a Shadowguard's promise was to be filled by any means necessary.

Four times, well, five now, the King Below had been defeated and each time it had been through total commitment to one's cause. I wasn't about to betray that path now.

Despite the fact you are one of the creatures they hunt, the Trickster said, *or should.*

Do you intend to annoy me for all eternity? I asked. *If so, I may reconsider falling on my sword.*

Only as long as you amuse me. The Trickster's tone was less mocking and more direct.

I shall endeavor to be as boring as possible then. I sneered.

Ha! The Trickster laughed. *Now that's the Riverson wit I so adore!*

Not quite the reaction I'd been hoping for.

Raising up my sword and ring as focuses for the dark magic within me, I began speaking in a tongue so foul and horrifying that the very air seemed to shudder and shake with its malevolence. My knowledge of Demonspeak, it seemed, had improved as much as my swordsmanship.

Regina held out her sword, horrified. "What are you doing!?"

That was when the dead Great Blue roared as its body returned to a twisted parody of life, its left missing eye unchanged. The creature had no life-force left in it but the fraction I'd returned to it. That power, however, was enough that it was bound to me now and would obey my every command.

The Great Blue stretched out its neck for us to mount and lowered its wings in a gesture of submission.

"I am getting us transport."

Regina looked revolted. "I am not riding that...thing. I have grown up around dragons all my life and this is a mockery of everything good about them."

I agreed. "It's also an offense against the Lawgiver."

"That too."

I crossed my arms and waited.

Regina was a smart girl. It didn't take long for her to realize if one lies down with Ice Demons, one shouldn't complain about getting chilled. "Fine. *Will* it obey my commands?"

"I assume so."

"You *assume* so."

"Would you prefer I lied?"

Regina smiled. "You are not at all what I expected from Jacob the Bastard."

"You could call me Jacob."

"I see...Sir Jacob."

"You seem to know a lot about my past."

"My uncle taught me well." She walked over to the Great Blue and sat down in the front rider's seat. "He is one of the ones I seek to avenge."

"I am sorry." I did not know the man but I admired his commitment to his daughter's education.

"Not as sorry as the Usurpers will be." The anger washed from her as I could sense her emotions inside. She wanted revenge and hated these Nine Heroes badly but I could also tell she was not comfortable with these emotions. Regina wanted her cause to be pure and her emotions prevented it from being so.

I knew something of that. In the end, I had abandoned pure causes as impossible. Victory, in the end, was what mattered.

"I'm sure. May I ask you questions about what has passed in my absence?"

"I am no historian but I shall share what I can."

"That is all that I ask."

Saddling myself, I tried to remember how to ride dragonback. Gladys Stonebrooke had never taught me more than the basics of the art, being more content to watch her Knight Paramount squirm.

"Hold on tight," Regina said, pulling on the reigns and sending the monstrous undead dragon into the air. "Huh, it still responds like a living beast."

"That appears to be going around," I said, awed by her capacity to manage such a monster.

"Dragonriding is a skill which runs in the family. Eric is said to have tamed the first dragon at the Battle of Three Brothers."

Gladys had done so and would not be pleased, wherever she was, to find out history had left her behind. "So, what may I ask did Prince Eric the Unsteady do to become King Eric the Great?"

"*That's* what they called him in your time?"

"I know I did." Jassa had actually coined the phrase and Eric had been too terrified to chastise her over it. Mostly because she'd said he'd drown in his own vomited blood if he ever thought about crossing her.

His guards hadn't bothered to intervene.

"Hard to believe," Regina said, as if the idea of him not being Eric the Great was somehow impossible to believe.

"It seems history is recorded very differently than how I remember it."

"Tell me how it really went," Regina said, the two of us flying against the wind. I held on tightly, watching the magnificent mountains part way below.

"You begin. I'd like to know how my time is remembered."

Regina seemed uncomfortable lecturing me about history I'd lived but did so anyway. "Alright. After smiting Kurag the Foul and driving away the King Below, he took up the latter's crown and expanded the Anessian Empire threefold. He brought to heel the Fir-Bolg Kings of Fireforge and drove the Formor back to the sea. With Saint Jassa, he reformed the Grand Temple and set himself at the head. Heathens throughout the land cast down their idols and proclaimed him protector of the faith."

I had not liked Eric, who was guilty of every single outrage they had assigned to me. It was said half the bastards from Grogway to High Square were the product of his exercising of lordly rights. I wouldn't have held this against him given my own origins if not for the fact he'd ignored his responsibilities to them and hadn't even paid for their upkeep or apprenticeship. He was a coward, fool, and liar with no honor.

Yet, he'd also been useful.

As I sat there on dragonback, feeling the freezing air, I couldn't help but remember more details about our past together. Eric had been a cunning manipulator, if nothing else, and done much to rouse the public against the King Below's forces. In my head, I heard one of our conversations replay.

"You and the Shadowguard need allies. They don't believe the King Below is real. They think it's just a Formor trick." Eric's voice echoed through my mind.

My own voice responded, filled with disgust. "I have seen what you do with your allies."

"Only when they outlive their usefulness. You need me to win." The sheer slime of the man revolted me.

Yet, my reply had been, "I'll do anything to win this war."

"Oh, my dear friend, this war is never going to end."

"There are no Fir-Bolg kingdoms anymore?" I asked, picking up on one of the more curious details she'd shared.

"A few scattered plots of land contained a pitiful remnant of their ancient ways. The majority live in Fire Districts now. In his mercy, King Eric gave pardon to those who converted and agreed to serve." There was a trace of bitterness in her voice as if she wasn't quite ready to believe it had been all that merciful.

I wasn't sure how to respond. The Fir-Bolg had never been popular with the Southern Kingdoms' peoples because of their frightening strength and great horns, but they'd always been our allies against the King Below.

"You should not judge a man by his ancestry," I said, frowning at her description of putting them to the sword.

"We are the products of our blood and heritage," Regina said, as if she was stating the obvious.

I was no descendent of the High Men of ancient Terralan. The

Fisherfolk of Riverford were one of the 'mongrel' races of the Southern Kingdom's born from intermixing along the Borderlands. We were a mixture of Anessian, Gael, Indras, G'Tay, and a dozen other people long since forgotten.

I'd been treated as vermin for my first few years in the Grand Temple by the Old Blood lineages and only found acceptance in the Shadowguard where kicking a man's teeth in for disrespect was permissible. I almost asked if the legends portrayed me as one of the Fisherfolk or had recast me as a lost scion of the High Men.

But I was afraid of the answer.

"The Fir-Bolg did not deserve such treatment," I said, simply, as much for posterity as anything else.

How much had been forgotten?

Or lied about? The Trickster offered. *Much. History is a tapestry of justifications and lies. Aren't you glad I exist? If not for me, you'd have to make everyone else villains.*

"I'm sorry," Regina said, her face scrunching from the cold wind blasting against it. "This must be terrible for you."

"It is."

"To have lost your family, friends, nation, and very time is beyond the pale. I have only lost my family and feel like I might break at any minute." Regina looked over the side of the dragon to the lands below.

"I somehow doubt you will. You strike me as a strong woman."

"You are kind."

"I only speak the truth. Though I do not believe warmongering is ever the answer, I respect you believe in your cause and are willing to do anything to achieve your aims. These are admirable qualities and the mark of a true Shadowguardsman."

"Thank you. I dreamed of being a heroine like Saint Jassamine or Gladys Stonebrooke the Fair. I wanted to be a knight in the service of the people like you."

I had to suppress a snort at Glady's title. Knight Captain

Stonebrook had been many things but 'Fair' was not one of them. Still, she'd had three husbands simultaneously by the end of the war so maybe she simply wasn't my type.

"Didn't you describe me as a rogue?" I asked, smiling.

"You don't seem very roguish."

"Just dead."

That killed our conversation. Regina kept her eyes on the ground from that point on as we passed from the Storm Giant Mountains into Lakeland.

CHAPTER 5

The unimaginatively named Lakeland was a nation I remembered fondly. It was a land decimated by the King Below's Ice Demons during the First Great Shadow War, but which had been reborn into a kingdom with three hundred or more lakes. Supposedly, there was one for each Ice Demon killed by the sidhe High Lady Ethinu when she turned upon her Formor father.

The Shadowguard tended to dwell around the borderlands, Winterholme port cities, and fortresses in the Northern Wastes, but they had a lovely castle near Lakeland's great city of Accadia. It was a pleasant pastoral land and one I would often spend many hours puffing away on smoke-weed while the men underneath me flirted with fishermen's wives. While settled for centuries, Lakeland was a land of peace and prosperity. What I witnessed passing over the lands was anything but.

"*What in the World Below?*" I asked, staring down at the sight which greeted me.

The most notable quality of Lakeland was I didn't see any lakes, or rather, I saw a single lake nearby the distant towers of Accadia. The majority of the domain had been drained dry with great black pipes stretching across the land and man-made reservoirs replacing them. All of Lakeland's forests had been cleared for farmland as a dozen or more cities were visible with sheets of black smoke pouring out into the sky above.

Weird kettles with wheels went up and down metal and wood stitched roads, carrying cargo in great amounts. I saw twenty-foot-tall stone golems, the kind once used to decide the fate of wars, being used to construct buildings and carry cargo on their back. There were *hundreds* of them moving about below. Some were assisting in the carving up of the mountains beyond for coal, several ones I'd known from my youth now flat-out missing. My background in magical craftsmanship and military engineering let me understand what most of them were, even if they were more advanced than anything I'd yet before seen, but it was bewildering to see how much had *changed*.

"Is something wrong?" Regina asked, confused.

"What have you done to this place?" I asked, staring below. "It looks like a toy shop crossed with a wizard's kitchen."

"Tharadon's Cradle is the richest land in the Empire. It used to be part of Lakeland but has since been annexed. It produces most of the tools and metal goods in the Southern Kingdoms. The Tinkerer Mages and Steam Sorcerers have done well by the people here."

I'd never heard of either but I knew the first name. "Tharadon the Black? The Great Wizard?"

"You knew him? All I know is he died during the Fourth Shadow War. Your War, I guess."

A flash of memories almost caused me to fall off the back of the dragon.

Tharadon fell backwards, clutching his chest. It was hard to see how bad the bleeding was given the color of his robes but I'd struck him well. His staff was on the ground, broken in two, and he looked at me with judgmental eyes.

We were in the top of his tower overlooking Accadia. The room was filled with hundreds of beakers, diagrams, and models for the devices the Great Wizard had worked on for decades. I'd already silenced his two apprentices and no one else was nearby. I'd leave my sword behind, collected from a Formor chieftain, and a banner once he was dead. Tharadon's neutrality in the war was a threat to us all.

Or so I told myself.

Killing him had been pathetically easy. A simple matter of disposing of his focusing device and then striking. The charm against magic given to me by Valance was working wonders, too, protecting me against all retaliatory curses.

Not that he'd tried any.

He just stared.

"You Shadowguard are all fanatics," Tharadon hissed. "You'll do anything to win."

"Yes," I said, holding my dripping blade. "We would."

Tharadon laughed. "You may bring my students into this war and my creations but you won't change the fact the war isn't what's important. It's what comes after."

"There is no after."

I plunged my blade into his chest again, this time twisting it.

"Yes, I knew him," I said, staring off into the distance. "He was a great man."

The revelation I'd killed one of the Great Wizards should have shocked me to the core but it didn't. I didn't possess all my memories but I knew who I was. War was an ugly business where the strong survived, the weak perished, and only by ending it quickly did you guarantee the latter could live in peace. We *needed* his students and their devices.

But if that were true why did I feel so sick?

Because who knows how many others you've killed for that exact same reason? The Trickster taunted.

Many, no doubt.

Perhaps Prince Eric's sisters? You were close to him, it seems. At least in legend. Perhaps you killed them to gain his favor?

I remembered my vision of the two dead children under the Grand Temple's steps. *Never would I harm children!*

Even to save the world?

Never. I felt confident of that, at least, which reassured me.

Then what a poor Shadowguard you were.

His words shouldn't have troubled me but they did.

"So, Accadia isn't a part of Lakeland anymore?"

"No," Regina said. "Though it's just up the river and is a good place for rallying the Lake Lords and Philosopher Mages. If there's going to be any chance against the Empress and her minions, it'll require the great wonders they build here."

I tried to imagine a battlefield filled with those gigantic stone statues fighting alongside dragons and who knew what else. I found my imagination failed me. "It sounds like something from before the First Age."

"Oh, we've long surpassed them," Regina said, causally.

"That's a grand claim to make."

Regina continued, "Someday the knowledge of the Great Wizards will spread across the land and every common man will be able to work the wonders of magic."

"I doubt that's a popular view with many nobles."

"Some fear the loss of their privileges."

As well they should, the Trickster said. *A king exists as long as you need someone very good at killing to keep other people very good at killing from taking your wealth. When that's not a problem, why have a king at all?*

Because it is the way of things, I answered.

Ha!

"So you're going to present them the broken sword and hope it, combined with their weapons, will let you rally an army to overthrow the Empress?" I asked, letting the wind blow in my face. It was strange but death seemed to make the world feel sharper rather than duller.

"That is the basis for my plan, yes."

"There have been worse. Can this Lord of the Lake be trusted?"

Regina paused before responding, which was never a good sign. "His line is new nobility with little love for the Empire. I also know his wards intimately. He can rally the merchant princes and robber barons of Lakeland across the border to fund a war. The promise of returning Tharadon's Cradle to their care would be enough to get them to donate any amount of gold."

She was now involving foreign powers in her plans. "So you intend to carve up the Empire like a cake now too?"

"You wound me, sir."

"I am sorry," I said, placing a hand over my heart. "I, too, have known great loss. If you seek to avenge your family's death by any means necessary, I honor and respect such a quest."

"It is not for revenge but justice. This is a just war." Regina sounded like she was trying to convince herself rather than me.

On my end, I had never known a just war, not even during my struggle against the King Below. That had been for survival but had still resulted in more innocent blood being shed than any man should know in a thousand lifetimes. There was something about Regina's demeanor that enticed me to want to follow her, though. It had been a long time since I'd known such passion in a soldier.

"You have my oath. I will aid thee in any way I can," I said, surprising myself. "This includes fighting your war."

"You only need transport me to Accadia, Sir Jacob. This is not your fight."

"Nevertheless, I will aid thee if you'd have me."

"Thank you," Regina said, sounding touched. "Though, I do not know why you would make such an offer. You have much to deal with already."

Truth be told, it was as much because I had no better direction to walk as admiration. Regina seemed honorable enough, but that was little reason to involve myself in her struggle. History was full of honorable nobles, peasants, heroes, mercenaries, and kings on both sides of wars. As Shadowguards, we were supposed to remain above the petty affairs of state which divided lands.

Yet, I was a monster and her family was dead.

Perhaps those were reasons enough.

Or you just like killing, the Trickster whispered. *Don't be afraid to admit such. I like it too.*

Regina paused. "One thing I would make a request of, though."

"Yes?"

"When you first approached," Regina scrunched up her nose, "it was like feeling the hand of the King Below reach into my chest and clench my heart. I felt sick, dizzy, and wanted to die. On the ground, there were some ice flowers present and yet they wilted at your presence. I have seen the smoking charred bodies of children, my brother, my uncle, and known this was likely my own fate. I have also faced Formor, Spiderfolk, and a few lesser demons. None of this filled me with as much terror and revulsion—"

"You have made your point."

Regina blushed, frowning. "I don't think I have. All of those feelings disappeared when you adopted a human guise. Indeed, you felt as fair as you looked."

"I look fair?" I asked, surprised.

"Oh yes." Regina looked back and nodded. "Did you not know?"

I had never been counted amongst the comeliest of the Shadowguards' warriors, which had been Sir Garris, let alone the rest of the world.

Her words surprised me.

I think you'd be surprised at how wonderful evil can look, the Trickster said. *If one is to adopt a human guise, one should always go royal than shit-stained peasant.*

I am a shit-stained peasant and quite proud of it.

You're a ghost who feeds on souls of the living. I'd take the good looks, dear boy.

In the words of Gladys the Fair, fuck you, God of Evil.

"No," I said, simply. "I did not."

"What I mean to say is it would be convenient if you could keep to this seeming as opposed to your, uh, other one," Regina explained, sounding like she was trying to avoid saying otherwise.

"Because it would not do to let your supporters know you are being supported by a force of ultimate darkness."

"You saved my life and for that I am grateful. You are also a hero who deserves to be honored—"

"You needn't defend your decision. I will do so."

"Thank you." Regina surprised me by asking another question. "So, Prince Eric *didn't* slay Kurag Shadowweaver and drive off the King Below?"

"That's been bothering you?"

"I was raised with that legend on my mother's knee. Finding out he was not the hero he's been touted as is a shock."

"One should never meet one's heroes." I tried to figure a way to say her ancestor was an irredeemable bastard without offense. "I can't speak of the latter because I was dead at the time, which is a strange but true statement. However, I can say I find it very unlikely. Eric was a cunning politician and an excellent lawmaker but he was not known for his swordsmanship or strategy." He was also a lecher, murderer, and worse.

I remembered Jassamine handing Prince Eric the blood-rune-covered sword for the first time. It had been she who presented Hopebringer to him.

I blinked. That couldn't be right.

Why would *Jassa* give him such an evil weapon?

My head hurt just thinking about it.

"Who defeated Kurag Shadowweaver, then?" Regina asked. "I used to act out the battles with the other Shadowguardsmen's children. My mother and father were both members, you see. They would often speak of Eric's epic duel with him."

"I did."

Now it was Regina's turn to be surprised. "*You?* Oh, well, I suppose that makes sense. How did you do it?"

"With a sword," I answered.

Regina snorted.

"I wasn't making a jest. In the final battles of the war, the Shadowguard all wielded magical blades crafted by me and Jass...Saint Jassamine. The weapons could break the spells protecting their masters, banish ghosts, and cut through armor like cheese. I defeated Kurag by spell and blade. It was not especially heroic, merely the case of someone setting out to kill someone and doing so. Great battles are for stories."

"Says the man who claims the Shadowguard Knight Paramount defeated the Lord of Despair in single-combat with a magic sword."

I smiled. "Point taken."

"Do you think Saint Jassamine drove off the King Below then?"

"Yes."

She did, the Trickster surprised me by admitting. *After I struck you down, she was quite vexed. Of course, I left the field of battle with your spirit. I think I got the better part of the deal.*

Jassa is revered across the world now. I weakly tried to defend her loss. The pain of knowing I'd never see her again was almost breaking.

Yet, chose to let Poor Prince Eric take the credit, the Trickster observed. *I wonder what she bargained from him in order to let that happen. Who is the puppeteer? The one behind the curtain or the one pulling the strings?*

I grit my teeth. *I look forward to finding a cure for my condition, just to be rid of you.*

There is no cure for death, the Trickster's words echoed a line from the Codex.

"I am honored to have you fight at my side," Regina said. "The Empress has no chance."

"Let's hope not. Now will you tell me—"

I trailed off before I could say anything else to look at the coming form of Accadia. Accadia was a massive city in the middle of Lakeland, now the Empire's, territory. It was formed on a series of five islands linked together by bridges and stretching forth to the shores beyond. Accadia was linked to several rivers now by a series of dams and a source of great trade throughout the land.

Accadia was filled with thousands of tiny little wooden buildings with arched roofs, glass, and other signs of prosperity. In the center of the town was a large stone keep, larger than any constructed in my era save the Imperial Palace, with white-stone and ornamental pointed towers. Great stone dragons were built into the side of said towers, making it look more like a work of art than a fortress.

The city was beautiful.

It was also under attack.

Gathered around the city's northern side and moving to secure the East and South were ten legions of Imperial troopers. Hundreds of Imperial gryphons, wyverns, chimera, manticore, and lesser dragons maneuvered through the air. I saw banners of iron armor, circular shields, hawks holding eyes, green fists, red-hourglass spiders, and lightning hammers signifying the Great Houses of my day had joined in this attack.

The air was filled with bolts of lightning, fire, glowing rune-covered ballista, explosive rocks, and worse. A mystical barrier around Accadia caused most of these to fall to the ground harmlessly as they retaliated with terrifying sounding metal tubes belching rocks as well as their own magic. A hundred of their gigantic stone men had already gone out to battle the Imperial armies, but half had been destroyed.

"Lawgiver," Regina whispered. "We're too late."

CHAPTER 6

I had seen battles this size before precious few. It appeared Empress Morwen was not content to wait around and allow her enemies to gather a force capable of opposing her, but striking first before such treason could sew its seeds. I wasn't sure this was the wisest course of action, since an execution for a crime was justice whereas the death of someone plotting such was murder. Countless rebellions had grown from individuals prematurely striking out at their foes.

Not that such helped the people of Accadia.

"Bastards and hellspawn!" Regina shouted, pulling the reigns upward and nearly throwing me off the dragon's back. "We must join the fight!"

I stared at the massive battle and shook my head. "I do not know what the stories tell of me or a Wraith Knight's power but I cannot defeat an army. The Dark Lords had armies of their own to fight the Southern Kingdoms."

Regina was no longer paying attention, however. Her eyes were focused on a group of gryphon riders coming at us, wearing black armor and a tabard for a House I did not recognize. It was a bloody ring of thorns made from a Hawthorne bush.

They sported glowing rune-covered lances charged with electricity, which I recognized since it had been by hand those devices had been introduced to the battlefield to slay the King Below's Nightterrors. These were far more advanced devices, however, as they I saw white bolts of lightning shoot from them toward us. One struck against the heart of our dragon and nearly caused its reanimation spell to fail.

"Murderers and sons of whores!" Regina hissed, her eyes developing a fury of a thousand burning pyres. "I strike at thee in the name of Whitehall's ghosts and the one true Emperor!"

She then turned our Great Blue dragon at them and kicked its side to speed it up.

"Regina, what are you doing?" I asked, trying to sound calmer than I was.

The Great Blue went faster and faster, maneuvering with a speed I did not think possible as the black armored knights fired more bolts in our direction but they missed by feet thanks to Regina's skill.

Their leonine eagle mounts joined in formation to maximize their assault, but broke into a dozen different directions when Regina crashed through, proceeding to leap off the side of our mount only to land on the back of an attacker.

Huh.

I hadn't seen that before.

Regina stabbed the knight in the neck with Hopebringer before flinging him to one side, taking up the bow and arrow attached to his gryphon's saddle. She was able on gryphon-back as dragon, maneuvering it well before firing an enchanted bolt which sailed many times faster than normal into the heart of another attacker. The spell on its head detonated and turned both rider as well as gryphon into a ball of flame.

War craft had advanced since my time, it seemed.

Hearing a gryphon call from my high east, I turned around to see a group of four gryphon riders descending on me, aiming their explosive bows. I turned my dragon around and kicked its neck with my spurs. The creature breathed out a geyser of magically-generated ice. Three of the warriors and their mounts died instantly, falling from the air like frozen statues.

One of the warriors was more skilled than the rest and dodged the Great Blue's attack before twisting his lance forward to pierce us head-on. The lance's charge must have been wearing thin because he did not attack once more with magic but attempted to go head-to-head.

I responded by dropping my comely visage, showing the true terrifying creature which lay beneath. The gryphon rider was still a hundred feet away when his mount reared back in terror and he was thrown backwards, his saddle straps catching him but throwing off his attack. I then ordered my dragon to bite them both in half, which the Great Blue did in two swift motions.

I had forgotten how pleasurable combat could be.

And that thought filled me with shame.

Turning around the Great Blue, I saw Regina had killed two more of the gryphon riders but her mount was badly wounded and another four riders were circling around for the kill. I had not come to her aid only to allow her to die now and brought the Great Blue forward as its icy breath once more shot forward. In my hands, I conjured my black bow and fired into the hearts of the warriors who met me on the aerial fields. I was not a good dragon rider but a mount's size and power had a quality all its own.

I killed three of the gryphon riders.

The fourth drove his spear into the heart of the Great Blue and the magic reanimating it failed, sending us spiraling to the ground. I did not know whether it was possible for a ghost to die a second time, but feeling my body shake in the onrush of wind, I sought to cut myself free before landing against the ground below. I managed to but had nowhere to go except up, floating a few feet before the creature, which struck the ground seconds later.

I, however, didn't.

Regina's gryphon, wounded as it was, held me in its talons. The fact the creature was clawing and gnashing at me with its beak showed it was perhaps not the best means of rescue, but I stretched out with my hand and calmed its mind. That was a fanciful way of saying I dominated its mind but I wasn't comfortable with all the dark magic at my disposal. I was even less comfortable with being eaten, though.

"Are you alright?" Regina said, nocking her bow back one last time to put an arrow through the visor of the last mounted knight. The gryphon and he vanished, once more, into a fiery explosion and I wondered how many such arrows they had.

"Never better," I said, trying to heal my painful talon wounds. "We should do this more often!"

"Sarcasm does not befit a hero, Sir Jacob."

"I fear you shall be disappointed then."

Regina helped me back up onto the back of the gryphon as I saw it was flapping its wings just a few dozen feet above the ground. I resumed my comely appearance, though I felt weakened doing so. It seemed creating a body used up more energy than I expected and I was already starting to feel weak.

Your sword used to channel energy from me but now channels energy from, well, nothing. Only the Crown of Weeping Gods, blood sacrifice, a new divine patron, or the Tower of Everfrost can provide you the energy you need to stay in mortal form, the Trickster said, foregoing his usual joking around. *I recommend the blood sacrifice one, personally. There's a never-ending supply of offerings around you!*

I do not intend to be a Wraith Knight long enough to need many more of those.

Keep telling yourself that, my friend. The Trickster's condescension had a twinge of regret to it, which I didn't expect.

"Who were those men?" I said, placing my hand and using half of my remaining strength to heal the gryphon's wounds. I wasn't sure if we were still heading to Accadia but, either way, we needed mobility.

"The Knights of Bloodthorn," Regina said. "A hand-picked group of warriors who serve the Imperial Steward. They were each trained by him and serve as his scouts and agents. Jon recruited them from his tribe in Winterholme."

I could see she was holding back. There was more to this than the gryphon riders being a particularly elite group of soldiers. "I see. But who are they to *you*?"

Regina's face darkened then turned to a look of shame. "As Commander of the Imperial Legions, it fell to Bloodthorn to destroy Whitehall and its peoples. His knights would have been a part of it. Forgive me, Jacob, I have wronged you and put my vengeance over our mission."

"Thank you for calling me Jacob. I've never been comfortable with titles."

Regina blinked. "How very strange."

Despite my concern for her well-being, her revelations bothered me. Winterholme produced some of the fiercest riders in the world (or had in my time at least). It was a harsh land which had been invaded four times (and probably a fifth) from the by the King Below's armies.

Worse, it was far enough North the Formor never stopped invading in order to settle the land and takes its peoples as slaves. Unbroken by centuries of war, devastation, and ruin, the Winterfolk had emerged a proud but grim people. If this Jon Bloodthorn was one of them and had risen to be Imperial Steward, he was a formidable individual.

"Where to now?" I asked.

"We need to plan our next move." Regina's hesitation told me she was as confused as I was.

"So you have no idea." I couldn't help but observe.

"Up is fine for now."

Regina took us back into the skies, to the outskirts of the battle. It was large enough, even with the majority of Accadia's forces retreating behind the city's barrier, to provide a reasonable degree of anonymity. Several more mounted warriors came to challenge us, most from the invaders, but Regina made short work of them.

I, instead, devoted my efforts to understanding the battlefield. While I was unfamiliar with the majority of weapons being used, one was a hundred-foot-long spider-legged nightmare which belched black smoke, but I could guess the majority of their functions. Every battlefield was like a complex puzzle and years of experience had given me insight into solving them.

And whoever was running the defense was *an idiot*.

Regina stared down at the towers below. "We must figure a way to pierce the barrier of Accadia without bringing it down. I shall deliver the sword Hopebringer and help rally the troops against this horde of evil which threatens to consume the spark of freedom. Tyranny mustn't prevail this day!"

I gave her a queer look then shook my head, pointing at the Northwatch Tower and the spider-machine assaulting it. "We need to go there. The barrier runes on the walls are about to be shattered by that device. The majority of the attack is a diversion to hide it before they plunge their heavy troops through."

"Are you sure?" Regina retrieved a spyglass from one of the gryphon's saddle bags.

"It's what I would do." I knew much about sieges, magic, and weaponry. The knowledge had come at a hideous cost but it was mine to call upon. Tharadon's notes had been something I'd studied extensively and there were…other sources. Things the King Below had fostered and nurtured even if I forgot the specifics.

Regina stared through her spyglass at the machine assaulting the wall. "Draamach, the Spider's Bite."

"I am unfamiliar with it."

"A siege weapon designed by Elevin the Mad to break the spells of protection laid into cities' foundations. I did not see it until you drew my attention. Runes of obscuration must be welded into its sides. Thousands of lives sacrificed on a gambit to bring this siege to an early end. What base treachery!"

"Impressive."

"We must destroy it before it ends this siege before it has begun." Regina brought forth her gryphon to move forward, the mind-controlled beast responding better and more clearly than any natural mounted one. It was deprived of fear, instinct, and pain which let us maneuver it through the explosion-filled skyline.

Accadia's barrier was holding back flames, liquid solvents, rune-covered rocks, and terrible alchemy-born creatures, but I could tell the assault weakened it. Such barriers existed in my time, albeit less grand, and had to be constantly reinforced by magicians.

We could not pierce it ourselves, not even with all of my power, but we flew to the Northwatch Tower anyway. There, hundreds of Accadian guardsmen were doing battle with the town's militia from *inside* the barrier, having sabotaged the fire tubes which should have been blasting away at the oncoming Draamach.

"You were saying about treachery?" I said, perhaps too flippantly. I was starting to respect this Jon Bloodthorn. He had obviously arranged for traitors to be placed in the guard or flat-out bribed them into turning.

"This is a dishonorable way to wage war," Regina hissed. "We need to get to the High Captain. Thomas is a friend of mine and can assist us if he still lives."

The barrier was under assault from Draamach and by the looks of things had minutes remaining.

"Pass through," I said, staring at her. "It should be permeable to individual flesh and armor in its weakened state. I will deal with this machine."

"What?"

"I will fight war dishonorably," I said. "For you."

I leapt off the side of the gryphon and landed thirty-feet below onto the back of the gigantic metal spider. It was a massive thing, the product of intricate yet artistry-less smith-work combined with magic and machinery. I was reminded of the great siege towers and weapons of my time, products of Fir-Bolg and sidhe craftsmanship mixed with Tharadon's converted designs. This was not a device designed for the pantomime of war fought between nobles with jousting lances and duels.

It was a device for killing.

I shook my head, thinking about Regina's condemnation of Bloodthorn's tactics. It was the great lie old men told to boys that war was glorious. In truth, war was the act of butchering men and women who were no different from oneself. There was no honor in combat, no glorious test of skills between evenly matched foes. A proper battle was won before weapons had been drawn, attacking an opponent who was weaker than oneself and killing them with minimum risk to oneself or one's troops.

That did not encompass the War Sickness, that condition which afflicted so many individuals who lifted blade or bow. If you allowed the darkness, misery, and emptiness inside you then it was possible to make it pleasurable. Indeed, you had to do so if you were going to survive, but this was a honeyed trap. Because if you did too much and for too long, you became war sick and there was no exit from the labyrinth of shadows you found yourself in. The lucky ones were those who became revolted by war like Warmaster Kalian and screamed at loud noises or the sight blood. The unlucky ones were those who unable to stop fighting and would not if they could.

Like me.

Lifting Chill's Fury above my head, I struck down at the heavy steel plating of Draamach's roof. The monstrous metal spider was striking with a hideous battering ram attached to its bottom, striking the barrier repeatedly with enough force to level a castle.

The creature's unnatural movements made me unsteady but when the first blow of my blade caused the steel to freeze and become brittle, I struck until I fell through the resulting hole into the war machine's interior.

What followed was something I am ashamed to speak of. There were a hundred men inside the three layers of Draamach. There were soldiers to protect against invasion, engineers, and operators who used a combination of levers as well as buttons to manipulate the strange weapon. They wore uniforms adorned with gold buttons and were a mixture of each race which inhabited the Empire.

I killed them all.

None of the soldiers' blades or dartguns was blessed by the Lawgiver nor did any of them know magic related to combat. None even sported a silver dagger, which would have been a basic necessity for troops fighting during the Shadow Wars. As such, their attacks were as drops of rain against a slavering wolf. I cut them down like wheat with Chill's Fury, stole the life-force of others, froze more with a torrent of cold from my palm, and mind-controlled the rest into killing their companions. Within minutes, the entirety of the crew was dead.

That was when I crashed the mechanical spider into the traitorous troopers fighting on the side of Northwatch Gate. This was like shutting the barn door after the horses had escaped. It was a useless gesture except for killing a small number of enemy soldiers.

There, the barrier had fallen.

CHAPTER 7

I emerged from the "head" of Draamach, my armor drenched in blood and halfway between ghost and man.

I had more than enough life energy thanks to all those I had killed but there was something about spilling blood which seemed to bring out the beast within me. To others, I imagined I looked like a black-cloaked specter of death who was both a part of this world and not. Several of the charging Imperials hesitated upon seeing me, then were run over by their fellows or bashed to the side.

This was not my war, a conflict which had nothing to do with the Shadowguard, my oaths to defeat the King Below, or even the nation with which I was born. Yet, I jammed Chill's Fury into the ground and unleashed a horrifying wave of freezing energy which washed over the charging troopers. Dozens died because I chose to involve myself in Regina's conflict. From there, I killed every single one of the Imperial vanguard who approached me, cutting them down one after the other in a whirlwind of death.

I had been a great swordsman during my final days as Knight Paramount but my skill had improved dramatically. I remembered fleeting glimpses of my time as an undead horror, training with Wodas the Dark Lord of War as well as the Nameless Dread, Lord of Fear. I moved like a dancer, slicing through bodies from above before spinning around to bisect others.

I parried those swords, mostly ancestral weapons, which could harm me before cutting down their wielders. Many times, I unleashed spells, coming within inches of fading away, only to drain away more life-force to empower myself. The corpses became a pile at my feet, but even my determination to prevent the Imperials from taking Accadia was nothing but an attempt to hold back the ocean with a teacup.

One man struck me in the shoulder with a silver-pointed spear that stung like the King Below's blade and another struck me in knee with a blessed dart from his smoking metal tube. These two had been wise enough to take weapons capable of striking at the King Below's servants which, for now, included me. I managed to kill both men, heroic and valorous, but they weakened me so the next two who picked up their arms were ready to strike at me. I might have been able to kill them but the two after would finish me.

"So be it," I muttered, lifting my blade to die in battle. I fought for several long minutes, holding off my talented opponents as each of my sword thrusts became slower.

That was when the Accadian barrier was restored.

"What the..?" I said, falling back a step.

Smoke poured from the mouths of a hundred invaders, turning into a sooty cloud which merged with the runes in the city wall and sealed the hole in Accadia's defenses. This blackness invigorated me and I struck down my remaining attackers by beheading the first, then sticking my left hand onto the other's face.

I drained from him every year of his life, transforming him into a withered pile of skin and bones which collapsed to the ground. My injuries did not fully heal but I felt stronger and more alert. The sudden death of a hundred of their fellows plus the cutting off from their forces demoralized the invaders who had come forth. Most enemy soldiers cast down their weapons and were taken prisoner while a few chose to fight on until they were killed, an inevitable fact in any conflict.

The spell cast was the darkest magic, used several times during the sieges of High Gillead or Kerifas. Yet, despite this, I was grateful to whomever had used it and I caught sight of her while the Accadian defenders rounded up their prisoners.

She was beautiful.

Possessing skin of burnt sienna, large dark brown eyes, and long curly black hair, she reminded me of Jassa. It was interesting to contrast her and Regina, though I felt guilty about doing so. They were as the Sun and Moon. The sorceress was dressed in a fitted black dress with a tight corset to accent her features, a pair of bronze bracelets on her wrists and a simple necklace of the same style around her neck. Even in my time, the latter were the chosen symbols of the Lakeland merchant class.

Her features surprised me because they were similar to the High Men of Old. Seeing one as a merchant's daughter amused me to some extent as it was a well-known fact the nobles of the Southern Kingdom had no more High Man blood than anyone else. Still, she looked more a queen than most I had met in my day.

Beware that one, the Trickster said. *Hers is a power which is raw and untested but it could cast down gods.*

Is her blood so powerful? I asked, wondering if that was why she'd been able to slay a hundred men at once.

No, her will. The Trickster sounded intimidated, which surprised me. *Valance was born of a potter and a swineherd yet it was he my brother chose to smite the Terralan for their perfidies. It is her intensity which reminds me of him rather than her lineage.*

I shall be cautious, I said, wondering if he was playing with me. Then I realized, *of course he was,* which didn't mean he wasn't telling the truth.

As the woman approached, I noted the black ghostwood staff in her hand topped with a red orb which resembled an eye. On her left hand was a small demonsteel band of twisted thorns which resembled the one around my own finger.

Strangely, there were no soldiers to accompany her and they seemed to avoid her as they went about their business trying to restore the North Gate's defenses.

"Hail, Kurag Shadowweaver, Lord of Despair," the woman said in a pleasant husky voice.

I felt uncomfortable looking at her. "I am not he."

The sorceress scrunched up her nose as if I was denying murder while bathed in the blood of my victim and holding a viscera-covered weapon. "As you wish. I am Serah Brightwaters, daughter of the Brightwaters family and niece to *Lord* Walys Lakelord." She said her uncle's title like she was cursing.

"That was the Breath of Ruin," I said, looking at her. "Where did you learn such a spell?"

"It is said by some my great-grandmother was raped by a High Man in the service of a Dark Lord, if not a Dark Lord in disguise, and afterward introduced her into the black arts. He converted my family to the ruinous worship of the King Below and they practiced all manner of obscenities to birth their final product in me."

I shook off the blood from Chill's Fury before sheathing it. "And what do you think?"

"I was born this way," Serah said, meeting my gaze. "People have hated me from the day my dark magic manifested as a child and justify their loathing by claiming I or my ancestors must have done something to deserve it. I do not hide what I am, however, but practice my arts openly. If I am to die, let it be proud of whom I am rather than lying I am something I am not."

I nodded. "That is courageous."

"It is stupid, according to my brother and family who have suffered trying to protect me. Many times there have been those who would roast my flesh alive in a pyre to the Lawgiver or cut out my tongue before giving me to ruffians. I am not the first woman born with dark magic but I am one of the few who has lived to enjoy it."

I thought of the many witchcraft trials which had been conducted during the war. Families put on trial for one or more of their children manifesting signs of being Shadowkind. Those who had interbred with the Formor or Shadow Races were under suspicion the most, but also those who simply displayed types of magic different from what was considered holy. As a Shadowguard, I'd often been called to officiate and explain light magic was not a sign of holiness nor was dark magic a sign of demonic influence. That spell, however, was one created by the Dark Lords. She was also reacting rather calmly to my 'true' identity.

"A snow-white haired woman with silver armor was with me," I decided to change the subject. "Possibly riding a gryphon. Do you know her location?"

"Yes," the woman said. "Sir—"

"Jacob."

"Ah," the woman smiled. "So the legends are true."

I stared at her. "Given what I've heard of legends in your time I sincerely doubt it."

"It depends where you hear them."

"Have you seen my friend or not?"

"If you mean Lady Regina of fallen Whitehall then yes," Serah stepped aside and gestured down the bloody ramparts of the dead. The smell wafted upward and I was enough of a human to be sick. Few legends ever spoke of the fact men tended to empty themselves when they died. It was just another inconvenient fact for those who wished to send generations off to die in muddy ditches fighting for other men's causes.

"I have known Regina since childhood," Serah said, gesturing to one of the body covered ramparts for me to follow. "We have been friends, rivals, and more."

Serah smiled.

"She is an impressive woman," I agreed.

"As am I, Dark Lord."

"That may not be the best title to refer to me by." I looked over my shoulder.

"Because they would burn you alive on a pyre made from Codexes, hymnals, and pews?"

"Yes."

"So be it," Serah said. "But I am the only person who knows who you are and how you became the way you are, Lord Jacob."

I stared at her. "We'll have to talk about that."

"I think we should."

"After we find my fr—"

The two of us followed a trail of enemy corpses which looked like they'd been cut through by some sort of unstoppable juggernaut, which did not stop until it reached its goal. We passed Regina's slain gryphon at the halfway point before passing on to more corpses.

"I confess, I'm impressed," I said, staring at the ruin she'd left.

"I'll be less so if we find her dead or dying at the end."

"Is she always like this?"

"The Gods Above and Below gave Regina two great gifts: great ability at war and passion. Both burn so hot, though, they might well consume her."

I look at the hundreds who had been killed by this conflict, soldiers on both sides. I had contributed a good number of the casualties and couldn't say if I'd made the bloodshed worse or better for my intervention.

"I see your point." I was starting to like this newcomer, even if the idea of someone wearing her status as a user of evil magic proudly was mind-boggling.

The two of us reached the site where a dozen men armed men lady dead around Regina and a wounded man she was cradling. The men around them wore stylized armor with tabards bearing a mark similar to those of a Lakeland merchant house. The man Regina cradled wore something similar but far fancier.

The symbol on their tabards was a boat with a sail and three rivers running behind it with gold coins forming the sides of a square. They dead men did not wield broadswords or spears but more of those metal tubes, one long one on their backs and the small ones I'd seen used in the battle from afar. Their swords were different too, leaning and more for stabbing than slashing. Even their armor seemed more for show than actual combat.

How much had changed in this world?

Oh much, the Trickster said. *If they ever figure out how to make rune pistols without magic, you can say farewell to swordsmen on horseback, castles, and armored knights.*

Pistols, I thought the name. *Strange name.*

Like a crossbow bolt the size of a marble, the Trickster said. *One of the many, many results of Tharadon's research.*

They seem to have improved archery and crossbows anyway. I couldn't get the image out of my head of Regina's arrows causing gryphons to explode.

Yes, magic does make things a tad disjointed. No sooner do advances make old devices obsolete than someone magics them up into something better. Someday, you'll be able to make an arrow magic so powerful it'll destroy the world. The Trickster made a noise sounding like clapping his hands together. *I do hope I'm there for it!*

I approached the wounded man, getting a glimpse of his face hidden by his helmet. He was very similar in appearance to Serah, though he had shaved his head and possessed a well-trimmed goatee. I saw he'd suffered a number of arrow wounds, his rune-covered armor having blunted the worst of them. His armor also possessed several dents from where the metal balls described by the Trickster had struck him.

Regina, by contrast, was covered in blood from face to waist, but I was grateful to see none of it was hers. Beside her were both Hopebringer and a sword she looked to have stolen from one of the soldiers behind us. There was an arrow buried in her back, but she didn't seem to notice it.

Regina spoke in a soft, calm voice. "Hush now, Lord, and know the traitors are dead. Your sister has sealed the breach and laid waste to the forces within. We have won a great victory for you."

"Thomas is not a Lord," Serah said, frowning. "Neither my brother nor I have inherited the title our uncle gained for selling this land to the Empire. Also, if this is a victory, I'd hate to see what you'd call a defeat."

"Does he need assistance?" I asked, looking down at the man.

Regina frowned. "I think we should get him to—"

"Heal me, Oh Dark One, with your dark witchiness!" Thomas said, waving his hand. "You can't be worse than Serah."

I looked around. "Does *everyone* know what I am?"

Serah shook her head. "My brother is sensitive to the shadow thanks to the fact we shared a womb. To those not blinded by the light, you are a star of night in the day, absorbing all light around you. It is beautiful to behold but invisible to most men."

"Yes, yes," Thomas said, waving his hand again. "Get with the healing. I didn't just fail miserably in my first military command to die here."

I lifted my hands and whispered a sentence of Demonspeak, which sounded painful to my ears. Regina shoved Hopebringer's hilt into his mouth to keep him from biting off his own tongue as the process healed a dozen internal injuries invisible to the naked eye. He had been dying, the only thing keeping him alive being his suit of impressively-crafted mystical armor.

Serah looked at me. "Thank you. Healing is not one of my strong suits."

Regina pulled the weapon hilt from his mouth. "I still say we should have waited—"

Thomas interrupted, blinking rapidly. "That was terribly painful!"

"Don't get horribly injured again," I said, dryly.

"Good idea!" Thomas said, struggling to climb to his feet. "I am Lord, not really, Thomas Brightwaters of House Brightwaters, High Captain of the Principality of Lakeland but not the actual Lakeland down the river. We'd call it East Lakeland to separate it from West Lakeland, the country, but apparently that's too simple."

"Our uncle sold Accadia to the Empire in exchange for a title," Serah said, frowning. "Our parents did not agree and were executed for it. This was before the Tyrant Empress came to power."

Regina stood up, cleaning off Hopebringer before sheathing it. "I have come to speak to your uncle about raising a resistance to the Nine Usurpers."

Thomas looked out to the army beyond the walls. "I think the time for secret meetings has passed. I do, however, approve of you bringing a Dark Lord to fight one of the Nine Heroes. I wouldn't have thought you that clever."

Regina blanched. "He was sort of an accident. But he isn't a Dark Lord. Not really."

I raised my hand to intervene. "Whatever I am, I am allied to you now. I would request you keep my identity hidden for the time being, though, as much as can be at least. I suspect people would react *poorly* to our cause if they knew my identity."

"Is it our cause now?" Serah asked. "You might find my uncle's courage has fled him with the arrival of the Empire's armies."

"He must help!" Regina said, clenching a fist.

"Well, I hope he does," Thomas said, gesturing to the troops. "I should probably appoint someone to take charge while I'm away. Make a speech or something."

"Can you make a speech?" I asked, raising an eyebrow.

"Oh yes!" Thomas said, smiling. "It's about the only thing I'm good at."

Oh this was wonderful. A Dark Lord, an idealistic deserter, a witch, and a High Captain who couldn't command his troops. All we needed was some animate luggage and we could be one of Terrance Pritchard's farces. What had I gotten myself into?

The answer, of course, was war. It was always run by idealists, idiots, and cynics.

Just not often so literally.

"Show me to your uncle when you're done."

CHAPTER 8

It was a good speech.

One of the best, actually.

If High Captain Brightwaters wasn't a very good military commander, he was an excellent orator and used a delightful selection of platitudes to reassure the soldiers under his command everything was under control. Thomas talked about how they would soon drive the enemy back and force a withdrawal.

Which didn't seem likely at all.

Serah, meanwhile, coordinated with Regina in fixing the royal mess he'd made of the city's defenses. They re-armed the sabotaged rune canons (as I learned they were called) on the North Gate and replaced the lost as well as traitorous soldiers.

Furthermore, they broke up the existing squadrons amongst more loyal groups so any treasonous thoughts which may have been spread could do little good. I, in the meantime, wandered through the infirmary, healing the injured before wiping their minds of the darkness they heard. Several times, when a soldier was too injured to heal, I drained away his life to help others. Toward the end, I heard people muttering I was a messenger of death.

Which wasn't far from the truth.

About an hour later, when the Imperial forces had pulled back for the time being, and more competent Captains were put in place, they arranged for a group of jet black horses for us to ride through the city on. They reared at my presence but Serah calmed them down with but a wave of her hand, allowing me to mount one.

The four of us joined an honor guard as we were led from the towers of the gate to the town below. By the sounds coming out from beyond the doors, the townsfolk of Accadia were not happy at the presence of an Imperial army at their doorstep. If a Lord had done their job properly, such anger would manifest as hatred for the enemy and desperate hope for victory. By the shouts and obscenities, it seemed they were more inclined to blame the Lakelord and his family. When we rode out into the village, crowds were already gathered and kept at bay only by the presence of armed men.

I decided to distract myself from this dreary fact by questioning my companions. "So how does a Shadowguard, a High Captain, and a sorceress become a trio of good friends?"

"You mean a fanatic, an imbecile, and a witch?" Thomas said, helpfully. He seemed immune to the verbal abuse coming from the crowds around him.

"I am not a fanatic," Regina said, softly. She looked deeply uncomfortable with the rage being directed at her. "I have my reasons."

Thomas looked back at Regina, a sympathetic look on his face. "I heard about Whitehold. I'm sorry. But you've always been passionate about everything you do. You almost broke my arm playing stickball."

"You were playing wrong," Regina defended.

"It was a decision of our uncles to spend our summers together," Serah said, taking the conversation from her brother. "Regina was raised in the Northern Wastes by her Shadowguard parents for most of her formative years. So, when she returned to the South, she was not fit for polite company, which means she was perfect for spending time with us."

"I did not place much value in the frivolity of gossip, embroidery, and dresses," Regina said, frowning. "This, apparently, is a horrific offense in the Empire."

"Almost as much as not putting much faith in the sword," Thomas said, frowning. "I am a lover, not a fighter."

"And yet you're High Captain," I said, frowning.

Thomas nodded. "It's terrible, isn't it?"

"Yes," I said, looking down at the terrified throngs below. "It is."

"I did not much care for her," Serah said, the first hint of a smile coming to her face. She did so as the crowds called her a witch and said she'd brought the wrath of the Lawgiver down upon them all. "Regina was insufferably sanctimonious at the best of times. Overly religious too. The Gods Above have never treated me with respect so I never treated them with such in return. But, eventually, we came to a mutual understanding."

"Oh, is that what you call it?" Thomas said, grinning.

"Mind your tongue," Regina growled.

I looked between them, surprised. "Ah."

Regina looked embarrassed. "Such things must be shocking—"

"We had such things in my time too, Lady Regina," I said, wondering what it was about people who always seemed to think their generation invented sex.

"It was not a long lasting relationship," Serah said, looking forward. "Our differences were too great and she soon turned to adoring handsome knights while I took to my books. Thomas, however, remained the one person we could always count on."

"I love you both," Thomas said, avoiding a cow pie thrown by a peasant. "Who else would put up with me?"

"You seem awfully calm at the situation here," I said.

Thomas cheerfully waved to the peasant who threw it. "The people have resented my uncle since he brought the Cradle into the Empire and doubled their taxes. I understand how being invaded hasn't improved their mood."

"Why is the Empress attacking?" Regina asked.

"Probably because she knows Lord Walys was planning to work with the Lakelords to overthrow her. That is why you're here, isn't it?" Serah said.

Regina looked down. "Yes."

Serah sighed. "Always thinking with your heart instead of your head. Most girls get over the romanticism of war by the time they start bleeding."

"They *murdered*—" Regina started to hiss.

"I will save your city," I said, interrupting.

"Excuse me?" Serah and Regina said, simultaneously.

"I will save your city with a minimum loss of life," I said, looking at the throngs of desperate scared people. "For their sake."

"You are a curious Dark Lord," Serah said, frowning.

"Please stop calling me that."

"How?" Thomas asked, smiling. "Not that I would understand it."

I looked between them, taking each one's measure. They had their strengths and with such I could form the backbone of an army. "I will force the Empire into a position where they must either negotiate with you for a settlement or withdrawal, necessitating the former. I got a good measure of their forces and yours, even if I don't understand everything, and know your position is not indefensible."

"And if the Empress' terms are my uncle's head along with mine and my sister's?" Thomas asked, blowing a kiss to a trio of Great Mother priestesses praying at a shrine to Saint Jassamine.

I stared at the statue of my lover then shook my head. "I will do my best to see you stay in power, but if the price is your lives, I will see you transported to a kingdom far away with a fortune in valuables to keep you content until the end of your days. I've made such deals before."

"I find those terms acceptable," Thomas said.

"*I* don't," Regina said, looking at me appalled. "We can win this battle."

"This battle? Yes," I said, knowing it was unlikely but possible. "This war? No. This is a castle under siege and you have no allies to relieve you or indications of long-term military preparation. The citizenry is not on your side either and while you can keep them down with troops and intimidation, that will infect your soldiers. Do you want a hanging a day to keep order?"

Regina clenched her fists then breathed out a sigh of distaste. "No, I don't."

"Then allow me to negotiate on your behalf," I said, knowing it wouldn't be that easy. This Jon Bloodthorn seemed to be a clever strategist given his trick with Draamach and foresight to bend troops ahead of time. He had to know time was on their side and that would impact negotiations.

I would have to chastise their troopers and demoralize them to get any sort of suitable terms.

Thomas made a circle with his hand. "Can't you just, make a plague to wipe them out of something? I recall one of you did that during the Fourth War—"

"It was the Second War," I said, sighing. "The famine and disease spells used by both sides created the Great Barrier Desert."

"Oh, right."

"I cannot believe we're discussing surrender," Regina said the last word like she was cursing.

"Some wars are won with blades, others words," I said, sighing. "Besides, you wish to avenge your family, correct?"

"Yes," Regina said, blinking.

"Then let us find the people involved and kill them," I said, simply. "There is no need to drag all of the Southern Kingdoms into the conflict. We'll sneak into their palaces under the cover of darkness and slay them each, one by one, and let their inheritors sort out the business of rulership."

Regina looked disgusted. "Secret killing is a vile business."

"So is starvation and we might be facing that," Serah said, shaking her head. "We only have stores for three months. Just promise me you'll take me with you when you do it."

"Pardon?" Regina asked.

"Your family was always good to me," Serah said, softly. "Why would you think I would not want to help you avenge them?"

Thomas looked disgusted. "So, he's going to negotiate to save our asses only for you to do the one thing which will result in them seeking our blood for the rest of time?"

"You could always condemn me, brother," Serah said, chortling. It was as if his reaction was funny.

"Like Below I will." Thomas snorted. "I am at your side, sister, no matter the cost. I will, however, make sure to hire a flesh mage to sculpt us some new identities and then the four of us had best make for G'Tay. I hear the women are comely and the men look like bears, so I should be a shoe-in with them."

"You miss the part where the bear-like men would object," Serah said, smiling. "See, Regina? You were never alone."

"Thank you," Regina said, looking both stunned and relieved.

Right before another cow pie hit the side of her face. To her credit, she simply cleaned it off and ignored it.

I wasn't sure dealing with the Nine Usurpers would be as simple as tracking them down one-by-one and killing them but I was hoping slaying both this Empress and her Steward would satisfy Regina's bloodlust. Regicide was an awful crime which was condemned in the Codex as a strike against the Lawgiver himself but that didn't mean it didn't happen all the time. Hopefully, they had successors who could easily slide into place and this wouldn't trigger its own brand of chaos and civil war.

This is all a great deal of effort for a woman you've just met, isn't it? The Trickster observed.

I am following my instincts.

You have no instincts, the Trickster said, *just the memories of them. Admit it, this is just an excuse for killing. If you didn't have a war to fight, you'd have nothing at all.*

I didn't dignify that with a response.

The four of us soon arrived at the foot of the Lakelord's castle. It was built on an island just off the shore of the lake with a series of bridges connecting it to Accadia. Walls had been raised with magic in-between of the bridges, creating an impressive albeit impractical series of fortifications.

The castle exterior had been modified with many unnecessary balconies, terraces, and ornate windows. There were other signs it was more a palace than fortress, which wasn't a problem since if the Empire got into the city, the war was over already.

We were conducted to a private garden filled with more flowers than I'd seen in my life. When I approached, they began to wilt, so I kept myself to the center away from the boxes and hoped no one noticed.

"Do you really think this is for the best?" Regina asked, surprising me.

"Which part? My plan? Surrender? The world as is?" I asked, feeling philosophical. "If this is the best of all worlds, I would seriously question the Lawgiver's plan."

"Attempting to surrender," Regina said, frowning. "Lord Hugh Whitetremor was not a warlike man. He was a lover of music, poetry, and sidhe culture. I never gave him the respect he deserved. He would have surrendered were the cause hopeless. Yet, it wasn't just he who was put to the sword but every man, woman, and child in his city."

"I will take their measure," I said, sighing. "I am sorry for your family."

"I want to believe they are in a better place. However, it is difficult to reconcile that hope with the violence of their deaths," Regina said, biting her lip.

"The Path never promised us an easy life, quite the opposite. It is not in this world we shall be rewarded," I said.

"Personally," Thomas said, butting in. "I prefer to take my rewards in this world. The world would be saved a lot of trouble if people cared more about drink and sex than revenge."

Regina's eyes grew dangerous. "This *isn't* about revenge."

"A pity," Serah said. "Revenge I could understand."

The Lakelord arrived at that moment, accompanied by his retinue. Regina, Thomas, and Serah all bowed their heads despite being nobility. He was obese with a large fur-trimmed coat, gold necklaces, and a dozen jeweled rings on every one of his fingers.

Lord Walys Brightwaters wore a beret with a red feather on his head and was a good deal shorter than his relations. He was a member of the High Men, though, and this would have gotten him respect across the lands.

If Regina was hoping for a fair audience, however, that was quickly dashed. "You! This is the fault of your kinsmen! I never should have listened to them. You have brought an army to my doorstep and ruin to my—"

"How dare you!" Regina shouted, the entire room going still. "My father and mother laid down their lives in service of the Empire! My uncle and his sons supported your entry into the Great Houses when every other one wanted you hung for you being a turncoat to your own people. Tirelessly, House Whitetremor defended you only for you to treat me as such upon my entry? Where were you when Jon Blackthorn led his men to hew and slay all those who once called you brother?!"

The Lakelord blubbered, taking a step back.

Serah burst out laughing.

Thomas added, "Now is not the time for recriminations, uncle. The invaders are at the proverbial gates and they do not seem inclined to share the view you are an innocent victim in all of this."

"I was misled!" the Lakelord said. "House Brightwaters—"

"Is twelve years old and born from treachery," Serah said, crossing her arms. "Our family was once revered as the greatest merchant house in Accadia. Peasant stock and proudly so. It was you who wanted to make us nobles. This?" she gestured to the walls. "The armies? *This* is the price of nobility. To be a King or Queen requires you to murder and slay whoever threatens you."

The Lakelord looked down. "Perhaps if—"

"If you think to turn over Regina to the Empress, you will perish and all of your defenders," I said, my voice solemn.

The Lakelord stared. "You threaten me in my own home? Guards!"

I stretched out my power and all of the flowers in the courtyard died instantly as a great shadow passed over my face. "I am....Tharadon! Returned from the realms of darkness and ice to defend my homeland! You stand before a Great Wizard, mortal! Do not speak to me as if you are an equal!"

Taking one look at me, all of the Lakelord's guards threw down their weapons and fled.

Regina stared at me, openmouthed.

The Lakelord fell to one knee. "My Lord, I had no idea! Please, deliver my castle from the hands of the Empire!"

"I shall, but I need complete obedience."

"Anything!" The Lakelord clasped his hands together. "You shall have anything!"

Huh.

I hadn't expected that to work.

Good, I suppose.

"If they ever write songs about this, I hope they change my Uncle's role," Thomas said, sighing. "He's not exactly covering himself in glory."

Regina looked over her shoulder at me. "It seems the songs lie...a great deal."

CHAPTER 9

I wondered if I was going insane or was just surrounded by lunatics.

Yes, the Trickster said. *Undoubtedly.*

That was probably the best answer.

Choosing to impersonate Tharadon the Black was a ridiculous idea, but the way blubbering Lakelord believed it. Then again, desperate people often chose to believe ridiculous things.

"Save my people, Tharadon." The Lakelord clasped his hands together. "I have done...questionable things in my pursuit of a better life for my family. I do not wish the people to pay the price for it."

"Don't put this on us, you old fool," Serah said, growling

"I note you don't want to pay the price either," Thomas added.

"You were the best hope for a rebellion." Regina shook her head. "I am ashamed of what you have become."

"The Empress is too powerful to oppose, Regina," Thomas said, coldly. "Defeating the King Below has been accompanied by many reforms which are popular with the people. She has bought the allegiance of many vital nobles and played the others against one another. You will need to strike at her image if you wish to defeat her." He paused. "Or just kill her, I suppose."

"Do not speak such things!" the Lakelord shouted. "She has eyes and ears everywhere."

"Obviously, because Bloodthorn has brought her army here," Serah snapped. "What did you *do*?"

"With the Empire's armies propping up the other Usurpers and their tyrannies, I thought it might be best to consider approaching those resistant to her. We could be Lords of the Southern Empire or elevated to a Great House ourselves. In time, perhaps even Emperor." The Lakelord rose and started pacing, regaining some semblance of dignity.

"Stop," Serah spoke, feeling her face. "It was not enough you wanted to be a nobleman but now you dream of a seat millions have died pursuing."

"At least you came to the right man," Thomas said to Regina. "This seems to be a house for treason."

"I do not care about such things," I said, conjuring a staff of shadow and altering my cloak to appear as hooded robes of midnight. "I came here only to bring justice and protection unto the people of the land."

"Right...Tharadon," Regina said, looking back at me. "That's... what you are here to do. Yes."

Goodness, she was a terrible liar.

"What must I do to save my kingdom?" the Lakelord asked, forgetting he ruled only a principality.

"Go forth and order your men to fetch me the Book of Balance from the Church of the Lake and the Holy Brand of Saint Ignius. Summon forth a council of the city's master wizards, builders, and engineers. Make preparations for a speech which will be heard by all of the people in your city."

The Lakelord rose to his feet and nodded. "It shall be done, Great Wizard."

"Go!" I said, slamming my staff on the ground.

The Lakelord bolted out of the room, his guards following.

"The Book of Balance? The Brand of Saint Ignius?" Regina asked.

"It'll be hours before anyone realizes it doesn't exist," I said, sighing. "Assuming the rest doesn't keep him occupied."

"You don't actually have a plan, do you?" Thomas said, sounding defeated.

"My goal remains to force a settlement," I said, calmly. "The safety of the people here is my primary concern."

"The Imperials are not trustworthy," Regina said, coolly. "Remember that."

"It would help if I knew more about who I'm dealing with," I said, dismissing the staff and the shadow robes. "Who is this Jon Bloodthorn and what sort of influence does he wield? The Steward of the Empire is a position which has had varied powers depending on the strength of the Great Houses."

"He is a madman," Regina replied, growling. "A murderous thug and a barbarian."

"Very helpful." Serah sighed. "I think he's asking for specifics."

"That *is* specific," Regina said. "If you wish to kill him, I am at your side."

"And you say this is not about vengeance." Serah grumbled. "Focus on saving the city. Please."

Regina looked over at her then nodded. "Alright."

"Allow me to share what I know of the man." Thomas raised an armored hand. "Jon Bloodthorn was born the son of a Winterholme barbarian and a Dryad of the Living Forest. His mother dipped him in the River of Souls as a babe then raised him on the nectar of the gods. As such, he is stronger than any man alive and swords bounce off his skin like raindrops. He has been a mercenary, a pirate, a thief, and a king with his crown set aside to serve Morwen the Revered Strategist."

"They are not lovers," Serah said, interjecting. "This is important to remember. She is like a goddess to him."

Thomas continued. "Jon slew the Dread Wolf Glamdraag with his bare hands and the Nightterror mounts of the Dark Lords so the other heroes could get to the King Below's side to fight them. He is Commander of the Imperial Armies by virtue of his power not lineage and beloved as an invincible warrior. It is said he conducts his business from a throne composed of the dragon skulls he collected from the arena battles he's won."

I stared at him. "How much of that is actually true?"

"Says the Knight Paramount of the Shadowguard who slew a Dark Lord, won a hundred battles, designed much of the weaponry which won the Fourth War, and killed a dragon by himself this morning," Regina said, rolling her eyes.

"*Now* who is being snotty?" I asked, dryly.

"I can't testify to the River of Souls and nectar of the gods part, but his skill as a warrior is true enough as are his magical defenses," Thomas said, sighing. "Part of the reason Bloodthorn's so popular is he's a champion of the arena. He's killed numerous dragons and wild beasts for the entertainment of the Imperial City's masses. I've been to a few of the matches myself. The Empress has used these victories to solidify his reputation as a hero."

"So his death would deal a great blow to their morale?" I asked, thinking on it.

"Undoubtedly," Thomas said. "As a peasant knight, the Great Lords hate him but have lost too many sons to duels and failed ambushes to strike against him openly. Poison and other methods have failed as well. Should Jon Bloodthorn fall, the armies would immediately start to quarrelling over who is in charge."

"Some things never change," I said, remembering the Fourth War. It had been like trying to organize a pack of wild dogs.

"I'm not sure it would have the desired effect," Thomas said, looking ill at the sight of the dead garden around him. "Despite the massacre of Whitehold, the costly foreign wars, the raised taxes, and harsh new religious-based legal system, many still think of the Nine Usurpers as the Nine Heroes. If Bloodthorn is struck down, his army will want to avenge him and whatever they plan for Accadia now will pale to what they'd do to it in his memory."

I was dealing with a popular military commander with an almost mythical reputation and immense personal skill in battle he liked to show off publicly. The beginnings of a plan started to form in my mind. "And if Lakeland were not responsible for his death but a new enemy? Or a very old one?"

"What do you mean?" Regina asked, now paying attention.

"I mean to say, what if I declared the King Below was alive and then challenged him on his behalf?" It was a foul idea, but had its appeal.

"That is..." Regina started to speak. "Actually, brilliant."

Thomas looked over at Serah. "If a Dark Lord working for the King Below could kill Bloodthorn, it would drastically undercut the Empress' claim to popularity. If she didn't kill the King Below then she isn't really all that important. It would also deprive her of a valued general."

"You're a better strategist than you let on," I said, nodding.

"Oh, this? World Above no, this is *politics*!" Thomas said, smiling a beautiful set of white teeth. "Lying, manipulating, and corruption! My specialty!"

"It doesn't deal with the actual *army*, however," Serah replied. "Let's not forget that."

"Your strange devices and machinery are impressive enough that an actual siege would be a protracted bloodbath," I replied, looking between them. "If Bloodthorn falls, we can use that and the threat of the King Below to negotiate a treaty. They'll want to preserve as much of their military as possible. If it doesn't work, I can use my abilities to keep killing in secret until we reach a commander who *is* willing to negotiate."

I was getting far too comfortable with a Wraith Knight's abilities.

"There's still another problem," Serah said.

"What's the other problem?" Thomas asked, turning to his sister.

"Defeating Bloodthorn may be impossible," Serah replied. "He's killed Dark Lords before."

"They came back," Thomas said, as if that made it better.

I grimaced. "Actually, it would appear the resurrection powers of Wraith Knights are overstated."

"Oh," Thomas said, frowning. "That's not encouraging."

"Jacob, could we speak together alone?" Regina said, sounding concerned.

"I'll try not to listen in," Thomas said, putting on a brave face despite the fact his city was about to be destroyed. Either that or he genuinely wasn't concerned.

"Try and finish soon," Serah said, looking toward the wall facing Accadia's North. "The mood of the people is not good. While there's nothing they can do to lay siege to our castle, it would not take much effort for a rabble-rouser to open the gates. My barriers only function so long as no one invites the invaders in."

"You have done well to protect these people." I reassured her. "Do not think that is unrecognized."

"You, Sir Jacob," Serah said, "are the only one who does."

Regina took me to a corner where she looked up to me. "I cannot allow you to do this."

"I thought we'd addressed this. I agreed to fight for you."

"There is a difference between choosing to lend your sword to a cause not your own and fighting the most dangerous man in the world."

"No. Both involve the risk of death."

Not that I wasn't already dead.

Regina looked down. "I was blinded by my need for retribution. Seeing Serah and Thomas endangered is a rooster crowing in my ear that my actions have consequences. You are a good man and I don't want to see you wounded or slain."

I looked at my hand, then the dead garden around us. "I am dead, Regina. There is nothing for me to risk. All those I loved are bones in the ground and the world I came from is half-remembered stories. When I awoke to this new world, minutes before you arrived, my first action was to try and impale myself on my sword. I couldn't bring myself to commit suicide but it will be no great loss should I destroy myself."

I remembered more of my career during the Fourth War. I remembered how my desire to annihilate the King Below's forces had become an all-consuming obsession. I remembered the mass-executions, the use of forbidden magic, and the bloody-handed way I'd pressed forward at all times. No method was too extreme, no alliance too sacred, and no weapon too powerful to utilize. In my head, I saw a massive graveyard of a hundred thousand swords replacing tombstones. I'd contented myself with the delusion I'd been a good man by never ordering the deaths of children, but how many had died because their fathers and mothers hadn't come home? No wonder the King Below had made me his lieutenant.

Regina placed her hand on my chest. "There is hope."

"Is there?" I asked, overwhelmed by the force of the memories.

Regina nodded. "You may scoff at the stories but my uncle's books contained much wisdom. There was a Wraith Knight who was redeemed."

I stared at her. "I have not heard of such a thing."

"The Lost Three are not spoken of outside of sidhe histories." Regina hand pulled back and her cheeks flushed. "The Four were originally Seven. The Lost Three's names were stricken from the ranks of the histories because they successfully rebelled against the King Below. Sidhe do not like to remember their shame, while humans loathe the idea any Shadowkind can be redeemed. Two of them have had their names lost to history, but a third escaped and lived a life as a smith for the Great Houses."

"Who was this man?"

"Co'Fannon," Regina said.

My chest tightened. I knew that name. For I'd slew him to steal his secrets, much as I'd done with Tharadon.

It seemed I was a killer of heroes.

"The Tower of Everfrost contained a way for him to turn back into a sidhe," Regina said. "We can find that method."

"Everfrost is located in the Eyes of the World beyond the Northern Wastes," I said, staring at her. "It is built over a hole which leads to the frozen center of the underworld. You would go with me to such a place?"

"I am a Shadowguard. I do not fear the cold."

I was struck she that she was as willing to aid me in a mad crusade as I was to aid in hers. I had no intention of dragging her to certain death, of course, but still honored her commitment. "You are an impressive woman."

"Thank you," Regina said, looking down at her hand. "I can fight Bloodthorn. You do not need to risk yourself on my behalf."

"You will need to if I fall in battle."

Regina looked at me, as if trying to figure out what to say in order to dissuade me. Finally, she said, "Alright. You must promise me you will triumph, however. We must journey to the frozen north together."

"I swear," I said, placing my hand over hers. "If I survive, I will go to the north."

I did not mention it would be with her.

Regina held my hand tight. "Do not become an oathbreaker."

"I shall not." I had hope now. Regina had given me an answer for my situation. I would go to the heart of the King Below's tower and seize his power for myself. I would match power for power and bring about peace for both myself as well as the Southern Kingdoms.

What could go wrong?

The Trickster was silent.

It was time to face Bloodthorn.

CHAPTER 10

Sneaking out the city with a cloaking spell, I walked a good halfway across the battlefield. A rainstorm had turned the surrounding grasslands into mud, causing the thousands of bodies from Bloodthorn's assault to sink into the ground. After his initial plan with Draamach had failed, he'd tested the defenses of the cities, using conscripts to determine where the rates of fire were at their weakest.

These losses were minor compared to the strategic information he'd gleaned from such a movement but I couldn't help wonder what sort of commander felt it was justified, especially when I stepped over an open-eyed sixteen-year-old boy. Above my head, the air filled with magical fire and explosions with the sky streaked with light. It was beautiful, in a morbid way, like the fireworks the Indras used in their celebrations. Someone had clearly adapted the children's toys into something more lethal, though. The barrier was holding, but barely and I wondered if Serah would have to start making regular human sacrifices to keep it up.

And whether that was wrong.

You are attracted to the woman, Regina. Tsk-tsk-tsk. The Trickster sighed. *How easily you forget your lost Jassa.*

I am dead, she is alive, I replied, wondering if it would be better simply to ignore him. *Nothing can happen between us.*

That's not what I said.

When I was far enough away from the city where it wouldn't look like I was coming from it, but not yet near the battle lines, I proceeded to draw a summoning circle in the mud. It was unfortunate my dragon was slain, for I needed something dramatic for the next stage of my plan. Something straight from the chorus of a players' troupe narration, daring the audience to imagine things beyond their ken.

I settled for a Nightterror.

Speaking the dark language, I drew upon the thousands of recently slain souls around me to feed the circle without the benefit of human sacrifice. The storm clouds above clashed and thundered, shooting down a bolt of lightning which struck the center of my summoning circle.

From the bolt appeared a pale demonic stallion with shimmering wisps of frost for hooves and a body made out of living ice. Its eyes glowed with witchfire, trailing white mist generated within the hollow insides of its unnatural body. A pair of shadowy black wings stretched out from its side even as I felt it radiate a diabolical resonance which would kill most men who approached it.

Nightterrors, or Nuckelavee as they were known as the Northern lands, were the souls of damned mortals wrapped up in the power of the King Below. It was said there was only one way to avoid the terrible pain of freezing to death forever in the World Below or wandering around in the dark and that was to sell yourself to the King Below's service. The Trickster was just that, though, and turned such spirits into horrible monstrosities.

The Nuckelavee looked upon me and breathed out a cone of cold which would strike most men dead in an instant. I did not even feel a tickle for my body was long dead and what I wore was merely the semblance of dead.

The creature did not wait to see what its attack had wrought and sought to take flight so it could slake its thirst for the living. The Nightterror did not get more than two heads off the ground before it was forced to settle back down in the ring.

"Are you quite finished?" I asked, impatient. "I'm not sure my cloaking spell will hide us both for very long."

"You are not Kurag," the Nuckelavee said, its voice manlike and hateful.

"I'm glad you noticed," I said, frowning. "You are to serve me until I dismiss you."

"You bring no offering of the living. No pledges of gold or murder. Not even a plea for my obedience. Why should I serve you?"

"Because I intend to kill Jon Bloodthorn."

The Nuckelavee snorted out a puff of frost. "I am yours to command."

Climbing upon my mount, I soared into the air, dependent on the cloaking spell for a few minutes more before removing it. I then unleashed the full power of my presence upon the Imperial Army, my terrible mount illuminated by the rapid succession bolts of lightning behind me.

It was said, at their height, the Dark Lords could defeat an entire army purely through terror. Indeed, most wars were won through morale for a conflict only ended when one side was either intimidated into submission or wiped from the world. Since I didn't want to do the latter, I endeavored to be as frightening as possible.

Taking up a visible position before the North Gate, I enhanced my voice to carry through the whole of the army. *"Fools and weaklings, why does thou make war upon each other when your true foe lies to the North? The ever-reaching hand mocks your efforts, stretching forth its fingers to all corners of the realm to sound his recovery. Did thou think it was possible to slay a* **god***? Nay, you have been played upon by one who would see you slay each other like fatted pigs for a feast. For the meal is my master's and he is ready to dine. The King Below lives as do his servants, laughing at your charlatans pretending to be heroes. The War of Light and Shadow can never be won, only fought."*

I was answered by a host of a thousand arrows, rifle-shots, and spells from those who had thought the King Below dead. I lifted up an amulet given to me by Serah, which conjured a barrier around me. She'd created it before my departure, saying she'd had to empty out the castle dungeons. I did not like to think of such.

The attacks struck against the barrier and bounced off, making them seem useless and ineffectual. My barrier was not a thousandth the strength of the city's, which had been created by hundreds of mages working for years, but it served its purpose. I could feel the doubt, fear, and horror wash through the ranks. They had truly thought the long nightmare of the Great Shadow Wars was over, but I had brought it back.

"Forgive me, milord," the Nuckelavee said. "I have misjudged you. You truly are the Lord of Despair and I am at your service."

That was like a hot knife to my heart. I pushed away the shame, though, for wars were won this way. If I had to be evil, then I would evil, if only to see the night pass to the day.

I pulled Chill's Fury from its sheath and caused it to blaze with witchfire, the only flame which burned with cold. *"I would challenge the one amongst you who claims to be one who has bested my brothers and sisters. He who has the impudence to say the light is stronger than the dark and flame is not but a flickering candle to the eternity of the night. I call upon thee, Jon Bloodthorn, Barbarian-Son and Wolf-Killer to do battle with your greater. If timorous be your soul then stand down and stay warm another night. A coward's death may be years in the making."*

A long metal tube with men operating levers and dials at the bottom raised from the center of the army at me. It made a massive noise as it fired, shooting a great ballista bolt of steel at my face. No fool, I retreated into my cloaking spell while conjuring an illusion of myself in its place. It seemed the rune-covered bolt passed right through me, further demoralizing them.

By this point, I'd already used up half of my magic. *"Is your response? So be it. From Everfrost to the Fire-Mountains of Lost Terralan, I shall speak of the callow end to the race of man's courage."*

A wise man would have ignored my entreaties and allowed them to pass into the wind. A wise man did not rise to power over the Imperial army by his own hand, though. No, that required a bold man and bold men lived at the end of a spear. They risked death every day for great gains and the price for such was to never show weakness lest they lose it all. Countless warlords became kings only to die as criminals when they lost the devotion of their men.

I was almost disappointed when Bloodthorn's voice bellowed forth from below, also enhanced by magic. It meant he was no different. "Your taunts, specter, are no more than words. You are but the sad will-o-wisp of a passed age, raging impotently at the dawn. Where is your army? I see no kingdom behind you? And your god? Gone like a foul dream the world has awakened from. Three Dark Lords were struck down at the Battle of Everfrost and I was there when the Empress stabbed through the Trickster's visor with Hopebringer, causing the ancient horror's spirit to rise up and burn to nothingness in the sun's rays. Your power is broken, empty, and false. Lord of Despair, I say that hope has rendered you impotent. Seek no more to spread lies of your god's survival but return to the darkness beyond death. Torment the living no more!"

He was eloquent, but a silver tongue would mean little with a knife in his throat. *"My armies blacken out the sky with their arrows, the* ground with their armor, and the sea with their ships. You may meet me on the killing fields, Wolf-slayer, or be struck down where you stand, but I shall present your head to the world as proof of what happens to mortals who claim they have slain gods."

"They cease to bandy words with ghosts!" Bloodthorn called upon, before his mount emerged from the front of the army. That is when I got my first view of my opponent.

Jon Bloodthorn was a man of Winterholme with of mixed human and giant blood. He stood seven-feet-tall if he was an inch, a mountain of muscle and long flowing black hair with scars criss-crossing what was visible of his body. A gigantic wolf's head and pelt was around his helmet, draping over his shoulders. If this was not the legendary Dread Wolf he'd slain, it was certainly meant to invoke it.

Contrasting to the elaborate heraldry and decorated armor of the knights around him, Jon wore Formor armor. Like its makers, Formor armor was thick, gray, ugly, and strong. A sword as tall as long as most men was sheathed on his back and I wondered if he had been the one to deliver the killing blow to the King Below.

Nay, that was his Empress, the Trickster whispered. *Men have always underestimated women. It's one of your species less charming qualities.*

Jon was sitting on the back of an exceptionally large gryphon. By its elaborate plumage and the golden crown on its head, I took it to be the Gryphon King. Ironically, this lowered my respect for the man. Gryphons were a holy species of the Lawgiver, dotting every Temple from here to the Borderlands, but a greedy and cruel species in truth.

They had given the barest minimum amount of help during the Shadow Wars and in my time, there was talk we could have ended the conflict in a fortnight by the gryphons bringing us to Eyes of the World. Then again, perhaps I was simply hoping for a swift end to a war which had consumed the World Between's peoples like kindling.

The fact Bloodthorn chose to ride on the back of the Gryphon King as well as have his personal guard use its subjects, spoke of a man who trusted too easily. Still, he was far from the barbarian king spoken of in the tales by Thomas and his Uncle. He was worse, since his attire spoke a man confident of his outside status but wise enough to equip himself properly.

Bloodthorn's squire removed his blade and presented it to him. He then drew a sword which glowed with an unearthly light before catching fire. "Come down, damned soul, and face a man forged like steel in the fires of adversity. A man who is not afraid of the winter's chill but slept naked in the snow and learned to wrestle leopards for his food during the long, hungry months. Your god has given you fear and eternal life as a spirit but the Ancestors have given me life as a living man with a strong arm to swing this blade. We shall see which of their gifts is stronger."

"Beware," the Nuckelavee said. "I was at the final battle at the foot of the Eyes of the World. Bloodthorn struck down demons, men, and chieftains carving a path for his brethren to reach the King Below. The Namelesss Dread sought to impede him but for all her mastery of the blade, she fell to his rune-sword."

"All he can do is kill me," I said, my voice like a normal man's.

"Which send your soul to the World Below," the Nighterror said, a hint of bitterness. "A fate I would wish on no man, even as I seek to strike at the hateful light within all things mortal."

"Then we had best not die."

This was theater, a puppet-show for onlookers. I simply hoped, for once, the villain won.

I brought the Nighterror down to meet Bloodthorn.

CHAPTER 11

The proceedings for a formal duel were largely unchanged from the fall of the Terralan Dominion. Even so, as they prepared the trumpets to announce when the two of us would be able to engage in battle, I was unnerved by the fact Bloodthorn was only a few dozen feet across from me, yet unafraid.

Despite having no squire or accompaniment and his army a hundred yards away across a field of corpses, Bloodthorn was as calm as a man waiting at the dinner table for his next meal. When I had faced Kurag, my heart had been turned to ice and it had taken everything within me to transform that emotion into unthinking rage.

Equally calm was the Gryphon King, who I realized had a glassy-eyed, empty look. A glance at the great beast's reins and saddle told me the Imperial Steward had used magic to seize control over his mind. It made me wonder if the whole of their race had been similarly broken or the gryphons followed their monarch, unaware he had been bound with sorcery.

Clutching my sword hilt tightly, I awaited the signal to begin our deadly duel. If I could strike him down quickly, then it would be a massive blow to the armies' confidence. I would probably die in the resulting counterattack, the rules of war rarely applying to Shadowkind, but it would massive undermine the enemy's morale. I would try to escape, though, if for no other reason than to guarantee my promise to protect Accadia.

Much to my surprise, Jon Bloodthorn spoke before the trumpets sounded. He was still clutching his flaming sword to one side as if it were the most natural thing in the world. "Tell me, how did such a man as you come to be in the service of a petty weakling like the Lakelord?"

"*I serve no man but the King—*"

"This is not the opera we just enacted, Jacob Riverson."

I changed my voice back to its normal tone. "I do not know how you know my true identity but I have broken free of the King Below's control. I have friends within Accadia and fight for their safety."

The Trickster snickered in the back of my mind at the words *broken free*.

"The Golden Sorceress gave us your identity when she told us not to pursue you," Bloodthorn said, as if I should recognize said title. "As for your friends, you would have done better to come to me in private and begged their pardon. The Lakelord and his heirs have no future but the headsman's ax, but I have no desire to turn Accadia into an abattoir. As much wealth as will be carried off when we take this man, I only unleash the fury of my men when my quarry resists. Had the Lakelord an ounce of spine, he would have surrendered rather than used his people as a shield."

I narrowed my eyes. "Perhaps he knew what sort of mercy you showed the people of Whitehold."

Bloodthorn's lips curled into a bitter smile. "There was no mercy shown to Whitehold. Not only did I slay the Whitetremors, I slew their servants, their peasants, their guests, their swords, and their singers. I burned their libraries, poisoned their gardens, torn down their statues, and wiped my ass with their tapestries. I turned that centuries-old city into a torch and those not slaughtered were carried off as slaves. My only regret is I did not silence their Lord's niece but have sent word unto the Shadowguard to do so."

My fury became a blizzard in my soul. "And yet you speak of pardon."

"I did it for peace."

"Language has changed it would seem. When I was still alive, we did not speak of wasteland and call it empire nor did we speak of death and call it peace."

"Oh? I think our definitions are very similar." Bloodthorn said. "I have seen the horrors of war and the burdens it places upon the common man. When my Empress was crowned, a hundred lords called their banners and prepared to strike her dead. A hundred more joined said alliance when they heard of her taxes to build roads as well as aqueducts and schools. Half as many for restrictions of their ancient rights. When I made a bloody ruin of Whitehold, the trumpets of war fell silent. If so old and proud a lineage as the Whitetremors could be treated as vermin, they realized their own houses as vulnerable. They are cowards, these lords and ladies of the Empire, and I merely showed them how real war is fought."

Bloodthorn's words were not too far from what many Shadowguard spoke as ways to handle the re-conquest of cities which had fallen prey to the Northern heathens. It felt the execution of one man could save a hundred, if suitably horrible. The death of one city served much the same purpose. I had adopted the former philosophy but never applied the second. It had cost me victories, much to my shame. Yet, I could not and did not forgive Bloodthorn for it.

Instead, I focused on the worshipful tone he used when speaking of his Empress. "Yes, she spoke of your pragmatism. Your loyalty too.

Morwen said you would willingly give your life for her cause. Which is good because making peace with those lords you have terrified will come at a cost."

Bloodthorn looked confused. "What do you speak of?"

I gave a short chuckle. "Your trust is misplaced. I have already made a deal for the protection of my allies. She sought me out in Accadia via thought-whisper to serve as her assassin. It is no coincidence you were sent here for the threat of the non-existent King Below's return who will unite the whole of Empire behind her—at the mere cost of your execution."

"You lie!" Bloodthorn hissed.

"Do I? I intend to kill you upon these fields. What reason have I to deceive? You have become an embarrassment to the Gryphon Throne. It would be better for you to die here, today, on the fields of Lakeland at my hands than continue to sully her reputation. Dozens of great lords will pledge their armies to her in order to have your steward's position."

Bloodthorn's gaze narrowed and he sought some sign of my lie before curling his lips into a sneer. "You shall meet your end, today, spirit."

"Die betrayed and alone." After all, why would I lie? To plant a seed of doubt in his mind which would not have time to grow into a mighty tree, but was only needed to stretch out its roots. I also hoped to cause the child-killer some degree of pain, even if I fell here today. On some level, I knew even if he won, he would always wonder.

For was I not the Lord of Despair?

I'm pleased you have accepted such, my knight, the Trickster said. *Now you just need to realize you're the King Below.*

I didn't have time to ponder that thought before the trumpets blared.

Bloodthorn lifted his blade as the Gryphon King reared, flying forward at me with whatever magic kept the leonine eagles afloat. The Nuckelavee turned to the side and charged, allowing me to bring up Chill's Fury and parry Bloodthorn's blow as he made a strike at my neck with the flaming blade.

The light and dark magic within our weapons exploded as it contacted, causing the entire battlefield to be showered with supernatural force. A thick gravy-stew like fog spread over the ground while the wailing of the damned could be heard around us.

Despite the size of his blade, Bloodthorn wielded it with one hand and with the speed of a rapier. It required every bit of my skill to hold back his furious assault of strikes, each possessing the strength of ax and the speed of a panther. The Nuckelavee managed to keep pace with the Gryphon King even as it proved to be slightly more maneuverable, giving me a chance to strike at the space between Bloodthorn's neck and helmet.

Chill's Fury proceeded to spark against his skin as if striking a piece of solid metal, which sent me reeling backwards. I moved out of the way to avoid Bloodthorn striking off my head, only for him to redirect his sword through the neck of my Nuckelavee mount. The creature let forth a hideous wail as it was decapitated, sending it back to the World Below. I was thrown back on the ground, rolling amongst the fog.

"Flesh magic," I grumbled, recognizing the spells. They were magic from Natariss, woven into the body with tattoos. That was the source of Bloodthorn's reputed invincibility, giving lie to his whole claims of being bathed in the River of Souls. I sincerely doubted he was half-Dryad too, which made me wonder if any of his history was true.

Bloodthorn brought up his gryphon to claw at me, the ends of its talons covered in blessed silver enamel. I dodged out of the way of them before proceeding to conjure a globe of withering darkness, drawing from the deathly energies about this place. I then hurled it at Bloodthorn's mount, suspecting any spell would bounce across his skin like raindrops.

"Fool! The Gryphon King is protected against all hostile magic!" Bloodthorn said, swinging around to take a strike at my head with his blade. That was when the Gryphon screamed and took into the air, trying to flee from the battle.

"It wasn't hostile," I said, hissing. "I cast aside the spells you wove against it."

That was when Bloodthorn landed on the ground, falling thirty feet on his right arm. The warrior was on his feet within moments, favoring his injured side. In the distance, I could see hundreds of other gryphons rising from the Imperial army and flying away. Whatever spells woven to keep them under control had been tied to their sovereign.

"Replacing those will be difficult," Bloodthorn said, coming at me with slower strikes. My parries weren't much faster, though, the spell having taken much out of me. Worse, the heat of his blade seemed to drain away my very substance. While I held back a dozen strikes, Bloodthorn's sheer power forced me back.

"You shall not triumph," I said, hissing. "This is the day of your death."

"I do not fear my death," Bloodthorn said, taking a step back as we encircled one another. "In Winterholme, there is no greenery or joy, only grim darkness. The King Below has invaded us five times and stripped away all but the rawest nature of man. If I die today or a decade from now, it will be with blood on my lips, a curse on my tongue, and a life lived by steel. What more can a man ask for?"

"Then why serve your Empress' cause?" I said, taking three fast steps forward and locking blades with him. I drew on what little remained of my mystical strength to give me a brief boost in my strength. If I did not defeat him soon, I would be little more than a wisp of air, powerless and damned.

"Because she dreams of a world where life is not a forge but a promise!" Bloodthorn shouted, knocking away Chill's Fury and swinging it around to cut me in half.

I threw myself underneath his injured side and came behind him, placing my hands around his neck and draining away the spells of protection woven into his skin. The immense power gave me solid form once again. I also got a taste of the magician who'd cast them.

Fire...

Flame...

Love...

Sadness...

Regret...

Once they might have been lovers, but Bloodthorn did not follow those he took to his bed. They were an endless series of soft caresses and empty words. He respected her only as a warrior and leader. She was wrong, though, for Bloodthorn longed for someone who could ease his troubled mind.

An equal.

Yet, the caster had treated him ever as nothing more than a subordinate.

Which bred distrust in his heart.

She was a creature of civilization.

While he was one of the wilds.

That was when Bloodthorn slammed the back of his head into my newly created nose then hurled me over his shoulders with his left hand. He brought down his flaming sword again, only for me to roll away before grabbing Chill's Fury once more.

"You move like a snake, ghost," Bloodthorn hissed. "Stand still so I send you back to your master."

I threw myself back on my feet, holding forth my sword. I knew his weakness now. "You're no longer protected by the flesh-magic the Empress wove into your skin."

"As if I needed sorcerer's tricks to kill the last thirty wizards I've slain," Bloodthorn hissed, growling.

"The Empress told me about your weakness," I hissed. "I wouldn't have been able to unmake the bindings without her knowledge."

I was gambling Bloodthorn hadn't taken the six years of training in craftsmanship and rune-work I had from my time at the Grand Temple. Nor had access to the secret arts of Co'Fannon which made my unbindings so effortless.

Did he believe me?

I could not say, only that he lost control for a brief second and swung his blade too wide. I once more moved behind him, predicting he'd step forward to avoid being vulnerable to a swing from blade.

Which allowed me to conjure a dagger of inky-black shadow in my left hand and drive it into the barbarian's neck. The dagger dissolved seconds later, but the shadow seeped into his neck like a hare down a hole. Bloodthorn stumbled forward, dropping his sword. The flames disappeared from the blade and he stood, a titan brought low by a trick. I could see his veins turning black while the blood gushing forth became a foul-smelling brown.

"It was a good death," Bloodthorn said, falling to his knees at last. "I ask you make it clean. Do not..."

I dropped Chill's Fury and picked up his sword instead. The weapon felt profaned by my touch but I lifted the Terralan weapon and drove it through the center of his skull, splitting his helmet in two. The Imperial Steward was dead and, with it, some small measure of revenge was taken for Regina's family.

I felt guilty being the one to take it, even as I knew what was to come. The Empire had never honored warriors of the King Below. They were considered to be heretics, blasphemers, and enemies of the world. One might duel with them for the sake of personal glory but representatives were rarely treated with anything resembling respect.

Assuming they weren't killed outright.

The Imperial Army had witnessed their commander's death at my hands. Such an insult could not go unavenged. I was not surprised when war horns blew and the sky filled with missiles of fire. It was like watching a river of shooting stars rushing toward me.

They were going to burn me alive.

"So be it," I muttered, picking up Chill's Fury and raising it in front of my face. I didn't even attempt to flee, instead throwing what little strength I could into a barrier I knew would be useless against their sustained barrage.

The ground exploded as the barrage fell like raindrops, my vision blurring as columns of flame shot up all around me.

Blackness took me.

I hoped, this time, I stayed dead.

CHAPTER 12

I did not know if I died for a second and final time on that battlefield because I found myself floating in an endless starry sea of memory. I dreamed of the present, I dreamed of the past. A ghost did not need sleep, food, or rest, but they could dream.

My memories were blocked while I was awake, coming to me only as a cold trickle stream as I was reminded of events and past dealings. While in this state, though, I relived them in crystal clarity. If I was undone, it might be my afterlife to spend the rest of eternity reliving the best and worst moments of my life. If so, it could have been worse. Oh, a time when I was young and free!

One memory soon drowned the others out. It was ninetieth year of the seventh age of the New Calendar, the Age of the Serpent. I was a man of twenty-three and the Fourth Great Shadow War had not yet begun. Instead, I was a Temple Knight serving in the Grand Temple.

Oh to describe the Imperial City to one who has never seen it? It was the greatest and most horrible city on the World Between, a place of surpassing beauty and terrible corruption. The Inner City was made of marble, colored glass, bronze, and possessed bronze statues larger than buildings. The slums were hideous, possessed of poverty which rivaled anything I'd seen on the Borderlands. Slavery was the only escape for many. As gentle as I'd found my indenture under Warmaster Kalian to be, it was not so for most citizens and yet still preferable to death by starvation.

Even so, Temple Knights were often sent in as part of their graduation to kill one of the homeless to show they had a killer's instincts (and to cut down on the city's mouths to feed). I'd bought the corpse off a family who'd lost their father to a tavern brawl instead. I doubt I'd have gotten away with it if he hadn't been a Fir-Bolg. It had resulted in the rather disgusting sobriquet of "Jacob Horncutter."

Even in my time, they'd been viewed with disdain.

I was thinking of horrid night when I walked through the gardens of the Grand Temple. The air was surpassingly sweet and the voices of the castrated choir boys sang the Hymns of Light. Great banners decorated the sides of the half-mile circular courtyard, bearing scenes from the Codex or depictions of the Burning All-Seeing Eye.

The gardens were the largest in the city and carefully maintained by over a thousand slaves, populated by magically controlled animals who defied their nature to act harmless or proper at all times. Leopards acted like house cats, cassowarys behaved as decor, and goats walked alongside predators with no fear. Fuck, they even shit in specific spots to avoid spoiling the mood.

It was in here priests and priestesses of the Temple could intermingle safely, as the gardens were to be a reflection of the World Above's Gardens of Otherworldly Delights. I did not know of such things, but it was hard not to deny the beauty of the Elder Trees, those two entwined white trunks, which grew together long ago and at the center of the Grand Temple's Courtyard. It was in front of them on a bench that I saw Jassamine Nightsbane.

Jassa was twenty-four, a year older than me, wearing modest white cotton priestess' robes with plain golden trim and a hooded grey cloak. A plain unadorned ghostwood staff lay to her side, twisted like the Elder Trees, showing her initiation into the higher mysteries of light magic. She was a lovely girl with olive skin and twisted hair which hinted at High Men ancestry, though such did not give her status in the Grand Temple. Whereas most of the initiates here were children of the Empire's nobility, Jassa hailed from the lands of Natariss to the Far South.

Which made us both outsiders.

"You look troubled, Jacob," Jassa said, not looking up from her book.

"How could you tell?"

"Because you are always troubled," Jassa said, smiling. "Not since you took your vows have you known a peaceful night's sleep."

"You would know," I said, whispering.

Jassa's smile became embarrassed. "We mustn't speak of such things. Such liaisons are forbidden."

"Liaison is a fancy word for what we do," I said, then paused, realizing how that sounded. "I prefer love."

"Sit by me, please."

I did so, without hesitation. My black silk cloak covered my similar pants and shirt. I was off-duty and dressed for travel throughout the town. Other Temple Knights might dress like peacocks but if they were going to treat me like Shadowkind, I might as well wear my darkness on my chest. Besides, not a single one of them knew anything but honor.

"You, alone, have brought me comfort since coming to this awful place," I said, not looking at her directly.

"It is not the place, but the people. We must be cautious. The others break their vows on a nightly basis. They have turned the Grand Temple into a whorehouse, the priestesses into painted strumpets, the clergy into coin counters, and the Temple Knights into drunkards. Yet, they have friends and protection. We do not."

"I've been dealing with people saying I smell of trout and garbage since I came here. They still call me Jacob the Bastard," I said, curling my lip. "As if I could help where my sire put his cock."

I refused to call the man whose seed had created me 'father.' Fathers did not sell their sons into bondage, even if my burdens had been light.

"Better than your graduation title." Jassa shook her head. "Your Fisherfolk is showing. Such language is unbecoming a Temple Knight."

"My apologies."

"We must be cautious, Jacob, there are spies everywhere in the Grand Temple. The Imperial City is not safe for outsiders, despite its reputed cosmopolitan nature."

Jassa spoke the truth. The Imperial City was a cesspit of treachery and vice. Most of the residents were Borderlanders, Fir Bolg, Gael, Indras, Lakelander, Trow, Winterholme, or some hybrid thereof, yet the majority of the power rested in the Imperial elite.

It didn't matter if your family had lived in the Empire for a dozen generations, all that mattered was if you were of "proper" breeding. The Imperial's arrogance extended past the nobility to the common craftsmen and traders.

I had gotten so sick of watered down drinks and overcharged burnt food, I'd started eating at Fir Bolg restaurants in the Fire District. There, the people called me fire-friend and I only had to avoid poisoning myself with the spiciness of their food. It was times like this I missed Kalian. No one had dared treat him as anything less than a friend of the Emperor himself while alive.

"I don't see why anyone would want to spy on me," I said, putting my hands on my knees. "My life is an open book."

"Your lack of secrets makes you suspicious," Jassa said, shaking her head. "You have also made enemies."

"Really?" I narrowed my eyes. "Who?"

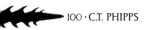

"Sir Hugh Smalltower and Sir Llewyn Mane for example," Jassa said, trying to look inconspicuous. "You have humiliated them to the point they seek your blood."

"Those teet-sucking twats?"

Jassa shot me a dirty look.

"Again, apologies," I said, frowning. "I know they can't fight forth s...much during practice but that's hardly a reason to want me dead."

"You humiliate them on a regular basis. Despite their epic breeding and wealth, they look like fools compared to you and they have been passed over for promotion to Knight Captaincy. Sir Hugh is responsible for the duel you fought last month."

"Which one?"

"The one where you killed your attacker?"

"Ah," I said, remembering. It had been some sort of gruddy flea knight who had done his very best to pick a fight with me. I'd remembered trying to go easy on him, only for him to keep escalating it until I'd been forced to shove my blade through his neck. It had been only the third man I'd ever been forced to kill. That had gotten me a stern lecture from High Priestess Marissa. Apparently, Temple Knights weren't supposed to slay men over tavern duels.

"I should tell Sir Llewyn he needs to get a better quality of assassin," I said, shrugging. "Right before I call him out."

"You mustn't," Jassa said, moving her hand over to mine, not looking at me directly. "They are only second and third sons of minor houses but should you reveal their crimes or, worse, kill them, then you would make a host of enemies you cannot hope to face."

"I'm not going to sit back and let them strike at me. That's not the way I was raised." That was a lie, I'd been raised to always turn my back on those who would harm me. My sire failed to realize that only invited stabbing.

"I wish you had been raised with more sense," Jassa said, removing her hand. "But Llewyn will be found by bribed city-guardsmen tomorrow in a brothel with the possessions of one of the many bodies dumped in the harbor every week. Llewyn will be encouraged to name Hugh as his accomplice because he is a coward."

I blinked, realizing she'd just described a plan to eliminate them both. "You want to falsely accuse them?"

"Their families will pay for their release but their time at the Temple will be over and their reputations destroyed irrevocably. At best, they will be sent to the front lines in hopes of redeeming their honor."

"I'm not sure I like that." I wasn't used to seeing this side of Jassa. The last time I had was when she'd gotten six men to give their sworn testimony they'd lain with a rival priestess named Layna. They'd hung her. Said woman had been a blasphemer, only becoming a priestess for the wealth and position it brought her, but I found such an action excessive.

Jassa shook her head. "One must learn to fight for scraps of meat when in a pack of wolves."

"Alright," I said, sighing. "I'll do as you say."

"It is good you say that because you are going to hate what I have to say next."

I grimaced. "What?"

"I need you to confess to our affair before the Grand Cleric."

I was silent.

"Jacob?"

"I'm sorry, I was just trying to figure out what we've done to warrant you deciding our deaths."

"They're not going to kill us."

I wasn't so sure about that. Both Jassa and I were sworn to oaths of celibacy as part of our vows to the Grand Temple. We were oathbreakers, though ones who had broken said vows only with each other while everyone from the lowliest priest to the Grand Cleric had made a mockery of them since before our arrival. The Grand Cleric had three children, one of which was a High Cleric and the other the leader of the Holy Temple Army. High Priestess Marissa was known to use comely priestesses and choir boys to win votes for the Grand Cleric's agenda in the Great Assembly. Indeed, there were whorehouses which catered exclusively to the supposed holy men of the city. Yet, as the late Priestess Lanya proved, the punishment for being discovered was dire. The corrupt might have no shame but the Grand Temple would do anything within its power to preserve its image as the Lawgiver's righteous fist.

"It is as you say, we're outsiders," I said, remembering the Grand Cleric's recent speech about cleaning up corruption. "I have no friends here."

Strange how that seemed to only involve his political enemies.

"You have more than you know," Jassa said, staring forward. "Besides, they will need every sword in the kingdom soon. The Dark Lords ride anew."

I opened my mouth then closed it.

"I know better than to ask if you're kidding," I said, breathing out. "This is a disaster."

"Indeed," Jassa said, clenching her fists tightly around the copy of the Codex in her lap. "The Dark Lords have already destroyed several Winterholme cities but those who wish to deny the danger believe it is merely raiding. That is why you must confess."

"What will that accomplish?"

"You must accept reassignment to the Shadowguard. I, on the other hand, will be banished from the Temple. From there, I can begin work amongst the nobility to start organizing them. They often seek advisors from renegades or defrocked priestesses. I have already made contact with the Mysterium."

That was troubling. The Mysterium were the Emperor's magical secret police and while their power had waned in recent years, they were still formidable. About their only redeeming feature was a fanatical devotion to the Lawgiver and that was diluted by bizarre superstitions about Dark and Twilight magic leading one to the King Below's service.

"Forgive me, but surely we should work from within the system? I don't respect the Grand—" I paused as a trio of priestesses walked within earshot and continued when they left. "—Cleric but even he has to see the danger."

"I have received a vision from the Lawgiver."

That gave me pause. The last vision had been a century and a half ago, if you discounted lackwit farm boys touted by tithing men seeking donations. "Are you *sure*?"

"As sure that the sun shall obliterate the night every morning. The Lawgiver has sent the darkness to consume and debase this land as punishment for our crimes. Only when we have scourged it with fire and faith shall we be able to build something anew. We shall reform the Grand Temple by casting it down and replacing it with a building far grander and more suitable for one of his stature. Both of us shall be rewarded for this with immortality and power unimaginable."

I wasn't sure how to respond to that. "A-alright."

"You are scared."

"Yes."

"You should be," Jassa said, sighing. "It will become dark before the dawn. However, my vision was clear that we will be instruments for the Lawgiver's will. You will take command of the Shadowguard and turn them into his sword. I will work to arrange a suitable shield for the faithful. I have seen you will suffer greatly for this, as will I, but this is the price we pay for the good of humanity." I was surprised she that word instead of one more encompassing.

"And what does this mean for us?"

That was when Jassa's proper attitude vanished and she turned to me, looking at me with a gaze of adoration.

One I shared.

Jassamine's words were honey to my ears. "Nothing in the world could tear us apart, Jacob. Not even death."

I wanted to kiss her then, surrounded by observers or not. "You are beautiful beyond imagination."

"There will be time enough for love when the evil of this place is cleansed with fire."

How literal those words would prove.

The image of my dream shifted to the burning remnants of the Grand Temple gardens as Jassa's body faded away, leaving me surrounded by corpses. A half-dozen dead Formor surrounded me as I chopped the head of another clean off.

Formor were foul fish-like things with nose-less faces and ears, but great eyes which were twice or three-times the size of a normal man's. Their skin was gray and scaly with a terrible rotting smell which clung to one's clothes days after one fought them. Their armor was black and ugly but thick as well as powerful. The Sword and Skull was emblazoned on their tabards and showed their allegiance to the King Below.

My own armor was similarly black but bore the tabard of House Tremor's thunderbolt hammer. In my hands was a blessed sword of the Lawgiver, soaked with blood. "To arms, my Shadowguard!"

"Save some for the rest of us!" Sir Garris, the long golden-haired man, said. He shot an arrow over my shoulder into a Formor trying to sneak up behind me. The arrow struck its throat and knocked it down, causing it to drown in its own blood.

"I fear we will all have our fill of fish tonight," I said, looking around the bloody ruins. "Much of the city is burning."

It was but a year later and the Dark Lords had launched a surprise attack which had managed to penetrate from the harbor. Not in Seven Ages had the Imperial City been sacked, even during the height of the King Below's reign during the Third War.

"Well, it's good we have a fisherman, then!" Garris slapped me on the back.

I smiled, no longer resenting their jibes. "We must secure the relics as well as the Temple treasury. We will need every penny in this place if we're to buy forces to pay the Dark Lords back for this treachery."

"What of the priests and priestesses? Most of them are locked in the main chapel. The fire will reach them soon. Then there will be no saving them."

I looked over to the servants on the ground, male and female raped with impunity before left to die. The clergy had abandoned them to their fates while seeking refuge in the hallowed but defensible halls of the Lawgiver's inner sanctum.

"Let them burn."

CHAPTER 13

I moaned, feeling the on rush of memories swirling through my head. I was close to breaking the dam separating my past from my present. The more I wandered about, the more I recalled the greater whole of my life. My time at the Imperial City had not been pleasant but it was the key to many other memories which were now sharp and vivid. Soon, I would know everything, but for the first time I wasn't certain I wanted to. I had been judgmental and full of fury as a young man. The Empire had been weak and decadent, but that didn't justify my brutality. One thing I had learned during my campaigns with the Shadowguard was that people panicked during times of crisis. They did horrible things which would haunt them for the rest of their days.

I was no different.

"Are you awake, Sir Jacob?" Serah asked, surprising me. I hadn't expected to awaken at all, really.

I was in a foggy mist of shapes, shadows, and mist. I didn't know where I was or what I was doing. I then realized I was lacking a body once more. Focusing, I once more conjured form from the ether. I found this gave me a splitting headache. My body also ached from scars, ones not physical, but inflicted upon my soul. My reservoir of power was restored, at least before I'd become flesh again, and did not seem weakened by my battle with Bloodthorn.

I was naked underneath a set of black silken bed sheets with my attire in a chair across the room, cleaned. It made me wonder if I'd been nothing but a blackened shape this entire time, an indistinct collection of darkness which someone had taken the time to retrieve from the fields of honor and carry to a bed.

The room around me was chilly, almost as cold as the mountaintop, with all of the light in the room being provided by a witchfire blaze in the hearth. The light provided was a strange blue-white glow, giving the room an eerie illumination.

The décor was lovely with ornate, finely-carved Gaelwood furniture and a portrait of the Lakelord overlooking the fireplace. Lush tapestries decorated the walls, extolling the virtues of House Brightwaters even if they were too new to give the impression of anything but recently-elevated aristocracy. A suit of ceremonial armor, untouched by war, was lying in the corner wearing a tabard bearing the Imperial Gryphon clutching the sun in its claws.

Ironic.

Serah was sitting in a chair, wearing a pleasant black dress with a low-cut bodice and a silver heart shaped locket around her neck. She was reading from a book entitled *Legends of the Fourth War*. "I am pleased to see you are awake and solid once more. I was afraid I could fill you with shadowstuff forever and it would leak from your body like a sieve."

I felt her presence inside me and the feel of her magic. Serah was a woman like an almond, bitter on the outside but sweet within. I could sense many terrible ordeals weighing upon her soul. Far more than a wealthy young merchant's daughter of high breeding should experience. There was an affection and curiosity toward me, too, which I found to be...unsettling.

"You cared for me?" I asked, surprised. "I thought myself doomed in the fury of Bloodthorn's armies."

"You would have been if not for the fact Regina rode out on a mechanical hippogriff, dodging flame and explosion to retrieve your body. Bloodthorn's three sons flew out to meet her, the last gryphon riders in the Empire in all likelihood, only to meet their end at her hands. Regina brought you to me and I have been using my meager knowledge of necromancy to patch together the withered remnant of your spirit."

I looked at my hands and nodded. "You have done a good job."

I grimaced as a thought occurred to me.

"Is something wrong?" Serah asked.

"Regina's actions have revealed I was an ally of Laketown," I said, cursing. "That will not bode well."

"Perhaps you should have factored into account she is unwilling to abandon a friend and ally. Had you died, it's quite likely she'd be planning a trip to the World Below to wrestle you from the jaws of the Dread Wolf's ghost. I admit, I am impressed by your heroism as well. Few individuals are willing to fight for Laketown amongst its people, let alone complete strangers. I found my body yearn in a most unseemly manner by the sight of you killing Bloodthorn before our gates."

I blinked, surprised by her boldness. "I thought you only—"

"Like Regina, I am a lover of both men and women," Serah said, a half-smile on her face. I suspected she found my surprise amusing. "Thomas introduced us to both when he took us on a tour of the best and brightest brothels of the Empire and Lakeland."

"I...see." Such things weren't unknown to me but they were far more open about it now than in my time. I tried not to think of Serah and Regina that way since, given my unclothed state, it would be most embarrassing.

"I confess I was never quite as lucky with men as he, though. It is said he was able to charm the clothes off the most cloistered knight."

"The reputation of cloistered knights is greatly exaggerated, or at least was in my time."

Serah snorted. "I'm surprised, I thought I might shock you. Perhaps there is some of the stories in you after all."

"I hope not."

Serah laughed. Her expression turned grim. "I have a request of you, Sir Knight."

"Ask it, and if it is in my power, I will grant it."

"That is a foolish thing to promise."

"I do not think you are inclined to ask for something unreasonable."

"Then you don't know me for I am *most* unreasonable."

"I will be the judge of that." I put my arms over my chest.

"I wish to go with you to the Tower of Everfrost."

I paused. "You're correct, that *is* most unreasonable."

"I can give my reasons for wanting to do so."

I pressed my hands together. "Serah, if I may—"

"Are you going to lecture me about the dangers of dark magic? About how it is not a toy? About how I could damn my soul or become a creature of evil? If so, I have been called such my entire life and it has only made me more determined to master my powers. The Tower of Everfrost contains the knowledge to let me move from being a slave of my destiny to its controller."

"Actually, I was just going to say I hadn't any plans to go to the Tower." Serah blinked. "Oh."

"It is, quite possibly, the last place in the world I'd want to be."

The Tower of Everfrost was located at topmost point of Northern Wasteland, in a place called the Eyes of the World. It held a place of singular evil in the mythology of men, being a tower erected in the

World Below before its master built upon it until his forces could enter the World Between.

I did not know if such was literally true but every Shadowguardsman had heard stories of it and the terrible black city surrounding it. The King Below gathered his armies at Everforst each time he rose to power and fled there when he was defeated. It was a city inhabited by demons, heathens, and Shadowkind with uncountable atrocities associated with its name. In all of history, only three Shadowguard had ever been taken there and returned.

I supposed I was now the fourth.

Thinking about the Tower was painful. I could remember fragments of my slavery within it. Periods where I was able to see through my eyes, but unable to move or think of my own volition. I was witness to unimaginable decadence, wealth, torture, and atrocity worked in equal measure. I recalled the greasy black metal towers, the never-melting frost which covered everything, and unimaginable numbers of prisoners who had been broken to the Dark Lord's worship. I recalled the fresh-young mortals delivered to me so I could sup on their life-force and raise their undead forms as my servants.

I recalled the taste of the young.

My heart seized in horror and I had to grab the sides of the bed to avoid going into a seizure. Serah, stunned by my reaction, stood up.

You monster! I shouted in my head at the Trickster. *The things you had me do!*

Yes, The Trickster said. *Things worse than any of the horrors you committed as part of the Great Shadow War. That was your punishment, to repeat your sin over and over until you learned your lesson.*

I'll kill you! I screamed in my mind.

Perhaps, the spirit replied lazily. *Wouldn't that be wonderful?*

"Jacob, are you alright?" Serah said, placing her hand on my shoulder.

I closed my eyes and struggled to control myself. Beads of sweat poured off my forehead, freezing against my skin. "Bad memories."

Serah blinked, then sat down. "I'm sorry."

I took a deep breath. "Why do you even want to go there, anyway?"

"The Night Queen's Library," Serah said, looking at me intently. "It is a place of unimaginable lore and power."

"Evil lore."

"What makes lore good or evil is how we use it. I want to show the world Dark and Twilight magic can be a force for good in the world."

"It's still a mad quest."

"Not if I have a Wraith Knight accompanying me. The King Below is dead and his forces scattered. Now is the best time to invade his former domiciles."

I wasn't sure there was ever a good time for that. "I can understand that but I can't imagine a reason to return to that hideous place."

Oh Lawgiver, what I had I done there?

Horrors unending, the Trickster said. *I would apologize but I cannot feel anything but spite, sorrow, and hate.*

Then I spite you, childkiller! I feel sorrow to have met you and hate at everything you have done.

The Trickster was silent.

"Not even to end your curse?" Serah asked, putting her book aside.

My head turned rapidly. "Explain."

"The King Below is dead so his power is broken, even if scattered fragments of his essence still lie around the world. However, that power is still present in the artifacts he left behind. The Crown of Weeping Gods, forged by Co'Fannon is a channel for all his dark energies. It was taken to Everfrost after the battle and is there for recovery. With it, you could break the curse on yourself and return to life."

"Regina mentioned such," I said, pausing. "I take it she got the idea from you?"

"I have discussed going there with her on many occasions in the past two years," Serah said. "Each time, we agreed the trip was impossible. Now? I'm not so sure. Your presence provides solutions to previously insoluble questions. I am sure we can restore you from the dead and send you to live a proper life as a man."

"Given my body is dust and bone, I'm not sure that's possible."

"Resurrection is not impossible for those who wield the power of the gods, just difficult."

"I have been told otherwise."

"You have been lied to."

Imagine that. I was aware of the risks to what she was proposing. The location she described was the heart of evil on this world, a fortress filled with uncountable legions of monsters and horrors. I would have dismissed her suggestion out of hand, like I'd brushed off Regina's, if not for the fact I was a monster myself. Alone, I'd been willing to go, but it occurred to me with a sorceress of Serah's power that it might be possible for both of us to get what we wanted as well as increase my chance for success. I wasn't sure about bringing Regina with us, but if she'd gone to such lengths to rescue me then I owed her that much. "I will go to the Tower of Everfrost. With you."

"Thank you."

"I would be remiss, though, if I did not ask why you want this."

"Have I not said?"

"You are beautiful, rich, and powerful. An old library in a tower built over a gateway to the Hundred Hells seems an odd thing to worry about." Of course, I didn't know what the state of Acadian's military was. Had the Imperial forces retreated? Somehow, I doubted that. Lady Brightwaters might be planning to flee for the North.

"I am not so beautiful as you may think."

I looked at her, wondering what she meant. Serah was, along with Regina, one of the loveliest women I'd ever seen. Jassamine was the only woman who compared and that was because of love. "Oh?"

Serah sighed and made a gesture with her hand, causing the glamour which covered her face to fail. The beautiful woman vanished and was replaced with a rather plain-looking girl. She was still of

High Men origins, but lacked the sculpted cheekbones and majestic bearing of before. There was also a long scar running down the right side of her cheek.

I blinked. "I don't see much of a difference."

Serah snorted and took a pillow to swipe my arm. "You are a terrible liar, sir."

"A great deal of beauty is artifice and I do not see much cause for you to change yourself. You are a formidable woman who need not look like the silly women who spend hours appearing as statues."

"A glamour takes ten minutes and I've found men are less inclined to burn a beautiful woman at the stake than they are an old crone."

"That is not your problem."

"It was my grandmother's. Such was her fate."

I wasn't sure how to react. "I see."

"My mother's family contained many witches even if they prayed every night for the darkness in their magic to go away. My mother was lucky enough to marry up because she was beautiful. My grandmother, however, was poor and captured by farmers who saw her shadow dance during a red moon."

"I'm sorry."

"You did not kill her," Serah shrugged, feeling her scar. "I suppose you wonder how I got this."

"I rather like it." Which was no lie.

Serah looked at me, surprised, then smiled. "I got it from a servant girl when I was twelve. She was terrified of looking after my room and kept a knife on her at all times lest I steal her soul or something despite being the same age. One day, she panicked and cut me. I'd been yelling at her about the linens or something."

"Unfortunate."

"More for her, my family paid a judge to have her hanged and when the dead girl's parents railed at us as harborers of Shadowkind, they had their house burned down with them. My parents were many things, but not good people."

"A grim story."

"Do you understand why I must go? With the power of the King Below, I could change the world for the better. I could also help Regina in her quest for revenge. She is one of the few people I have ever cared for because she treated me as a person."

"I will help you. I swear it."

Serah stared. "You, too, now have my devotion."

I wasn't sure how to react to that. "How is the military situation?"

"A third of the Imperial army has withdrawn back to their leaders' home territories in fear of retaliation by the King Below. All of the gryphons in the Empire's service have rebelled but a scant few which remain loyal to their masters. There is also great confusion within the ranks over who is to lead the campaign against the city. They have sent a missive saying they will not sack the city and let its inhabitants go free if tribute is paid as well as some other minor concessions."

I nodded. "This is good."

Serah looked down. "Not really. One of those concessions is your head."

CHAPTER 14

Serah's pronouncement the Imperial Army was bargaining for my head didn't have quite the reaction she expected.

"Hmm," I said, nodding in agreement. "That sounds like a fair exchange."

"This may surprise you, Sir Jacob, but cutting off your head would kill you."

"I'm not sure. Lately, I've been going about much of my day without a head, organs, or limbs. One of the advantages of being dead is it becomes very hard to kill you."

Serah narrowed her gaze. "This is serious, Sir Jacob."

"Just Jacob, please. The honors of knighthood have never rested easily upon my shoulders."

Serah smiled then shook her head. Her expression turned serious. "I believe my uncle is going to take the Imperial Army up on their offer."

"He should," I said, not in the least bit disturbed by the threat. "One life to save thousands? He'd be a madman to refuse."

My response was motivated less by altruism than the fact I had no intention of offering my life up for the Accadians for a second time. Not because I was afraid of death, though I'd discovered a surprising will to live on the battlefield. Fighting Bloodthorn had been one of the most difficult battles of my life and I'd been on the defensive the entire time. The fact I'd fought so hard to survive and wanted nothing more than to live in those final seconds before the Imperial Army's retaliation struck had been an awakening of sorts. I did not want to die and would not go to the executioner's block willingly.

No, instead, I would deliver them an already dead man's skull tainted with dark magic. If they wanted Chill's Fury, I knew enough about blacksmithing and sorcery to create up a reasonable facsimile. I had used many such tricks during the Fourth War and had no reservations about continuing to do so.

"That implies a trustworthiness to the Empire which does not exist. As soon as they execute you and open up the gates, they will march into the city and do what they planned to do from the beginning." Serah put aside her book. "One cannot deal with the honor-less as their very nature inclines them to treachery."

"One does not need honor to deal fairly during accords." I frowned. "The system is designed to protect the interests of both parties. If the Empire broke such an agreement then no one would have any reason to honor with them again. It's a matter of practicality versus decency."

"This is not the Anessian Empire of your time, which according to the histories I've studied was a decadent and ruthless militaristic state—"

"*Finally,* someone performed serious scholarship. I was worried the whole of human history had been distorted beyond all recognition. It was also full of treachery, intrigue, and unbelievable bastards. The slimy kind rather than the heroic ones like myself."

Serah suppressed another smile. "But the Old Empire was *so* known for its intelligence in resource management. The New Empire has vast mercenary legions and its own Imperial forces separate from the Great Houses' forces. Only the fact they're preoccupied elsewhere, propping up the other Nine Heroes' regimes—"

"Eight Heroes," I interrupted again.

"*Eight Heroes*' regimes, has them not be the ones to lay siege to us," Serah said, softly. "The Empire has not been seriously challenged since the days of Eric the Great and Saint Jassamine. After they defeated the Fireforge Kingdoms and forced the Fir-Bolg to convert to the Lawgiver, everyone started sending the Imperial City tribute. It is said the treasury spends thirty times more on their militaries than all the other Southern Kingdoms combined. The Great Lords and generals are used to riding over anyone who opposes them and I fear your humiliation of them today will only inflame their desire to teach a lesson."

That was grim tidings. It also changed our positions considerably. I was a fool to make promises to the Brightwaters I couldn't keep. Even more so for attempting to jump back into the realm of politics and strategy after a two-and-a-half-age absence. "What would you suggest I do, fair damsel?"

Serah paused, looking annoyed at my continued use of that word. Then sighed, smiling. "You are hopelessly endearing. You know this, right?"

"I have been told that."

"I would have you go to the Hall of Artifacts in the basement of the castle. Tharadon's Mirror is located there and it could take us directly to the Eyes of the World. Let us abandon this place and leave the city to the Empire."

I kept my expression even. "I am not going to abandon your people."

"They are not *my* people." She then added, "We would, of course, take Thomas and Regina with us."

"So, your brother's plan, except dump them in the middle of a frozen wasteland thousands of leagues from civilization filled with every monster imaginable."

Tharadon's Mirror had been an amazing discovery which I'd put to terrible use in the service of the Shadowguard. Its power costs were tremendous, requiring a hundred wizards working from sunrise until sunset or a year of charging on its own, but which had done an immense wartime service by teleporting assassins or glass balls full of death gas across the continent.

The discovery it was in the Lakelord's possession rather than the Mysterium surprised me and I couldn't help but wonder if Bloodthorn had wanted that artifact amongst other booty. If the Empress wasn't aware of it, then it was a shocking oversight on the part of the Empire's secret police.

Assuming the Mysterium still existed.

Serah blanched. "Well, perhaps we can drop them off in Indaras or wherever first. I'm sure my brother can charm his way into a wealthy lover's bed with minimum fuss. That's assuming he hasn't already converted a massive amount of our funds to precious stones already."

I crossed my arms. "I made a promise to protect your city."

"Great Wizards preserve us!" Serah threw up her hands in disgust. "*They are going to kill you.* Do you understand that? My uncle is going to send you a pot of tea poisoned with blessed verbena and wrap you in silver chains. He'll decapitate you with the family sword, someone who is fighting for his stolen lands, and then he's going to let in the army which will put his head on a spike. They will burn this city to the ground and use its wealth to pay off their debts so they can keep borrowing money to burn cities to the ground elsewhere."

Her passion surprised me. "Why is this so important to you?"

Serah slumped her shoulders. "Is it so hard to believe someone damned from birth might want to prevent a greater injustice?"

I pondered how I was going to respond before deciding to speak from the heart. "*Beware the weavers of shadows, the conjurers of ice, and the manipulators of destiny. They are Shadowkind and deserve nothing but scorn, hate, and derision.*"

"Canticles 2:8," Serah said, bitterly. "I have lived my life suffering from that passage."

"Canticles 2:9 talks about how it is an offense against the Lawgiver to use one's right hand to shake hands because it is the one used to wipe one's ass."

Serah snorted. "That one doesn't get as much attention."

"The Grand Temple divided the kinds of magic into light, dark, noon, and twilight magic at the Third Council of Starbourne. Learned men determined that Twilight and dark magic use was to be closely monitored for its dangerous nature but there was nothing inherently sinful about it. Many Shadow-weavers and ice mages were instrumental in fighting the King Below's armies. Many fire and light mages served as his emissaries. The common people, however, had different ideas. Folklore and superstition had built up dark magic as a scare-specter behind every incident of curdled milk or dead cow. It had been that way for eight hundred years in my time and I doubt it's changed that much. You are not damned, Serah. You are a beautiful, wonderful, and charming woman who if I was not a ghost and in mourning would have been honored to take dancing."

"Dancing? How sinful!" Serah said, feigning shock. "Canticle 10:31."

"I hate that passage," I said, smiling. "Do not confuse the hate-speak of the ignorant as the way of the Lawgiver."

"And if the Council of Starbourne along with a bunch of other old men and women said dark magic was evil?" Serah asked. "Say after King Eric's reforms?"

"Then I would say fuck them and the ass they rode in on. Pardon my Fisherfolk."

Serah reached over and placed her right hand on mine, giving it a squeeze. "You remind me very much of Sir Roland of Fireforge."

"Oh, who he was?"

Serah grinned wickedly. "He was the first man Regina and I shared."

Dark Lords shouldn't sputter.

Serah's grin became actual laughter. "You should get dressed. Thomas is undoubtedly trying to prevent my uncle from making the second stupidest decision of his life and Regina from killing him for it."

"She wouldn't do that."

"I know her *a bit* better than you."

"So I've heard." I waited.

Serah stood, unmoving.

"Ahem." I cleared my throat.

"Yes?"

"Would you please turn around?" I said, looking down at the bed sheet which was protecting my modesty.

"Why?" Serah asked, gazing at my conjured form intently. It would seem Regina hadn't lied and women *did* find it pleasing.

I frowned.

Serah rolled her eyes, stood up, and turned around. "You're much more entertaining in the legends."

"So I've heard," I've repeated, slipping out of the bed and changing back into my clothes. I caught Serah peeking at me several times during the process, but decided to let it go. Flattered as I was, I'd never been subject to much female attention in my life. I had lost the love of my life recently.

It didn't seem real I would never see Jassa again. Despite the fact centuries had passed, I only remembered a few terrible moments between my death and awakening on the mountaintop. Indeed, as painful as the hole in my heart was, I was surprised it wasn't worse. The loss of Jassa seemed more like an old, scarred wound. I couldn't help but feel like my dreaming mind knew things my waking one didn't.

The Trickster actually giggled.

The King Below shouldn't giggle, I chided. *Have some dignity.*

What is the point of knowledge and power if it is not to lord over those who possess neither?

To help others? I suggested.

The hand offered in assistance is just one less to defend yourself with.

I was less disturbed by the Trickster's statement than the fact I'd said similar things during the Fourth War. I hadn't yet recovered all of my memories but I was getting closer. Each reminder of my past, great and small, triggered another set of them. Like a child's building blocks, stacked in a line, they tumbled forward in a row, but unlike said objects they did so at their own pace and leisure.

It was maddening.

Stretching my gloves on as the last of my apparel, I said, "Can you tell me what it is I have missed, these two ages past?"

"That is no small request."

"I wish to know what has come to pass so I know where to step forward."

Serah nodded. "I owe you that much."

"You owe me nothing."

"I owe you my brother's life. If not for you and Regina, then the Northgate would have fallen and with it everyone defending it. I could defeat a thousand men and it wouldn't have made a bit of difference."

"Then consider the debt repaid with this knowledge."

"Your advisor I shall be."

It was dangerous company I was choosing to keep. Serah Brightwater *was* a beautiful, charming, and wonderful woman but she was also ambitious. Wizardry was like a sword, it conjured dreams of empire and revenge in those who wielded it. Warmaster Kalian had learned the ways of light Magic from the Fir Bolg Sun Priests but it was something which had never sat well with him. Magic inborn was as natural as water flowing down a riverbank, but magic learned required an indomitable will to shape the universe through thought alone. I often wondered if that was why so many clerics and Temple Knights tended to religious fanaticism or naked ambition.

I also wondered if that was why magic had come so easily to me, easier than swordplay or blacksmithing.

I wasn't sure if I was going to Everfrost but it was my only lead on a cure. If I was honest with myself, I had to admit ambition was not limited to my new companion in our small group. The Crown of Weeping Gods was a legendary artifact which had twice fallen into the hands of mortal men, unleashing power undreamed of from the Age of the Tuatha to the Fall of Balor the False King Below.

With it, I might be able to resurrect myself permanently and banish the Trickster from my mind. If he was truly just a ghost, I might even bind him to a rock and toss it in the middle of the ocean or obliterate him outright so he could not even taunt the living anymore. Anessia the Third had used the King Below's stolen armor to become an invincible juggernaut on the field of battle, smiting the Fifty Kings in order to re-forge the Empire. The King Below's sword, World's End, had been purified by Saint Gilead to slay a thousand demons.

What could I do with a tower *full* of such treasures?

No, Serah was not the dangerous one.

We both were.

You want to be a hero, the Trickster whispered, *and the only way you know how is through war.*

I promised Regina I would cast down the Nine Heroes. Your tools are a means of doing so. I am strong enough and wise enough to resist your lures.

Of course you are, the Trickster said. *You were last time.*

I drove away any thought of my mind's unwelcome guest and went to the door. "I am ready to speak with the Lakelord again."

Serah nodded. "Just don't claim to be Tharadon again. I don't think that's likely to work a second time."

"Maybe I'll go for Valance the Red."

CHAPTER 15

The castle was full of whispers.

Walking down the dark, moonlit halls of the Lakelord's castle, I could hear the sounds of servants talking amongst themselves as well as guards. A gift of my state as a Wraith Knight, it seemed. They spoke of the Lakelord making a pact with the King Below, of how he was under the control of a Dark Lord, or how this was all a plot by his evil niece to lead them to ruin.

The guards, a more cynical bunch, thought the High Captain Thomas was using mummery and illusion to achieve the same effect. Most of them didn't believe in the King Below and thought he was merely turning around the Empress' own use of scare-legends. Others had a problem with that because they didn't think the Lakelord was that intelligent. Quite a few were planning to flee the castle or plotting mutiny thanks to my presence.

I could hear them all.

"The situation is not good," I said, walking alongside Serah.

"My uncle does not inspire loyalty amongst his followers," Serah said, holding her ghostwood staff she'd retrieved from behind the bedroom fireplace. She clutched the object of power tightly, as if she expected a fight. "If he ever had their respect, it was forfeited when he turned traitor and brought us into the Empire. If he had their loyalty, it was lost when the Empire showed up on their doorstep. If he had their strength, if only paid for by gold, it was lost when they realized he not only had a witch for a niece, but a Dark Lord protecting him."

"I am sorry."

"You apologize so very much," Serah said, shaking her head. "If you are to make a deal with my uncle, do it from a position of power. Terrify him into believing only you can lead him from this shadow and to deal with the Imperial forces from behind the barriers. We can salvage this, but only with Thomas and Regina both. Claim Tharadon is protecting us to the public as a whole and the Dark Lord is allied with the Empire."

"That makes no sense."

"Lies don't have to make sense. They just have to be something the public will believe," Serah said, placing her hand on my shoulder. "Appear to the public in your form and they believe you are their returned Wizard-King because you are beautiful. We'll open the treasure vaults and pay double to the soldiers as well as volunteers who join our cause. No one wants to ascribe evil motivations to those who are lining their pockets. Once the Imperials leave, we can get proper reinforcement from Lakeland."

"You make it sound terribly easy," I said, sighing.

"Money does not solve all your problems, but turns many problems into ones which can be solved."

"A proper Lakeland proverb."

"We created Lakeland as a place where free-men could do business without lords and ladies stealing two coins out of every ten. Tharadon created Accadia as a place knowledge could be studied freely without fear of heresy charges or use in the arts of war. Those two lands are natural allies. My uncle forgot that, but the people haven't."

I paused. "I killed Tharadon, you know."

"I know," Serah said.

I did a double take. "You know?"

"One of the Shadowguard wrote a book called *The Truth of Heroes*, which explained how you did many terrible crimes in pursuit of saving the world. The murder of Tharadon, the butchery of Kosswood, the slaying of Co'Fannon, and assisting in treasonous activities designed to propel Prince Eric up to near-absolute power. It's the only book I've read which portrayed you, not as a lecher, but a dour and serious man involved in the Temple Reformation."

"Sir Garris," I said, guessing my old friend to be responsible. He, alone, had been the one to know many of those things. "What happened to him?"

"He recanted. His books were burned. A few copies, however, remain in the right libraries if you know where to look."

I didn't question how that was achieved. Serah seemed like a resourceful woman. "I see."

"Do not mourn him too much for it came with a palace, title, and a chance to live with his lover until the end of their days."

"That is good at least." A second passed. "Am I really *dour*?"

"Extremely."

I passed by a hallway mirror and blinked as I saw myself for the first time since my resurrection. Before I'd died, I'd been a plain-faced sort of man with weathered features, dull olive skin, stringy hair, and deep sunken eyes. Jassa had encouraged me to grow a beard, in part because it hid some of the less attractive features of my face.

In my place was a smooth-featured man with long shining black hair, rich olive skin, and smooth features which looked like they'd been chiseled. My deep, soulful eyes seemed to encapsulate the world now. It was like the paintings done of royalty which left off all the pox marks and flab, only brought to life as a living sculpture.

It was a strange sensation, to be handsome.

"See something you like?"

I smiled. "Just artifice."

"That is all beauty is."

I looked over at Serah, taking note she hadn't restored her glamour. I couldn't help but feel the stirrings of desire within me. The same way I'd felt for Regina. Serah was a formidable woman with a powerful will and drive. Like Jassa. "You remind me of someone."

"Oh?"

Before I could make a complete ass of myself by saying something I shouldn't, we were interrupted by Thomas dashing down the hall. He had changed from his suit of ornamental armor to a gold-buttoned vest, fine breaches, and a white silken shirt which probably cost as much as a decent horse.

"Oh thank the Lawgiver I found you," Thomas said, taking a deep breath. "The situation is bad."

"Oh really, I hadn't noticed," Serah said, mock aghast. "Between the siege, demands for Jacob's head, and Whitehold being destroyed has something worse happened? Did one of your lovers discover you were unfaithful? Is a gold button missing from one of your shirts?"

Thomas looked disgusted. "I make it quite clear to all of my lovers I am never going to be faithful and I would *never* wear a shirt with a missing button."

"Clearly, I have wandered into a comedy troupe by mistake," I said, gesturing down the hall. "Could someone please direct me to the heirs of Accadia? I'm supposed to meet with them to prevent the end of the world."

"Yes, because that's so much more serious." Serah rolled her eyes.

"And to think you called me dour."

"Regina has called our uncle out," Thomas said, drawing both Serah and my attention.

"Oh Hundred Hells," Serah said, feeling her face. "Of course she has. Where is she?"

"This way, my beloved sister, Your Darklordship."

"Never call me that again."

The three of us headed through a pair of ornate double-doors, past a pair of guards who seemed startled at my presence. The interior of the room opened up to a grand ballroom which would have been the envy of anything in the Imperial City two-hundred-and-fifty years ago.

The chamber was three-stories tall with a set of four grand staircases in every corner, leading up to the balconies on the sides. Images of Dryads and Satyrs frolicking were carved into the side of the white wooden paneling around each of the balconies while rainbow crystal chandeliers hung from the ceiling. The chandeliers showered the room with spinning prismatic light.

In the back of the ballroom, against the North Wall, an entire symphony of Clockwork Golems looked a hundred times more advanced than the kind we'd had in my day. They had cellos, flues, tubas, and several instruments I didn't recognize with a mechanical conductor. The entire thing, even in Tharadon's Cradle, must have cost the equivalent to a small kingdom's treasury.

Even so, it was not the extraordinary wealth on display which attracted my attention, but the rather despicable amount of military force contrasting to it. Each of the balconies had guards carrying crossbows with strange gear-mechanisms which seemed designed to load bolts automatically. A few had rifles. Others still were carrying old-fashioned bows, though they were done in a decidedly sidhe-esque style. There were perhaps twenty in all, and I wondered if they were for the Lakelord's piece-of-mind or to ambush me.

Perhaps both.

In the center of the ballroom were two eight-foot-tall golems made of glass-steel shaped like Temple Knights. Both looked like something from a stained-glass window brought to life. They were made from blue glass-steel for their faux-armor, red for the symbols on it, and green for their false flesh. Both were carrying huge white glas-steel swords, which caught the light the same way the chandeliers did. The Burning Eye of the Lawgiver was emblazoned on both their chests along with a tiny maker's seal. These golems had, obviously, been made for the protection of cathedrals, but it appeared the Lakelord had purchased them for his own protection.

Beneath the two giant glass statues were Regina and the Lakelord, both having a passionate argument which I was surprised I hadn't picked up on earlier. Then again, I wasn't yet used to my powers.

"You dare bring this disaster down on my head!?" The Lakelord hissed, shaking his pudgy fists. "Ungrateful, incompetent, child of traitors!"

Regina slapped him across the face, almost sending him to his knees. It said a great deal about how the Lakelord's soldiers viewed him that only a few raised their crossbows, only to put them down almost immediately.

Regina shook with fury. "Ungrateful? You were on your knees begging to look after me during my summers! It gave other nobles the impression you were something other than the jumped-up coin-counter you are! That you were friends with a family of true rank and nobility. As for incompetent, you have led your city to ruin and the only reason you have any hope of survival now is the Imperial army has been chastened by Jacob! As for traitor? Why I—"

I cleared my throat. "May I cut in?"

All of the guards in the balcony moved their weapons toward me.

Well, that answered a few questions.

Regina spun around and pointed at the Lakelord. "This man is a fool! Thomas, relieve him of his office and throw in a dungeon."

"I'm not sure I can do that," Thomas said, rubbing his chin. "Though the idea is tempting."

"You might be able to pull it off," Serah said, calmly. "I fear my uncle's bought loyalty is still loyalty, however. He has kept up his bribes and payments, if nothing else. Even if we are now deeply in debt to several banks across the river they're less than pleased he's hidden behind the Imperial Army until now."

"You have spoken your last insult to me," the Lakelord whispered, rising up on his feet. "I was willing to endure your haughtiness and sneers when you were of good family or a useful symbol to rally fools around but you have forfeited those privileges, Regina Whitetremor. You have shown yourself to the entire Empire to be a servant of darkness and evil. As for you, my heirs, I have indulged you to my limit. Do you think I became Prince of Thradon's Cradle purely through sniveling and treachery? I appeared harmless because a fat merchant invites fewer daggers but I slit countless throats and burned dozens of buildings to bring us into the Empire. I will deal with the Great Houses outside the way I have always done. I will offer hostages, beg, bribe, blackmail or steal to keep my position. If you have to marry some noble lord, Serah, so be it. If you have to marry a noble daughter, Thomas, it will be done. If I must clap you in chains, Regina, naked and mind-fucked for the Empress to give to her son then I'll do that too. I am the Lakelord and I am not to be dismissed!"

"What a grandiose way to describe your cowardice and treachery." Serah shook her head. "Are we supposed to be impressed?"

"You are supposed to obey!" the Lakelord snapped. He looked up. "As for you, Dark One, you have brought shame upon my household and ruination. All is not lost, however. I will bind you with chains of blessed silver and deliver you to the Empress along with Regina. You will become a living monument to the Nine Heroes' triumph, carted out for holidays and children charged a half-penny to gawk at in the Grand Temple dungeons. You have dishonored the holy name of

Tharadon and made Brightwaters a joke. However, they will give me a Great Lordship for capturing the last remnant of the King Below's evil and call me a righteous man."

I stared at him, my voice lowering an octave. "I wish I could say this was the first time I've heard a man threaten rape, treason, and betrayal of his offspring in the same sentence as declaring himself righteous. Sadly, it's not even the fifth. You are a poor example of a friend, ruler, and uncle. To be noble comes not from the blood but one's deeds, which you have sown a bitter harvest with."

A wiser man would have seen how foolish such a statement was. I had no respect for the Lakelord, though. He was the only thing worse than the corrupt, vile, and petty nobility I'd known training as a Temple Knight: one of those who wanted to join them. I should have realized from his speech he was not a fool to be trifled with. No, he was a fool whose pride had been wounded and now would attempt to satisfy its demands with blood. Bullies and street toughs were drawn from the ranks of those who were powerless. While the Lakelord had power, he hadn't enough he would not attempt to lord it over others weaker than himself. Such men could only be pushed so far.

As I had just done.

The Lakelord's eyes turned red as his trembled with a fury far darker than Regina's earlier outrage. He glared at Serah, Thomas, and Regina in equal terms before taking several steps backwards. Once he was behind his Temple golems, he growled like an animal. "Kill them all! Remove this stain from my family! These witches, deviants, traitors, and monsters! I command you as your lord!"

Thomas tried to speak up as the guards responded to his command. "Gentlemen, ladies, do not listen to him—"

One shot faster than the others, burying a bolt in Thomas' throat.

Serah screamed out his name as all of the rainbow crystals in the room went dark. A wave of terrible black energy washed from her and wiped out every candle, fireplace, and electric lamp in Accadia. In the darkness, crossbow bolts, rifle-shots, and bows fired wildly as I pulled Regina and Serah away from their strike. I could see perfectly in the darkness. On the ground, Thomas bled to death within moments.

Witchfire flew from Serahs' fingertips as she screamed a curse in Demonspeak. The Lakelord's body was consumed in the resulting cone of white flame, transformed into a frozen mass in an instant.

It then exploded, showering the ballroom floor with chunks of icy gore.

The lights returned, the wave of darkness passed.

Battle was joined.

CHAPTER 16

E verything went to hell in a moment.

I summoned up a barrier spell to protect us from the next wave of crossbow bolts, darts, and arrows, even though some had runes. The air around us turned to fire as these detonated, but my barrier held still.

The death of the Lakelord and Thomas changed everything as there was now no one in the city who could take command. Serah was a Kinslayer now and even if the people were willing to follow someone who wielded black magic, they wouldn't be able to overlook such a heinous crime. The world couldn't have changed that much.

I didn't blame her in the slightest, though.

"Die screaming!" Serah shouted, conjuring a globe of darkness then hurling it at one of the balconies before conjuring and throwing another. Both balconies exploded, casting out their residents onto the ground below. Serah began another invocation in Demonspeak, generating a murder of Hellcrows which flew through the air to start biting away pieces of flesh from the assailants above. This, at least, gave us some respite from our attackers.

That was when my barrier was shattered by the blessed sword of the first Temple Golem. The now-late Lakelord had not only purchased them from a holy sanctuary, he'd left them with all the blessings intact. Its sword glowed with a brilliant white light visible only to my undead eyes, filling my heart with fear and driving me back.

Its partner then swung at Serah.

Which compelled me to block it, meeting the holy blade with my own cursed one.

"I will take the one on the left!" Regina called, slamming Hopebringer into its glass-steel frame. The powerful enchantments on the blade remained intact, causing it to pass forward like stabbing cheese. Cracks appeared all across the torso of the monstrous thing before Regina began to twist.

"Understood!" I called, parrying the graceless monster's blade back before seeking out its animation runes. The craftsmen who created these holy weapons had concealed them well, protecting them under an extra-layer of glass-steel to hide them from opponents like myself. The holy magic glowed like a fire in the night to me and I slammed Chill's Fury into the first of them, destroying it despite its protections.

There were eight more.

The mechanized orchestra played in the background, triggered by the excess amount of mystical energy flying through the air. The song they played was "The Milkmaid Fair", which had been a bawdy and lewd drinking song in my time but had apparently been rewritten to something cleaner by the dignified way the band played.

Screams filled the air as Felbeasts and Hellhounds burst from where Serah swung her staff, drawing energy from each of the men she killed to send out more monsters. She paid attention to her own safety and I had to conjure a literal shield of shadow to block an arrow aimed for her head, still fighting my Temple Golem. Half of the crossbowmen were slain, however, and a few had fled.

"My entire life I have sought to do the right thing with only Thomas believing I could be something more!" Serah screamed, her voice echoing with two parts grief and one part fury. "If you wish me to be a monster then a monster, I shall be! I swear my allegiance to the black, the cold, and the damned since they are the only ones who show any decency!"

I was five runes down on my Temple Golem when Serah struck with such force into hers that the creature fell into a broken pile of glass-steel on the ground. She stabbed into the back of my opponent, which gave me an edge to conjure a spell of abjuration, causing all four remaining runes to dissolve at once. The Temple Golem ceased its movement in an instant, falling over like a puppet whose strings had been.

Well, a nine-hundred-pound puppet, at least.

Seeing their efforts with ranged attacks were getting nowhere, the remaining guards fled from the balconies and joined together at the other end of the ballroom, drawing swords to engage us with blades. All of the blades were plated with silver and hastily blessed. It was a poor effort since, unlike the Temple Golems, they had not been made with the proper rites or by truly faithful priests.

One of them made the foolish error of calling out, "Disgusting creatures of the pit, the Lawgiver's justice will find you all!"

"You have spoken your last invocation," I said, spinning around Chill's Fury and using it as a focus to summon a blizzard around the charging soldiers.

They screamed as they flew through the air, were frozen where they stood, or simply fell to the ground blinded. Serah's monsters vanished with the last of them falling to the ground, her rage and the source of their existence spent.

Regina walked over to the survivors disabled on the ground, and methodically cut each of their throats. One asked for mercy, only to get a stony rebuke. "You shall get the same mercy you gave Sir Thomas."

Then she made it a point to stab him in the leg and twist the blade before cutting his throat.

I took a deep breath, curiously undiminished despite my copious use of magic. "This was a bloody business."

There were perhaps forty bodies spread throughout the ballroom, many officers included, and that was not counting Thomas or the Lakelord. Serah's revenge had enacted a heavy toll on Accadia's defenders and I did not think it would be soon forgotten. I did not have time to ponder what my next move should be because, behind me, Serah burst into tears.

I turned around to face her and saw Serah, a woman who had displayed amazing courage in the face of overwhelming odds, break down. Her tears ran down the side of her face, freezing into ice as they fell off her chin. She leaned heavily on her ghostwood staff, as if she wanted to fall to her knees beside her brother's body but couldn't bring herself to sacrifice that final bit of dignity.

She was too strong for that.

Or proud.

Or both.

So I hugged her.

Serah's body stiffed in my embrace but I knew there were many times after the worst of the battles I'd fought where I needed a comrade in arms or Jassa to give me this comfort. Man or woman, there was a simple universal need for the love of another being. I was a ghost made flesh, a monster that did not belong in this world.

But I hope she would accept my sympathy.

Much to my surprise, Regina joined the embrace.

The three of us held each other.

"Thank you," Serah said, her voice sounding confused. "I am better

now. If my dignity is to survive, however, please let go."

Regina let go first.

I did as well.

Serah looked down at her brother's body. "We do not have much time to waste. The entire castle will have heard our actions here and will rouse the rest of the guard."

"I am not afraid of them," Regina said, clenching a fist with her left hand. "If any seek to harm—"

"We could knock down the whole of this castle between us, but I do not wish to. I desire to be gone of this place," Serah said, lifting her staff. "I will not leave my brother's body to be despoiled by the mad dogs who will seek to blame him for this catastrophe, though."

Serah spoke the words of magic. This time, however, the words which flowed from her lips were not those of Demonspeak. Instead, they were those of Illumination. Her magic drew from love and light rather than the dark place. A golden flame covered Thomas' body and consumed it within seconds. Despite it being antithetical to my nature, I couldn't help but let the warm glow wash over me.

Gentle teasing...

Annoyance...

Defending the other against all others...

Nights drinking...

Hangovers...

Broken engagements...

Love...

I only got a small taste of everything Thomas Brightwaters had been to his sister but it was some of the purest emotion I'd experienced since my resurrection. I regretted the fact I hadn't known the man better and would never get the opportunity now. It also reminded me of a very clear fact: as long as I was a Wraith Knight, a creature of darkness, people would die because of me.

I'm glad you finally agree, the Trickster said. *Too bad we both know you're not going to abandon your few anchors of sanity left. You're too much of a coward for that.*

I had no response.

Which left the Trickster grinning in the back of my skull.

I was a coward.

"It is done," Serah said, looking at the ashes which had once been her brother. "We must leave now."

Regina looked over at the dead guardsmen. "I don't suppose you have any idea of where to head next. It appears my idea of raising a revolution against the Tyrant Empress was as foolish and naive as you said."

"You have my support," Serah said, coldly. "The Empress of her cronies are as responsible for Thomas' death as my uncle. I will take away everything from her and when she dies, I want Morwen to know I was the one who did it. The Anessian Empire will *suffer* for this, I swear by all the gods above and below."

Regina placed her hand on Serah's shoulder. "I understand and accept your promise."

It was an irrational response. The Nine Usurpers had nothing to do with this save on the vaguest level but I could understand anger needing an outlet. I could have asked them to think clearly but who was I to judge? I had made a thousand graveyards in the name of peace. Such a man had no advice to give on letting go of anger, hatred, and spite.

"Serah had the plan to use Tharadon's mirror to journey to the Eyes of the World," I said, interrupting their blood-fueled plans.

Regina looked disgusted. "Why would we go there?"

"A cure for Jacob's condition," Serah said. "If such a condition is said to need one."

"It does," I said.

Regina looked to the doors and saw a servant staring in at us. He bolted away at her gaze, shouting about murder.

"One direction is as good as any other when trying to survive a storm," Regina said, picking up a sword and crossbow from the dead warriors on the ground. "I swear a bond of friendship to you both, through thick and thin. An oath which supersedes all others. As a traitor to the Shadowguard and the Empire, it's not like I have any other loyalties."

"I need no pledges to know you are my truest friend and more," Serah whispered. "You both have done more for me than any but family. More so in some cases."

"You have both shown me more kindness than the shadow of the man I was deserves," I said. "By all rights, you should have met me with flame and silver. I will not forget this. Where is the mirror?"

Serah pointed to the floor. "The artifact room is directly below us. We'll have to—"

I proceeded to hit the ground with Chill's Fury, causing a five-foot-long circle of marble to freeze then crumble away. The resulting hole revealed a fabulous combination of art gallery and treasure room, radiating out an aura of magic even stronger than the power I'd felt from Serah minutes before.

Jumping down, I found myself in a large stone chamber with dozens of items looted from the Fourth War or even older time periods. There were the pieces of Tharadon's broken staff, his mirror, Eric the Unsteady's armor, a dress allegedly belonging to Jassa which was nothing like she'd ever worn, a vellum book of black magic written by Kurag, a bow belonging to High Lady Irigid, and a golden chalice which made me dizzy just looking at it.

All of these items were marked with little plaques and mounted for display. This was in addition to numerous works of art I knew had been looted from the Imperial City or other civilizations which had fallen to the King Below's forces. Quite a few belonged to the Grand Temple, Imperial Royal Family, or Great Houses I'd seen marching outside on the fields of battle.

"Or we could do that," Serah muttered, dropping herself down from the edge.

Regina jumped down. No sooner did they both land that I could hear the distant echo of explosions and detonations like thunder. It took a second for me to realize my enhanced senses were not picking them up. They were happening loud enough Regina and Serah could hear them. Both of them stiffened their backs and exchanged a troubled look.

"Those thrice-damned morons," Serah said, holding tight to her staff. "They've lowered the barrier to surrender."

"They're attacking anyway?" I asked, horrified.

"You expected more?" Serah's bitterness infused every syllable.

I looked down at my feet. "Yes."

"Don't," Serah said, heading to the mirror. "We won't be able to head directly to Everfrost, interference from the King Below's powers is too great. We should be able to arrive within traveling distance, though."

Tharadon's Mirror was a simple-looking device, lacking the flourishes so many wizards put on their devices. It was nothing more than a six-foot-tall piece of quicksilver with an adamant inlay. Only those who were familiar with the intricacies of alchemy, magic, and craftsmanship could perceive the hundreds of spells woven together into a single complex wonder. Given a decade, I might be able to unravel its secrets but I doubted any other artificer was capable. It was probably why this century wasn't filled with a million such devices.

Regina stared at her. "You can rally the city troops, Serah. We can save it."

"No," Serah said, placing her hands on the mirror's surface. "This city has taken enough for me."

A silver-white energy passed from her hand and the mirror's surface became an image of a snowy wasteland.

Serah stepped through.

Regina followed.

I heard more explosions, closer to the castle now. I could imagine the screams, death, and carnage happening outside. The city was being

bombed before they invaded. The Imperial army would take their revenge for Bloodthorn. Could I help? No. I had done enough to ruin the Accadian's lives.

I walked through the mirror.

CHAPTER 17

The three of us arrived through the portal seconds later, only to find ourselves on a hilltop overlooking a vast ghostwood forest. The evergreen trees of the mysterious white pines were covered in snow and the sun was setting, making me wonder if the trip was not instantaneous or if we'd just travelled a great distance to the East.

We were now in the Eyes of the World, the northernmost tip of the planet and the land above the Northern Wasteland. Very few rangers of the Shadowguard ever made it this far, since we were already deep into the Shadowkind's territory.

Stories back home portrayed the Eyes of the World as an endless barren land of evil, if not the entire northern continent, but I'd always been aware of its many beauties. A truly barren wasteland wouldn't be able to support the vast number of nonhumans and wild men which formed the basis of the King Below's armies.

Even farther to the North, where the snow never melted and it was always winter, at the top of the world, there was the Tower of Everfrost. Even this far away, I could feel the power of the place radiating outward. It was like an eerie black song of Demonspeak, one of which I could almost make the words out of.

Then, like the world was taunting me, I could hear the words sung by women I knew the voices of: *"Come hither Black King of the North, rest your weary head against the stones, and rise anew with sword in hand."*

I shook my head, trying to drive away the eerie song. I would say I was going mad, but such was too hopeful a thing to contemplate as true.

"Walk with maids of blackened sun and hidden moon, hand-in-hand, a trio of the damned. Skip across the skull roads and watch the black roses bloom."

Be silent. BE SILENT.

"Tis the hour of your doom."

I put my hand to my temples, closed my eyes, and took several useless deep breaths. The music faded to the back of my mind, another taunt by the Trickster, a way of showing his power over me grew.

I would not let him take me. I would seize his power at the Tower of Everfrost.

I would be free.

Turning around, I saw Regina holding Serah by the shoulder. Both of the women looked cold and I realized they needed spells of protection to survive the ensuing journey. Serah probably had her own, but I walked over and whispered two spells over both, covering both in an aura which would keep the cold from bothering them.

Much to my surprise, the spells felt far more powerful and instead of lasting weeks, I felt they had somehow altered both women so they would never fear the cold again. The presence of the Tower, even at this distance, already affected my magic.

"What was that?" Regina asked, looking up.

"A protection spell," I said. "It should keep you from the worst of the cold."

"Forever," Serah said, smiling. "We will find our magic greatly enhanced here."

She seemed cheerier about the prospect than myself.

"Is it possible to resurrect my brother?" Serah asked, looking up at me. "The necromancy of the Dark Lords is said to be great."

I should have seen that question coming. In life, I would have been horrified by the question but now I searched my memories for an answer. "I would need his corpse and, even then, I doubt I have the skills. The actual Kurag might have known such magic, but I am but a pale imitation."

"I think you sell yourself short," Serah said, looking down. "We shall have to work on getting your skills up to speed. If impossible, I will do it myself. The Tower of Everfrost should double or even triple our gifts."

That did not bode well.

"Surely, your brother is with the Lawgiver," Regina offered.

"My brother did not believe in the Lawgiver."

Both Regina and I stared at her.

I like him already, the Trickster said. *I often wished to disbelieve in my opposite.*

Serah gave a half-smile. "I always thought he was rather stupid for it, given everything around us, but he said it was more believable some wizard in funny armor was using the King Below's name to rally the Formor and tribals. Well, more believable than two all-powerful beings were battling it out on our world when there were so many others out there. Thomas always looked for the trick or the lie. I think it came back from his days when he traveled with an acting troupe. Those were good times."

"I'm sorry," I said, wondering how strange it must be to have an undead monster comfort you.

"Why? You didn't kill him. My uncle's men did."

"Then you killed him," Regina said, shaking her head as if she still couldn't believe what Serah had done.

"I did," Serah said, absorbing the weight of her action.

Kinslaying was one of the three Unforgivables in the Southern Kingdoms. You could not kill someone of your own blood or have it ordered. You could not slay a messenger flying under flag of truce. Finally, it was forbidden to spill blood in one of the sacred places to the gods. Any of the gods.

You could rape, kill, torture, flay, or toss a baby in a river, but these were all things which you could recover your honor from. I'd been accused of raping Jassa to save the Grand Temple the embarrassment of initiates having willing sex under their roof but that had just landed me in the Shadowguard. Yet, there was no place in the Southern Kingdoms for Serah now.

No place but Everfrost.

"It must have been difficult," Regina said, showing surprising compassion given her background.

"Yes," Serah said, looking away. "But satisfying."

The silence was long.

Regina turned to me. "How long will it take to reach Everfrost from here?"

I thought about the distance. "Provided we move on spirit-steeds, I'd say about a month."

"A month?" Regina said, surprised. "Is there no way to move faster?"

I shook my head. "I would not trust a Nuckelavee or other demonic creature this close to the Tower for so extended a journey. The Trickster still has influence, living or dead. Ghostly horses are all I risk. If we had a dragon we could get there in a week's time but I don't see the likelihood of finding one here increasing any time soon."

"A month is fine," Serah said, breathing out. "It will give us time to get to know one another."

"I suppose there is that," Regina said, smiling. "Though I know you better than any other person on this world, Serah."

"Except the most obvious thing," Serah said, sighing. "But your blindness there is something I have become accustomed to."

"Pardon?" Regina asked.

"A subject for a later time," Serah said, looking away.

"What will we do for food?" Regina asked.

"I have lived off the land before," I said, contemplating our options. "I do not think I require the same sorts of sustenance I used to. Even this far away from the Tower, I feel as if I am no longer fading away gradually. We only need to gather enough food and water for you both. Which should be possible in this place."

"I am a Shadowguard and can hunt my own food," Regina said. "The rest of my order may have fallen to indolence and sloth but that doesn't mean I have."

"My needs are simple," Serah said, straightening her back. "I am used to a certain kind of luxury but I will attempt to keep my complaints to a minimum. This is a quest for knowledge and power, neither of which have historically come cheaply or without suffering."

"What do you wish to achieve with such, may I ask?" Regina asked. "I have long known you have wanted to increase your control over the mystic arts but any ambitions beyond that have been opaque to me."

"Freedom, my dear Regina. Freedom from fear. Freedom from the rules of right and wrong. I will test my limits before breaking though. This dark magic has been a curse for too long and now it will be my blessing. I meant it when I said if I could not be a force for good then I would be the scourge of life they imagined me to be."

"Do not let their ignorance poison you against the common folk." Regina put her hands on her hips. "The ignorance of a few should not be used as a weight on the scale for the many."

"Even if it is the ignorance of the many I am concerned with?" Serah snapped back. "What I hope to find in the Tower is power.

Power to change the world no less. Because the world *needs changing*."

"I am sure you will use your powers for justice," I said, speaking before Regina could. Serah still suffered the trauma of losing her brother and anything she said now would be influenced by that pain.

What she needed was trust. I only wish such a lesson hadn't been learned the hard way.

"Thank you," Serah said, sucking in her breath. Due to my spell, her breathe was no longer visible in the cold air.

"Fine," Regina said, clearly not happy about having her objections dismissed. "I trust you, Serah, you know that. I would not have come to you and Thomas if I didn't. I certainly wasn't coming to see your uncle because I believed in him."

"We dance on the edge of a knife," Serah said, reaching down under her dress to remove a dagger from a hidden sheath on her leg. Holding it in her hand, she cut the end of her thumb and drew a droplet of blood.

"Serah—"

"Let me finish," Serah interrupted. "Both of us were possessed of our entire lives before the Empress' rise to power. Now, our futures have been cut away like pieces of stone from a sculptor's block until it resembles only a single thing. I have no desire to harm the innocent or inflict harm upon the undeserving, but this path before us is going to be layered in corpses. To defeat the Empress, we will have to not only kill her but her supporters as well as break the public's faith in her. Killing Jon Bloodthorn was a first step but it did not end his influence over the army. Jacob struck a blow to the Empress' credibility when he claimed the King Below was still alive. We must *smash* their remaining respect to pieces and scatter it across the floor. It is not enough to kill them. We must make sure they are remembered as cowards, fiends, and murderers who brought down a horrific plague on the world. It is an old G'Tay proverb you should make funeral arrangements for yourself when planning revenge. Most believe this is a warning against revenge but it is a statement you should devote yourself completely and utterly to it. To the point you are willing to sacrifice your life and the lives of others to its completion. I have lost what is most precious to me, Regina, as have you. I am willing to make that sacrifice. Are you?"

Serah let the blood dribble from her thumb on the snowy ground.

Regina stared at the knife, clearly contemplating what Serah was asking. Whether she was willing to sacrifice everything she was as well as her future for the sake of destroying the eight remaining usurpers. Regina made her choice and grabbed the knife before cutting across her palm. "I will sacrifice everything that I am, could be, and was to this cause. You shall find no fire burns hotter than my desire to cast down my foes. Whitehold and Thomas will be avenged, no matter the cost."

Regina's blood co-mingled with Serah's in the snow. Both women turned to me.

I took the knife from Regina. "I have sworn such an oath before and did so during the Fourth War, promising to sacrifice everything up to and including my soul to bring ruin to the King Below's designs."

"And so you did," Serah said.

"Did I?" I said, looking at the knife. It was a fine blade, excellently manufactured, and of Riverford manufacture. Serah must have picked it up from my people's descendants on a trip or through traders. "What you see before you, this bloodless shadow of a human being, is the product of my oath. I dread the prospect of recovering my memories for I am certain it will reveal an ocean of atrocities my spirit was forced to do on the King Below's behalf. Yet, even as I think on that, I know they would only be custard to a pie of bodies I made all too willingly. You stand here, willing and eager to throw away your futures to deny someone else theirs. I do not disapprove. I have no right. I will be at your side for this is where destiny has taken me. I would ask for a favor from you both, though. A boon for our nascent friendship and saving your lives as you have saved mine."

"What?" Serah said, narrowing her eyes and tightening her grip around her staff. She was displeased with my response to their blood oath.

Regina, by contrast, looked ashamed.

"When you throw all of your logs on the fire of revenge, I ask you keep a single twig behind. A small part of yourself you hold fast to, apart from this scheme, which will be there on the small chance you succeed and lay waste to your enemies. A part of you, which will be able to grow and love as well as live past the moment victory is in your grasp. Too many seekers of revenge are undone when they achieve their aims, left little more than shadows as metaphorically true as mine is literal."

"Did you keep such a thing?" Serah asked, all but an accusation.

"I did," I said, half-ashamed. "She had a name."

Jassa.

Snowflakes began to fall as a light storm began to intrude over us. The silence around us was maddening, only the incessant low-level singing in the back of my mind being audible. Despite being an exemplar of everything terrifying under the bed and hiding outside the window, I had never felt more terrified than under the gazes of the two women before me. It was like bringing flowers to Rosemary Cotton when I was fourteen.

Regina looked ready to argue but stopped before a word was uttered. Turning to Serah, she gave her an inquisitive look.

Serah relaxed. "I will try and keep such a twig, Jacob. I have occasionally known a root which was quite pleasurable. Yours runs deep through my soil and if I cannot think I will be with the one I care for, knowing they crave different things, then I will try not drag them down with me. I will also try and live for the joys of stretching out my flower petals to the sun as well as supping the nectar from the rain."

"That sounds remarkably dirty," I said, half-joking.

"I was just thinking of how Thomas would want me to behave in this situation. If I were to die, he would have drunk a lake of ale, pissed away a fortune at dice, and fucked every whore in Accadia. He would not want me to make him a noose around my neck, even if I am not so inclined to his largess."

"You are too valuable to waste on the Nine Usurpers," I said, cutting my finger and letting a shadowy drop of blood fall to the ground with theirs. "We will make a toast to all of our departed friends in the finest restaurant with the best food money can buy when victory is our hand. I will be a man again, Regina a Princess, and you a wizard beloved by all."

"And we might also have a hen which lays diamonds while we're wishing," Serah said, laughing. "Reserve your strength, though, I may have need of it in the coming days."

Regina opened her mouth to object.

"I am in mourning, too, I fear," I said, placing my hand over my heart. "Not that the offer is not a severe temptation. I do, however, require my paramours to buy me drinks first."

"How un-chivalrous of you. I like it."

Regina rolled her eyes. "You two. This is going to be an interesting month."

"In good company, at least," I said.

I turned around and spoke words of magic which summoned forth three horses made of living ice. Spirit Steeds were not sentient, even animated by the mindless elemental spirits leftover from heathen times when they served forgotten gods. They were, however, Twilight magic which would tirelessly take us North.

To the Tower of Everfrost and the Crown of Weeping Gods.

CHAPTER 18

We travelled through the snowy hills of the Eyes for weeks, taking in the sights of the strange and foreboding land. The Northern Wasteland was both beautiful and terrible at once. I saw ancient frozen castles, ruined cities inhabited only by ghosts, the skeletons of terrible beasts half-a-mile long, abandoned eldritch machines of nebulous purpose, and terrible battlefields where snow never covered the thousands of still-fresh corpses created during the Great Shadow Wars. Several times we saw Formor villages but, aside from a couple of times where I snuck in to steal supplies for my companions, I avoided these.

The journey across the ice deserts, glacier mountains, and ghostwood forests proved to be a surprisingly pleasant one. Aside from the stark environment and ominous surroundings, the Eyes of the World were not all that bad of a place to live. There was ample game to be found in the woods, plants which grew year-round, and fish which did not seem bothered by the cold. The inhabitants seemed welcoming too, several times fresh deer being left near our campsites by dire wolves or Spiderfolk.

We sat at one of those campsites, after weeks of travel, but now only a day's ride from Everfrost. I did not know if its visibility from such a massive distance was an illusion created by its inherent magic or if the location was genuinely that big but it had steadily grown as we'd approached it.

Now the tower and its surrounding city loomed like a mountain range over the ghostwood trees about us, forming an impossibly vast wall which stretched in every direction. We had but to pass through the Gates of Light's End then ascend the Stepstones of the Damned to the Mouth of Bahlor. Which, aside from being excessively overwrought in their naming, were not that intimidating.

The three of us had no need of flame to keep us warm, my magic continued to protect us from that, nor did any of us get tired as we travelled. However, it was necessary to cook my companion's meat and the light from our fires kept away most travelers. The Spiderfolk and Dire Wolves still encircled us, though, keeping watch on our movements, but seemed uninterested in attacking us.

Both Regina and Serah wore ill-fitting Formor armor, heavy furs, and leather armor underneath I'd stolen for them. They didn't need such clothing, but neither had felt comfortable in their previous clothes after escaping Lakeland Castle.

Regina still sported Hopebringer, though, and clung to the blade fastidiously despite her original plan having been stabbed to death. Serah, by contrast, was mostly quiet. The death of her brother still weighed heavily on her heart and the fact it had come at the hands of her uncle only made worse. Despite this, she came out of her shell and finished the Song of Eveningtide, a beautiful melody about a woman and her ghostly lover.

Both Regina and I clapped as she finished it.

"That was beautiful," Regina said, smiling.

"Thank you," Serah said. "My voice was the only thing my parents didn't want to beat out of me."

"You did not deserve the treatment you received," Regina said, reaching over to pat her shoulder.

Serah flinched then shook her head. "I am not one to complain too much. It informs my actions but I am going to the Tower of Everfrost now. It is my hope the libraries are still intact. It is said to be the greatest collection of science and learning in the world. The things I could learn there are beyond imagination."

Regina frowned. "I have heard one look at its books will drive a man mad."

"I think we're all mad here," Serah said. "Or have you not noticed?"

I laughed.

Regina shot me a dirty look. "I will be glad when our business at the Tower is concluded. We are on a goodly quest to free the world from tyrants. You have slain Jon Bloodthorn. That is one of the Nine Usurpers dead. When the other eight are slain, then the lands shall know peace."

Serah stared at her. "Yes, because the regicide of the world's rulers is going to usher in an age of peace."

Regina's gaze narrowed. "You would have me ignore their crimes?"

"No, I want them dead. All of them," Serah said, gritting her teeth. "But for myself, not the world."

"That is a cold view of the world," I said.

"We are in a cold place," Serah replied.

I poked the rabbit roasting on the fire with a stick. "On that cheerful note, let's move on to something more depressing. Our backstories. We have shared many stories these past three weeks, let us share more."

"Agreed," Regina said, looking at me. "I know what the legends say about you which are—"

"Completely untrue."

Serah said, "A pity. Some of them were quite saucy."

I smirked.

Regina frowned.

"What of you, Regina? I have heard you speak of your time with your parents in the wastes, your time with Serah and Thomas, plus several war stories. You speak little of Whitehold, though. If it is not too painful, I would know more of that place."

"My story is boring." Regina looked down, bashful.

"Yes, well, I'm sure we can enjoy the minstrel and ale at this inn."

Dire wolves howled in the distance.

"You're far too funny to be an embodiment of evil," Serah said, smiled. It was the first true smile I'd seen in a week-and-a-half.

"He's not an embodiment of evil, merely cursed," Regina said, a little too quickly. "He will be a man someday again."

"I see no curse," Serah said, shaking her head. "But you should answer his question. Start with how you came to be with your uncle."

"I was born the daughter of Shadowguardsmen as you know," Regina said, looking up. "My mother was a great warrior and enemy of evil. My father was a medic, despite being the son of a great lord. They were killed in a Formor ambush while on patrol in the ice desert."

Regina stared out into the woods. "I grew up in a place like this, living in a Shadowguard fort. It was the last. All the others had been abandoned for decades, the lordlings and princelings of the new Guard not wanting to risk themselves in the frozen wastelands. I remember hiding under my parent's corpses to escape the Formor seeking survivors."

"What happened?" She had mentioned her parents had died but not how.

"I was found." Regina looked up. "The Formor Captain spared me and a boy-child who had been traveling with parents. They dropped us nearby the fort with a message that the King Below had returned to his full strength and the Great Shadow War was once more upon the races of men. I was sent to live with my father's family."

I blinked, surprised by her story. The Shadowguard was rarely so gentle to the children of Formor. I had thrown up the first time I'd realized what was expected of me after a raid upon one of their villages. From that day forward, I'd avoided any raids on their infrastructure. The sight of Formor cubs, elders, and those left to guard them burning in a pyre haunted my nightmares long after I'd seen entire cities put to the sword for collaboration. It was the first time I'd learned children would suffer no matter what during war and my only grace was I'd never killed any.

Only ordered the sacking and burning of cities which resisted re-conquest, causing thousands of children to die. Much better, the Trickster said.

He wasn't wrong.

Reigna sighed, dreamily. "I wish I could describe to you the beauty of Whitehold. King Eric's secondson, Matthew Elf-Friend was an enthusiast for the culture of the sidhe. While rebuilding the Empire for his brother the Emperor, he made sure to do countless castles and parks in their style. Whitehold was his masterpiece. The townsfolk were taught to dress in sidhe-styles, speak oghman, and follow sidhe law. Elf-lovers and those with their blood from all over the Empire flocked to live there."

"It sounds like I'd slit my throat after a week there," I said.

I was not a fan of the sidhe or their High Lords. During wartime, they would waste thousands of allied troops to rescue a single member of their kind while providing the barest minimum of help which required risk. They spoke of human, Fir Bolg, giant, and dryad lives as transitory things compared to their immortal glory. I once saw a Lesser Lord use a column of Fir Bolg refugees as target practice for his men. When I'd confronted him about it, he'd claimed he was 'cleansing the world of detritus.'

In the end, I'd invited him and his men to have a feast at a Temple to the Great Mother, locked them in, and burned it to the ground. That had been two Unforgivables I'd broken with my men but the sidhe had been so incensed by the 'Fomor' doing it (once I'd left the appropriate evidence), they'd contributed an extra ten thousand archers to help us clear Heartstone Pass.

See, it's that kind of initiative which made me choose you, the Trickster said. *That and your hypocrisy.*

Regina laughed at my words, unaware of my dark memories. "The sidhe, themselves, always hated Whitehold when they visited. You could tell they found the enthusiasm offensive. My maternal grandmother, who will look younger than me when my grandchildren are dead, loathed girls who altered themselves to appear more like elves. She called them perfumed swine and rats dressed for a ball. I called her *var'ash'narhal* in her language, which means—"

"I know what it means," I said, chuckling. "That was cheeky."

"I bet you were the darling of Whitehold," Serah said. "Its white rose."

Regina snorted. "I raised witchfire and damnation every chance I could. I was a child of the wilds and they had put me in one of the most effete courts in the Empire. Like a sidhe, I was expected to know dancing, embroidery, philosophy, singing, harp, and how to use a bow as well as a sword. Never mind that sidhe men and women get a century or two to learn these things before adulthood. I loved my uncle but I couldn't help but think he looked ridiculous in his imitation Highlord clothes and magic-sculpted features."

I tried to imagine that but found myself laughing instead. "Lord Whitetremor sounds like an interesting man."

"Uncle Hugh was," Regina said, checking the rabbit. It was almost done. "The Last Great Shadow War was the shortest and still lasted a decade. He fought on the side of Emperor Thelion with bow, sword, and spell. He loved me as his own daughter and made sure my training in weapons was matched only by my education in responsibility. I think he would have taken me to fight with him during the final battles at the foot of the Eyes if not for my mistake."

"Your mistake?"

"I fell in love with his son, Gewain."

"You fell in love with your cousin?" I asked, surprised.

"Is that so strange?"

"To commoners? Yes," Serah said, amused. "Thomas and I always found your relationship with him strange."

"Says the woman of High Man blood."

"Too much stock is placed in that," Serah said, turning away. "I am who I am because of what I choose, not because of a quirk of lineage."

"You are who you are because of both," I corrected, feeling oddly jealous of this Gewain. "He must have been an impressive man."

"The most beautiful man in the Empire, the gentlest, and the wisest," Regina said, softly. "I pledged my love to him but he rejected me."

"This part I knew," Serah said, smiling. "She was inconsolable. Regina spent two months wandering from whorehouse to whorehouse seeking men and women who reminded her of Gewain."

Regina blanched, embarrassed. "You didn't need to tell him that."

"But you're such a funny drunk," Serah said, the smile turning pained. "We both know how the story ends, though."

Regina nodded. "Gewain perished with everyone else."

That took me aback. I had forgotten about that fact of her story. "I see."

Regina's look grew grim. "My uncle did not hold the Lawgiver's worship to an orthodox level and allowed the veneration of both the High Lords as well as ancestor spirits as is an old sidhe custom, even if they have abandoned it. Much lore declared blasphemous by her Steward was also present. Uncle Hugh also refused to recognize Empress as anything more than the late Emperor Jorge Tremor's Queen. He wished, instead, to crown their son."

I did not need to know the details but I suspected Regina needed to tell them. "Go on."

"I received the message by dragon-rider," Regina said, her voice quaking. "The Empress had always been a friend to the Shadowguard and had kept us separate from the purges in her court, of the lesser houses, and the Temple. I regret, to be honest, I did not care about what she was doing as long it did not affect me. Then, I flew my dragon over Whitehold and I saw ashes. What it had taken my family two centuries to build, she had destroyed in two hours. It was a lesson to the other houses. An effective one for, within days, hundreds burned their verbatim books, swore themselves to her and the Temple, and sent her hostages."

I could only admire her courage now and respect her desire for revenge. "Your thievery seems more justified now."

"It wasn't before?" Regina asked, weakly. "You remind me in many ways of Gewain. Which is strange since you could not be more different than the star-filled night to the sun. Yet, both are beautiful."

Serah cast her an unpleasant look.

I almost laughed. "Thank you."

"What is your story, Dark One?"

I looked up to the moons above and the ringed planet behind them. "It all begins in a muddy shack on the river..."

CHAPTER 19

T he memories of my homeland were powerful, stronger than any save of Jassamine. I could smell the air, taste the fish, and hear the sounds of the woodpeckers against the nearby forest. I saw flashes of my family, however little I'd thought of them during my time at war. I even missed Malcolm Riverson, pathetic old monster he'd been.

"The Fisherfolk, at least the ones in my time, lived on the edge of civilization. If we were not quite the Borderlands then we were in recent memory of being part of such territories. We were the descendants of those unwanted by the rest of the Southern Kingdoms as well as refugees from the lands beyond the Barrier Mountains. We did not possess a king, lord, or standing army. Clothes were always dyed in the deepest black and our focus was on religion."

"That is a strange way of living," Regina said, blinking.

"Not so much when you know the whys of such," I said, remembering the darker aspects of my life with them. "For the Fisherfolk believed in peace. Not like other men who hope for it and prepare for war but as a way of life. They were not warriors and carried no weapons, even in defense. They believed the Great Mother made all life sacrosanct. We produced no killers, soldiers, or slayers. Murder was as rare as gryphon's teeth and was usually an accident during good-natured brawling."

"Your home sounds divine," Regina said, smiling.

"It sounds foolish," Serah replied.

"It was both. It meant peace amongst ourselves but that also that we were easy prey for those who didn't share our beliefs. To set down one's weapons was to invite attack and we invited many. Worse, our love for life was mistaken for weakness. I could not count the number of brigands, mercenaries, and petty warlords who considered us a source of supplies. The good ones merely took what they wanted and left. The worst stayed or abused for the pleasure of it. We had extensive underground tunnels because we needed places to hide our stores so we wouldn't starve and to protect the most vulnerable. Even then, that always didn't work as many soldiers will search thoroughly for prizes."

I clenched my fist. It had been a week before Malcolm sold me into slavery that I'd stuck a fat pig of a deserter with a pitchfork for one too many insults and leers toward my sisters. I'd hidden his body well but my sire had acted like I'd been in the wrong. Even my sisters had looked at me like I'd become something which was no longer their brother.

"The Riverfords are no longer that way," Regina said, looking down. "I'm sorry to say."

"What do you mean?"

"It means they're a place of brigands, mercenaries, and warlords but it's the Fisherfolk who now do it. They're nicknamed the Daggerlands," Serah explained. "It turns out if you beat a dog too much, it eventually breaks or goes bad. When my brother and I were actors, visiting Joy was like visiting a brothel owned by pirates in the middle of a swamp. What religion your people possessed fell away with the ravages of time."

I burst out laughing.

Regina frowned. "Is something funny?"

"River's Joy was my hometown's name," I said, smiling. "It would be my luck that it become that way."

"You don't strike me as the type to enjoy such a life," Regina said, bringing the conversation back to its subject.

"I didn't," I said, remembering my sire's many beatings and attempts to instill in me a peaceful heart. "In the end, I did something, something Malcolm Riverson couldn't forgive."

"What did you do?" Regina asked.

"I killed a man." I shrugged. "My sire contacted my mother's brother, Kalian, who had ventured outside of the Riverfords to join the world. Kalian had returned changed, prone to nightmares and screams when people touched him unexpectedly. I would say he was suffering the War Sickness but he was averse to blood than desiring it. Kalian was famed as a hero both inside and out of the Riverfords, though. Malcom had me branded as a thrall and given to him with instructions I was to be kept close watch on. If I ever left Kalian's side before he freed me, I'd be executed. Even in the Riverlands we had masters and servants. Kalian was my master and I was the servant."

Regina placed her hand in front of her face. "Your uncle, that's... monstrous."

Serah, by contrast, said, "It seems to have worked out for you."

"Yes. For Kalian was more a father to me than Malcolm ever was. Kalian knew much in the ways of war, though he was constantly haunted by guilt and self-loathing for the battles he'd participated in. He also never married for reasons of inclination and needed an heir. I'm certain my sire would have never allowed me to become his slave if he knew it was Kalian's intention for me to inherit his fortune."

"So your story has a happy ending," Regina said, nodding.

"The beginning has not yet begun, I fear."

I thought of Kalian teaching me swordsmanship, riding, and literacy. He hired tutors for me when we arrived in the Imperial City. There, he spent most of his time with his lover, David, but I'd learned a staggering amount regardless.

Those had been good times.

Times before the war.

"In the end, Kalian's war guilt overcame him and he officially freed me before sending me to the Grand Temple with a letter of recommendation. The Grand Cleric himself received me and gave me a blessing." I didn't want to tell them about Jassa. That was too personal, too private, and the decades which followed were one long nightmare.

One which only ended recently.

"What happened to your uncle?" Serah asked.

If I had any tears left to weep for Kalian, they were gone now but my eyes were as moist as a ghost could make them. "When he heard of the next Shadow War and the rising of the Dark Lord, he knew he would have to return to the battlefield. He was a symbol of courage for what he'd done during the War of the Fire Kings." I paused. "He sent me, my mother, and his lover each a letter before walking into the nearest lake with stones in his pockets."

The camp site was silent for the next minute. Our rabbit was done.

"Uncle Kalian's funeral was attended by every race in the Southern Kingdoms. A High Lord and two kings gave a speech."

"I'm sorry I've never heard of him," Regina said, frowning. "He sounds like he was a formidable man."

"The War of the Fire Kings was the last war in my lifetime where honor and decency were expectations rather than fancies. Where the rich and entitled fought in the front rather than the back," I said, shaking my head. "My uncle started in the war as nothing more than a foreign sellsword but rose to the highest rank in the Empire. He could have been a great lord but chose to leave his position for the peace of a commoner's life. It is not right such a man should fall prey to battle-trauma."

"I, too, knew someone like Kalian," Regina said, placing her hand over her heart. "Her name was Fiona and she was the Battlemaster of my father's household. She was sidhe but did not possess the same level of arrogance so many of my grandmother's ancestors did. Fiona had served with House Whitetremor since before there was one. It was she who pounded me into the piece of steel I later became. It was Fiona who taught me the best way to wield a sword was to learn when to keep it sheathed." She looked embarrassed. "Not that I have ever followed said advice."

"You sit here with a witch and a Dark Lord as friends," Serah said, reached over and patted her knee. "I think she did a magnificent job."

"Thank you," Regina said, frowning. "I remember one night, before I joined the Shadwguard, she insisted on taking both me and Gewain out on dragonback. She took us to the neighboring territory of House Rogers. There, we saw the burning of the city's Fire District. Men, women, and children butchered in the streets as their possessions were stolen with the full support of the law."

"Why?" I asked, surprised.

"Because they were Fir-Bolg," Regina said, as if it was self-evident. "It has been centuries since they had their own land, Jacob. You asked of what happened to the Fir-Bolg, the same thing happened to countless other Lightborn races and they did not have the benefit of being placed in city slums. Eric the Great, who does not seem so much to me now, turned his sword against all who did not follow the strict worship of the Lawgiver as proscribed by him. For many lesser lords, those not of human or sidhe blood were suspicious by nature. Under the Empress, it has gotten worse. Ironically, because she believes they should be brought fully into the fold of the Lawgiver's light."

"I see."

Regina looked to one side. "I couldn't help but think Fiona was wrong that day. She held us back, having brought us to see how unjust and unfair the world truly was. However, we had dragons. If we wanted to, we could have rained down a terrible vengeance on those looters, murderers, and rapists. We could have protected the innocent."

"And started a war?" Serah asked. "House Rogers is the most powerful in the Empire."

Regina shot Serah a withering look. "What use is power if it is not to protect others?"

"That is a simplistic worldview," Regina said, removing her hand.

"That is the right worldview and the only people who say otherwise are those who hide behind platitudes." Regina's eyes flashed venom as she balled her fists.

"Regina," I said, hoping to stave off an argument. "I, too, know what it is like to be helpless when there is something horrible happening."

"I am not a child. I know the world is...complex. I have also seen what the countless compromises, reliance on noble obligation, and avoiding conflict has wrought. The world is rotten to the core and everywhere I turn to seek some calling to make it better, I find more maggot-ridden interiors. The Shadowguard were my last hope. Someone needs to set fire to the plague house of the Southern Kingdoms and build anew."

"That is a bit radical," I said, feeling hypocritical saying so. "Even if I agree with you about the world's institutions. They don't appear to have gotten better since my arrival."

"Only the Grand Temple has improved because of Saint Jassa," Regina said, sighing. "I would sacrifice everything to see the world made better."

"You have," Serah said, looking at her. "You have burned every bridge imaginable, Regina. The Shadowguard, nobility, and others all think will think you have sacrificed your honor for working with us."

"Honor is a word people use to defend shitting on good." Regina snorted. Getting a sour look on her face, she looked away. "Gods, I need a drink."

I pulled the rabbit from the fire and started carving it up onto metal plates. "Alas, we have melted snow and more melted snow. I saw some jars of Formor brew while looting through their goods but the stuff smelled like piss and probably tasted worse."

"When I wish to get drunk, I rarely care about taste," Regina said, taking one of the plates. "It also wouldn't be first time I have gotten knees-up on Formor brew either. Last time I ended up nailing my undergarments to the Whitehold Temple wall."

"Now that sounds like an interesting story. More interesting than mine," I said, handing Serah her plate.

"You should finish your story, Jacob."

I stared at the fire, thinking of Jassa. "There's not much to tell, really." I lied. "I proved to be a poor Temple Knight. Despite my faith and skill at swordplay, I was unable to turn a blind eye to the corruption. I found someone I cared about greatly but our destinies led us in different paths. So I ended up joining the Shadowguard at the start of the Fourth War and ended up fighting against the King Below for ten years. There was a lot of hammering and studying sorcery in the meantime. They made me Knight Paramount, I killed Kurag, I died, the end."

"Surely, that's glossing over much," Regina said, frowning.

"It is," I said, biting my tongue. I had grown close to the two over the past three weeks and wanted to tell them the whole of my story. I was afraid they would turn against me, though. My suppressed memories were breaking through the closer we got to the Tower. I already recalled things I wished I didn't.

It was five nine years into the Fourth War and we were now two of the most powerful people in the Empire. People bowed in my presence and I was the one who handled all of the Crown Prince's war councils.

I was wearing an all-black uniform, as befitting the Knight Paramount of the Shadowguard, but it was significantly more dressed up than the normal attire of my organization. I had a golden burning-eye broach around my neck and an embroidered patch on my lapel which marked my position.

Numerous medals hung across my chest, symbols of my accomplishments in battle, even if several of them had been awarded for questionable deeds. A long coat covered my body, its pockets containing cold iron nails, Saint Esau's wort, and wards written on folded-up paper to ward away assassination spells.

Jassamine, by contrast, was wearing the gold and white robes of the Mysterium's Archmage. It was a symbol of how high she'd risen in the Mysterium. She'd reformed the Emperor's secret police and transformed it into a cold and efficient engine of order.

Both of us had turned our influence to reforming the Grand Temple and using its resources to help fight the King Below's forces, which won us more influence, which we used to influence others to fight the King Below's forces, and so on.

"The Empire does not need a strong ruler like Edorta or his siblings, someone who thinks their blood gives them special insight into running a country." Jassa's voice was low but her tone resolute. "We need a pliable candidate for the throne, someone who is dependent on us to protect him from his enemies yet charismatic enough to serve as a rallying cry for reforming the Southern Kingdoms."

"I do not like, Eric," I muttered, walking beside Jassamine in the halls of the rebuilt Grand Temple. "He is a weak man and unworthy of inheriting his father's mantle."

"That is why he needs our full support," Jassamine said, holding tight to her staff.

"It seems backward to weaken the Empire to strengthen it."

"I am not limiting my ambitions to the Empire," Jassa said, shaking her head. "The Southern Kindgoms are full of heresy, superstition, poverty, slavery, and petty divisions. We can use the Empire as the basis to spread Imperial culture and unite the lands under the aegis of the Lawgiver. It will be bloody business but if we are to be free and equal, we must be the same.

That is why I have had you burning those libraries and making sure the right people make it back from the front while the wrong...don't."

"We should be focused on defeating the King Below."

"We have gained as much as we can by pressing him," Jassa said. "The aftermath of the war is what matters now."

"There is no after," I repeated my mantra.

Jassa took my hands and joined her fingers with mine. "There is us."

It had been a sobering realization Eric the Unsteady had been not been leading the Empire astray but it had been we, Jassa and myself, who lead him to ill-deeds. He had been Jasamine's puppet, content to write what she wanted and leave the ruling to her. If he had become Eric the Great, it was surely at her behest.

If so, did that mean Jassa was responsible for what had happened to the Fir-Bolg? How many other races had suffered under her actions?

I needed to sit down in a library and read up on the past two Ages.

For a month.

You could always ask me, the Trickster said.

No, I replied.

As you wish.

"There is more, but it is a story for another time." I lifted up piece of rabbit to chew on. Food was ash in my mouth but I often went through the motions for my companions. They were uncomfortable eating otherwise.

We were eating in silence when I felt a cold, almost impossibly powerful presence wash over us. Something I hadn't felt since facing the King Below himself. Both Regina and Serah dropped their forks while I dropped my plate.

A somber, gravelly, yet bemused voice spoke. "Greetings Lord Kurag, welcome back."

I knew the voice well.

"*Creature,*" I whispered.

CHAPTER 20

Drawing Chill's Fury, I spun around one easy motion and aimed it behind my back at the source of the voice. The blade did not meet flesh, however, and came to a stop a few inches away from the face of a newcomer.

A short newcomer.

Standing four-foot-five yet radiating more dark energy than I'd felt outside of the King Below and his Dark Lords was a wizened old Formor in ratty demon priest's robes. He had saggy blue-gray skin with large bat-like ears, a too-wide mouth, yellow-eyes which seemed sunken into the back of his elongated face. Formor were an ugly race, though this one was less hideous than most with a kind of impishness which reminded me of a pug dog.

This particular Formor was also wearing a heavy star metal chain around its neck, ending in a medallion which contained the skull and sword of the King Below covered by the dual-masks of the Trickster. The symbols of all the other Gods Below, smaller in size than these two, formed a circle around the main two. In light of the Trickster's claims he was all of the Gods Below, I had to wonder if this "holy" man knew his deity was a being of many faces.

All beings are, the Trickster taunted. *You just haven't yet realized I am one of yours as you are of mine.*

Blinking, a name came to my mind for the being who had just addressed me.

Creature.

Which wasn't so much a name but a title.

The King Below had given it to him and the being before me had cast aside his original name to be the God of Evil's designated servant.

His creature.

In the ghostwoods behind Creature, I could make out two more forms. The first was as lovely as Creature was hideous. I was not a lover of men but the figure was a perfection of feature which transcended mere sexuality. He had lovely brown skin, angular features, almond shaped silver eyes, and long hair which hung down to his waist. There was a fierce wildness to his presence which seemed to draw one's attention and he was not standing in the snow so much as walking on top of it.

Of course he was a sidhe.

This figure was dressed in a magnificent work of art, armor composed of living silver which clung to the body and a cloak of star-filled night which moved in dramatic ways with his every movement. Contrasting with his near-perfection was a hideous bow made of bone, sinew, and black magic and a Dire wolf fur quiver on his back.

I knew this man, too.

Curse, son of Ruadan. A Dark Elf.

He was a Prince, of sorts, and the last descendant of Bryes the Betrayer by his bride Irigid the Incredible.

The third figure clung to the shadows, but the darkness hid nothing from a Wraith Knight. She was a Bauchan, one of those rare products of human and Formor mating which bred true. They tended to exist on the edges of civilization, living as hermits or bandits or, rarer, as members of communities which accepted them on the basis of their actions than blood. While wrapped up in heavy scarves and a wool coat over her armor, I could make out a shapely female form. Her skin was gray like Creature's with the same yellow eyes but her features were almost entirely human but for the sharp point to her ears. My experience with the Bauchan taught me she probably had teeth and nails capable of rending a man. Her name, I knew, was Payne and she was a Bone Knife. One of the order of mystical assassins which served the King Below.

We were in august company tonight.

"Hello," I said, looking at Creature. "I'm afraid I don't answer to the name Kurag anymore."

Regina looked ready to take on all three and reached for her sword hilt. I put her chances against three of the most dangerous people on the World Between at, well, actually, she could probably take out two but the third would definitely kill her.

Serah wisely said, "Hello, sirs. How are you this fine evening?"

Creature gently pushed away the tip of Chill's Fury with forefinger. "It's been quite a shit time for the past fortnight, to be honest, Lady Brightwaters." Turning to me, he said, "Should I refer to you as Lord Riverson, instead?"

"Jacob will do," I said, turning back to Regina. "I don't think they're going to kill us, Regina."

"Why's that?" Creature asked.

I looked back at him. "Because while you could individually take any of us out, all three of us would destroy you with power to spare."

"Force, the basis of all honest diplomacy," Creature said, chuckling. "I'm glad to see regaining your free-will hasn't removed all of your good sense, Lord Jacob."

"What do you want?" Regina said, removing her hand from her sword hilt.

"The same thing everyone wants," Creature said, gesturing for his followers to come out of the shadows. "To enslave all creation and rule over the Three Worlds as their undisputed master."

"That is not what everyone wants." Regina glared.

"Really? I thought it was just they didn't think they could pull it off," Creature said, frowning. "Are you sure? I'll have to change my whole belief system. Oh dear, oh dear."

"Just what we need: a sarcastic Formor." Regina sighed, relaxing.

"All Formor are sarcastic complainers," Payne said, walking forward. "Just as all true sidhe are obnoxious."

"They are no true sidhe anymore," Curse said, trailing up the newcomers. "The *true* sidhe settled this world alongside the gods as equals, coming from worlds where magic and science were as one. They had populated ten thousand worlds with their creations and refined reality as a musician does a song. They raised flying cities, killed armies by themselves, and were worshiped wherever they walked for the gloriousness they embodied. The diminished peasants playing at High Lords on the Eternal Isles aren't worthy to call themselves heirs to ancient Tuatha."

"See?" Payne said, gesturing to him.

"What?" Curse replied, looking confused. I couldn't tell if it was an act or not.

"Curse is usually better at keeping his opinions to himself," Creature said.

"He really is," Payne said, looking back at him with an admiring gaze. "He's the modest sidhe I've ever met. He can go whole *hours* without sounding condescending."

"How does a sidhe manage to survive amongst the Children of Balor?" I asked, genuinely confused. The Formor hated the sidhe more than anything else on the Three Worlds, which was impressive given the Formor hated everything.

"He can be very charming," Payne said before her voice lowered. "He has other qualities too."

Curse looked embarrassed, an emotion I'd never seen on him before.

"I turn anyone who tries to hurt him into jelly while Payne slits their allies' throats. The few leftover are ones Curse can deal with on his own," Creature said, shrugging. "Formor respect power and all of us have it in abundance."

"Why do you protect him?" Regina asked.

"I owe him a blood debt," Creature said, curling his lip. "During the First War, when I was young and stupid, I got myself captured by a group of human slavers who were torturing Formor to death. Curse put an end to it and set me free. Mostly because his grandfather was allied with the Formor, but the debt still stands. When his father fell, I gave refuge to the last of House Bryes and let him marry my daughter."

We all looked at Payne.

"I overlook his hideousness," Payne said, dryly.

"My grandfather, High King Bryes, believed peace was possible between the sidhe and Formor. That the two races had much to offer one another if we were not torn asunder by religion and racial strife," Curse said, speaking wistfully. "It is my desire to fulfill his dream."

"Wasn't he overthrown ten Ages ago?" Serah asked. "Then forced to drink three hundred vases of cow's piss?"

"Poisoned cow's blood," Curse said, frowning. "Though, honestly, I'm sure they prettied up the story."

"They also massacred his followers to the man," Serah said, adding to the story. "The last of the Unseelie died centuries ago."

I knew, because it was at my hands. "Apparently, we missed one."

"I didn't say I was successful," Curse said, looking up at the Peace-Weavers in the night sky. "The road to peace is a long and winding one, not always taking the most direct route."

"And more often leading to a dead end," I said, putting away Chill's Fury. "I know who you are: Creature, Curse, and Payne. You are three of Kurag's lieutenants and high-ranking members of the King Below's armies. You will find no friends here."

"If I wanted friends, I would have set out a tea-set, some scones, and thrown some doilies around the campsite," Creature said, pointing at me. "What I want, Lord Jacob, is to offer you an alliance."

"No," I said, resolutely. "You don't."

"Jacob," Serah stared to speak. "We don't know how many of them there are."

"They're alone," I said, staring down at Creature. "Formor don't seek alliances. They fight until one side is subordinate to the other. If they've come to us, it's because they're desperate."

"Or maybe you're just stupid," Payne said, drawing a curved dagger of dragon bone from a belt around her waist.

Regina went for her sword again.

Curse had his bow notched with an arrow in it before she was halfway there, pointing it at her chest.

I snapped my fingers and his bowstring snapped.

Curse stared at his now useless weapon.

Creature snorted.

"Most effective!" Creature said, clapping his hands. "I seem to recall I taught you that trick."

"You did," I said, trying to force down the memories of spending time with Creature. They reminded me there were times when the controls on my mind were not absolute. I couldn't deal with that now, or ever, in all likelihood.

"We need guidance and safe passage into Everfrost," Serah interjected into the conversation. "Perhaps an alliance is not such a bad idea, if it is made clear we are the ones in charge."

"We? You gain alliances quickly, Lord Jacob," Creature said, looking between them.

"I will ally with them only so long as they promise to harm no innocents while allied with us," Regina said, her voice resolute. I had no doubt she was entirely willing to take on all three by herself. Plus, however many reinforcements they had nearby.

"Innocents?" Curse asked, laughing. "My dear, where do you think you are?"

"I am nobody's dear," Regina said.

"You should work on changing such," Payne said. "Everyone should have a beloved. Even one as homely as you."

Regina opened her mouth, stunned, but no words came out.

Serah looked both amused then offended then amused again.

Creature pressed his fingers together. "You are right, Lord Jacob, we are desperate. I am willing to offer our service to you if you're willing to help us. That includes not killing the 'innocent,' which you'll have to define since I haven't seen such a creature in many a year. As your, well, the late lord Kurag's Castellan, I am fully capable of opening the pathway to Everfrost to you and giving you safe passage from the Frostiron clan which inhabits the region. I am happy to avail you of my considerable wisdom regarding your circumstances and the King Below's treasures—which is why you have come, is it not?"

"Our business is ours," I said, not trusting him in the slightest. Creature was close to two-thousand-years-old and a wizard of incredible power. I wasn't going to let his small statue fool me into complacency.

"Knowing your business would allow me to help you perform it." Creature made a reasonable argument. "If it would reassure you, though, then let it be known none of my group holds any lingering loyalties to the King Below."

I'm hurt, the Trickster said in my head. *Not surprised, but still hurt.*

"And why is that?" I asked.

"Because the King Below is dead," Payne said, sneering. "If he was too weak to survive then he is too weak to follow. Those are the rules

he laid down to us when he first took us over during the Pre-Age."

"Yes, well, might makes right is a rather poor philosophy if you're not the strongest one around," Creature said, making a tsk-tsk noise. "The Formor clans are scattered and only the Frostirons make their home in Everfrost now. When the King Below was slain, it was like a great weight was lifted off our shoulders. Unfortunately, the first thing everyone seemed to do upon this weight being lifted was try to yolk everyone else. The civil wars these past two years have been quite devastating."

"My heart beats for you," I said, staring at them. "Oh wait, no it doesn't."

The Formor were a race bred for war. Once, they might have been something else. While the holy texts taught they were creatures of darkness created by the King Below, learned minds argued they were a species from another world brought by the sidhe before the fall of Terralan and who predated the majority of the modern races.

A few even argued they were natives of this world the same way the Fir-Bolg claimed to be. Whatever the case, what they were before had been obliterated by millennium of enslavement. Art, civilization, culture, and anything but the most violent of sports had been beaten out of the Formor in order to prepare them for an existence of fighting the King Below's enemies.

I had studied them for years during the war and every observation I made was they were a culture which began as well as ended on conflict. If Formor had any redeeming features, it was they were clever and industrious peoples who savored life as if there was no tomorrow. Even so, these qualities were put to use by the King Below and Dark Lords to make them better warriors. Life was war so best to enjoy it before dying.

They had no honor, not even as Regina thought of it.

Creature looked at me. "Then let us speak plainly, Lord Jacob. Help us and we'll help you."

That I could understand. "What do you need?"

"Help reclaim Everfrost." Creature looked back at his children. "Something worse than the Formor has taken it over."

Oh joy, and just when I thought this was going to be easy.

CHAPTER 21

I find it difficult to believe there's anything worse than the Formor," Serah said, curling her lip in disdain.

"Says the *witch*," Payne said, adjusting her scarf across the bottom half of her mouth. I saw the barest sign of heavy scarring there. "I can *smell* the black magic on you."

"I have been persecuted all my life because of the belief I'm a servant of the King Below," Serah said, narrowing her eyes. "I have chosen to ally myself with one of the Dark Lords because of it. Yet, so far, Jacob has done nothing but protect the people of the Southern Kingdoms. I've seen what the Formor do to cities during the Last War."

"The Empire and its allies are no better," Curse said, sneering. "What they do to those who befriend the Formor or even surrender rather than fight to the death. Every atrocity the Formor have inflicted has been matched and reversed. Believe me, I'm a sidhe, I know how horrific the conflict has gotten on both sides."

"You will find comparing yourself to the Empire wins no friends here," Regina interjected. "However, we will help you both for our aid and the fact every race deserves to be free from the hands of oppressors."

Serah did a double take between Curse and Regina. "Excuse me?"

Regina looked to Serah then me. "We must hold ourselves to a higher moral standard than the Nine Usurpers. What better place to begin than assisting those who have every reason to hate us as much as our enemies?"

"Literally, with anyone else," Serah said. "Anywhere."

"I thought it was your idea to get their assistance," Regina said.

"That before I knew it would involve rescuing them from a new foe," Serah said, putting her plate aside. "I can play the diplomat when the time calls for it but if Everfrost is under the control of someone new, I suggest we speak with them instead."

"What do you think, Jacob?" Regina asked.

Oh lovely, they were putting me in the middle.

Creature pointed at each of us. "Are you three mated? Because, if so, that would explain a great deal."

"No," I said.

Not yet, the Trickster said.

Don't be lewd, I said back to him.

You can marry them first, the Trickster.

Creature and Payne exchanged a look before looking back at me. I wondered if the Formor wizard and Bone Priestess could hear the Trickster's voice.

"I think we should find out what we'll find when we cross through the Mouth of Bahlor," I said, deciding on the middle path which would please no one. "If we choose to help or not, it would be better to be informed."

Creature bobbed his head. "Very good, milord. After the King Below's death, all of the spells keeping Everfrost protected from the elements fell. The countless enslaved wights, revenants, shamblers, ghosts, and bonies were banished to the World Below. The demons went wild, killing or enslaving at will. Every clan chief declared himself Warmaster and a few demanded to be worshiped as the King Below once was. All they managed to do was kill each other in honor duels, leaving the victors too weak to fight their subordinates. The Dark Lords could have sorted it all out but only you survived the Nine's assault. Even then, it was impossible to locate you. It seemed the King Below sent you to the farthest reaches of the World Between and we lost contact with you afterward. Most of us thought you dissolved."

"I should have dissolved," I said, looking down at my gloved hands. "I don't see why every other spirit was freed except for me."

I know why! The Trickster said. *I'm not going to tell you though.*

It was times like this I wished the God of Evil were more mature.

You really don't, the Trickster said, his voice gaining a hint of ominousness.

I ignored him. "I can't say what happened to me but if I've truly been gone two years, it has been spent in a state between life and death. I suspect I've been gathering my essence this entire time, slowly putting myself together piece by piece."

Or I was, the Trickster said. *You could just be the suit of clothes I'm wearing to anchor myself until I can reclaim my crown and rule over the world once more. But what are the chances of that?*

Very small given you are a dead bodiless spirit, I retorted. *An empty echo of a long forgotten age.*

At least, that was what I hoped.

Payne finished whispered something to Creature before he muttered something back. I wasn't paying attention and missed what was being said. It increased my suspicions they could hear the Trickster, though.

Creature sighed. "It would have been better if you had awakened and returned a few months earlier because the tunnels underneath

Everfrost poured out the Spidefolk. These kinsmen of the night who bear the torsos of sidhe and the bodies of arachnids."

"We all know the Spiderfolk," I said, annoyed with Creature's flourishes. "They don't seem worse than the Formor. I met a number of pleasant ones during the war, including a few shapechangers. They have always chafed under the King Below's power."

"Because the King Below was a vicious cruel bastard," Creature said, surprising me. "He was even worse when he was in his Trickster guise."

He's talking to me you know, the Trickster said. *You should kill him before he reveals my presence to the others.*

No, I said. *Now be silent.*

Strangely, the Trickster obeyed.

Creature blinked, as if acknowledging something unseen. "If it were the Spiderfolk alone then it would be nothing the Frostirons couldn't handle or any of the other clans which stayed in Everfrost. However, the Spiderfolk were driven by a darker force. They fought as slaves, sapped of their own will and terrified of what was behind them in a way not even the Dark Lords could muster. They wielded true names against us."

I was speechless. Name magic was the most difficult and powerful form of magic. It was to light and dark magic what mastering a sword was like to playing with sticks. To master one true name was a feat worthy of a master wizard and to master three was to make one a rival for the Great Wizards. It was supposedly due to being given the true names for earth and fire by the Lawgiver that Valance had been able to bring about the Fire Judgment.

They were not things to use casually.

"How?" I asked.

"Yes, how?" Serah repeated, sounding a little *too* interested.

"T'Clau, the Namer of Names," Creature said, saying the word like a curse. "An ancient power from the Pre-Age. She is said to be able to view every being in the universe's true name in her cauldron.

This gives her power over even the gods. She has dwelt in the caverns below Everfrost, between this world and the World Below, since the death of Gods Between. Now, she has turned against us."

I had heard of T'Clau, but knew very little of her. She was mentioned in Tharadon's notes as a being the Great Wizard had consulted in order to learn the true names of iron and lightning. He did not speak much of the meeting, only that it had involved a "terrible price" and cost him his apprentice Kalinda.

I was an accomplished wizard even before my transformation into a Death Knight but only knew the shape of those names with both Tharadon's and Co'Fannon's knowledge.

"You are not doing much to persuade us of helping your cause," Serah said, tightening her grip around her staff. "Indeed, the fact this T'Clau wields such power gives us more incentive to seek her directly."

"Is she hurting your people?" Regina asked, leaning in.

Serah shot Regina a nasty look.

"Abuse?" Payne said, lowering her scarf to reveal hideous burns. "You might call it such. You might also call it tortures. I was given the choice between having fire venom poured down my throat or to cut the throat of cubs. The Formor will perform any deed if it means victory but the lives of the young are sacred."

"A familiar mantra, eh, Lord Jacob?" Creature said, showing he knew me better than I was comfortable with.

"The commands for tortures, executions, and worse come daily. We cannot resist because the true names apply to any and all Formor in hearing distance. While no Formor would harm a child—" Curse paused, as if catching himself. "While no true Formor would harm a child, there are those willing to violate the Unforgivable. The Spiderfolk also lack our reserve. They follow T'Clau's every command, I suspect because their own children suffer if they do not obey." Curse sounded offended.

I found it hypocritical given the amount of suffering the Formor had inflicted. Then again, if I disregarded every person who complained about their side suffering despite the suffering they caused, I would live in an empty world indeed. I would also not be able to listen to myself.

"We will help," Regina said, clenching a fist in front of her chest. "I swear it."

"Oh for the Lawgiver's sake." Serah felt her face with her free hand. "Are you going to do this often?"

"Do what?" Regina asked, feigning innocence. I'd known her long enough to know when she was lying.

"Really?" Serah called her on it. "You need me to explain why this is a terrible idea?"

"It's not a terrible idea," Regina said, taking a bite out of her rabbit. "If we leave T'Clau alone then who knows what nations she'll attack. If she truly knows an endless number of true names then the world is at her mercy." Regina spit out of a piece of fat and put it away, showing decidedly unladylike manners. A fact I'd gotten used to over our three weeks of travel together. "T'Clau may start with the Formor and Spiderfolk but anger has a way of expanding. I know that more than anyone. Besides, anyone who would harm children of any race has clearly left the Path."

I wasn't so sure. I had leapt head first into Regina's quest for revenge on the Nine Heroes and was now involved in a war against the entire civilized world. While I didn't regret doing so, since it had led to developing fast friendships with two women I was honored to associate with, I couldn't help but believe I'd acted rashly.

Even stupidly.

Looking at Payne's wounds, marring her once-legendary beauty amongst both races, I was unmoved. She was an assassin who had done terrible things to countless people in the name of an evil god.

But she'd been willing to suffer for children. Children who were in danger.

Fuck.

"Alright," I said, taking a deep breath. "I'm already regretting this but I will help you against T'Clau."

"Jacob..." Serah said.

"Please," I said, looking again at my hands. They were the hands of a ghost pretending to be a man. "I ask you not to try and talk me out of this."

"I would never abandon Regina," Serah said. "Nor would I ever abandon you."

I was touched by her loyalty. I had fought with some Shadowguard for almost a decade and received less. Even stranger, I knew I would follow her into the World Below just as I had done with Regina and would continue to do so.

"I feel the same."

"Now that we've got such matters out of the way," Creature said, drawing attention back to him. "I promise to assist you in any way to navigate Everfrost and its many dangers. You can take any of the King Below's treasures there."

"No," I said, deciding how I was going to play this.

"No?" Creature said, sighing. It was clear he'd expected this but had been hoping for better.

"You will swear your eternal loyalty to me as well as the loyalty of the Frostiron clans for defeating T'Clau. I will be your king, autocrat, and god."

"That's outrageous," Payne growled, putting back up her scarf. "You are a spirit not a god."

"Jacob, this seems excessive," Regina said, not understanding why we needed to take such a drastic action.

I still planned to kill the Nine Usurpers on an individual level, but it seemed increasingly clear we would need a keystone to build our positions up to handle the aftermath. I wasn't going to make the same mistake I'd made during the Fourth War by focusing entirely on winning rather than what would come next.

The Formor were powerful weapons and I would have been a fool to not make use of them or their desperate situation. I also didn't want them stabbing me in the back by making use of exact words in our deal. If I was their ruler, they would be forced to act in my best interests unless they intended to challenge me for leadership. I was confident I could kill any Formor foolish enough to try.

"We do not need your aid that much," Curse said, staring daggers.

"I think you do," I said, staring right back.

Curse looked away first.

Creature surprised me by laughing and clapping his hands. "I approve, Lord Jacob. You have sensed our weakness and decided to capitalize on it. You realize, though, setting yourself up as our king comes with the responsibilities thereof. You will tying yourself to the destiny of the Frostiron clan and once such oaths are sworn, they are not easily set aside?"

"Father, you can't be serious," Payne whispered, stunned. "He is—"

"What? Not a Dark Lord? We *know* what he is," Creature said, his accent almost a hiss. "It would be foolhardy to not let events play out as they are destined. Your terms are agreed to, Lord Jacob. I speak for the Frostirons and several other lesser clans. Rid us of T'Clau and their allegiance will be to you until you are no more."

Payne turned around, keeping her arms crossed. Curse fumed.

"I am going to deal with T'Clau, free your people, and then ascend to the Tower of Everfrost. I am going to claim the Crown of the Weeping Gods and the King Below's other objects of power. I will regain my humanity and bring low the Nine Usurpers as well as anyone else who strikes my fancy." I felt strength in my purpose and a rising sense of pride. "I am not going to start a war with the rest of the world and anyone who is under my command will follow my rules about proper conduct without question. Those who obey will receive my protection, guidance, and judgment. Those who refuse will be driven from Everfrost or wiped clean from this world. I am the harbinger of the new way. Is that understood?"

My words seemed to come from a dark place inside me, burning with passion I'd long thought extinguished. It was an amazing feeling, having something to live for again. Regina had pointed the way but my destiny was only now taking shape before my eyes. A chance to build something new and grandiose. I would not be the slave of the past or the Trickster's manipulations. Instead, I would build on the foundations to make something new.

Something good.

"And you two?" Creature said, glancing over at my companions. "What is your take on your Dark Lord's vision?"

"I do not approve of everything he says," Regina said, frowning. "Indeed, I disagree with some of it quite strongly."

That hurt.

"I owe him my trust, though, and will be there by his side," Regina said, looking at him. "Someone has to protect him from his bad decisions, after all? Why not the person he does the same for?"

I looked back at her and saw something in her eyes I hadn't recognized before. It was more than attraction, which I'd seen from the moment she'd first seen my conjured human form, but a desire for a deeper bond.

What surprised me was I desired one too and wondered what it would be like to press my lips against hers.

To make her my partner in all this.

Had I truly forgotten Jassa so quickly?

Worse, my feelings weren't limited to those two women.

I was starting to feel something for Serah as well.

This was not a complication I was prepared for.

"I am glad he has chosen to conscript your people," Serah said, distracting me from my thoughts. "I don't think you are trustworthy in the slightest and will betray us at the first sign of weakness. That is why, I don't intend to show any."

"You think highly of yourself," Curse said. "You are not the first witch in Everfrost. Nor even the thousandth."

"I am, however, the first Serah Brightwater and I will be the last."

"So we are in agreement?" I asked them, unsure how I should proceed now that I realized I was falling for them both.

Strange how the plans of Wraith Knights and gods can go astray due to simple meddling of the heart.

They both nodded, oblivious to my shameful thoughts.

I needed to become human now, more than ever, if for no reason than to rid myself of this unnatural spiritual greed.

"We should leave then," I said, rising from where I sat. "Sleep this close to Everfrost is foolhardy, even with the protection spells we've woven around the campsite. Creature found us easily enough so I wouldn't be surprised if T'Clau can. If she isn't aware of our presence, we need to strike quickly before she can use our true names against us."

"To the Gates of Light's End then," Creature said, gesturing to the pathway they'd come. "We were just returning to the city after months of searching fruitlessly for a champion. Finding you must be a blessing of the Trickster."

I could feel the Trickster grinning in the back of my head.

"Perhaps," I muttered, suddenly uncomfortable with all of the decisions I'd made to reach this point. I steeled myself, though. This was not the time to ask questions. This was the time to act. "Let us go to war."

CHAPTER 22

The Gates of Light's End was a gigantic outer wall of permanently frozen ice, magically enhanced to be harder than iron and kept from thawing. The Gates had a massive pair ice sculptures depicting both the Trickster and the Lawgiver on opposite sides of the open entrance. The Great Mother was noticeably absent despite the fact she held a place of importance every bit as noteworthy as those two.

The Trickster resembled nothing so much as a demonic-looking sidhe with a lute and clawed fingers, not too dissimilar from the seeming he'd visited me with on the Storm Giant Mountains. He looked happy, despite his impish grin, and not at all like the godlike figure who ruled over the Northern Wastelands from the Black Throne.

The Lawgiver, by contrast, seemed even more sinister than the Trickster. Dressed in the holy vestments of the Grand Cleric, his long spidery hands were folded across one another as his long-bearded face held cruel penetrating eyes. It was a depiction of Old Man Law as a pitiless judge and patriarch, the unchallenged ruler of the cosmos who did not share equal partnership with the Great Mother but dominated her as his subject.

I had never been fond of that depiction.

"Strange the Formor would give such a respectful place to the Lawgiver," Regina said, seemingly undisturbed by the depiction. Then again, she wasn't a former Temple Knight like myself and might miss the subtleties of such. It was also possible this heretical depiction was the more common one in her time. It had already been gaining ground in my time, desiring to reduce the importance of the Great Mother and the Lawgiver's children with her to mere servants or representations of the One God Above All.

A notion I found ludicrous.

"The Tower of Everfrost was constructed during the Pre-Age when the sidhe, Formor, Dryads, Giants, and Fir Bolg were the only races on this world. Then, the Lawgiver and Trickster were worshiped equally by all races. The sidhe venerated the Lawgiver as the Lord of Summer and the Trickster as the Lord of Winter," Curse said, looking up at the statues. "That was before the arrival of the Terralan and the Dark Days which followed."

The Stepstones of the Damned beyond the gates proved to be a somewhat pleasant set of shiny white circular cobblestones set in a pleasant incline plane. Surrounding the wide road leading up to the massive walls of Everfrost was a collection of tremendous bones, which reached a hundred feet in the air.

The gateway was a half-mile off but I could see the gigantic skull of a hideous deformed giant Formor. It was the size of several buildings piled on top of one another. This was the Mouth of Bahlor, the mythical God-King of the Formor who had been their general during the First War. The Formor, to honor their patriarch, had made his bones into a pathway for Everfrost's visitors.

Beyond the ribs were vast farmlands of Mandragora, Bloodvine, Razor-root, and other disgusting but nutritious staples of a Formor's diet. The space between the two sets of walls played tricks on the eyes as if it occupied more space than was actually present. In my mind, it seemed like the fields were far vaster and enough to feed several large cities.

Yet, all of these fields were unoccupied.

It was disturbing to say the least.

"This place is curiously unattended," Regina said, looking around. "If you're walking us into a trap—"

"Then you'd die," Creature said, interrupting. "Not even you can defeat the entirety of the Frostiron clan."

"I wouldn't try," I said, looking down. "I'd kill you and declare myself ruler."

"Huh." Creature blinked. "That would probably work."

"You rule by the strongest?" Regina asked, disturbed. "That is a poor policy."

"Yes, because humans are so much better," Payne muttered. "You may coax it in terms like honor or divine heritage but it is the sword which determines who is the ruler in your lands."

"I did not say we were different, merely that it was poor," Regina said. "A good ruler needs principles and strength."

"The Formor do not have time for principles, I fear," Creature said, sighing. "What Curse calls the Dark Days were the heyday of the Formor. With the Terralan destroyed, we were ready to pour out onto all moongate-linked worlds with the terror-machines and magic of the World Below at our backs. We never managed to get past this one as the sidhe sacrificed almost the entirety of their species to prevent such. Nine in ten sidhe were killed but it broke the back of our invasion."

Creature spoke as if the subject was personally painful. Then again, given Creature's age, it was possible he was old enough to remember it.

"Your race was decimated?" Serah asked Curse.

"Decimated would be one in ten," Curse corrected.

"What do you call nine-in-ten?" Regina asked.

"Genocide," Curse said.

"Where are the farmers then?" I asked, bringing back the subject to its root.

"Trapped inside," Creature said. "The Spiderfolk under T'Clau keep them for her daily executions and tortures. They cannot farm, ranch, or feed their crops."

"That will kill them all," I said.

"I believe that's the idea," Creature said, frowning. "T'Clau is too powerful, though, for she knows the names of all the Formor. I am only protected by the fact I exchanged my name with another and my children because they are…unusual. Even then, T'Clau could control us both if she cared enough about our movements."

"I see." I wondered if she would be able to control me. "What is the history of the Formor?"

Creature looked back, as if my request was offensive. "That's a big request, milord."

"Depends on how you tell it. We have a long walk to those big mammoth tusk gates, though."

"True," Creature said. Silent for a moment, he then said, "Alright. If you must know, it is one long series of bloodbaths and misery. There, done." He gave me a sideways glance. "I could add some annotations in the middle but that about sums it up."

Curse chuckled. Payne looked annoyed.

Serah rolled her eyes while Regina just nodded.

"Perhaps *a bit* more detail," I said.

"As you wish." Creature looked straight at the giant skull of Bahlor. "Legend tells the Formor were created when the Lawgiver and the King Below waged their first war together. Having created the sidhe together, their children split between them with equal amounts on both

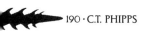

sides. When the King Below was cast down, all of his followers were cursed with hideous features akin to fish and sagging skin. They and their descendants would be accursed before the eyes of the Lawgiver forever. The Trickster appointed Bahlor to rule us along with his other Ice Demon brothers, each of them assuming Formor skins despite their ability to become mammoth monsters of legend. This was before the seven Unseelie High Lords were turned into the Dark Lords and subjugated the Ice Demons with spells. After that, our history becomes nothing but a long series of wars underneath them all."

I wondered what it was like to be cursed before you were born. "What do you think of that story?"

It didn't fit with the depiction the Trickster painted of his relationship with his brother. While I wasn't stupid enough to take anything he said at face value, I was inclined to believe the Trickster loved the Lawgiver in his own way. I was disturbed by that belief since it implied everything the Grand Temple had taught me about their relationship was a lie. If that were the case, how many other errors had the Lawgiver allowed to creep into his Codex? Were they errors at all or just lies?

"I think it makes the Lawgiver a colossal asshole for cursing his children's descendants like that," Creature said, cackling. "Of course, this is just the story the sidhe tell. I, for one, find humans and the sidhe to be disgusting looking creatures with your tiny little eyes and disgustingly warm skin. It's not much of a curse since we're so lovely because of it."

I smiled at his claim. "Do the Formor tell a different story?"

"Oh, we have many versions of our origins. They vary from clan to clan," Creature said, turning around and using his staff to walk. "We were a once-proud-empire from another world brought low by the sidhe. The Terralan engineered us as slaves from other races. We were born from the blood spilled by the King Below when he killed the Gods Between. I'm inclined to believe we're a people born like any other, from the muck and the mire, who came to worship the gods on our own."

"Do you think you could ever have peace with the other races?" Regina asked, showing a surprising amount interest in the Formor.

Creature pondered that. "I suspect it'd be easier to do the latter if they weren't constantly trying to murder us."

"You've allied with the King Below in many wars against the Lightborn races," I said. "The Formor are usually the aggressors, seizing vast amounts of land in Winterholme and other coastal regions."

Payne snorted. "It's amazing how persuasive an argument sounds when it begins with: *do you want to live someplace other than a frozen wasteland?*"

"And that justifies all the murder and killing?" Serah surprised me by asking. I had thought it would be Regina who would ask such. "Many of my ancestors have died fighting in the Great Shadow Wars. Peasants who perished unloved and forgotten in the muddy killing fields created by the armies of a mad god."

Creature just looked at her, as if daring her to say that wasn't what every other race did for land, religion, or both.

"I believe he has made his point." I was also intrigued by Creature's story. "Do the Formor really worship the King Below, despite the fact he's the God of Evil?" I had difficulty understanding that concept. If I was to deal with the Formor fairly, I had to know what motivated them.

"Evil is a relative term," Creature said. "What one race calls evil, is usually strength or necessary ruthlessness when it's being done to their enemies."

"There is…wisdom in that," I said, frowning.

It was strange trying to think of the Formor as anything other than monsters to be exterminated. I found it even stranger to think of them as people with their own thoughts, feelings, and desires. I still believed the King Below to be a figure of absolute evil but I couldn't help but wonder if the Formor were no better or worse than the men of the Southern Continent. If they'd only been misled by the King Below, then perhaps it might be possible to reconcile the Shadow Races with the Lightborn just as Curse and his ancestors believed.

Hahahahaaha. The Trickster snorted. *Oh, my, I knew there was a reason I liked you.*

"The King Below was powerful, ruthless, and charismatic," Creature said, shrugging. It was as if my question was asking whether the sun was bright rather than if they venerated a monster vilified across the three continents. "What more do you want from a god?"

"Justice?" Regina suggested.

Curse said, "A god is just by its nature of being a god. Only men can be unjust."

"Yet, we are made in the gods' image," Regina argued.

"Only kings and queens are," Curse replied. "After all, they rule with impunity. We are but the dust in their path."

"I don't believe that," Regina said. "A King and a Queen are mortal. They can die like anyone else. They can make mistakes or be wicked. The only difference is the magnitude of their action's consequences."

"Tell them that," Serah said.

"Will the Formor accept me as their King?" I asked, hoping Creature's insights would help me consolidate my position. He seemed reasonably alright with the idea of my takeover and it wasn't like his position could get worse. "You have, but I'd like to know the general people's mood."

Creature looked at me appraisingly. "You're strong enough to be king, I expect. My people are in bad shape and you would hardly be the first Dark Lord to rule over us during our master's recovery. However, whether you possess the most important quality to be a Formor monarch remains to be seen."

"And what quality is that?" I asked, pondering whether I could stomach ruling over the Formor long enough to use them, let alone direct them to follow the Path.

Creature lifted up his gnarled cane and poked my leg with it. "Whether it's more dangerous to defy you than serve."

Something about that struck me as funny. "I'm starting to like you, Creature."

You'll need absolute strength to rule the Formor and the other Shadow races, the Trickster said. *Only I was able to unite them and that was because my power was absolute.*

Says the man who was defeated five separate times by mortals, I pointed out.

Oh, I wouldn't say that, the Trickster said. *Victory is very much in the eye of the beholder. I convinced the Terralan God Kings to undermine each other with intrigues until they were all paranoid of their own shadows with the power to destroy the world. It was the reason my brother chose to destroy them. I didn't lose the Third Great Shadow War either. After a hundred years of ruling over all of the Southern Kingdoms, I realized no great heroes were going to rise to defeat me so I abandoned my empire.*

I refuse to believe that, I mentally growled.

It's no fun if there's no challenge. The Trickster laughed. *Tell me, would you be seeking the power you're looking for here if not for the promise of a good war after?*

I clenched my fists. *I will not rise to your bait.*

For now.

"Are the Formor in such bad shape they need a Dark Lord?" Regina asked Creature.

"We are as the ice deserts have made us," Creature said, sighing. "Violent, decadent, and possessed only of our pride. I have seen the King Below retreat to the World Below five times. Each time, it signals a new period of murder and bloodshed as the clans fight to avenge past wrongs or have enough food to last the winter when there is not enough for everyone. Formor clan kills Formor clan only to band together when the Shadowmen, Spiderfolk, or Trow come calling. The Formor are a polygamous race because it is better to love everyone you love and bind them all in the compact of marriage than trust a single union against the horrors which exist out here."

"I'm sorry." Regina said, surprising me with her compassion.

Creature shrugged as he walked. "Your pity is welcome but I would prefer your friend's power. Rulership by a tyrant is not a good solution to our woes, but it is *a* solution. Until you make the snow bloom and the winters less freezing, I'll settle for killing T'Clau. We may be exchanging one warlord for another but that is our history in short. Besides, I don't think you want to kill us quite as much."

"No, I don't," I pointed out. "I don't know what I'm here for."

"You came here for power and weapons to kill your enemies." Creature sounded understanding. "It is as your race says: War makes Formor out of us all. My race was afflicted by the War-Sickness long ago. So were you. We both can't stop so we might as well fight together."

"Have you tried?" Regina asked. "Stopping I mean."

"No." Payne, Creature, and Curse answered simultaneously.

"I see," Regina said.

"I fear you do not," Curse said, looking down at the step stones. "The shiny white stones beneath our feet? They are skulls of sidhe from the First War, filled with masonry mix and enchanted to never erode. This ancient road of magical angles and length is composed of the bones of my people."

Regina looked down, staring in horror.

So did I.

Serah pointedly stared forward.

We were all silent thereafter until we reached the Mouth of Bahlor.

CHAPTER 23

The Mouth of Bahlor had one of the most impressive doors I'd ever had the privilege of seeing the craftwork for. It was composed of steel three-feet-thick carved with hundreds of Frost, creating a barrier around the entire city which would be reinforced by human sacrifices buried into the thousands of watch-towers which encircled Everfrost.

Serah's barrier around Accadia had been impressive work but this was many times more so, the result of a deity's power and necromancers working for millennium with unlimited resources. The doors were unguarded because, really, why would you need to guard them? No being on Three Worlds could enter through these doors without knowing the right spells to do so.

The artistry was rather impressive too with the door possessing hideous black demons slaughtering naked innocents, menacing looking snowflakes (I hadn't even known such was possible), and gorgeous demons of both sexes engaged in lewd acts. If one was going to be serving the powers of evil, I supposed it was best for Everfrost's artists to embrace such wholeheartedly. Of course, the Skull and the Sword was predominately displayed on the front of the door with an additional snake going through one eye and around the blade.

"I don't suppose you know the password?" I asked, looking down at Creature.

"This isn't a story, Lord Jacob," Creature said, sniffing the air. "The doors open when the masters of the city want them to and close when they don't. We had to go over the side of the walls."

I looked up the sixty-foot-walls. "I suppose I could summon a Nuckelavee."

"That would alert everyone to our presence," Creature said.

"We're not going in stealthily, we're going to kill everyone," Serah pointed out.

"You can do both," Payne said, frowning.

An argument broke out before Regina examined the door and said, "Can't you just command the door to open since you're a Dark Lord?"

Everyone stopped at once and looked at me. It was rather funny.

"Worth a try," I said, drawing Chill's Fury. "Also, I'm not a Dark Lord. I'm *the* Dark Lord."

I swear I could feel Serah rolling her eyes behind my back.

I held the blade forth and said, "The Lord of Despair commands the doors to open, show the way to Everfrost, and bar us no more."

"You could just have said open," Curse muttered.

I was starting to hate my new companions.

We got an answer to whether or not Regina's plan worked when there was an immense grinding of gears. The Mouth of Bahlor's gate opened and I felt an immense wave of evil energy pass out from within. It was crippling cold, filled with hate, rage, and venom. Regina clutched tight to her sword, Serah turned her head, while the Shadowkind seemed to enjoy it.

For me, it was like a welcome home.

I felt stronger than I'd ever felt before in my life.

I also felt the Trickster diminish within me, as if he was sugar dissolving in a glass of water.

I didn't like the implications of that.

But I walked forward.

Beyond the wall was the city of Everfrost and the Tower lying in a valley a hundred-feet below the Gate's entrance. The Tower was the heart of the city and something which was difficult to describe being beautiful, terrible, and horrible at once. It rose from a deep crack in the ground like a fingertip reaching forward from the top of Wraith Knight's gauntlet.

Looking at the Tower was difficult because it was like the road in that it did not occupy a static amount of space. Instead, it seemed to change every time you looked at it. This was not because the tower was changing but because human eyes, even Wraith Knight ones, were not meant to perceive the totality of its existence. It existed in this world, the World Below, and probably other realms not known to man.

If I concentrated hard, I could see it existed in multiple times as well, but processing how that worked was difficult. There were thousands of fang-like teeth jutting out of the sides, demon statues, and spectacular stained-glass windows which seemed to catch the sunlight in spectacular ways.

To one side of the tower was a giant dragon's skull whose mouth poured forth a waterfall drawn from the River of Souls. I could sense the World Below beneath our feet as the crack the tower rose from was more than a simple hole but a gateway between universes. Even so, that was less dark energy than from the tower itself.

Within, The Crown of Weeping Gods waited to be claimed.

The rest of the city was impressive in its own way, created by combining technologies known only in the World Below or lost to the rest of the world with the almost tribal primitivism of the Formor. The houses, mostly, looked like the ones in Accadia only warped into circus attraction mirror proportions

Strange cables crackling with lightning were spread throughout the districts, often connecting to glowing balls. There was an observatory, an Aetherium, and several places where the laws of reality seemed suspended like free-floating islands hovering over other parts of the city or places where rubble was floating in the air. In the heart of the residential district, if you could call it that since Everfrost seemed to move in ways similar to the tower, there was an acre-sized orrery depicting the movements of the solar system's celestial bodies. It seemed to combine the merits of a sculpture with complete indifference to the people who lived nearby it.

A large industrial district existed in one part of the city, similar to some of the factories I'd set up with Tharadon's research was present only a hundred times larger. Gigantic smoke-stacks, furnaces, and weird piping to rival what I'd seen in Lakeland were present. All of the great machines were shut down, though, including a monstrous armored golem which looked a hundred feet tall.

"This is a weird fucking city," Serah said, surveying it with me.

"You speak the truth," I said, staring down. "I see no people despite the size of it."

"There's a curfew," Curse explained, looking down on the city with disdain. "The Spiderfolk's troops number in the thousands. If you thought this would be easy, Lord Jacob, then you are a fool. I do not see what one man can do against an army."

"Then you are the fool for it is *two women* and one Wraith Knight." Serah sniffed the air.

Regina cleared her throat in her fist. "*Do* you have a plan, Jacob?"

"Yes."

"Oh good!"

It was just rather…dark for my tastes.

Oooo, I like dark, the Trickster said. *But you probably guessed that.*

I was about to explain my plan when I felt the prickling sensation of power in the air, great power which was undisciplined and uncontrolled. A properly-trained wizard, created whether by will or by birth, felt like a bonfire in the night. These were more like torches, erratic and strange energies held by people who

The Spiderfolk climbed up the side of the cliff-face we were located on, hollowed up and riddled with passageways as it was. They moved down the walls above us as well. A third group started up the stone road which lead down from the gateway to the city below.

There were dozens of them, probably a hundred or so, each wielding the power of True Name magic. I found myself impressed as a few dozen wizards with far lesser magic was capable of turning the course of major battles. They were wielding halberds, spears, nets, and crossbows.

As mentioned, Spiderfolk had a resemblance to sidhe. While I found the idea of the Formor being cursed elves to be ridiculous, the Spiderfolk were almost too-plausibly so. They were spectacularly beautiful in some ways with soft brown skin and shining low black hair which trailed down to their waists, both men and women. Some of them wore armor which looked to be steel woven like spider silk but most were bare-chested. Without being vulgar, they were akin to centaurs or merrow in the fact both men and women possessed visible human sex organs before the animal parts of their bodies began. The Spiderfolk were capable of breeding with the races of humanity and often did so, creating hybrids who had the beauty of elfblooded but inhuman agility as well as a facility for Twilight or Dark magic.

The animal portion of their bodies was arachnid but not all that similar to the spiders which might live in one's cellar. Indeed, aside from the fact they had eight legs, they weren't spider-like at all. Instead, they were armored limbs and a thick exo-skeleton plated undercarriage which was immune to most sword thrusts. Given their upper torsos were their most vulnerable parts, I was surprised to see so many were unarmored.

Many of them wish to die, the Trickster said. *T'Clau's vengeance has been fierce, involving forcing many to do harm to their own loved ones or do things against the Spiderfolk's rather strict moral code. Well, as strict as anyone who thinks I'm the prettiest maid in the fair can be.*

As they approached, I said to Serah, "Draw on the power of this place. Name magic is incredibly strong but this place is the fountainhead of Dark and Twilight magic. It will not be pleasant. I need you to be our defender. I have a plan but it is going to take all of my power."

"I understand," Serah said, her voice somber. "Though, honestly, I'm anxious for a chance to demonstrate my full power."

"We should flee." Curse clenched his teeth. "Fighting this many Spiderfolk is suicide."

"I'm eager to see what Lord Jacob does," Creature said, placing several black iron rings on his fingers.

They were objects of power, every last one of them.

"Please lend me your strength in the next few minutes, Creature," I said, frowning. "This will be rather…big."

"We should try to talk to them," Regina said, once more showing why she was the best of us.

Not that such is particularly difficult, the Trickster pointed out. *Objectively, you're all evil bastards but her. You're just deluded about yourself.*

I object to the idea I'm deluded about being evil, I said. *I'm quite aware I am.*

I was going to fix that with the crown's power.

"They are slaves in mind as well as body," Payne said, answering Regina's statement. "Death is a mercy."

"Most slaves cry out for freedom, not death," Regina said, placing her hand on her sword. "They are victims like you."

"Is she always such an insufferable Sally Sweet Treats?" Curse asked.

"You have no idea," Serah said, holding her staff defensively.

The Spiderfolk were not charging but moving into position around us, which I hoped (but did not expect) might lead to a peaceful settlement. It was more likely, however, they were attempting to get a proper tactical position for attacking us. If they really were under the control of influence of their true names, there was nothing which could be done for them since nothing in the four forms of magic could match it.

In front of the group emerged a huge mutated Spiderfolk, standing twice as large as a normal member of his race with four arms rather than two, and a hideous face covered in bone-spikes. Its torso was covered in blood runes and each hand held a glowing enchanted curved blade forged by, well, me.

I recognized the weapons as one of the thousands I'd created for the favored servants of the King Below while under his control. The King Below had made ample use of my skills an artificer and those blades, in particular, drained a portion of the life-force taken from every mortal killed back into their wielder. While in small amounts it resulted in greatly increased strength, long-term use had something of an unpredictable effect.

As this Spiderfolk had learned.

"We do not wish to bring you harm," I said, suspecting I knew the answer.

"The Witch Who Lives Behind Your Eyes does not know you," the Mutant said, his speech slurred. "You will die. Slowly."

Well, that was informative.

The Spiderfolk began speaking the True Name of Fire almost simultaneously. It made the entire world glow as the air became hot around me, challenging the frozen nature of the land. The sky began a rainstorm of fire, dropping flaming death like hail stones. A black sphere of shadow shielded us, conjured by Serah

It was a testament to the sheer power at her command the barrier she summoned held against the first wave of the Spiderfolk's onslaught. Even so, I could see the protection spell begin to buckle as another wave fell.

They speak the name of fire like rainbow birds, echoing what has been forced into their minds while not understanding, the Trickster said with distaste. *I am offended as a magician as well as a god.*

Creature focused a massive amount of energy inside me while I gathered the near-infinite reservoir of power around me into Chill's Fury and slammed the blade onto the ground. A tidal wave of witchfire washed over the Spiderfolk, knocking many over the side of the cliff and killing others outright.

The feeling of channeling that much Dark magic was intoxicating. All of my human feelings, things like conscience and morality, vanished in the ensuing rush. The deaths of so many Spiderfolk gave me power to strike again and I unleashed a second wave onto the disorientated warriors, sending more spiraling away in the gale forces of the blizzard conjured from my blade.

I wanted to kill them all.

I *could* kill them.

That was when I took a fireball to the face. The pain of having my flesh from my body was matched by the fact the fire struck at my spirit simultaneously. My armor burned, my cloak, my hood, and my skin. I lost my eyes, hands, and more with much of my conjured form going up like paper. Muscle and tissue disappeared along with part of my bone. It was less like I was made of blood and meat than dry kindling.

Then I started to heal.

The bone regrew, flesh knitted itself from the shadows, and muscle re-wove into a coherent whole.

I felt it all.

Another Spiderfolk attempted to summon flame to fight me, only for me to reach out in rage and suck away his life-force. I greedily drank it before conjuring a forest of black shadowy tentacles from the ground which impaled more of the now-routed attackers. Even so, I was soon grabbed by the claw-like pincers of the Mutant. It had not only survived but seemed unharmed by all of the freezing death I'd unleashed.

Lifting me up by the neck, it pulled back its sword arms, only for Regina to wrap her legs around its chest and stab repeatedly into the side of its neck with Hopebringer. I noticed a dozen Spiderfolk to the side of the group and realized we'd been flanked, only for Curse, Payne, and Regina to have fought them off. The Mutant gurgled as Regina stabbed repeatedly, allowing me to finish healing by draining away its last bit of life-force. My clothes and armor repaired themselves as if they were part of my body.

The Mutant dropped me, causing me to roll against the snowy cobblestones of the ground. I ended up not a foot away from Creature who looked down at me with a skeptical look. "That was just the gate guards, Lord Jacob. If this is your plan, I think your reputation as a strategic genius is overstated. More will be coming soon."

I rose up from the ground and wiped away the snow on my clothes. "That won't be a problem."

"Oh?"

I sheathed Chill's Fury and tapped once more into the terrible energies around us. I had time now to do the spells properly. Every single one of the dead Spiderfolk around us began to rise from the dead. All of their eyes glowed with witchfire. Within a minute, the entirety of the force which had been attacking us but moments ago arose.

Nothing would stop me from getting the Crown of Weeping Gods. *Nothing.*

Turning to them, I gestured. "Go ahead of us and create more troops to animate. Serah, begin summoning your shadow monsters. We need an army and for every one of theirs which falls, ours shall grow stronger. I expect you to help, Creature."

Reinforcements for the Spiderfolk began to arrive, only to be assaulted by the new army of Deathless.

"Huh," Creature said, blinking his over-large eyes. "I may have underestimated you. I won't do that again."

CHAPTER 24

The next five hours were carnage as the Spiderfolk proved to be competent as well as deadly. The ever-growing army of Deathless under my command were not the shambling horrors of campfire stories, though. Deathless maintained all of the skills and intelligence they had in life, as well as the power to wield magic.

For all of the true name magic we faced in the street-to-street fighting, we gained sorcerers for every one of our minions we lost. Our forces were not limited to the ones I created with necromancy, either. Serah's shadow creatures were vicious, unpredictable, and twice as powerful as in Accadia but she maintained perfect control over them.

What surprised me, though, was Regina's skill in compelling Formor to join in the fight to retake their homeland. Not only did she speak the Formor language like a native, but she managed to win over more allies than Creature, who didn't even try to lead the Frostirons to rebellion. The Formor had been disarmed by the occupation and subjected to terrifying torture to cow them into submission but once word started to spread the Spiderfolk were doomed. Two Formor died for every Spiderfolk we killed, even with the aid we were providing them, but I didn't hesitate to raise them as Deathless either.

It was close to noon by the time the Spiderfolk retreated to the Tower of Everfrost. Most of the Deathless I'd created were destroyed and hundreds of Formor lay dead or dying. We'd inflicted devastating losses upon our enemies. Indeed, they were almost *too devastating* since ten percent of an army being killed was a ridiculous amount of casualties in most battles.

We'd killed almost half of the Spiderfolk.

The fact they were fighting to the last was not a situation I wanted to deal with. Worse, barricading themselves in the Tower of Everfrost meant the place I needed to get to most was now the least accessible.

"This is too easy," Creature said, sitting in an uncomfortable looking wooden chair in the Stone and Anvil Tavern and Inn. A large mug of pitch-black swamp water masquerading as ale was in his hands. I had chosen to pass on the tavern's specialty.

"What do you mean?" I asked, pondering our situation.

We had set up an informal command center in the surprisingly human-seeing establishment. Aside from the excessive amount of taxidermy animals on display, blood stains on the floor, and weapons lining the wall for easy access, it could have been any drinking hole in the Southern Kingdoms. Our group rested around a wooden table I'd assembled numerous maps and figurines on while a dozen armored Formor Captains were spread throughout the room.

I could feel the hundreds of Deathless I'd created patrolling the territory we'd successfully taken as the rest of the Formor started seizing weapons from the dead or now abandoned armories. Disturbingly, it didn't weaken me to be connected to so many abominations against the Lawgiver. In fact, I felt stronger for having so many. The act of dominating another being seemed to strength the enchantment which kept my spirit bound to this world.

Something to think about.

"If it were merely a matter of fighting against an army then we wouldn't need you," Creature said, sticking his tiny feet on the table. "A bunch of Spiderfolk calling down fireballs, lightning, and poison gas isn't something to fear. An army of mages is a challenge, not a chore."

"He's right," Curse said, pacing about the room. "T'Clau should have sent her people to destroy us by now. She has access to our true names, *everyone's* true names, which means there's nothing stopping her from killing us outright."

"Then why hasn't she?" Serah said, poking at a plate of still-writing worms with a fork. It was, apparently, a local delicacy. "I think you overestimate her powers."

Curse doesn't, the Trickster said. *She could kill any one of this group at will but we're protected by her ignorance. T'Clau is not omniscience and needs to know what name to look for in her Cauldron. Your companions are strangers in this land and we are merged. If it was either you or me, T'Clau could wipe us away with a gesture, but I am wearing your flesh so she doesn't know to look for the name of a being who is both Jacob Riverson as well as the Trickster. It's how we were able to kill the Gods Between despite them having power over us.*

We? I asked, wondering who'd helped him.

A story for another time, the Trickster said. *T'Clau has not yet begun to stretch her power against you and when she does, you will be unable to defend these people. Creature, Curse, and Payne will try to kill you if she wills it. They are known to her.*

Then why hasn't she done it yet? I asked. *Serah raises a good point. What you're describing is not the actions of a sane military commander.*

Who said she was sane? I imagine she hates the Spiderfolk as much as the Formor. This is work of a sadistic torturer who takes pleasure in the suffering of her slaves as well as enemies. The Trickster chuckled. *Like recognizes like.*

"Jacob?" Regina said, finishing her third swamp ale and second plate of bore grubs. "Are you alright?" She then belched into her fist. "Excuse me."

Serah stared at her, dropping her fork and pushing the plate away.

"We may be in trouble," I said, looking at them. "It will not be long until this ceases to amuse T'Clau and we're forced to endure the full brunt of her power. I don't think we will be able to defeat her and even if we do, it will be with many Formor casualties."

"Our people are used to such things," Paye said, sitting in a corner of the bar where she was nearly invisible due to the angle of the light. "One does not win a war without a willing to make sacrifices, thousands if necessary."

"That doesn't mean one should not avoid as many as possible," Regina said. "We should take the fight directly to this demoness."

"Nature Lord," Serah clarified. "If it was a demoness, I might be able to control it."

Nature Lords were unique beings worshiped by the Fir Bolg and primitive human tribals in heathen lands. In olden times, they were worshiped the same way the Gods Above and Below are now. Some of the heretical branches of the Grand Temple even went so far as to declare them lesser gods worthy of veneration the way the Lawgiver's Messengers were.

The Nature Lords, supposedly, had ties to the Gods Between, but were mysterious as well as private entities. The Shadowguard had records of encountering them but precious little raw data. The advice for fighting them boiled down to *don't*.

Curse went behind the bar and pulled out a bottle of imported black Ashlands wine along with a dainty elvish crystal glass I was surprised the Formor had on hand. Filling his glass, he said, "For once, I agree with Sally Sweet Treat."

"Please stop calling me that," Regina said.

"We need to go to T'Clau's lair and slay here directly," Curse

threw his empty glass over his shoulder, letting it shatter against the ground. "We can cut the heart out from this invasion and seize the Cauldron for ourselves."

"T'Clau knows us," Creature said, shaking his head. "Other heroes of the Formor have gone down there and emerged as broken shells of their former selves. Grim had no skin but still lived, Gentle had mouths where her eyes should be, and Fang was forced to butcher then eat his own children. We cannot participate in any attack against her."

Curse slammed his fist against the table before getting up from the table.

"I have it on good authority T'Clau does not know my, Regina, or Serah's true names." I was taking an awful risk trusting the Trickster. If he had arranged all of this so we'd go down there to die horribly, well, then he'd just be acting as he was spoken of in the Codex.

"Good authority?" Curse asked, turning around.

"Authority I trust," Creature said, keeping his gaze focused on me. "Let nothing more be said."

Curse took a long sip of wine.

"You want us to kill a goddess?" Serah said. "I know some things about T'Clau from my studies but that is a tall order, even for us."

"The High Lords of the Old Sidhe killed Ice Demons and the Dark Lords have killed the King Above's Archmessengers, I cannot think this is fundamentally different," I said, not at all confident in our chances.

Hopebringer can kill gods, the Trickster said. *I should know. Besides, she's not truly immortal like my kind.*

Says the dead god, I pointed out.

Who is talking to you, yes, the Trickster said. *Though, I admit, the Nine Heroes having my true name helped.*

What? I asked.

I did mention a cauldron, the Trickster said.

Oh, how delightful. T'Clau played some role in the King Below's demise. Why did I suddenly feel like I was playing right into a complicated revenge scheme?

Because you're only half a fool, the Trickster said.

"We had best move quickly," I said, looking down. "If this Cauldron doesn't provide divination powers as well as true names, it may give us some time but it won't give us much."

I was more concerned about Regina and Serah than myself. After all, if it was as the Trickster said, I had nothing to fear from her.

Oh, I didn't say that. Knowing just half your true name will allow her to rend you to nothingness. The Trickster made a tsk-tsk noise. *Trust no one, especially me.*

That was redundant advice.

But useful.

"Can you give us directions to her cavern, Creature?" I asked, wondering what I was going to do after I seized the Crown of Weeping Gods. Once we defeated T'Clau, there would be nothing to stop me from taking its power and becoming human again. I was suddenly aware of just how many frightening possibilities that opened up.

And how devastated I'd be if either of my companions perished.

I needed to talk with them about how I felt.

Even if it proved an embarrassing mistake.

"I can—"

That was when all of the Formor captains in the room began to melt. The screams which filled the room were beyond terrifying, like you'd expect if you could hear a man as his flesh slowly sloshed off his body but was able to feel every second of it.

We drew our weapons, but there was nothing we could do. The Captains continued to scream even after they lost their lungs, skeletons, and organs and were nothing more than puddles of gore on the ground which oozed from their empty sticky armor into a single coherent pool on the floor.

The oozing puddle rose and reshaped itself until it became a

hideous replica of a female Spiderfolk made of gore. The stench was terrible, combining every horrible fluid in the body with something else from another reality. I was dead yet the horror of it all made me sick to my stomach.

The entire process took an agonizing minute.

"Hello, Lord Jacob Riversun," the Bloody Horror spoke with a decidedly feminine voice. I had never seen magic like this before and hoped to never see it again.

Elementalism, the Trickster explained. *A lost art of sorcery between the four disciplines of my brother and I. This is a perversion of Water Magic.*

"T'Clau," I whispered, guessing her identity.

"That is one of my names." The Bloody Horror quivered like a glob of freshly cut sweetmeat. "It was not my name always but it is the one I wear now. Hateful, wretchedly, and with loathing."

Regina scowled and held out her spare sword, Hopebringer firmly tucked in its sheath. "You will pay for the atrocities you've done."

She spoke with such conviction, such strength of character, that it didn't strike me at all as the sort of thing only storybook characters would say. If anyone deserved to have legends written about her, it was Regina.

Brashness aside.

"One cannot work atrocities against monsters," the Bloody Horror said. "I have given much love, devotion, and joy to this world. They have given but ruin. If I have no more love to give then let my hate be shown unto those who deserve such pain. Let the hell they have brought to others be their final fate before I exterminate them all. All Shadowkind shall be purged from this world and it shall be better for it."

I grimaced. I had made similar claims in my life, even if I'd never taken steps to follow up on it. I could never harm Formor or Spiderfolk cubs. As such, I always let their families slink away from the battlefield even if it meant fighting them in the future. "That is not for you to decide."

"I have the power to enforce my will on the world. The only thing I cannot change by knowing the true name of is myself." The Bloody Horror's voice quivered . "I invite you to speak with me about the subject. Bring your companions, but not the filth you have chosen to roll around with."

"I feel insulted," Creature said.

Serah's eyes darted to the Formor wizard. "Shut up."

"You're...inviting us to our lair."

"Yes," the Bloody Horror said. "Come soon or I will order every Formor in Everfrost to kill themselves."

That was when Curse pulled out his bow and aimed it at his wife while Payne lifted her throwing daggers and aimed them at Curse. Creature, alone, seemed unaffected but his eyes became dangerous. Curse and Payne's eyes, by contrast, were utterly horrified but unable to do anything.

"We will," I said, raising my hands in surrender. "Please do not harm my companions."

"We barely know them," Serah said, pouring herself some of Curse's wine. "But I, too, would like you to do so."

Regina looked ready to charge the Bloody Horror.

"See you soon." The Bloody Horror collapsed into a pile of gore on the ground. Payne and Curse regained control over their bodies. They dropped their weapons and embraced, holding onto each other for dear life.

I envied that love.

Creature finished his mug and set it back on the table. "You realize, there's no way to defeat her now. She knows who you are."

"T'Clau needs to speak our true names," I said, calmly. "She can't do that if she's dead."

Creature blinked his cold dead eyes. "You never really fit in with us, Jacob, no matter what terrible things you did in your life. I would wish you happiness but we both know that is not how this story is going to end. There is no light in the dark."

"Then maybe someone should bring a set of matches," Regina said, looking down at him. "Despair is the final sin since it takes away a chance at a better tomorrow."

Creature, Curse, and Payne just looked at her as if she was deranged.

And she was.

But it was a madness we needed.

Serah got up. "Alright, let's go kill this thing. Then we're getting some food which doesn't move."

CHAPTER 25

The trip into the caverns beneath Everfrost was like moving down a pathway to the underworld, which I supposed it was. The ancient tunnels hollowed out by Formor miners and slaves were filled with disturbing carvings, glowing fungus, and pictogram art which told a story I did not understand.

There were also corpses.

Many corpses.

Creature hadn't exaggerated when he spoke of the damage this Namer of Names had inflicted. The tunnels were filled with hundreds of Formor with their juices sucked out of their bodies, left as nothing more than withered husks. There were other races too: antlered Fir Bolg, pale-skinned humans, Nockers, Trow, and those who had the mark of demon-blooded.

There were many Spiderfolk too. Strangely, these creatures

didn't assault us. Instead, when they saw our approach, they retreated down adjoining tunnels or fled. They showed none of the loyalty the ones above did and seemed glad at our approach. One of them even shouted a prayer of thanks to the King Below before throwing down his weapons and kneeling.

We walked past that one without a word.

"I get the impression this T'Clau woman is not very popular even with her own people," Regina muttered. She had a look of revulsion at our surroundings, which was appropriate even if all of the victims we'd encountered were former members of the King Below's armies.

"They are not her people," Serah said, looking surprisingly comfortable in the dimly lit tunnels. "The Spiderfolk are said to resemble T'Clau but were created by the King Below in mockery of her, not veneration. She is an older thing than the mortal races, dangerous and hostile to all forms of life."

"What do you know of her?" I said, lifting up Chill's Fury and conjuring witchfire around it to illuminate a particularly dark tunnel. "You mentioned you'd found things about her in your studies but, the interruption in the inn distracted me from asking."

Serah sighed. "I know little more than Creature. All I know is what he's told us. She is a former servant of the Gods Between. A Nature Lord who lives apart from the rest of her kind, hording over forgotten treasure."

"You've mentioned the Gods Between a few times but I confess, I've only heard of them from their brief mention in the Codex," Regina said. "Just another of the many victims of the King Below in the Pre-Age."

That was how I knew of them.

Serah smiled, pleased at the opportunity to educate. "The Gods Between are spoken of in more detail in several sidhe tablets I've perused. They're also mentioned in transcriptions from Pre-Terralan civilizations, before the majority of the modern human civilizations were brought through the moon gates after the First War. The Gods Between were kin to both the Gods Above and Below but dedicated to peace between both factions. They were linked to plants and animals the way the King Above is to light or the reverse for his brother."

Regina seemed surprised. "I've lived alongside the sidhe all my life and I've never heard that."

"You wouldn't have," Serah said, shrugging. "They are a legend forgotten by even the immortals. The Song of T'Clau is one of the few surviving fragments. I can't really repeat any of it and it doesn't make sense outside of elvish, but it speaks she knows the names of everything and everyone, giving her both knowledge as well as control over them."

"Well we know that's not true," I said.

"Oh?" Serah asked. "How so?"

"She wouldn't need a bunch of Spiderfolk to bully and abuse the Formor if she possessed that kind of power." I expected T'Clau was bluffing about forcing the entirety of the Formor to kill themselves. At least, I hoped she was.

"Perhaps," Serah said, sounding unconvinced. "It's also possible there's a whisper of truth in the din of lies. Either way, we should be cautious. I do not think this is a being causally slain, even by other monsters."

"I will face any horrors to help get Jacob back his humanity," Regina said, resolved.

"You honor me," I said. "Though I'd hope you'd avoid some of the things which can kill you instantly."

"You don't know her," Serah said, smiling. "She speaks nothing but the truth."

"I think I know you both pretty well now," I said, smiling. As bad as this situation was, I spent it in good company.

"Thank you," Serah said, looked down, embarrassed.

The three of us continued until we came to a series of winding tunnels which seemed to twist and turn in ways which weren't natural.

Entrances blurred into three different pathways, only to suddenly become one, while exits changed behind us.

There were times we walked through the darkness with nothing to illuminate our path but my witchfire blade and I could have sworn there was nothing around us whatsoever, that we were traversing through an endless void.

Still, we pressed on.

The three of us, eventually, reached a massive cavern which was illuminated by glowing fungus and witchfire pits which made the coliseum-sized chamber as bright as daytime. There were a few shadowy places but these were due to the heavy shade of stalactites and stalagmites which formed a stone forest above and below.

A clearing was to one side with a circular pit. Unlike the others, though, this wasn't filled with witchfire, but a green bubbling substance which poured out mystical energy like chimney poured smoke. The magic was neither light, dark, noon or twilight. Not even true name magic. It was something older and deeper, born from sorcery which had been woven into the fabric of Creation.

I'd never felt anything like it.

Behold the Cauldron of Names, the Trickster said, his voice bitter. *A chalice of that substance was my doom.*

I thought you said you abandoned your life as the King Below because it was boring, I thought, annoyed.

I lied, the Trickster said. *I do that, sometimes. I also tell the truth. Sometimes I misrepresent things. It's really whatever is most amusing. For example, your beloved Jassa is still alive.*

I rolled my eyes. "Be on your guard. I'm certain this is the beast's lair."

"Beast? *Beast?* You know nothing of the word, Jacob Riverson!" A shrill high-pitched, almost insane sounding, voice echoed through the caverns. It was the force from before, but far less rationale-sounding, for whatever value you could give to someone who chose to speak through the remains of the dead.

A hideous creature stepped through the stalactites, so disgusting it almost made me retch. Its top half might have once been beautiful with a voluptuous female form stretching down to her waist, bare-breasted, and long-haired. Her snow-white hair was streaked with dried blood, and her face was riddled with masses of scars as if she'd tried to claw it off. The monster's body showed poorly-healed cuts all over, forming crisscross patterns in a manner which reminded me of flagellants who despised everything about themselves.

The lower half of her body was to Spiderfolk as they were to people, a twisted mass of hideous chitin covered in abnormal growths and extra-legs which seemed designed for eviscerating those who came too close. Each of her lower limbs could probably slice an armored knight in half. The expression on her face was the worst part, though, as her eyes were red and face twisted in a mask of half-mad fury. She was elfblooded, like Regina, and the contrast of beauty to horror made the latter worse.

"You are T'Clau," I said, holding out my sword.

Regina readied Hopebringer while Serah held her staff defensively.

"I am she and not," T'Clau said, walking out from the shadows of the stone forest. "I was here when the Three Worlds were young and but a few spans older than your companions. I am both betrayer and betrayed, a thousand women offered unto the Cauldron of Names, each devoured and reborn."

Delightful. She was insane.

"We have come here to put an end to a great evil," Regina said, unafraid.

"I know all three of you," T'Clau said, looking between us. "I have seen the shadows of your adventures in my Cauldron and plucked your names from the aether. Do you know what a true name is? It is not the name your father and mother give you at birth but a perfect understanding of a thing. To know a true name means you must know their past, present, and future. I know each of you and wield power beyond imagination over your destinies."

"*No one* commands my destiny but me." Serah growled, taking a step forward. "Not god, not monster."

T'Clau let forth a peel of insane laughter. "Your destinies are interwoven with forces you can neither affect or deviate from. You are enslaved to your natures. The Nine Heroes have enslaved Regina with her hatred, you with your love of your companions, and Jacob with his desire for relevance. You could no more stop running to your doom than a tortoise might leave its shell."

"You seem familiar," Regina said, unexpectedly. "You also speak of the Nine Usurpers as if you know them."

"The Nine Heroes..." T'Clau spit after saying their name. "They came to me with the Golden Sorceress. They flattered me with gifts, promises, and tales of the King Below's injustices. They had the sword Hopebringer, blessed with the power of the Lawgiver and three-hundred years of murder, but they needed another weapon to make him mortal enough to kill."

"*Can* the gods be killed?" I asked.

"No," T'Clau said, as if the idea was ridiculous. "They can, however, be turned into mortals. Who, by nature, *can* be slain."

The idea was staggering. It also heralded a chance to rid myself of the Trickster forever. "How?"

"The Cauldron of Names," T'Clau said, her voice like a hiss. "It grants perfect knowledge of a person, concept, or thing's true name to they who offer a sacrifice unto it. A new T'Clau is born from each sacrifice, gaining the knowledge and power of the old one. It was the Cauldron of Names which compelled the Lawgiver and Trickster to murder the Gods Between."

We did not slay them for the Cauldron, the Trickster corrected. *We slew them because it was fun, or at least I did.*

"You gave them knowledge of the King Below's true name," I said, staring at her. "That is why they were able to kill him."

"No," T'Clau said, lifting two of her legs and shaking them with rage. "I did not. *She* did not. T'Clau tricked us and they betrayed me!"

"I am utterly confused," I said, staring. T'Clau was speaking as if she were two different people.

"*Now* I recognize you," Regina said, stepping forward and pointing with Hopebringer's broken blade. "Aegeta Silverhair."

The name seemed to send a shudder of revulsion through T'Clau as she took a step back into the shadows. "Aegeta is dead, betrayed, forsworn, and abandoned! Do not speak her name or you will suffer endlessly."

"You seem to be under the impression you haven't already threatened us with that," I said, unimpressed. "Who is she?"

Regina stared at the spider-demon and shook her head, as if she couldn't believe what she was seeing. "Aegeta Silverhair was one of the Nine Usurpers. She was an Eternal Isles moonsinger of the Peace-Weavers known for her gentle nature. She's the only one of their number who wasn't present at the final battle."

"Now I am even more confused," I said, wondering how a moonsinger became an epoch-old monster.

Serah, true to her nature, provided the answers. "That's what the sacrifice to the Cauldron does, isn't it? The only people who can pull true names from it are ones linked to it. It needs T'Clau the Namer."

Aegata emerged again from the shadows. "Yes. I am both she and the thousands of T'Claus before me. When the T'Clau before me refused to hear their entries, I was grabbed by my fellows and fed to its hunger."

I opened my mouth, appalled. "None of them were willing to sacrifice themselves?"

It was not the fact they would go to such an extreme measure, for it would be the height of hypocrisy on my end to condemn them, but the fact they chose to offer another in their place. War required great sacrifice to win but the moment you started making others sacrifice for you, it became the road to evil.

Isn't that the nature of war, my heir? The Trickster asked. *Making the other side sacrifice themselves until they give up?*

"I was the weakest," T'Clau said, staring up at the roof of her cavern. "I was a gifted singer and storyteller who helped raise their spirits through the darkest of days. I was a competent swordswoman, archer, and spellcaster but not a legend like the others. I was…their friend. Yet, none of them raised a voice in objection when the Golden Sorceress demanded I be sacrificed. I screamed to Morwen, who I had always admired, to Jon, who I had been lovers with, and to Fel Hellsword, who was my kinsman. All met my gaze with stony resolve."

"Monstrous," Regina said, showing sympathy a woman she'd vowed to destroy. Then again, if what T'Clau was saying was true, she had no part in the Nine Usurper's crimes. Albeit, she had committed far more heinous ones since as result of her madness. Could she be blamed for those? I wasn't sure.

"I am less sympathetic," Serah said, cool and calm. "If you had known your companions better, such a betrayal would have been obvious."

"T'Clau's eyes blazed. I thought she was ready to attack. "You know nothing, witch! Do you not think your companions would trade you for the power to command gods?"

"Would you?" Serah asked, turning to me. "I ask sarcastically."

"I have not so many loved ones left to do so," I said, not even thinking it. "I might offer myself up to defeat one such as the King Below, but never a loved one."

"Never," Regina said. "I would rather kill this monster, destroy the Cauldron, and end the cycle of offerings forever."

T'Clau curled her lip into a sneer. "With your true name, Jacob Riverson, you would be able to turn yourself back into a living man. With the true name of Jassamine the False, you would be able to summon her to you and bind her to be the image you have in your mind. She would love you every bit as much as you loved her. Regina

Whitetremor could have the names of my former companions, bringing them low in one terrible night of revenge. You cannot tell me you would not offer countless sacrifices to do so."

T'Clau's words gave me pause. It was one thing to condemn her when she was talking about giving up one of my companions, though the Nine Heroes were certainly quick enough to do such, but quite another to dismiss the idea of sacrificing others for true names in general.

There were countless horrible people in the world that would be easy to deliver to this place. We could win the war against the Nine Heroes, seven now, overnight. Who knew what would happen thereafter? With the true names of the world's leaders, I could bring a proper order to this planet and forge a lasting peace.

I saw nothing wrong with this until I looked over at Regina's face and saw one of abject horror and revulsion. Her look confused me until I realized she'd seen what sort of aftereffects came from enslaving the world under the wills of do-gooders. Had it truly been so long since I had cared about the individual in my desire to help the many? I also realized it would be very easy to start justifying using people like coinage, spending their lives whenever I needed.

I was ashamed.

Aww, just when things were about to get interesting, the Trickster said. *Tsk–tsk–tsk.*

I realized why T'Clau had invited us here. She could not help herself and hated the monsters she'd been raised to think of as monsters. I looked human, now, while my companions most definitely were. T'Clau hoped to have the company of people from the Southern Kingdoms. Perhaps even thought we might be able to free her from her curse and help her live a normal life. She might even be sympathetic to my condition.

But there was no redemption for her.

No forgiveness.

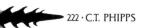

I wouldn't allow it. Not after what I'd seen.

"We are here to liberate the people of Everfrost. Nothing more," I said, taking a step forward. "I am uninterested in your Cauldron or your names. I only want you to leave these people in peace and return to the dark shadows from whence you came!"

It was a lie, but a believable lie, I hoped.

She had to pay for her crimes.

T'Clau reacted by letting forth a peel of hideous laughter. "You claim to have come here to help the *Formor*? The one group more wretched than I? The beings whose torment provide my sole diversion in this hideous state? You make good jests, sir!"

It was Regina who spoke up this time, her eyes blazing with rage. "They are a people deserving of respect and to live their lives without predators, the same as any other beings! You have abused and tormented them for the last time!"

"The Formor are a race of *vermin*," T'Clau snapped. "Every man, woman, and child in the Southern Kingdoms knows this. They have been a plague on this world since the moment the Trickster first raised them from the primordial soup of Creation. Whitetremor, I know your true name, which means I understand everything about you. I know they murdered your parents! How dare you speak to me as if you would not desire the name of their race to wipe them from existence!"

"I would not!" Regina snapped. "Even the lowliest being deserves a chance at redemption and I do not know what twisted road lead them here! The Trickster is dead and gone, which means the Formor can be made as other peoples! You punish them when you should be helping them!"

"That may be going a bit far, dear," Serah said, looking at her. "We're here because we need what they guard."

"Ah," T'Clau said, smiling a too-wide mouth full of sharp teeth. "The truth becomes apparent. You are not here for the muck people but the treasures they guard. Why did you not say so? I will open up the gates of Everfrost and leave you to plunder its wonders. They mean nothing to me. I only enjoy inflicting the pain I suffer daily on those who have inflicted it on others their entire race's history."

"I am inclined to accept her offer," Serah said, shrugging. "This is not our problem."

"The Formor need our help," Regina said, coolly.

"Lots of people need our help," Serah said. "Chiefly us."

I found myself torn. I had fought a decade against the Formor and their sibling-races, losing countless friends and comrades-in-arms to their machinations. I'd seen cities destroyed, temples desecrated, and children slain.

I had seen enough atrocities from men to know they were a difference in degree rather than kind but such was small comfort. I had seen armies begin as conscripted potters, coopers, and tailors only to be twisted by war into marauding brigands who were capable of nothing more than destruction.

How much more so were the Formor who had been abused and sculpted by the Trickster for millennium? If they had hope of redemption it was probably centuries in the future or under the firm guiding hand of a reformer, assuming they wanted it at all.

I was also less than inclined to trust the word of a creature which seemed spewed from my blackest nightmares. In the end, it was a choice of evils, so I chose the one I found least offensive. "Upon reflection, I am inclined to break an alliance at the merest mention of reward. My honor is blackened beyond cleansing but I have enough memory of it to know leaving the Formor to your mercies is a betrayal."

T'Clau narrowed her eyes. "Then cease to be."

She spoke my true name.

CHAPTER 26

N ame magic was the strongest magic.

There were many wizards who swore by it, even though they only knew one or two names at best and sometimes only half-of-one. They claimed it was the beginnings of all magic and mystical languages like Demonspeak or High Celestial were merely constructs based on the barest concepts therein. From the way I felt, they were right. Too bad I wouldn't get to use my newfound knowledge.

T'Clau spoke my name in a language which had a resemblance to both Demonspeak and High Celestial but so much more. I could not describe for you the syllables or intonation, only that in a breath, she managed to perfectly encapsulate everything about me.

All so she could order me to be no more.

Painful cannot be used as a descriptor for what seemed like reality trying to squeeze you out like puss from a wound. My flesh, muscle, bones, and organs felt like they were trying to rip themselves apart while something similar was happening to my soul.

It did not feel like she was killing me, such would have been a mercy compared to what was happening. No, instead, it was as if she was trying to *erase my very existence*. I felt agony not only now but in the future and the past, the torment of the moment sailing forth from my body in both directions as T'Clau sought to unmake everything I was and could be. My last thought as the spell ran its course was to wonder whether I would even exist enough to visit an afterlife or if the gods themselves would forget me.

I fell to my knees.

Unharmed.

"What?" I said, the sensation passing.

Oh, T'Clau, the Trickster said, the barest edge to his voice. *Did you really think you could manipulate the new King Below by saying only half his name?*

T'Clau barely got a chance to register surprise before the hilt of Hopebringer buried deep into her throat. Turning my head, I saw Regina had hurled it like a throwing knife. A feat I would have considered impossible before meeting her. Then again, the weapon was magically designed to seek its owner's enemies.

"Speak no more lies, False-One! You have earned your damnation!" Regina said, pulling off the bow from her back and notching a Formor arrow.

Serah, by contrast, began drawing on the dark forces infusing the cavern and conjured them into a glowing black orb which she hurled at T'Clau. The orb exploded against her. The resulting black ribbons acted like whips, flaying at her skin and tearing away mystical defenses which protected her from assault.

T'Clau's reaction was furious. Ripping out the blade from her throat, she struggled to say something but only achieved a gurgling gush of blood. A normal human would have been dead but normal humans did not bear divine curses. The monstrous spider-woman used two of her legs to rip free one of the massive stalactites beside her and hurl it in our general direction.

The two of us managed to duck under or to the side of the massive rock while she ripped up another one. Not able to throw a blade with the same precision as Regina, I ran straight at T'Clau, swinging Chill's Fury.

Chunks of chitin exploded from T'Clau's lower body as Formor armors penetrated into the side of her flesh. Serah, meanwhile, summoned forth waves of dark energy which strengthened me and weakened T'Clau. She had to duck out of the way of another hurled rock, even as I dodged between the monster's legs. I struck again and again, dancing between blows and delivering slashes which I hoped would kill the beast.

None of them seemed to do more than irritate her. A glancing blow from her right leg struck me in the jaw. I was sent spiraling to the ground before another reached over and grabbed my shoulder with a crab-like pincer. Lifting me up face-to-face, the look on T'Clau's face was more animal than person.

I allowed myself a moment of pity. "I am sorry for you. I know what it is like to be made into a monster."

T'Clau's response was to try and impale me with another of her legs. I managed to block the pincer with my blade, struggling to hold off her superior strength. Using Chill's Fury as a focus, I sent a current of black lightning through the demon's body. Only a fraction of the current passed onto me through her claw, but it was enough to make me convulse.

T'Clau threw away her advantage, literally, by throwing me to one side in disgust. I bounced against the cold stone of her cavern, weakened but alive. A blast of witchfire struck against the spider woman and caused horrific frost burns. Serah's magic had done terrible damage to the monster, but I wasn't sure if we were anywhere close to killing it.

That was when Regina recovered Hopebringer, making a mad dash for the weapon. She charged forward with the broken sword, cutting one of T'Clau's legs off with a single swipe. She struck again, sending the flaming mass to one side.

The ice-generating flames died out as Regina took advantage of the prone monster to stab into an artery by her heart. When the blade pulled out, a river of blackish ichor poured out and T'Clau had only time enough to wail once last time.

She was dead within seconds.

"I hate thee, I hate thee from here to the World Above to the one below and every world in-between." Regina continued stabbing and slashing the body, reducing it into an unrecognizable mass of bloody ribbons.

"Regina..." Serah started to say.

"Hate!" Regina screamed, driving Hopebringer's hilt into the skull of the T'Clau, showering her with the remains of the monster's brain.

I raised my hand to Serah, signaling her to leave her be. I had seen similar such breakdowns on the fields of battle. They were common amongst veterans and I'd suffered no less than three. They happened when one had seen too much blood and too many friends die.

Regina took a series of deep breaths, covered in gore. "Revenge is not so satisfying as I'd hoped."

"She was not amongst the ones who slew your family," Serah said, choosing a poor time to point out facts.

"I care not," Regina said, rising from the ground. "She chose to ally with the other Usurpers. I would kill them all, carve out their hearts, and feast on them like the cannibal tribes of the North."

What could one say to that?

"Seven remain," I said, simply. "I ask you to set down your revenge when they are finished."

Regina glared at me, the fury of her battle still burning within her chest. "You ask a great deal of me, *Wraith Knight*."

"Is it?" I asked, knowing she needed to let her anger out.

"They are followed by armies, nobles, priests, wizards, and peasants. They have disgraced the entirety of the world with their actions and anyone who follows them deserves to…" Regina trailed off. "I'm sounding like a crazy person, aren't I?"

"A little," Serah said, softly. "But who hasn't in this group?"

"I called to the highest hills of every corner of the Southern Kingdoms to kill every man and woman who followed the King Below and re-educate their children with the rod as well as Codex. To put to sword the whole of the Shadowkind races." I stared at her, sighing. "Now I see they are people and realize I was deserving of this shadowy cloak."

"You deserve nothing but happiness," Regina said, looking gentle despite the amount of gore covering her armor and face.

"What we deserve and what we get are two very different things. You, of all people, know that."

Regina stared down at T'Clau's corpse. "I loved Gewain. I loved him more than I loved my parents, my uncle, my honor, the Shadowguard, and the Empire. Even if he did not love me, that is how much I loved him and people like her took him away. Do you know what that is like?"

I nodded. "I do."

"As do I," Serah said.

I looked over at Serah, surprised.

Serah was not meeting Regina's gaze.

"Who?" Regina asked the question I did not want to answer.

In for a bronze, in for a silver. "Jassamine. We were lovers. More than lovers, in fact, but in love."

"You loved the Conqueror-Saint?" Regina asked.

I tried to put into words what I loved about Jassa. However, the first words which came to mind when thinking of her were not the ones traditionally associated with a lover: cunning, ruthless, and ambitious.

I had long admired Jassa's passionate commitment to the Lawgiver, bordering on zealotry. But those were not the words Regina wished to hear.

Instead, I said, "She was a formidable woman. One of the most passionate I've ever known. Empires rose and fell due to her influence. Jassamine set the world on fire with her words and her will was law. I was a leaf in the wind of her will and it was glorious just knowing her. To love her was a gift from the Lawgiver beyond measure."

Regina looked at me before beginning to clean off the blood. "The King Below separated you two with his blade."

"Yes."

She would not recognize you or you her, the Trickster said. *You were attracted to the flame and she the wood to burn. Now you are as ice and she is ashes.*

"How do you get over it? This pain?" Regina said, realizing she could not clean herself while still holding Hopebringer.

She threw the broken sword aside.

Serah looked down at it, then picked it up. She then pulled a cloth blanket from her knapsack and handed it to Regina.

"You don't," I said, sadly. "Though I have met some truly formidable women since then."

I couldn't help but wonder whether the Trickster had placed me in Regina's path, knowing it would turn out the way it did. He was a god, after all, and divinations existed for the more powerful wizards let alone one who had helped create magic. Had he known how I would react to her and, later, Serah?

And if so, why?

The Trickster was not given to kindness.

I am the kindest god of them all, the Trickster said, sounding sincere.

"And you, Serah?" Regina wiped her face. "Who was your lost love?"

"Don't you know?" Serah said, sounding wistful. "She was taken from me by war, though it was not by violence."

Regina looked confused.

I, on the other hand, understood.

Serah loved Regina.

How had I missed it?

"I will try and keep my heart open to new possibilities," Regina said, finally. "If you had asked me a month ago whether I would ever be fighting alongside a Wraith Knight in the defense of Formor with hopes of continuing to do so in the future, I would have called you a liar and challenged you to a duel. I am glad to be beside you both, though, for it is good company in a time when there is nothing else."

"It could be more," I said, looking between them.

Serah blinked.

"What do you mean?" Regina asked.

I grimaced, realizing I'd presumed too much. The flames of ardor were ones easily sparked between those of the proper inclination under combat, stress, and months in close quarters. However, I was a ghost and if I had picked up an attraction from either or both women then there was nothing I could give them. They were living women and deserved living partners, each other or another.

Another reason to find my peace, lest others be lead astray.

"Nothing," I said, sighing. "I was just thinking we have a sacrifice of sorts if we were to compel one answer from the lips of this vile hag."

"Do tell," Serah asked.

"A fresh corpse of the T'Clau itself," I said, pointing to the Cauldron of Names. "With some necromancy I might animate her head and toss it in."

Serah looked intrigue. "The magic would allow you to compel the head to give you an answer. It would then turn in on itself and destroy the Cauldron. That is if it works like a standard oracular device, that is. It's a creation of the gods so the usual rules may not apply."

"Please speak sensibly," Regina said, looking confused.

"You can cheat magic," Serah said, clutching her staff tightly. "Say, if a curse is for you to kill your eldest child. You could, instead, adopt an enemy older than your child and sacrifice him to the magic. However, the consequences for this would be unpredictable as the energies go in new directions thanks to the spell's intent being subverted. The curse might kill the caster or the target or cause an explosion."

"This magic is too powerful to leave in the hands of an enemy," I said, staring at the Cauldron. "We'd ever be subject to the possibility of a new T'Clau, too, who might resent the fact we'd killed her in a previous life."

"I know enough twilight magic to redirect the forces of entropy released to strike other areas, preferably the homes of our enemies," Serah said, walking over to the cauldron and beginning to draw sigils in the cavern floor dust.

"I have no idea what you're talking about," Regina said. "Either of you."

"Just watch," I said, severing the brutalized head of T'Clau and lifting it up by her hair. Whispering several words of Demonspeak, I restored a semblance of life. The resulting shambler hissed and spit, its eyes full of mindless venom.

Serah, meanwhile, spoke numerous intonations to Sidhe High Lords and Ladies as well as mathematical formula which was designed to focus the energies around her. She was a master of it and I couldn't help but stand in awe of her skill. I might have two-hundred-and-eighty years of magical experience but she was my better by far.

"It is done," Serah said, breathing hard. "The pool will become useless thereafter but should give you the information you desire."

"Understood." I paused. "Thank you."

"Anything," Serah said.

Regina finished cleaning off her face. "Do you have a true name you want to ask for?"

"Yes," I said, walking over to the cauldron. I had come here to Everfrost for power and an end to my curse. This way offered a

chance for both. Without availing myself to the twisted might of the Trickster. Holding the head over the bubbling, churning mass, I spoke a command, "Tell me the true name of Jacob Riverson."

I dropped T'Clau's head into the disgusting soup within.

I learned my true name in that moment.

I gained a perfect understanding of myself. My memories returned and I learned everything I'd been hiding from my conscious mind.

I screamed.

CHAPTER 27

The memories came as an avalanche, burying me in their power and intensity. I recalled things normal people had forgotten. Birth. Infancy. The awkward years from boyhood to man.

How utterly stupid I was as a young man. I hadn't so much forgotten that as I'd tried to forget. Some of the memories' flashes made me regretful in ways I hadn't expected. I realized my sire, no father, had been a kinder man than I remembered. He'd been frightened for me after I'd killed that mercenary, not condemnatory. I'd been too angry to realize "selling" me to Kalian had been his way of getting me out of the village before I got myself killed. I regretted I'd never be able to make peace with him. Or see my sisters again. Elizabeth, Nina, and Tara.

All gone.

As I relived my beginnings, I simultaneously recalled the other end of my life. It was as if my memories were a snake moving to eat its own tail. I remembered my time with the King Below now, clearly, from him sending me to the Storm Giant Mountains during the Final Battle of the Fifth War to his first bending my will with black magic. Strangely, those memories proved to be less repellent than I expected. The King Below had not kept my soul chained to the point of being nothing more than a marionette, like I'd expected. Instead, he'd just blown out my conscience like a candle and bound me to his will. I had been like a parody of myself, serving his cause, but otherwise unchanged.

The only thing he'd ever truly warped of my being was when he'd forced me to harm children. I had been willing to kill my former allies, torture, and destroy for the God of Evil in my transformed state but such action rebelled against even my conscienceless self.

The few times the King Below forced me to do it resulted in me going catatonic for months. It had won me friends amongst the Formor even as the Dark Lords grew sick enough of my resistance to leave that corner of my spirit alone.

On both ends of my lifespan, the memories grew darker. They were coming to the same point, a time so terrifying and hate-filled I'd buried it in the deepest part of my consciousness. My time with the King Below was like a terrible dream but I had the comfort knowing it wasn't me. No more than Regina without her conscience or Serah without her will or Jassa without her ambition.

But there were dark times when I was fully myself.

And there was no one to blame for my actions but the man I saw in the mirror.

Those were the memories I feared.

Tharadon...

Co'Fannon...

The creation of the Terrible Weapons at the forges of Twilight's End...

The use of the Death Mist on Kosswood...

And one memory at the bottom of them all.

No. No.

NO!

I refused to face it. My conscious mind did not want to relive the moment I betrayed myself and everything I believed in.

I knew what was to come.

I just didn't want to face it.

Please, I begged. *Have pity.*

No, the Trickster said. *Remember.*

It was the beginning of the first year of the Eighth Age, the Age of the Codex. It was the last year of the Fourth War and the tenth overall. There were still a few months before the final battle on the fields of Winterholme. The King Below's forces were concentrated there now, in full retreat from the forces brought to bear by the Southern League.

Which had allowed our attention to be focused elsewhere.

Lawgiver forgive me.

I walking through the halls of the rebuilt Grand Temple. Gone were the ostentatious furniture, gold candlesticks, and costly art. The puppet Grand Cleric appointed by the Emperor and his archmage had emptied the vast treasuries of the once-wealthy organization to fund the former's personal army. No longer required of the Great Lords to fund his campaign and their forces pressed to the limit against the King Below, the expansion of Imperial Royal power had changed the face of the Anessian Empire. The Mysterium had taken hostages from every Great House, arrested countless high priests, and begun a vigorous campaign of ecclesiastical reform. The Shadowguard had eliminated everyone who couldn't be arrested.

Now the Grand Temple was full of somber priests and priestesses chosen for their piety rather than connections. The Mysterium and Grand Temple worked hand-in-hand to administrate the Empire's newly seized territories while purging those who resisted the New Order. A new uniform legal code had been drafted under Prince-

Regent Eric, his father remaining on the battlefield where he was most comfortable. Emperor Edorta had never been a man for statecraft and was eager to leave ruling the Emperor to those who wanted to do it. We were, frankly, doing a better job than he ever did anyway.

The poor now were fed from almshouses, slavery was limited to seven years duration for Lawgiver worshipers, debt prisons were shut down, protections were given to second and third spouses, as well as expanding the rights of peasants who chose to serve in the King's Army. The mages' colleges were required to swear direct allegiance to the Emperor as well as pledge service to the Empire's improvement for a period of at least five years. Hersey was now punishable by death.

It was good.

Or so I thought at the time.

The Grand Temple's new halls were a monument to the reforms we'd made. The stained glass windows lacked their former ornate depictions of the rest of the Gods Above with only the Lawgiver shown now. A few simple shrines to the Great Mother at my behest but Jassa had believed the other gods were best venerated through remembering their service to the God-Above-All. The tapestries were changed too, being simple red banners with the burning eye in their center.

All the others had been burned.

"It's too quiet these days," I muttered, shaking my head. "I really need to get the practice of hymns reinstated."

I'd been suffering a strange disquiet for the past year. The destruction of Kosswood had changed something within me and left me feeling less enthusiastic for doing the Lawgiver's work. The collateral damage had been small, but the responsibility for the orders still rested with me. We were close to victory now.

So why did it feel so far away?

A younger initiate of the Great Mother, dressed all in black, walked up to me and curtsied. She wore a plain bonnet with no makeup but was still quite lovely. Jassa had recently started sending nothing but attractive females she kept firmly under her thumb to communicate with me. It had begun with my increasing hints to her we should take our relationship public and wed. I found the implications of her answer insulting.

"Milord," the woman said. "My name is Mara Gooddaughter. I am at your service."

I bit my tongue. "What does the Lady Jassa want?"

I wasn't in the mood to mince words.

Mara Gooddaughter frowned. "She requests your presence, Lord General, at your earliest convenience."

"Show me the way."

Mara curtsied again, the formality in the Grand Temple now stifling. She turned around and lead me down to the basement levels. The catacombs had been cleaned out of saints relics and tombs for Great Wizards were interred elsewhere.

Jassa had wanted to remove their status as revered figures but I'd argued sainthood encouraged people to think they could serve the Lawgiver in a direct capacity. We'd had many arguments about the subject. I'd finally given up.

Still, I was disturbed the Mysterium had adapted them to dungeons. That sent the wrong message to the faithful. It was amazing to think so much of this had occurred in the past few years, but the war had left a great power vacuum in the Imperial City. The Empire's confidence in its invincibility had been shaken and the five-hundred-year-old institution had been willing to do anything to repair its greatness.

"I owe you a great deal, milord," Mara spoke.

"Do you?"

"Oh yes," Mara said, presenting her right wrist. It bore the tattoo of a snake eating its own tail. They were those who had been born into slavery and were destined for it in perpetuity. There were other marks which informed she had been trained as a submissive in the concubine houses of Gael.

Rather than produce prostitutes, said houses specialized in permanently altering the minds of their subjects to become obedient toys to their owners. The Concubines of Gael were said to be any man or woman's fantasy if your purse was deep enough and they would love you all the more for however you chose to treat them. The Mind-Benders were all dead now, convicted of King Below worship and treason with their slaves freed. I hadn't regretted lying under oath to frame them at all.

"I see," I said, understanding why she'd been sent. "I hope you are enjoying your independence."

"It was difficult at first," Mara said, descending down the dark and spiraling staircase. Lightning lamps had been installed from Thradon's notes but, for whatever reason, were kept at third-strength. "Exercising one's free-will is like using a muscle. If you are kept from it for a long time, it atrophies. Many of us struggled with the pain of making decisions after having such done for us so long. That was when Saint Jassamine offered us positions in the clergy. The strict regime and rules are comforting with the hole in my heart filled with the Lawgiver's light."

"Saint Jassamine? A *living* saint?" When had she so utterly changed her opinions on the subject of divine honors? Enough she'd defied convention to take them before passing onto the grave as was tradition?

"Oh yes," Mara said, smiling. "The Grand Cleric bestowed both the honor of it as well as Great Wizard onto her yesterday. Her word is to be entered into the Codex as a new litany."

I was speechless.

"She could not have done this without you," Mara said, staring. "Even if your reputation prevents her from showing you the affection she desires."

I balled my fists, insulted in every possible way.

"You should marry, Lord," Mara said. "Once the war is over, I mean. You could be a Great Lord and a leader on the Warlord's

Council. You would not be subject to the same laws as others regarding licentiousness. It's part of your mystique."

"Do not confuse my legend with me."

Mara looked back, confused. "Of course, milord."

We reached the bottom of the stairs and found ourselves in an environment which was significantly less ominous than the upstairs or staircase. The Catacomb Dungeons, despite their name, were brightly lit with the downstairs looking more like a luxurious inn than a place where prisoners were kept.

The lightning lamps were turned to full strength while the ground was covered in fine carpet. Well-dressed servants, paid three times what they'd earn in the service of the Great Houses, carted around meals prepared by gourmet chefs to the prisoners behind the steel doors.

The servants were routinely searched as well as the meals but, otherwise, the prisoners were left with treatment better than most merchants could expect. Their quarters were filled with furniture taken from the Great Houses, copper pipe plumbing, books, and other luxuries which showed they would not be mistreated.

Unless the political situation changed.

This was just the first level and I knew the lower ones could get much worse. Heretics and enemies of the Reforms were offered either the cake or the scourge. If they took the former, they would be allowed to right condemnations of their former writings as well as monitored release with hostages. If they took the latter, they would confess to their crimes and accept the punishment they entailed. Eventually. The system worked so well many of the Imperial hostages had been transferred here along with the members of the Royal Family who had been used by rebels against Emperor Edorta's heir. People trusted the new Grand Temple would not abuse their loved ones and, as far as I could tell, only a few hostage executions had taken place.

That was when I saw a Mindbender of Gael.

His appearance was unmistakable with the shaved head, elaborately woven tartan, and the tattoo of a sun on his forehead. His hands were covered in the dozens of mystical rings his kind wore while another set hung from his earlobes. Around his waist was a thick leather belt with a dozen or more wands, each coded to assisting with a different sort of magic related to the mind. His arms were tattooed with the signs of a high wizard with symbols that said he'd personally reordered the minds of over two hundred people.

I opened my mouth in shock and would have been less surprised at seeing the Trickster playing a set of satyr pipes while dancing in the nude. Mara passed him by as if he wasn't anything noteworthy, the high wizard giving me a nod of respect as if I was his superior.

I choked back my bile. "What is it that *Saint Jassamine* wishes to speak with about?"

I had clearly entered a madhouse. The only thing missing was rotten fruit to toss at the lunatics and someone collecting pennies for it.

"It is not my place to say, milord," Mara said, frowning.

"You owe me," I said, my voice like ice.

Mara was silent as she walked, finally saying, "It is Grand Duke Rogers."

"The King's marriage brother?"

Mara nodded. "It would seem he attempted to spirit the Princesses from the Catacomb Dungeons."

"Why are the Princesses *in* the Catacomb Dungeons?" I had clearly missed a great deal in the past six months fighting the King Below. It seemed I needed to make a greater effort to travel back and forth on gryphon-back.

"Evil men desire to use them as rallying cries against the Reforms. They claim the Emperor is senile and the Prince-Regent is under the spell of a foreign..." Mara trailed off as if unable to finish the sentence.

"You can say whore." It wasn't like these accusations were new.

"I can't, sir," Mara said, embarrassed. "They claim it is necessary to arrest Prince Eric, force him to join a monastery, and marry the

Princesses to scions of House Rogers and House Archer. Even the Shadowguard would suffer punishments for their actions. Both the Grand Cleric's election as well as the charter for the Mysterium would be dissolved. I do not want to say what they planned for both you and Lady Jassamine."

I could guess. Beheading for me after torture and public shaming for Jassamine, after the removal of her tongue of course.

"I see."

This was grave news indeed.

We reached a pair of thick wooden doors, which were opened by a pair of Temple Golems made of gilded armor.

I passed through them.

To a room full of blood runes, human sacrifice, and horror. On the ground were the Princesses, Deborah and Ruth, both of them with their throats cut. Mystical symbols and circles were drawn around them, making a formal pattern for a powerful enchantment spell which harnessed the young ones' deaths.

A sword was in the center of this nightmare spell.

Hopebringer.

Mara followed me in as the golems closed the door behind us. "Saint Jassamine has taken steps to rectify the problem, however."

CHAPTER 28

The chamber was a Natariss ritual magic chamber, which was a polite way of saying it was a place where blood magic was performed. In addition to the absolute profanity of two ritually-murdered children on the ground, the walls were decorated in their mandalas and sigils designed to focus the power of blood magic. Blood covered statues of the Lawgiver and Great Mother were placed in strategic points around the chamber, amplifying the sense of utter blasphemy before me. The smell of incense, death, and terror was thick in the chamber even as the sight made me sick.

The Natarins were one of the great sources of heresy in the Southern Kingdoms, composed of Terralan survivors who had intermarried with pale-skinned savage human tribals. They'd formed their own religion distinct from the Grand Temple, but having roots in the same traditions. They despised the body and believed the physical world was evil, requiring the destruction of this universe in order to make a new one where the Lawgiver would be the only god.

Three Holy Struggles had been launched to deal with them, but they'd failed against their powerful blood mages plus the countless local diseases which only they seemed to be immune. Jassamine had fled from that country out of disgust for the ritual sacrifice of their third-born children and other atrocities.

Now Jassamine had erected a shrine to their blasphemies in the basement of the Grand Temple.

And *killed children*.

All to a make *a fucking magic sword*.

"You knew about this?" I asked Mara, keeping my voice low.

"They are the children of ene—" Mara didn't get to finish her statement because I'd already drawn my service dagger and plunged it into her chest.

"I'll take that as a yes," I whispered, feeling her blood wash out over my hands while she collapsed into my arms.

I dropped her to the ground.

Mara looked up, already half-dead and gone seconds later. The look on her face was one of confusion as much as betrayal, as if she didn't understand why I'd just done what I'd done. In truth, I wondered that myself.

I knew who was responsible and it wasn't her.

"That was unnecessary and wasteful, Jacob," Jassamine's voice spoke from behind one of the statues. "She would have done anything for you."

Jassmine stepped out wearing a more ornate version of her previous Mysterium archmage robes, almost completely gold with the Burning Eye embroidered on the foot of her attire. Her robes seem to glimmer in the room's lamplight, shining a rainbow of colors around her. Her hair was up and bound with a pair of G'Tay chopsticks even as her fingers were covered in focusing rings. Her staff was absent, which indicated she didn't intend to kill me. A few minutes ago, I never would have suspected she might do such.

"*What have you done?*" I asked, staring at her.

"Punished traitors and eliminated potential threats to Emperor Eric's reign. The Princesses were perfect rallying cries to our enemies as long as they existed. Deborah and Ruth were soft, pliable, and sweet children. Too much like their brother and we only need him."

"You have made yourself a monster."

Jassa smiled, the look not reaching her eyes. "I took a page from your book of tactics. An attack will be foiled against Prince-Regent Eric and signs will be left that the Grand Duke's men killed the Princesses. By the morning, no one will help Rogers or his allies. They will be pariahs and their kinsmen will beg us to take half their houses' lands."

I pointed at the bodies on the ground. People I'd known since they were in swaddling clothes. I'd brought them toys at Solstice, for gods' sakes. "I want no part in this! This...this abomination!"

It was like some horrible dream and I wished to the Gods Above and Below, I could wake up.

But the worst was yet to come.

"Your myopia does you no credit," Jassa said, advancing on me. "Do you think saying you have harmed no one not old enough to hold a sword absolves you of the murders of those who could? Do you think the Terrible Weapons you designed developed the ability to differentiate between ages? That the armies under your command never harmed a child? No matter how many they've left orphaned and alone? How many cities have you sieged, fields have you burned, and ruins have you created? To win this war, you swore you'd do anything and you balk *at this?*"

"Yes, I do!" I screamed at her.

"Your arbitrary line may give you comfort but I am past such illusions," Jassa said, raising her palm and calling forth the blade from the circle to her right hand. The signs of blood magic vanished in golden flame, burned away by the holiest of holies in sorcery.

Only the Princesses' bodies were left, proof of their murder by House Rogers.

After all, who would gainsay a saint?

"We are finished," I said, looking at the children, then turning to the corpse of the woman I'd just killed.

I was not so far from Jassa, it seemed.

"Jacob, my love for you is undiminished but you are a fool if you think I am so easily cast aside as that—or that I would let you shirk your responsibilities. I brought you here to witness the birth of this sword because you have an important role to play in the ensuing months."

I spun around, staring at her in disbelief. "You have just murdered two of the Imperial Royal Family! What do you think is going to happen when Emperor Edorta finds out? Do you think he is going to blindly accept your explanation? You will be found out, by wizards or priests or servants! They will strip you of every rank, honor, and privilege then they burn you as a witch!"

"You are right," Jassa said, walking forward, her golden robes against the ground. "Emperor Edorta will not let the deaths of his family go unpunished. He knows his brother-in-law is not the sort of man to do such an unspeakable crime even if he trusts me completely. This is why we must create a plausible story underneath it to feed him in private. Shapechangers, witchcraft, and mind-control are my thoughts. The information must come from you and you alone, Jacob, because he respects you for your martial accomplishments. He knows you would never harm a child."

I stared at her in disgust, wondering how I'd ever loved her. "You are mad."

Jassa stepped but a few feet away from me, passing over the Princesses' corpses as if they were nothing. She grabbed me by the face with her left hand and forced me to look at Mara. "Think very carefully about what you are sacrificing. This woman, who you snuffed the life of, is but one of ten thousand or more who have been freed by our actions and one of a hundred thousand who will know the breaking of their chains because of our actions. If I perish, or am disgraced, all of what we've worked for will be undone. The Royal Dragons will reign fire down on the impoverished masses and it will return, worse than before. Everything horrible you have done, we have done, will be for nothing."

I couldn't help but flinch at the cold dead eyes looking from me. Yet, behind her, were the bodies of two girls I'd known. They'd had futures they'd never know because of Jassa's madness. "Their names were Deborah and Ruth."

"I taught them to read, Jacob." Jassa looked up at me. "History will record their death as an infamous crime, but *good* can come from it. New laws can be made to safeguard those who have no protection. This is almost the end, Jacob. When the King Below is driven back to the North, he will enter hibernation for decades if not centuries. I have seen it in the flames. An age of peace and prosperity will begin which will last for two hundred and fifty-years."

"What else have you seen?"

Jassa looked guilty, for the first time. She had not flinched at the murder of children but what she knew was coming made her feel remorse. "I have seen much. Emperor Edorta must not survive. Prince-Regent Eric must distinguish himself on the fields of battle, which he can only do with this sword, and you must be there fighting at the vanguard."

"Edorta is my friend," I said, staring at those children. "He trusted me to keep his heirs safe."

"You failed," Jassa said, sad but remorseless. "Now you must choose whether your pride is worth the lives of everyone else we can save."

What she asked was more than one final compromise. It was to end my last illusion about myself. If I was the man to overlook, acquiesce after the fact, to the assassination of children to frame their family, then I was a monster. I was the kind of evil which I had struggled against my entire life.

There would be no forgiveness.

Looking at Hopebringer, I recognized the blade's craftsmanship. I had been trained as a blacksmith in my village before killing my first man and leaving with Warmaster Kalian. It had given me the basics for understanding Co'Fannon and Tharadon's ideals, even if I'd had to study to understand even a tenth of them.

Hopebringer wasn't a sword Jassa had picked at random. It was one of the ones I'd manufactured for the Shadowguard at Twilight's End, enchanted with perfect balance as well as weightlessness, plus the ability to kill even the strongest Deathless or demon.

I was a part of this horror already.

"There is no after this war," I said, realizing what I had to do. "I will do as you say."

The next few months passed in an instant because I'd decided, then, to die. The Battle against Kurag had not been one because of my skill in battle but because of my complete lack of concern for my own life. The Fourth War's final battle had been chosen as my way to reconcile myself to my guilt. It had been the instrument of my suicide, a way to die so I did not have to live with the horrors of what I'd brought forth. The King Below had sensed this despair, this acknowledgement I was damned, and used it to claim my soul.

Extinguishing my conscience had been a welcome release.

Gods Above and Below.

In my head, I was surrounded by endless darkness, kneeling on the ground. There was no light anywhere, only the all-consuming despair of my failure. I was no hero. I was a villain of the worst sort.

That was when the Trickster walked up to me, staring down at me. His attire changed from a jester's outfit to the black demonsteel armor of the King Below. His humanity was invisible, only shadows and witchfire eyes visible through his helmet.

"Kill me," I whispered.

"No," The King Below said.

I said, "I have nothing."

"I know. Yet, you could have everything. Good and evil are but directions. There is no stream of water polluted with mud which cannot be made clean or any fire which cannot be extinguished."

"I am extinguished, burnt out, and broken."

"As am I, for I loved my brother more than the stars, sun, and moon. When I came to this world with the other gods, I stood with him against all of the others and did my best to be what he needed. At the end, he chose to destroy me rather than acknowledge our love."

"Then we are both damned."

"Look upon the world as it is."

The King Below stretched out a spiked gauntlet into the void and I saw how the Southern Kingdoms had changed. In many ways, they were similar. Other ways were startling different with reservoirs, pipes, lightning lamps, golems, and labor machines spread as far as the Borderlands.

Slavery was a thing of the past, in legality if not actuality, with debt used as a means to keep the masses under thumb rather than title. Many of the worst privileges of the nobility and Grand Temple had been repealed in the wake of the decades following Saint Jassamine's reign. Men, women, and children lived as they always had--trying to survive the best they could.

It was a world worth fighting for.

Then I saw the Nine Usurpers at work.

Morwen the Wise, Jon Bloodthorn, Fel Hellsword, Silence, Armac the Binder, Marahi Crimsonmoon, Elevin the Mad, Aegeta Silverhair, and Thermic Redhand each were beings of extraordinary power gathered by a being of pure light. They were also broken, each of them, in a way similar to myself. They had experienced immense suffering and it had convinced them the world needed to be changed by fire rather than words.

Under them, the Mysterium had been reborn and the Imperial army had spread to every corner of the Southern Kingdoms. They manipulated the public opinion, speaking of foreign invasion and imminent threats from countless madmen who may or may not exist. They sneered at the Fir-Bolg who lived amongst them, whispering of how they undermined the Path as well as the quintessentially human and elven culture of the Southern Kingdoms. Torture had been banned for decades as a means of extracting confessions, yet its practice had been returned, greater than ever, as a means of rooting out Shadowkind. The Old Laws were being reintroduced, one at a time, to curb the so-called decadence of the modern world.

Worse, they believed they were bringing peace even as they were holding the world by its throat.

A burning eye loomed over them, directing their every action.

"The Lawgiver," I said.

"My brother had gone mad. In his quest for a perfect world, he has broken his white light into a thousand myriad colors of terror. As the chaos embraced me, so has the law destroyed him. Not even his family can save him for he will murder them as he did the Gods Between." The King Below paused. *"And me."*

"I don't believe you."

The King Below shifted back to the Trickster. "Do you believe the other visions?"

I whispered under my breath, "Yes."

"This world needs a villain to distract the heroes."

"It needs a hero to fight tyrants," I said, sighing. "Someone like Regina. Serah can help you. She must help, in fact."

"And you?"

"I am unworthy of either."

"So be it."

I awoke.

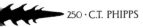

CHAPTER 29

Devastation.

Emptiness.

Loneliness.

Loss.

I let my body pass away into the nothingness of the shadow and embraced the fact that I was nothing more than a ghost. I thought my condition was a curse but, instead, it was justice. I had placed Jassa in a position of immense power and, by my actions, led to the deaths of the innocent.

I was a monster.

I was on my knees before the Cauldron, it's waters now black and useless. It bubbled with magic, but was nothing more than a container for foul and destructive magics. The Cauldron of Names was one of the last remnants of the Gods Between but it was too powerful to be trusted to anyone.

Especially me.

I was fully aware of my past now and every filthy, horrible, evil thing I'd ever done. Very few people had the opportunity to look at themselves with unbiased eyes and the Cauldron had stripped away the illusions I'd held about myself. That I was an honorable man, that I'd fought for the cause of the disadvantaged, and that I was anything but a murderer who's only solution was to kill again.

"Forgive me, Kalian," I whispered. "I have fallen from the Path."

"By the Great Mother," Regina whispered behind you. "You poor man."

"What?" I asked, looking up.

There, Regina stood, her hand outstretched as if she was trying to put her hand on my shoulder only for her to be frozen in place. Her expression was one of confusion and distaste. Hopebringer was dropped on the ground, like a piece of rubbish.

Serah, meanwhile, stood behind her looking thunderstruck. I'd never seen a look of surprise on her face before, but there it was, along with horror, and uncertainty. She clutched her staff.

"The Cauldron showed us your memories as you were struggling with them," Serah said, walking up to Regina's side. "I never imagined your past would include that."

Dear gods...

"I wish you had not seen that," I said, looking away. "What I have done is unforgivable."

"What your lover has done is unforgivable!" Serah said, stepping forward. "History is always written by the victors but it has recast a demoness in human form as its champion. So much of the Grand Temple's evils, today, date back to those days."

"Much good, too," Regina said.

Serah spun around and glared. "I speak of Jacob's actions as well as hers."

"He couldn't have known," Regina said, looking down at her feet.

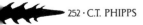

"I knew," I said, climbing to my feet. "I turned a blind eye to the dark path I walked. I can name all the horrible things I've done in the service of the so-called greater good. I called it the lesser evil but I forgot that is still evil. All that remains is for me to pass from this shadow to the next."

"You killed yourself before," Regina said, closing her hands into a fist. "You gave up!"

"Excuse me?" I asked.

"You should have killed her!" Regina shouted, surprising me with her venom. "You should have stopped what she was doing and saved her future victims. Instead, you wasted your life and turned the kingdom over to her!"

"I—"

Serah narrowed her eyes. "Spare us your self-pity, Jacob. Do you think you are the only one who has done things they find reprehensible? My hands bear the blood of countless people from not just Accadia's battlefields but others. I failed to protect my brother and the only thing keeping me going some days is the thought I might be able to see him again. I did not drag you this far, to the top of the world, so you could talk about how you deserve to die!"

I was speechless.

Regina picked up Hopebringer, took a good long look at the blade, and hurled it like a skipping stone into the tainted Cauldron. The sword which had killed gods disappeared, melting into the pool of acidic goop.

"Regina—"

"Shut the fuck up," Regina said, pointing a finger at my chest. "I am *furious* at you right now."

I took a step back and looked at my hands, shaking them in despair. "I cannot put away my feelings. No. It's worse, I did. I did for *centuries*. I let the King Below take my life and then let him take my mind. I *deserve* what happened to me. I've been fooling myself, lying to you two, about what I am. Can you not understand that?!"

I was surprised at how my voice rose.

"This is not something you can fix," I said, shaking with the memories of all that I'd done. "I am not one of Accadia's clocks. I am piece of glass."

"You are anything but glass," Regina said, reaching over to touch my hood. She leaned close and I thought she was going to kiss me.

Though I had no lips to kiss.

I wanted to conjure them, though.

An entire body to love her.

To let go of this darkness which wrapped around my neck and dragged me down to oblivion.

But I didn't deserve to be happy.

They did.

"Serah loves you," I said. "She loves you and wants to be with you."

Regina pulled away, looking like someone had slapped her. "What?"

My gaze flickered to Serah whose eyes widened in shock, narrowed in anger and embarrassment. There was also a flicker of her eyes to me, which told me she was confused and hurt.

I turned away from Regina. "I know you people surprisingly well despite just a month together. It is an old G'Tay proverb: you can spend a hundred years with a man, but won't know his true character unless you face down a dragon with him. We have faced down many dragons together. Serah loves you and wants to be with you. Not just in bed as a lover but by your side, forever."

Regina hesitated then looked back, clearly unsure of herself. Her gaze met Serah's before the latter looked down like a blushing maid.

"Serah, is this true?"

Serah muttered something under her breath which made me grimace. Which, given I was no stranger to salty language, was impressive. Taking a moment to compose herself, Serah said, "Yes."

"How long?"

Serah gave a smile which was stark contrast to her demeanor. "When you first cussed out my uncle after inviting you to tea with the Great Ladies visiting from House Archer. I was there beside him and saw the entire anatomically vivid description."

"So, within minutes of meeting me."

Serah sighed. "That's the romantic answer, I suppose. Truth be told, I can't tell you when it precisely happened. I was always attracted to you, but I treasured our friendship more. Even when we became lovers, I didn't want to lose that so I never asked for anything more than your company. You have always been there by my side, though, when everyone but Thomas and a thrice-damned moron skulking in a corner—"

Regina and Serah both glared at me.

It was like being back with the Shadowguard. Garris and Gladys never let me hear the end of it when I fucked things up.

Why did I abandon them?

"—considered me either a tool or a monster," Regina continued. "I realized when you returned and said you were going to plot treason against the Empress that I would follow you anywhere. I ask for nothing other than the chance to travel with you for as long as you permit for I—"

Regina interrupted Serah with a passionate kiss. "Why is it the people I most love are those who love themselves the least?"

"I..." Serah degenerated into an incoherent mumble. "You feel the same way?"

Regina stroked Serah's face. "I loved Gewain first even if he could not love me back. I tried to love others but I made the mistake of believing I had to abandon my love of him to do so. This quest of vengeance is consuming us all so I need to acknowledge the love I felt for him and the love I feel for you. The love I—"

Serah silenced her with a kiss, wrapping her arms around her neck.

I watched in silence, happy for them.

But jealous.

You could have love like that, my heir, the Trickster said. *Yet, you throw it away like trash and call it sacrifice.*

What do you know of love? I asked, disgusted. *You have made the world a ruin and replaced peace with desolation.*

People were doing that long before I came to this world, the Trickster said. *Also, though I will deny it later, I say unto you I know something of love too. Once, a very long time ago, I loved another being as much as she loved me. My brother, she, and I were as one with the worlds we blessed beyond measure.*

You speak of the Great Mother, I thought.

Yes, the Trickster said. *But my brother's jealousy grew and I knew in my heart I could deny him nothing. So I rid myself of my love for her and let him have all of her affection. I turned her away when she objected and, instead, devoted myself to becoming my brother's scourge. I thought their happiness would make me happy.*

What happened? I dared ask.

The mind is a machine of wheels and gears in constant need of maintenance. If you cut yourself from the oil and grease of life, the parts wear down until they are nothing. I have loved no one but my brother so long I have forgotten what it is like to love anyone. I am twisted, empty, broken, and done. The Trickster sounded almost wistful. *The worst part is, I'm aware of it and unable to change. I am the horror which mortals fear and have not the madness to rejoice in that state nor the strength of will to change.*

You are acting this way to make me sympathize, I said.

Oh, dear Jacob, you sympathize because you are not alone, the Trickster said.

He was right.

I knew what I had to do.

If a monster I was, a monster I would be.

For the world.

Serah and Regina were still kissing when other presences entered into the cavern. My senses were sharper than ever in my wraith form

and I could feel the distinct presences of Curse, Payne, as well as their father. They'd also come with a small army of Formor. There were Spiderfolk too, moving in the tunnels in the walls and coming out of the holes throughout. There were even more crawling around on the ceiling.

Regina pulled away. "They come to honor us."

Serah looked skeptical. "Yes. That's why they brought a small army. You realize, Creature never had any intention of honoring his agreement with us."

"I did," I said, having hoped for better but expected the worst. This I knew. This I could deal with. "However, I imagine he never expected us to be able to beat T'Clau either. We were a convenience for him to gain some measure of revenge. Now he'll be afraid of us. He also knows I have a power inside me he's sworn to respect."

Not that I put much faith in Formor promises. They were too much like human promises. People tended to honor them only so long as it served their best interests or were easy enough to do so. Still, the Trickster had been the Formor's god for millennium so that had to count for something. I wasn't sure if Regina and Serah had seen my meeting with the King Below

"What are you going to do?" Regina asked, holding Serah's hands.

"Talk with them."

Regina blinked her blue eyes, opened her mouth, closed it, then said, "Don't get killed, Jacob."

Serah nodded in agreement with Regina.

"I won't go to my death again," I said, staring at them. "I promise by you both."

It was the strongest oath I could swear.

Bastards and hellspawn, I loved them both.

When had this happened?

I walked out to meet Creature, finding him standing in front of a collection of Formor cloaked mages and armored warriors. Curse and Payne were present too, looking uncomfortable. The mages were wearing Black Sun amulet around their necks, which indicated they'd been born with the ability to wield light and noon magic.

Unlike humans and Dark Magic, the Formor considered these disciplines perfectly natural as well as useful for war. It was clear they'd been brought to help deal with them. The Spiderfolk, by contrast, held back behind the stalactites as if they were unsure how to approach me.

Conjuring a throne from shadows, I sat down in front of Creature. I imagined without a face, it was quite intimidating. I also let the power of fear radiate off of me. The same force which had caused Regina such discomfort before I'd created a body to remove said feelings. "As you can see, we've defeated T'Clau."

"For which the Frostiron tribes and all of the lesser tribes in the city are immensely grateful, Lord Jacob," Creature said, placing his hand over his heart and bowing his head. "However, I must regret to inform you that I have spoken to the other clan chiefs and determined our relationship has outlived its usefulness."

"As I recall, you swore to make me your King."

"I actually just agreed to serve you. But yes, I'm a liar. What a terrible little scamp I am," Creature said, grinning. "So sorry."

I sighed. "That just doesn't work for me. Kill yourselves."

I was filled with more hatred, self-loathing, and horror than I'd ever been in my life. I also had two-hundred and fifty years of magical training as well as the fact *I was under the Tower of Everfrost* to empower my spell. Creature, Curse, and Payne clutched their chests with the latter falling to her knees. The others simply slit their own throats, stabbed themselves, or rolled their eyes into the back of their heads before falling over.

Shrugging off my spell, Creature looked back then back at me. "Hmm."

I snapped my fingers and the reinforcements Creature brought rose from the ground, now re-animated as Deathless. I concentrated

and sent out a command to every man, woman, and child in all of Everfrost. *"People of Everfrost, T'Clau is dead and I am your ruler. Know that I will rule you without a hint of mercy, pity, or friendship. Your lives are mine to do with as I see fit. I am not the King Below, though. Those who serve will be rewarded, those who betray me will be destroyed. Those who betray those who would be betray me will be richly rewarded. You have failed miserably under Creature, suffering poverty and abuse. I will bring you riches and power beyond your wildest dreams but my price is absolute obedience. If you do not serve me well, you will die, but your children will be unharmed. When they are adults, they will have the same ultimatum. You will obey both Lady Serah and Lady Regina as you would me. Now get to work repairing my city."*

Curse had his bow aimed at me while Payne had her daggers drawn like short-swords. Serah and Regina had come to reinforce me as the Deathless were all ready to join in the fight against the three. So were the Spiderfolk.

To help me.

"We will serve you, milord," a black-skinned Spiderfolk woman with white-hair said, coming up behind me. "All of the Spiderfolk. You have freed us from a great tyrant. Please show us mercy, though. We did not serve T'Clau willingly."

Spiderfolk had a very different culture than Formor.

"I have no mercy," I lied. "Obedience brings rewards, though."

The woman nodded.

"Put your weapons down," Creature said to Payne and Curse. "He's passed the test."

"What test?" Curse asked.

"The test of being stronger than us," Creature said, chuckling. "Which is the only test which matters when you're a king. We are watching you, though."

"No Creature, I am watching you," I said, getting up. "Show me to the Crown."

CHAPTER 30

Entering the Tower required journeying over a bridge made of black rock which seemed made of a frozen corral-like substance. Wraithrock crystals, often used in the production of magical items, grew from it organically.

Along the sides of the bridge, I could see into the immense pit leading to the World Below. Gargoyles, Lesser Demons, Sincubi, and Ice Ravens flew around the hundreds of tunnels carved into the walls. I rode on a Nuckelavee while the others rode spirit-steeds and giant wolves, forming a procession through the city. The Fomor were not happy with my presence, but quite a few seemed relieved *someone* was in charge now.

I wouldn't be able to have their complete allegiance until I claimed the Black Throne and Crown of Weeping Gods, however. They were symbols, like the Tower itself, of the King Below's power. A monarchy's strength derived from such things as much as force of arms. If I didn't possess them, the Formor would go back to fighting each other and peace would never touch this land.

That would not do at all.

The Spiderfolk, at least, opened the main doors to the Tower willingly. The massive twenty-foot-tall doors grinded with the same gear system as the kind in the front gate, revealing the castle's eerie soft interior. Hundreds of their kind formed a procession along the bridge, bowing or outright prostrating themselves before my mount as I passed.

The Spiderfolk seemed far more amiable to my rule than the Formor. I'd spent quite a bit of the past hour reassuring them I was not going to engage in any massacres or revenge. Indeed, I was going to have more trouble from the Formor since they were anything but interested in peace with their former tormentors.

I had to promise swift punishment and brutal example in order to keep the peace between the two. Walking the tightrope between my own inclinations for peace and not showing any weakness was going to be a difficult road. The Formor would not change overnight, or in a year, or even a generation, but perhaps I change their children as well as their children's children.

I had time, after all.

The Endless Winter shaped the Formor and it is as fundamental to their nature as the firmament, the Trickster said. *I could have made their lands a paradise or given them the tools so they did not need to fear starvation but instead let them remain hard and cold. Who are you to decide to defy nature?*

Myself, I said.

Then know it will be their choice they change, not yours.

"You shall have to give us the two copper tour," I said, entering into the otherworldly palace.

The Tower was like no other building ever constructed by man, elf, or Formor. The ancient Formor warchief, Orkis, had written of it as:

A place constructed of stone, living ice, and crystal where time has no meaning nor space. A man can wander the halls for months or become an old man in one room while his friends dine on fish and ale in another. It was raised from the depths of the World Below but every generation of Shadowkind have added their own additions to the palace, competing with works from the future and races long dead.

The King Below comes from another world, let us not forget, and we are but the latest in a long line of subject species he has enslaved across uncounted epochs. To look upon the Tower's interior is to see a museum to the universe's secret history.

He was not exaggerating.

Words fail me in describing it but if I may try, I shall say it was like being in the center of a gigantic cavern with its own separate city away from the one surrounding it. Stalactite palaces existed at the bottom of the antechamber as bridges made of ice ascended up a spiraling interior which seemed to go on forever. Along the walls were temples to the King Below, armories, statues to various ancient beings long dead.

Free-floating islands hung above the bottom of the chamber, containing their own tiny-looking villages. I would swear the tower interior was only few acres in size, yet some of the islands were several miles long. A miniature sun of witchfire, which gave off no heat, illuminated the top of the chamber and its light reached every corner of the chamber.

It was exactly as I'd remembered it.

"It's more like the two silver tour," Creature said, looking up.

The entirety of the group was struck by the Tower's beauty, which was both wondrous and terrible. The fact the Spiderfolk had managed to seize it from the Formor was impressive but I wondered if T'Clau realized what she'd had in her possession. Given she was living in a cavern to keep watch over the Cauldron, I very much doubted it.

"I expected the Tower to be less...." Regina trailed off. "Grand."

"Oh?" Payne asked.

"More tortured souls, wailing of the damned, and all that," Regina said.

"Why would he torture his faithful?" Payne asked.

"Because he's an asshole," I said, staring up.

True, the Trickster said.

We all dismounted our horses and handed them off to ghostly servants, the spirits of those pledged to serve the King Below in this life and the next who had not vanished with the others freed by his death. The Spiderfolk holed up here would want to speak with me as would the other Shadowkind leaders but there was time for that after I seized the Crown.

"Let's just head to the throne room," I said, gesturing up a smooth walkway made of green crystal. "I assume that's where the object is?"

"Yes, Lord Jacob," Creature said, still getting used to taking orders from me. I could see the little monster plotting behind his eyes.

Good. That made him predictable.

"We'll walk the rest of the way," I said, staring up the side.

Serah stared up at the Witch's Sun above, which was about a mile away. "I'm not quite up for that much walking."

"You won't feel a thing," I said, sighing. "It takes some getting used to, but perception is reality here. That or everything is an illusion. Or both."

Serah seemed to comprehend that, nodding. "I understand."

"You do?" Regina asked.

"The Tower of Judgment is much the same in the City of Light," Curse said. "Needlessly grandiose."

"You've been to the City of Light?" Regina asked, doing a double take.

"Of course, I have. I'm an sidhe. The Messengers allow us free passage to the World Above." Curse paused. "Well not me, probably."

"Probably?" Regina said, horrified.

"Like you'd be welcome?" Curse asked.

"I serve a good cause," Regina said. "The Lawgiver will understand." Curse snorted.

"Onward and upward," Creature said, ascending up the stairs. "Let's start us off with some of the more fun locations." He pointed to a large door carved with my face on it. "That way leads to the Forge of Fallen Stars, it's where Lord Kurag would create his many works of destruction and beauty. It's powered by the heart of a star that the King Below stole from one of the Peace-Weavers' Messengers. I imagine it will be getting much use of it in the near future." Creature had a knack for passively insulting me.

"You were a smith?" Regina asked, blinking as we ascended up past it. "I mean, when you were enslaved by the King Below."

"I was the greatest smith of my Age," I said, wondering if I could use it and my abnormal knowledge of engineering as well as smith-work to repair this place. "After a fashion."

"Really?" Regina asked, taking position beside me.

"How did you get such abilities?" Serah asked. "None of the stories of you mentioned that quality."

"Of course, they mention the stories about my sex life but the fact my primary contribution to the war after the third year was making weapons," I muttered, trying not to think how I'd acquired my abilities. Knowing my true name prevented me from forgetting anything, though. "I stole them. I stole the knowledge which made me the greatest smith of my Age."

"Ooo, I love stories about stolen knowledge," Creature said, smiling his cracked jagged teeth. "Do tell!"

"There's not much to tell," I said, looking uncomfortable. "The war was going badly and we were running out of resources to defeat the King Below."

"That's because you're not supposed to win the Great Shadow Wars. You're supposed to fight in them. There's a difference,"

Creature explained, acting like he was talking to a small child. "You Shadowguards always seemed to miss that."

"I know this story," Curse said. "It's a dark one even by my standards."

Payne looked at her husband. "Now I'm interested."

"It was said the sidhe had secret magics and technologies which rivaled the Old Terralan and could be used to destroy entire legions. Items which could invoke the Great Magic," I said, feeling ashamed. "We—"

"Is this before or after you killed Thanador?" Creature interrupted. "Because the King Below and I laughed about that one. The greatest mind of ten Ages, snuffed because you wanted to use his discoveries for killing. You single-handedly set back mechanimagical development an Age."

"If he didn't want his inventions used for war, he should have never invented them. All knowledge will eventually be used for killing. It is axiomatic." I found myself curiously defensive about my evil deeds, even now.

"Agreed!" Creature said, smiling. "Now you're talking like one of us!"

Sadly, I couldn't deny his words. "This was before. We discovered the next phase of our plan in Tharadon's research. In his notes were communications with the legendary High Lord, Co'Fannon, Lord of Smithcraft and Prince of the Sun. He who made the Crown and the Death Knight's swords."

"Oh yes," Creature said, smiling. "I remember Dear Old Co. How is he?"

"He's dead."

Curse looked appalled. "A Great Wizard and a High Lord? I refuse to believe it. No mortal could be so lucky and stupid. Which is saying something given what your race gets up to."

"It's true, I'm sorry to say."

The details were, as always now, fresh in my mind. Co'Fannon had been seduced by the Night's Queen into teaching the King Below smithcraft and rune-secrets they'd learned from the Lawgiver. He'd only discovered the horror of his mistake after the Second Great Shadow War. The sidhe banished their High Lord, thereafter, sending him to a distant world reachable only by star bridge.

I actually was the one who seduced Co'Fannon, the Trickster said. *I have no consort, children, or allies like my brother. I'm spectacular as a sidhe woman. Would you like to see?*

No.

I remembered the betrayal now like it was yesterday and wondered how many memories of mine were not so much missing as suppressed. "Prince Eric funded our expedition. I took twenty of the greatest Shadow Warriors alive and Jassamine. We went through the moon gate, claiming to be messengers of Tharandor, and defeated him in battle once he learned of our plan. All died but three yet we laid him low. As he was dying, Jassamine used a mind-stone greater than any in history to steal away all of his secrets. She could not contain them all and gave unto me his secrets of craftsmanship."

Garris never forgave me for that mission. Thom Stone-Hand, Mathew Birdeyes, Robetta the Fire-Walker, Jim Burnheart, Sonja Unicornrider, the Rake, and so many others perished because of our desire to steal Co'Fannon's secrets.

Gladys would have perished as well, if not for the fact she'd been recalled to the Imperial City before the mission to train their new force of dragons. If not for her, Garris would have lost his mind. The best Shadowguards of an Age sacrificed to acquire weapons which would do our job for us. The world would have been a better place if I'd died there along with Jassa.

Better, I imagine, the Trickster said. *Or maybe millions of other people would have died. Then maybe those people would have had babies that were never born. That's the funny thing about immortality, everything mortals do always ends up fine if you take the long view of it. Well, fine, and irrelevant.*

Curse looked insulted. "I don't believe you. Co'Fannon was a High Lord and you were just a man then."

"Your elvish is showing," Regina muttered.

"My elvish is always showing," Curse said.

"Well don't whip it out for strangers," Payne said.

Curse glared at her.

I laughed at that one. "Believe as you will, Curse. With the knowledge of both Tharadon and Co'Fannon, I created blades capable of cleaving stone like butter, machines which could send darts across an ocean, flames which could be shot from tubes by men without magic, armored carriages which could protect entire squadrons, and gas capable of laying low a small city."

The last had been used only once.

I had underestimated its power.

The memories of Kosswood made my mouth grow dry and I wished for my amnesia to return.

"Ah yes," Creature said, nodding. "A thirty-year-war reduced to a mere decade. You must be so proud."

It had been like a sickness, the blood-lust and desire to defeat the enemy. I'd been terrified in the end, frightened beyond measure, because I knew I wouldn't be able to deny what I'd done when the battles were over. "The war wasn't supposed to end."

Creature patted me on the legs. "Well, if you feel like making any more horrors in the forge, it simply needs to be re-lit. We have a cranky old Grand Red in the basement named Smoke. Just don't get her mad and you'll do fine."

I remembered too much of my old self now. "The Shadowguard teaches you should do everything you can in order to win, then stop. I forgot that rule."

"Don't forget it again," Regina said, looking back to Serah. "Either of you."

Serah frowned.

Creature spent the next half-hour pointing out brothels, torture chambers, brothel torture chambers, museums to carnage, museums to history, museums to the history of carnage, and similar redundancies. Serah became absolutely giddy at the prospect of visiting the Night Queen's Library even as it proved to be larger than a town and more books than she could possibly read in her lifetime. Regina's interest piqued when she found out there was a dragon aerie with over a hundred of the beasts. She almost stabbed a bonie trainer when he tried to whip one, which was misbehavior. We settled on her punching him in his skeletal jaw.

We reached the throne room doors, next to the Witch's Sun behind us, I was well and truly sick of this place. The Trickster had a comical number of locations in his chambers from shops to saunas to research facilities. All abandoned, but signs of the methods the King Below used to stave off his ennui.

"It's like the damned Imperial City forum," Serah said, sighing as we reached the top. "Only with more undead and less trinket shops."

"I think we passed three," Regina said. "I'd say the creator of this place was insane but that goes without saying doesn't it?"

"I swear I saw myself leaving a room at one point," Serah muttered.

Curse and Payne seemed as bewildered by the place as Serah and Regina, which surprised me as I would have expected both to have visited regularly. I then recalled they'd never gone up above the sixteenth level.

"Beyond here is the final test," Creature said, looking at the doors marked with three rings bound together.

I blinked. "*What* final test?"

CHAPTER 31

I sucked in my breath and grit my teeth. Once more, my body was flesh and blood. I hadn't even felt the transition or loss of power this time, possibly because of my proximity to the Crown. "*What final test?*"

"Oh, did I forget to mention that part?" Creature asked, feigning shock. "How atrocious of me."

Curse sniggered.

"You are displaying poor gratitude to the three who saved us," Payne said, looking between her father and husband. "Both of you."

"Gratitude is a human virtue," Creature sniffed the air with both nostrils. "You have too much of your mother in you sometimes."

"You have too much of yourself in you and not enough anything else," Payne replied. I was surprised by her approval.

"Would you kindly explain the test?" I asked, guessing this would be my fate for the next few centuries: constantly tested by the Formor and plotted against in ways both great and small. As a form of perdition, it wasn't a bad one.

"As you wish, milord," Creature said, looking at the doors. "You may have noticed the Formor and its sibling species are not the most peaceful or selfless of races."

"I am stunned," Serah said, dryly. "My world is coming undone at this revelation. Oh woe. Oh woe. The sky is falling."

"Maidens weep at this revelation," Regina added, her expression bored. "Men tear out their hair while begging the gods to slay them."

Creature looked back. "You are a sarcastic collection of mortals. You may survive this place, at least for a little while."

"Go on with your story," I said.

"When the King Below fell, there was much denial, but even more ambition," Creature said, rubbing his star metal necklace. "None of the Nine Heroes would touch the Crown of Weeping Gods and servants were able to spirit it away back into Everfrost's gates. They could have sacked the city at that point, but chose to retreat on massive airships."

"Airships?" I asked.

"Extremely slow forms of travel involving gas bags and magic," Regina explained. "You're better marching overland."

"It was an elite force meant to reinforce the Nine Heroes. Their retreat made tactical sense," Creature said, shrugging. "They had the Master's true name, so they were able to force him into open battle without fighting the rest of us. Whatever the case, it was decided amongst the Shadowkind leaders whoever wore the crown would rule in the King Below's place."

"Is the Crown that powerful?" Regina asked.

"Yes," Serah said, as if she knew from experience. She lifted her left hand and displayed the demonsteel ring there. The Ring of Nefras is only a fraction of the Crown's power but magnifies my own abilities several times. The Crown is said to be even more powerful."

Regina did a double take at the revelation Serah wore one of the Dark Lord's rings. "*When* were you going to tell me you were wearing a Wraith Knight's ring?"

"Never?" Serah said, grimacing. I sympathized. I was in no position to judge someone for a sharp tongue and ill-considered words.

Let alone secrets.

"It bestows godhood on the wielder," Creature said, rubbing his hands together. "Or, as close to it as can be achieved with items alone. We all dreamed of becoming the next King Below and commanding the legions of demons beneath our feet as well as the uncounted hosts of the Damned. None of the demons tried to claim it, so why not us?"

"Let me guess, the demons knew something you didn't," I said, smiling.

"Don't look so smug," Creature said. "We didn't understand the Crown was cursed until the first warchief who put it on transformed into ice and exploded."

"You'd think the freezing to death part would have been enough," Curse said.

"The King Below never used half-measures in his examples," Creature said. "Either way, we figured out how dangerous the Crown was."

"How many died trying it on?" I asked.

"Forty-seven," Creature replied. "Beings of every race, profession, and status."

"One would think you'd have learned after the first few," Regina said.

"Greed makes fools of us all," I said, frowning. "Which is an unfortunate statement given I'm about to try the Crown on myself."

"Perhaps we should wait to examine it first," Serah said, clutching her staff tighter with a pained expression on her face. "We haven't come this far so you can get yourself killed."

Regina put her hand on my shoulder. I pulled away. I did not want her comfort now, because each time made me aware of just how much I didn't deserve companions like her and Serah. I wanted them to turn away from me, forget they'd ever known me, and find happiness with each other.

I'd have to drive them away soon.

Otherwise, I'd lose my strength to do so.

"I think I have an idea of what the problem was," I said, getting a clearer sense of why the Trickster was haunting me in particular. "Open the door, Creature."

"As you wish."

Creature walked up to the door and it parted for him without having to move a muscle. It opened up to a throne room surprising in its simplicity. The room was grand, standing at least half an acre in size but lacking any adornments. The chamber was made of smooth black stone with a polish that reflected the bodies of visitors from all directions.

There were only a few banners bearing the King Below and Gods Below's seals, but none of the usual decor which filled the Southern Kingdom's throne rooms. Yet, in a way, this conjured its own sense of power. The sense of power conjured by the room's austerity had a strength all its own.

A long, thick, vertical carpet led from the door to a raised dais with three steps. Upon the dais was the Black Throne and upon said throne's seat rested the Crown of Weeping Gods. Both items were like staring into the sun, the source of all my power, indeed my continued existence in this realm, but terrifying as well.

Both items were made of the same substance as Chill's Fury. Demonsteel. Demonsteel was one of the rarest substances in the world because not only did it have to be mined in the World Below, but the tempering process required dragonfire as well as techniques lost to all but the greatest sorcerer-smiths. It was, however, one of the most powerful channels for magic in Three Worlds. Only star metal and moonsilver were of comparable levels of quality.

The Black Throne was a memorable-looking seat, shaped into the image of a black dragon's claw reaching up from the ground to embrace the occupant. It emblazed with the symbol, not of the King Below or the Gods Below, but the Three Circles. The symbol of the King Above, King Below, and Great Mother working together in unity for the betterment of the universe.

It was outlawed in all civilized nations.

There was an inscription in the old tongue of Terralan, creating an additional circle around the Three Circles: *Tahavan maethicus regintus al mahaem. Katal ak mon ut katalas.*"Which, translated roughly, meant, "Power shapes the one who wields it. Master yourself or be so mastered." It was good counsel, albeit wisdom the Trickster had never followed.

The Crown of Weeping Gods rested on a dark purple pillow, unguarded by man or beast. It was a jagged piece of metal, looking like it had been cut from a larger piece of Demonsteel rather than shaped in a forge. Like the Tower, it did not wholly exist in this world and it was easy to guess that was because Co'Fannon had infused much of the World Below into it.

Gods shouldn't need to have their power enhanced but the Lord Master Smith had figured out a way to make it so. Like the Cauldron of Names, it was a source of terrible power and temptation for anyone who wielded it. There was even a legend amongst Shadowkind that the Lawgiver had turned against his brother due to the power it bestowed. That was why the Lawgiver had made his inferior Crown of the All-Seeing Eye.

Looking at the crown before me, I believed it.

The power was unimaginable.

Not so much, the Trickster said. *It is in proportion to one's willingness to give oneself to the darkness. The man who can wield the full potential of the crown is the one who is surrounded by endless nothingness for all time. To master the crown is to know all things must crumble to dust and all beings, inevitably, must die. The void consumes all in the end.*

Every mortal knows that, I said, pitying the Trickster. *I am sorry you did not.*

I'm going to destroy you, the Trickster said, losing his sense of melancholy in an instance. *Completely and utterly, so not a trace of the person you are remains. I will probably regret it.*

I'm flattered, I said. *I intend to send you to the darkness with the crown, you realize, deprived of your crown and empire.*

That is too pleasant a fate, the Trickster replied. *End me forever.*

"The Black Throne has its own power," Creature said, looking at both items. "It is linked to the rulership of every demon, Formor, Spiderfolk, or otherwise in Two Worlds. Every person who swear the Black Oath to serve the King Below in secret does so by the Black Throne and has their souls bound by its power."

"What happens when people try to sit on it?" Regina asked.

"I have not the slightest idea," Creature said, frowning. "We were smart enough not to risk it."

Serah walked up beside me. "But not smart enough not to kill yourselves with an obviously cursed crown."

Creature shrugged. "I love my people, but consistency is not a quality of our blood."

"It is time," I said, walking forward in front of the group to my destiny.

I understood, now, the King Below's plan. Slain by the Nine Heroes, he'd made sure one of his Dark Lords had been kept in reserve so that there still might be someone tied to him by his power. Through Chill's Fury, I was connected to the Crown of Weeping Gods and thus linked to the Trickster's power. Our essences intertwined and as long as I existed, the God of Evil would continue to bedevil this world.

He had played me like a lute, directing me through my vanity and desire for atonement. With Regina at my side, I'd been set on a jousting course with the Nine Heroes while Serah was the perfect tool for guiding me toward the Crown of Weeping Gods. I wondered if the Trickster was able to influence her through Nefras' ring into seeking it out. It was possible that was how he'd learned about Regina in the first place and timed it so I met her on the Storm Giant Mountains.

Events had continued to serve the King Below's purposes, ending in the death of T'Clau as well as the destruction of both the Cauldron of Names and Hopebringer. Both weapons used to kill the King below were now eradicated, making any future strikes against him pointless. I'd also won the allegiance, after a fashion, of the Frostirons as well as Spiderfolk.

When I sat down upon the Black Throne and placed the Crown of Weeping Gods on my neck, it was very likely the Trickster would seize control of my body. The King Below would be reborn and I would have undone all of the Nine Heroes' work.

Clever.

I could feel the Trickster chuckling. *It's also entirely possible this is all wild coincidence. No, that wouldn't fit with your need for me to be the all-powerful monster you want me to be, would it? To think the road of ambition and conquest you've paved here was entirely the result of your own choices. That you craved the affection and approval of your lady-loves so much you were willing to build an empire for them. That you want to be remembered as the Dragon-Which-Walks, the second King Below, rather than the bastard who couldn't be satisfied with a hard, but peaceful life. You'd be **responsible** then and we can't have that.*

"It ends," I said aloud, believing this road was one not of my own choosing. "Fate has led me here. I believe Serah and Regina can stop you."

I would do everything in my power to hold the King Below back and drag him to the World Below with me. With that, so would end the reign of the God of Evil forever.

A fitting end.

I ascended the dais and lifted up the crown, putting it on the throne's arms before sitting down.

Nothing happened.

"Well, that was anti-climactic." Creature frowned. "I was sure there'd be more exploding frozen wraith-chunks."

Regina kicked him.

Hard.

Creature fell over, planted face-first on the ground.

"Don't kick my father!" Payne growled, spinning around with her knives drawn.

"Tell him not to be such an ass!" Regina shouted back, her hand on her sword.

"That'd be asking him not to be gray and ugly," Curse said, laughing.

Payne's stare could have withered a man's gentiles and caused them to fall off.

Curse's head slinked back into his shoulders.

"Put your weapons away," I said, feeling my face. I should be dead but, for whatever reason, I wasn't.

Much to my surprise, Payne did, without hesitation.

She looked confused.

"Oh no," Creature muttered, getting up. "*That's* what it does."

Congratulations, Jacob, the Trickster said. *You now have bound the entirety of the Shadowkind races to you as well as all those who have sworn the Black Oath. You have more power and authority than any human king could ever dream of having. It will follow you even after you step off this throne.*

I lifted the Crown of Weeping Gods, staring at it. *I thought I was going to become you.*

The Trickster made a hmph noise in my head. *Yes, because I'm a riddle so easily solved as that. But if you really believe you are nothing more than a pawn of destiny, place the crown on your head.*

I stared at the Crown of Weeping Gods for a long time, realizing I'd let myself be a puppet this entire time. For the Grand Temple, for Jassa, for the Trickster, and now what I thought the latter wanted. The last time I'd made a choice for myself was when I'd killed that soldier and been exiled from the Riverfords.

It was easier to let other people think for me. I looked up at Regina and Serah, realizing how stupid and selfish I'd been. How I willingly endangered them so I wouldn't have to live with the guilt of what I'd done. I was a monster unworthy of love, there was no doubt of that, but the consequences of my action were my own.

It was time I became master of my own destiny.

I tossed the Crown of Weeping Gods to one side. "I do not take slaves or keep them. I believe in the Reforms and regret only that they became an excuse for bloodshed and tyranny. I order you to make your own choices and never follow my commands unless it is your will. I dissolve the Black Oath and the bindings."

The magic of the Iron Throne turned in on itself, snapped, and vanished.

"I will be your King," I said, staring at them. "But it will be if you desire such. You may choose to try and serve yourselves but you've had years to do that and all you ended up doing was epically fucking up both yourselves and others. I stand by my promise of prosperity but I will rule my way, not yours."

Creature, Payne, and Curse stared at me.

"You are completely mad, you realize that, correct?" Payne said, staring at me.

"Yes," I said, smiling. "Regina and Serah are your queens now. Equal to me as the moons are to the night."

"Um, Jacob?" Regina said, raising a hand in protest. "You might have asked—"

"We accept," Serah said, interrupting her.

Creature muttered something. "This is going to be an enormous pain in the ass to resolve. I accept on my behalf, though. I'm not going to allow another T'Clau to take us over and I wasn't strong enough to overthrow you, mad and stupid as you are."

"Good," I said, pointing to the door. "Go spread the word. I have business to attend to?"

"What kind of business?" Curse asked.

"I'm going to the forge. I need time to think."

CHAPTER 32

In the Forge of Fallen Stars, I hammered steel.

I hammered Moonsilver.

I hammered Daemonsteel.

I hammered darkness itself.

The pounding of hammer against anvil was a song I knew well. It was strange how life tended to move in circles. I had been born a fisherman's son, but apprenticed to a blacksmith and even after all the things I'd become thereafter: Squire, Temple Knight, Shadowguard, Knight Paramount, Reformer, Wraith Knight, and now King—I still loved the sound of shaping metal.

The Forge of Fallen Stars was exactly like I'd remembered it: a monument to function and simplicity. There were rows of shelves filled with metal samples, tools, and pieces of equipment I'd created for more complex work. A small library of rune schematics was indexed in a plain cabinet ordered alphabetically.

I had created the Forge of Fallen Stars during my time as Kurag and it was designed for maximum efficiency. The fact it had been created with the murder of a Messenger and there was a sixty-foot-long Grand Red Dragon's lair next door with a hole for her to stick her head through were the only parts I objected to now. The latter, mostly, because Smoke insisted on chatting with me as I worked.

"So what are you working on now?" Smoke asked, popping her gigantic bone-ridge-covered head in for the seemingly thousandth time.

Smoke's head was almost my size in height and twice again as wide, long with a massive mouth of teeth like steak knives. You could see little spurts of flame with her every word from inside, pouring out steam whenever the forge wasn't hot enough to match the Tower's eternally frozen atmosphere.

Smoke was one of the Demon Dragons, a race possessed by Fallen Messengers who'd offered their services to the King Below in exchange for freedom from the Lawgiver's edicts. Despite this, or perhaps because of it, she was a very personable entity with very little in the way of the Formor's aggressiveness.

"A sword," I said, pulling out a chisel to work on my masterpiece's final runes.

I had no idea how long I'd been down here and the Tower of Everfrost had a way of shaping time so it didn't really matter. The fact I didn't need sleep, food, rest, or water contributed to the fact I had little knowledge of how much time was passing.

There were no windows in the Forge either, leaving me to count the time passing in the amount of work I was doing, and I stopped counting soon after beginning. I was here to regain a sense of myself and the only way to do that was through creation.

My present work was a blade for Regina and had consumed me every bit as much as the thrones and a staff for Serah had. I'd been possessed by a fever since coming down here and the work I'd produced was greater than anything I'd ever dreamed of accomplishing.

I possessed only a fraction of Tharadon and Co'Fannon's total knowledge yet I'd taken the basis of Chill's Fury, analyzed it, and removed all flaws before perfecting its strengths. It was a masterpiece of creation and I doubt I would be able to match its greatness again.

"Is it a good sword?" Smoke asked, showing a childishness which belied the fact she was probably smarter than half the continent put together.

"Yes," I said, carving the true name of Regina into the runes before melting moonsilver over the signs, binding the sword to her power forever.

I had deduced both her and Serah's true names during my work.

As well as the true name for metal and magic.

I wasn't sure how I was going to deal with these revelations, but I'd put both true names to work in my creations for them. Finishing the last of the bindings, I plunged the sword into water taken from the River of Souls and felt the power of creation leave me.

I was done.

"It is a great sword," I said, taking a deep but useless breath. "A monument to craftsmanship."

Smoke lazily rested her head down on the ground before turning it to one side. "I think you need a little less craftsmanship and a little more industry in the Southern Kingdoms, to be honest."

"Oh?" I asked, feeling like I needed to sit down.

"Oh, yes," Smoke said, blinking her big yellow reptilian eyes. "The Southern Kingdoms are fascinating, from what I've seen when I go down there to take human form or fly over. There's all manner of amazing little machines and objects of power. However, each is hand-built and a unique work of art. Take ten magic swords and you'll get ten wildly different weapons with varying powers."

"I don't see a problem," I said, putting down my forge hammer and conjuring a chair of darkness to sit down on.

Smoke continued, "Formor are different. For every sidhe-forged sword of legend which can kill fifty men with one blow, the Formor manufacture a hundred magic swords that can kill two. All of them identical and easily trained with as well as replaced."

"And by comparison, pieces of shit."

I'd never been terribly impressed with Formor creations even if they were solid and dependable creations. Smoke was speaking the truth, though. Treasure-hunting was a common pastime amongst the mercenaries and lesser nobles of the South. You never knew when a dead man's blade or armor might mean the difference between being arrow practice or an invincible warrior on the battlefield.

Warmaster Kalian had taught me some strange things before sending me to the Grand Temple, including always checking out swap meets of villages. He'd found his legendary armor and lance for sale at bargain cost, allowing him to become the champion that would make him famous. It had been hell on tactics taking every individual's equipment into account when planning raids on the Formor.

Smoke turned her head back over. "Not always. Look outside and you'll see a city which thrives on individuals building on top of each other's works. Alchemists and forge-sorcerers down below horde their knowledge in like Tharadon, keeping it as a gift to dole out at Summer Solstice. Here, the sciences are freely shared and grow in strange new directions."

"I thought half of that outside was created from knowledge taken from the World Below?"

"Only half."

"So you want the Southern Kingdoms to become more like the Children of Orkis?" I asked, shaking my head.

"Not at all," Smoke said. "The Formor are limited by their culture of war and tyranny. They're not very imaginative, to be frank. I was just wondering what sort of wonders could be achieved if you combined the two. A united Northern Wasteland and Southern Kingdoms each building off each other's strengths. It could be a paradise of smoke and steel."

"As much as I love foundries, it's never fun to live downstream from where they're made."

"Say that again knowing every large town has a sewer to wash away refuse and hot baths thanks to Formor techniques you stole during the last war."

I blinked, and then burst out laughing. "That is a *very* good point."

The Formor had managed to carve out a reasonably comfortable existence, brutal overlord aside, in Everfrost. Many of the villages outside of the kingdom, though, barely scraped by at a Post-Judgment level. If the Formor's techniques were adapted for peaceful purposes, they might not need to conquer the South for resources.

Or maybe I was fooling myself.

I'd come down here to find myself and, after who knew how long, I still felt like I wasn't entirely sure who Jacob Riverson was. Despite knowing my true name, or perhaps because of it, I was aware of how much I'd drifted through life. I had lines I wouldn't cross, ones which hadn't prevented me from doing evil but I realized were necessary as well as important even in their hypocrisy. I also had faith in the Path, as far as I'd strayed from it.

I also needed Regina and Serah, which was awkward now since I'd pushed them into each other's path while feeling entirely inappropriate feelings for a friend. Both had come to visit me during my work and I checked up on them regularly with magic—as much as possible in this place as well.

They were together and taking on all challenges.

I approved.

Indeed, one was due for a visit anytime now. They had a way of showing up whenever I finished one of my creations. As if on cue, I heard Regina's footsteps coming down the stairs to my location. She had changed her attire to a very modest blue wool dress, white linen shirt, and her hair tied into a modest braid down the side of her left shoulder. It was attire related to, but different, from the kind the Reformer women of my era wore.

I found it very fetching.

"That's unexpected attire," I said, surprised. "I wouldn't think of you as taking off your armor around here."

Regina lifted a shield bracelet, hidden on her wrist. "I am not stupid. Still, armor is impractical for helping the Formor reform their medical care. They are very efficient healers but moving them from killing their elderly, deformed, and maimed will take some work."

I gave a pained smile. "They are free for the first time in their history. That will take some adjustment."

"Are they free?" Regina asked.

"No one is, really," I said, sighing. "But if they ever ask me to leave, I will."

"They would be foolish to do so," Regina said, keeping her expression even. "I've felt your presence checking up on Serah and I."

I looked down, embarrassed. "Yes, that one time--"

"We weren't doing anything shameful, just having sex," Regina said, having changed her point of view on the subject. She looked me in the eyes. "You've been here a long time."

"I haven't been—"

"Two weeks."

I blinked.

"Three months from my perspective," Smoke said, raising her head off the floor. "One project after another, complete and utter focus. I'd admire such dedication if not for the fact it was the product of a man running away from his problems."

"That is impressive," Regina observed.

I walked over to the sword I'd just completed and removed it from where I'd dunked it before wrapping its hilt in living shadow. The blade glowed with a light of its own as the runes carried the captured light of the heavens.

"For you," I said, turning the blade around and presenting the hilt to her.

Regina took the blade and stared at it, opening her mouth and gazing at it for a good minute as she tested out with several practice swings. Bringing it low, she struck my anvil and sliced through the front end.

"Jacob, this is an extraordinary gift," Regina said, staring at it.

"As my poor anvil just found out."

"Sorry." Regina flushed with embarrassment, then laughed. "I think you can get another one."

"True," I said, gesturing to the blade. "This is a sword similar to those wielded by the Dark Lords, but transforms the darkness it channels from the World Below into light. It bestows the wielder with strength, magic, and defense against attack the more it is used. Furthermore, the blade will be stronger with time."

It would also bestow immortality of a far kinder type than my own.

The world needed warriors like Regina.

Regina lifted the blade up and held it in front of her like a reversed cross. "Does it have a name?"

"I believe you are the one who should give it one."

Regina stared at it. "Starlight. Let it be a bringer of comfort and beacon to those lost in the night."

I looked at her, taking in her soft features and wishing I could wrap my arms around her. "Starlight it is. Though, the metaphor is a bit on the nose."

I handed Regina a sheath for her new blade, which would protect the wearing from losing any blood. She tied it to her waist and placed Starlight within. "It is better to be clear about such things rather than obscure. I am worried about you, Jacob."

"I am fine," I lied.

Regina's gaze cut through me like Starlight would.

"As much as an undead wizard knight can be," I said, frowning. "You know, who leads an empire of evil built over the Hundred Hells."

Regina looked at me, almost pitying. "I am not a good person, Jacob."

I looked confused. "Excuse me?"

"I've met you three times and say categorically you are the best person who has visited this place," Smoke said. "Not in chains, at least."

"Please stay out of this conversation, Smoke," I said.

"As you wish."

"I try to be, but it's s a falsehood," Regina said, sighing. "Every day I struggle with how much I hate the Nine Heroes and how many lives I am willing to sacrifice to bring them down. I was willing to start a war to destroy them and plunge Accadia into a conflict it didn't have a torch's chance in the World Below of winning. When I called to you on that mountaintop, I knew you were a Dark Lord, I was just desperate to survive. I was even willing to call upon the powers of darkness and when I saw you were amenable, I played upon your guilt to align your power with mine. I was willing to wield a Wraith's Knights powers against my enemies if it meant getting revenge. Which I have gotten a portion of, in no small part thanks to you. I also knew about Serah's feelings but I didn't want to hurt her. I would rather have her friendship and sleep with her than lose the former by breaking her heart. This despite the fact my heart belongs to another."

"I know." I had figured out quite a bit of that at the forge. Knowing the true names of those you cared for was an awful experience. It had taken weeks of hammering to get my feelings clear on the pair. "I also know Serah was trying to seduce me to get closer to the Crown of Weeping Gods. Before she lost Thomas, she was intending to seize it, and then banish me to the World Below. Serah loves you dearly but she also loves power and to go down in history as someone important. Serah is here not to reform the Formor armies or help me become human, but because this is a chance to be part of history. She's not above manipulating you, either, since she's the one who keeps sending you down here. Both because she wants to keep me on her side as well as to soothe your own feelings of longing."

Regina half-closed her eyes. She was silent for over a minute. "So where does that leave us?"

"I love you," I said, muttering. "You and Serah both. Not as a sibling or companion but as a man loves a woman." It would have been much simpler if I loved Regina alone but I couldn't deny my attraction to Serah's ambitious, calculating nature.

All too similar to Jassa's.

Regina's expression fell as she sighed. "You should have spoken up earlier."

I closed my eyes.

"Though I feel..." Regina trailed off. She put her hand over her chest. "I feel the same. I want to be with you."

I smiled.

"Which puts us both in a very awkward position!" Regina snapped. "I am *very* cross with you."

I opened my mouth, unsure how to respond to that.

That was when there was the sound of an explosion from outside the forge.

Followed by many more.

CHAPTER 33

My war never ended.

I grabbed Serah's staff and ran up the stairs to the Tower's interior. I had a chance, albeit a small one, of escaping this endless conflict when I'd first emerged from my living slumber. I'd chosen to fight in Regina's war, later in Serah's, and had begun my name. The Trickster had been right in this, though, I could not put down my blade because I'd been wielding it too long.

The War Sickness was upon me.

And I did not know a way out.

When we emerged from the Forge, it was to in the site of an ongoing battle. Massacre would be a better term for it as I saw the remaining Deathless I'd created were spread across the ground of the tower, half of them burned to ashes or torn to pieces with the remainder scattered.

A group of seven noon-magic-wielding undead threw bolts of fire at an assailant, only for three columns of dragonfire to strike them simultaneously and burn them to nothingness. I looked up to see the sight of what had destroyed them and, if not for the fact I was an undead, damned ice ghost, I would have said my blood ran cold.

The thing was horrific beyond description, seven yellow dragon heads rising from its massive armored base propped up by a dozen legs. From its mouth belched forth golden fire, incinerating Spiderfolk and Formor with causal malevolent glee. It possessed wings made of flame that sent forth waves of heat, scorching everything which tried to flank it as well as knocking away those who sought to attack with giant bats or ravens. A long tail stretched out from the monster's back, smashing through stalactite palaces and destroying everything it could. The creature was as large and half again as Smoke, who was an empire killer to herself.

Worse, as the Tower's Shadowkind warriors tried to retaliate, it deflected all attacks with a barrier stronger than the one protecting Accadia. I could feel the living inferno of Noon magic burning within it like a second sun. So powerful, it reduced the immense strength I drew from Everfrost by half and seemed to cause the entire tower to shudder.

"Great Mother," Regina whispered, staring at the thing in abject horror.

I could only hold my mouth open and wish to every god I was asleep and this was some terrible phantasm conjured by my unconscious.

But no, this was all too real.

Someone had recreated the Great Abomination of Natariss.

"Bastards and Hellspawn," I said, drawing Chill's Fury, even though I might as well have been pulling a bee's sting.

"Is that what I think it is?" Regina said, pulling out Starlight.

"Yes," I said. "It is."

"Lawgiver preserve us."

If their use of blood magic, human sacrifice, and heresy wasn't enough to divorce them from all civilized peoples then the abominations

were proof enough they were beyond redemption. The Natariss frequently fused human slaves with animal aspects or other animals together for various tasks. Many of the creatures which presently bedeviled the world today, both good and evil, owed their life to Natariss flesh-sculpting. The Great Abomination was the Natarins' attempt at creating a god.

Not content to communicate with the Gods Above the way all men did through prayer and meditation, they had sought to create a vessel they might summon an Archmessenger into so they could receive their guidance directly. Fusing dragons together, for they were considered holy by the Natariss the way gryphons were by the Imperials, they had succeeded in calling *something* from beyond. That something had laid waste to whole swaths of their land before moving onto others, becoming the doom which felled the ancient kingdom of Qadash and drove the Nockers into retreat underground. In the end, it had only been defeated by an alliance of sidhe High Lords working in concert with the four Dark Lords.

What madman would bring back such a monster?

You know, the Trickster said. *Or will, soon enough.*

Coming up beside us was Serah, who wielded her staff and was covered in blood, which (thankfully) wasn't hers.

"We have a problem."

"We noticed," Regina said, tapping her shield bracelet and conjuring a mystical suit of shadow plate armor over her body. It covered her completely and shielded her head in a faceless black reflective helmet, which left only her braid visible.

"We have to defend the people here," I said, tossing Serah the staff I'd made for her. It was every bit as powerful as Starlight but we did not have time for ceremony.

Serah caught it with her spare hand, intending to wield both it and her ghostwood staff at once. "If we die defending a bunch of orkis and scrumpkins, I'm going to haunt you both."

"Don't worry, I'll be dead too."

"That is not a comfort!"

This creature, formidable as it is, is but a distraction. Abandon the insects to their fate and go to the Crown of Weeping Gods. There, you will meet your true enemy, the Trickster said.

I was already charging at the abomination.

Why do I even bother? The Trickster murmured.

In the heart of Everfrost's power, I conjured a Nuckelavee without a ritual in front of me and leapt on its back, willing it to fly forward. The creature was less chatty than its counterpart and maneuvered through the three bursts of dragonfire the Great Abomination spewed at me.

As I got close, I lifted Chill's Fury and spoke the blackest magic I could do. A seven-foot-tall column of living entropy manifested around the end of my blade and I launched myself from the back of my steed to jab it into the neck of the central neck. The enhanced blade slid through the creature's barrier and stabbed into its neck, going through the other side but doing very little damage. Its blood covered me, though, and that provided a channel.

I pulled the massive amount of hellish energy suffusing the tower into the Doom Blade spell and spread it through the entirety of the monster. A storm of black lightning assaulted the barrier even as ran up and down my body, the barrier buckling underneath my attack. It also weakened the whole of Everfrost's magic.

Despite the fact Everfrost had been constructed by *a god.*

Who created this beast!?

I didn't get a chance to enjoy even this pyrrhic victory, though, because one of the Great Abominations' heads grabbed me in its massive jaws and clamped into teeth into my armor and flesh. I was shaken like a dog with a rabbit before the creature hurled my prone form through the air, sending it hurtling to the ground.

I would have splattered against the ground like an egg if not for Serah raising her old staff and speaking words of light magic that reduced the speed of my fall to a gentle descent. Still, I would have been dead with my organs leaking out of my body if not for the fact I was a ghost and let my physical form dissolve back into nothingness.

Serah was strong enough not to get distracted from her task, though, and cast aside her old staff to fully embrace my own. She called forth the energy of the Great Abomination's damaged barrier and channeled it to reinforce her own, which came in handy as the monster breathed forth dragonfire from all seven heads down onto her. Somehow, it held, but I suspected without the item, even a Great Wizard would have been killed.

Regina took advantage of the monster's distraction to charge forward herself, swinging Starlight and cutting massive holes through the monster's legs one at a time. The creature howled in agony, one of its heads coming down to bite her in two, only for Regina to dodge out of the way, mount the back of its neck and swing her sword to half-decapitate it and finish the job with her second blow. Regina threw herself off the monster's neck and rolled against the ground as it flew backwards. The headless stalk flailed about uselessly, spewing blackish blood which caught fire when it hit the ground.

That was when Creature and his children attacked.

The Great Abomination was struck by fiery-hot breath from the back of Smoke as the Grand Dragon was ridden by Creature. Creature rained down a veritable swarm of lightning, frost-bolts, witchfire, and hell crows summoned from the World Below all at once. Somehow, he'd successfully stored a dozen or so spells to release at one time. A trick I would have to learn from him.

Payne, meanwhile, threw one of her dragonbone daggers into one of the creature's eyes then struck another and another, missing only once out of seven. The daggers promptly exploded once they hit, blinding the creature even as they destroyed the priceless weapons. The Abomination attacked randomly with its blinded heads, breathing fire and death down at her position, but she moved from shadow to shadow using Bone Knife magic.

Curse? Curse simply peppered the Great Abomination with powerful explosive rune arrows from a safe position. The difference between him and so many other archers being his seemed powerful enough to actually damage it, at least with its weakened barrier.

Climbing to my feet, I looked over to see the ruined and maimed form of my mount, the demon having been bitten in half by two dragon heads working simultaneously. Summoning Chill's Fury to my hand with a spell, I ran toward the Great Abomination. The Shadowkind had started rallying to defend us, even as their attacks did little but keeping the Great Abomination's barrier from regenerating.

That was enough.

That was when Regina, having struck a second off the monster, was blasted full-force by dragonfire in the back. Her flaming body slid off the side of the dragon's neck and landed on the ground, continuing to burn.

I don't recall the next few minutes.

I remember screaming in anguish, slamming my sword into the ground, and freezing the entirety lower-half of monster in a glacier I'd never have been able to conjure if I'd been thinking rationally. Everything thereafter vanished into a red mist of running up the side of the ice and slashing at the necks, snapping heads, necks, and body with unchecked rage. Somehow, that didn't impact my skill at dodging or stabbing, though. Chill's Fury became a deadly instrument of revenge and I fought like a man possessed.

The blade seemed to draw strength from my suffering with each blow dealing three times as much damage as they'd normally do. Two more of the Great Abomination's heads fell to the ground even as the others were all grievously wounded by my attacks. The Great Abomination's barrier was gone and there was nothing protecting it from the full fury of my companion's attacks that focused their wrath against its body. The monster surprised me by retaliating with spells spoken in a deep, gravelly tongue, which killed more of the Shadowkind around us. It even tried to animate some of the dead, only to have those creatures seized from it by Serah's superior control.

In the end, though, the final two heads of the monster perished not by my hands but by Starlight being shoved through the creature's frozen lower half. The sword I'd forged hacked through the ice and carved a path through flaming gore to the monster's heart. Then the weapon was plunged into the still-beating organ to drain away the mystical inferno which kept it alive. The messenger, demon, or thing inside was killed, passing its strength onto the sword's wielder.

Regina.

Regina stood, naked and covered in flaming gore, seemingly unharmed. Her original had had burned away but a new set of moonlight white locks trailed over her shoulders. She breathed heavily, but looked like she was in shock, holding Starlight as if she wasn't entirely sure she still alive.

Sliding down the side of the monster's corpse, I landed beside her while Serah stumbled towards us.

"Regina!" I said, staring at her. "How..."

Regina, rocking on her feet said, "Would someone please cast a cleaning cantrip? That is in the arsenal of dark wizards, is it not?"

I conjured yet another shadow throne for her, which she collapsed in. Serah, upon arrival, cast the aforementioned cleaning cantrip and left her looking like she'd taken a less impressive hot bath. To preserve her modesty, I removed my cloak and conjured another suit of armor around her, this clinging to her body like a tailor-made dress.

Regina, after several more breaths, said, "It would appear your sword can protect individuals from fire."

"It would appear so," I said, acknowledging that. Given it was designed to fill her with light energy the way I was filled with dark and make her more alive--that made a certain amount of sense. I didn't entirely understand all of my creation's abilities it seemed. I would have to rectify that.

"Who could have created such a thing?" Serah asked, looking at the monster's remnants. "It took a hundred master mages a year and a half to create the original Great Abomination."

"There is one," I said, knowing who was a greater master of Natariss blood magic than all of their ancient masters and modern philosophers combined.

She'd have had centuries to practice too.

"We need to get to the throne room immediately," I said, realizing what the Trickster said.

Creature brought smoke down beside us. "Why do I have a feeling the ancient monster of legend, which isn't ours for once, is the least of our problems?"

I climbed onto Smoke's back as both Curse and Payne both ran up to get on as well. Regina got up, only for Serah to stop her. Regina gave Serah such a glare, the latter took a step back, and allowed her to join us on the mount.

Serah, by contrast, simply cast a spell to levitate upwards.

I was going to have to learn that from her.

Soaring through the air, our arrival at the top of the Tower was a lot faster the second time around. It was as if Everfrost wanted us to arrive. Given I expected the enemy of it and all said building stood for was about to seize ultimate power, that wasn't surprising. Smoke couldn't bring us past the witchfire sun, but we dismounted on the path leading up to it. The sun, which was the source of the immense mystical energy infusing the tower, looked faded and I knew something was cancelling out its power.

Something which was so antithetical to the King Below, I was barely any stronger than in Accadia.

What had happened to her?

Running up the path with the rest of my group in tow, I saw the throne doors were ripped clean off their hinges. Passing through the door without bothering to look inside, I stopped only when I saw the figure standing over the throne. She was standing over the Crown of Weeping Gods, working on an enchantment I expected was designed to unmake the legendary artifact.

Or break its curse to be harnessed by the King Above.

She stopped as soon as we arrived.

I sucked in my breath. "Hello, Jassamine."

CHAPTER 34

Looking upon Jassa was something I'd never expected to do again this side of the afterlife and maybe not even then. She was like a vision from the World Above and I may have been more right in that than I expected. Even if I couldn't look at her now without feeling a mixture of horror and disgust. Jassa had changed, that much was clear. No long was she the shy retiring girl from my early memories or even the fanatical murderess from my later ones. No, instead, she looked like a goddess. A terrible goddess of wrath and zeal but a goddess, nonetheless.

Her age was frozen in its mid-thirties, but there was a timelessness about her which made her look both young and old at once. Gone were all the imperfections of her features and her smooth olive skin was now a brilliant brown color which shined like the sun. Jassa's long black hair was curly and lustrous, capturing the light from the torches around us before reflecting it outward.

Around her were the flowing yellow-white robes of a Great Wizardess and, looking upon her, I knew her to be Jassamine the Golden. In her left hand was a carved white ghostwood staff, the six-foot-tall object topped with a crystal ball containing a shimmering rainbow.

Jassa was the most beautiful woman in the world but it was not the beauty of a lover or wife but the gorgeousness of a sunrise or storm. I had never felt so terrified in my life before, being in her presence, save perhaps once. That was when I'd been at the foot of the King Below, facing the immortal god-king with my deceased monarch below me. Jassa was no longer a human woman, looking upon her told me that much.

What was she now? And did I have the courage to destroy her? The memories of her murdering the Princesses left me feeling uncertain and confused. I'd chosen to overlook a monstrous crime because I loved her. My love had broken me and destroyed everything good inside me.

It had also driven me to suicide. I had gone to the fields of Winterholme to die, I knew that now. I had destroyed Kurag because I had fought like a man who had no desire to live. The King Below had recognized this and given me a gift by making me a Dark Lord: making me forget the horrors I'd turned a blind eye to. I was not the same man I was before. I was not going to let her harm the people here. I would stop her, no matter the cost.

I could imagine the Trickster laughing about this now.

Betrayal by those you love isn't funny, the Trickster said. *To me at least.*

"Jassa?" I stared at her, my voice like ice. "*How?*"

Jassa stared at me then looked up to the Heavens. "When I saw you struck down by the blade of the King Below, I ran to your side, only to meet my death soon after. Yet, where you passed into the hands of darkness, I walked through the valleys of frost and darkness to scale a mountain of light. The Lawgiver had witnessed my deeds done in the name of bringing peace and justice to the world, so he joined his essence with mine. I was reborn as a being of fire and brilliance. Look upon me, my love, and know that I am Jassamine, the chosen vessel for the God Above All."

I looked at her with eyes as both a creature of darkness and a man. I saw past her skin to the being underneath and was almost blinded by her brilliance. Hers was no mortal woman's soul, but a being which seemed to shake the very foundations of the world. It was like staring into the sun, its radiance threatening to burn me away. She told the truth. She was touched by the God of Good and blessed. It was also an inhuman light. I saw nothing but white emptiness within her. Within was an embodiment of perfection with no possibility of change, growth, or learning. She was as she was when she first joined with the Lawgiver and would nothing more forever

If this was the King Above's idea of good, I wanted no part of it.

"Indeed," Jassa said, proud and regal. "I am his reliquary, just as the Dark Lords were the King Below's. I exist to show the world's peoples the Path and cast down those who would tempt mortals away from it."

Funny, the Trickster said. *It was the King Above who told me to start tempting mortals in the first place. He's just upset I did such a good job. Ingrate.*

All of my companions stood there, silent, as if entranced by her presence in a way beyond words. I likely would have been the same if not for the fact I knew Jassa intimately and was carrying around the opposite of the Lawgiver's essence. One by one, the pieces fell into place in my mind. The Trickster had been manipulating me this entire time, not to rebirth him but to create a foil as revenge against his brother's plans. How much he'd foreseen beyond his death was difficult to say but I now knew the architect of the Southern Kingdom's woes.

"You are the Nine Heroes' patron," I said, sorting through the clues which had been there all the time. I should have realized there was a greater hand in all this the moment Bloodthorn had mentioned a Golden Sorceress. "They answer to you."

"I am the last of the true Great Wizards. The others have all failed their appointed tasks. I drove Valance to the distant shores and took his place. The heroes the stones by which a new Grand Temple will be built to the King Above All's glory."

I'd witnessed terrible things in my vision from the Cauldron of Names. Regina had not been exaggerating the rivers of blood being spilled. The Nine Heroes were killing people with a fury and speed only those filled with righteousness could perform. Empress Morwen and her armies were but one finger on a nine-fingered fist which was choking the life out of the world. I had killed one of her champions, but the loss of Jon Bloodthorn would not impact their ambitions.

She had to be stopped.

I had helped create this horror.

"No," I heard Regina whisper, her voice shaking in horror. "The Lawgiver *cannot* approve of what Empress Morwen is doing. You are a murderer of children and a betrayer of everything the Path stands for! You have slavery, superstition, and fear where the King Above is supposed to bring hope!"

I could but imagine what this was like for her. It was one thing to stand against the heroes the rest of the world believed in. It was another to know the gods of good were on your enemies' side.

"I am the truth. Your merciful and sympathetic god is the lie," Jassa said, beaming with inner righteousness.

Regina's eyes became fierce and she pointed at Jassa with her broken blade. "You are an abomination!"

Serah stared. "I complete my resignation and swear my black oath to the Broken Throne. By my choice do I spite thee, enemy of man."

"As if you were ever *not* damned." Jassamine let out a tinkle of melodious laughter, which sounded like a thunderclap. "For too long, man has endeavored to profane the gods with his petty wars and idolatries. They have raised false idols and kings which have distracted from the glories of the World Above while spilling each other's blood in his name. No longer! The King Below was sent five times to menace the world in hopes of uniting them against true evil. Let the New Path be the guiding light for all beings and justice reign. If a tongue speaks against the Lawgiver, so shall it be pulled from its mouth and if a heart turns from his glories, so shall it be ripped out! Let all monarchs be but criers for the Lawgiver's words and devoid of their own failings! Let all nations unite in the glory of worshiping He-Who-Is-Perfect!"

I was too stunned by everything going on to process what she was saying. Instead, I drove my thoughts inward.

Is what she says true? I asked.

Whatever I say will matter little. If you believe in my brother, you will carry his words even past him, the Trickster said. *If you honor him, you will do so even against him. Or you can simply walk your oath path. We were not the first gods and it was the Elder Ones who lead us to this place to educate your kind. We have strayed from that task. All of us except our sister.* He paused. *Sorry about lying about her survival. In my defense, it was funny at the time.*

The string of profanity I directed at him was more foul than anything I have said in two-and-a-half-Ages of life.

Regina fell back against the wall, sliding against it. This was too much for her to take. "What of mercy? Is there no place for it in the new world?"

"In the World-That-Is-To-Come, there is mercy beyond belief. Mercy that heathens shall be cast down to perdition lest they infect others with their horror. Is it not more merciful to correct the child with a beating than suffer it to grow astray?"

"The innocent are dying in your wars!" Regina choked out. "The Nine Heroes are tyrants. I beg of you, turn away from this path! Thousands of dead! Tens of thousands!"

"*Millions* will perish to remake the world in the image of our king and master. Yet, this should not to be mourned for the Lawgiver shall take up their spirits to his breast and give them a hollowed place amongst his cherubs. Mourn, instead, those who are not innocent who can only be purged by fire and blood."

It was useless.

She was mad.

Still, I could not bring myself to raise my sword.

I was as guilty of her.

Of the same crimes no less.

"And what of the Shadowkind?" Creature, the wizened old goblin, said, walking with his gnarled cane toward the glowing brilliance of my transformed lover. "Where do we stand in your *glorious* Lawgiver's plan?"

Creature's children, Curse and Payne, moved to the shadows behind them. Both of them were still transfixed by Jassa's brilliance. I could not blame them for such, because I was as much as them. Creature shamed me by his defiance.

Jassa smiled, her heart-shaped pink lips contrasting against her glowing skin. "The Shadow Races have been led astray by the King Below and his minions. Your physical bodies are tainted with his presence. Such evil corrupts and malforms the pure souls which lie within, souls which have suffered because of this Fallen World around them. Know that in this time of reckoning, the Lawgiver's infinite mercy shall be extended even unto the dogs and vermin. Kneel down, Creature, and be remade as a glorious being purged of taint. Go forth and preach the Path. Know the penitent shall be tempered in the forge of his glory while the prideful shall be turned to slag."

Creature looked up at her, meeting her gaze without fear. "I think not."

Jassa stared. "So be it, *worm*."

Her next words were a whisper and yet caused Creature to explode. Curse and Payne were finally shaken enough to rush to their dead father's burning remains.

"No!" I shouted, spinning around to look at the callous act of murder.

Jassa turned to me, ignoring the pair. "As for you, dear sweet Jacob, you have suffered beyond belief. It is your tribulation to have been used as the King Below's puppet to punish, rend, and maim those fools who the Lawgiver has turned his back upon. Yet, your suffering is about to come to an end. Bow down upon the ground and receive your salvation. Through the Lawgiver's power, I will restore you to life and send you on a new task. Your rewards will be great for you have suffered much."

I stared at Creature's ashes, both his children too stunned to move at their father's murder. I suspected the aura of light magic Jassa projected enhanced their guilt. They were being made to feel unclean for all the actions they'd done so that her offer might seem enticing. That the murder she'd just committed might seem like justice.

Creature and I had not known each other long and I had been raised to hate his kind but he had been an affable sort. He'd also been willing to die for his beliefs. "Do you think I have ever cared about *rewards?*"

Jassa's voice, for the first time, contained a hint of the woman she once was. "You have always only cared about me, winning the war, your creations, and the Reforms."

I looked down. *"Yes."*

That was mistake.

My greatest flaw.

But could I kill someone I'd loved and held in my arms? Someone who I had wronged by not directing her from the path we'd both walked?

"You could do this in the Lawgiver's service. Replace Jon Bloodthorn or T'Clau and I will forgive you." All trace of warmth left Jassa's face. "You never had the stomach to murder children, but every other conceivable atrocity you were willing to perform in order to build a force capable of throwing back the King Below. That strength is what we need now."

I was looking at a mirror. I had become a shadow of my former self, literally so, in the pursuit of defeating darkness. By seeking to fight monsters, I had become one. By opposing a king of ice, I'd created a Queen of Flame.

This was my fault.

"Do you believe in the Path, my love?" Jassa said the last two words like they were ones she hadn't spoken in centuries.

She probably hadn't. Not that she knew what love was. I had been blinded. Those who did things like this didn't know a damned thing about love. Regina had her hand on her sword while Serah had hers on her staff, but neither could move, Jassa's radiance keeping them still even as I could tell both women wanted to launch themselves at her.

"I believe in the Path," I said, whispering.

Jassa smiled.

"And I believe you and the Lawgiver have fallen from it!" I said, lifting my blade.

Jassa lifted her staff's bottom six inches off the ground and then struck it down against the flagstones of the room, causing a thunderclap and invisible wave of energy that threw me six-feet in the air before blasting me backward.

"The woman inside me pities you. The god knows you have made your choice. Disappear in the light of the truth like the fog obliterated by the morning sun." Her final words, I could hear, cracked as she spoke.

But she still conjured a brilliant nimbus of light which filled the room, blotting out all but shapes. It burned my armor, body, and clothes like they were bacon on a skillet. I became less and less substantial, the spells and life-force keeping me anchored to this plane burning away.

Yet, I kept my sword raised and took a step forward. "Good and evil cannot exist without one another for the path to the former requires the choice to be the latter. For without the freedom to do wrong, good is but an empty shell. We must know temptation, wrath, and desire for these things make as much a part of life as their opposite. Sacrifice has no meaning if you have no choice but to give!"

Jassa's radiance continued to burn me.

Oh, the pain!

I was once stabbed in the leg, the wound becoming infected with no light mages in ten leagues. Big Tom Brown had poured a mess of flesh-eaters into the wound to eat the infected tissue and let their venom cleanse the insides of my leg. The agony of that day did not approach a tenth of what I was experiencing now.

"Your lies will not save you," Jassa said. "I must hold fast against the temptations you represent."

"I have seen the truth! Turn away!" I spoke, lifting my hand out. "You were—"

Regina came at Jassamine with her blade, the entrancement spell broken. Jassa was not an drawing room sorceress, however, and with a single step she spun around and blocked the blow which would have been her death before hurling Regina to the side.

Jassa's strength had been enhanced by her possession as well, throwing my companion aside like she was a child. "Your betrayal stings me, Jacob, but no so much as this will."

Jassa turned her staff toward me and intensified the blast. I was struck by a rainbow-like pattern of greens, blues, yellows, and reds which caused me to feel start burning away. I became like paper in the fire, vanishing from this world. I could hear the calling and screams of the Forsaken in the World Below, begging for pardon or lamenting their loss.

That was when Regina swung Starlight from the ground into the center of Jassa's staff, cutting it in two. The crystal ball on the top exploded as all the magical energy stored within was released at once. The room filled with yet more light but the explosion propelled her backwards and sent me crumbling to the ground.

My tattered robes were filled with holes, my armor half-gone, and my body once more reduced to a memory. I had no face, hands, or form. I was but a substance-less given shape by my clothes. I would not last long, even in Everfrost, against someone who possessed the full power of the Lawgiver.

But I had to die for a second time, it would be for those I cherished.

CHAPTER 35

Despite my situation, all hope was not lost. A wizard, even a Great Wizard, was drastically weakened without their object of power. The human body could only channel so much sorcery without an intermediary between them and the Worlds Above and Below. Tharadon had been one of the most powerful magicians alive and yet had died easily enough when a sword was stuck between his ribs.

I was committed now.

Jassa climbed to her feet and turned to Regina, who was already up and charging. Jassa knocked away Starlight from her hands with a cantrip, a simple spell even an apprentice wizard could do. Much to my surprise, rather than go for Starlight on the ground, Regina brought her fist against Jassa's face before delivering the Golden Sorceress an uppercut to the jaw. I wasn't sure whether I approved of her plan to deal with a demigod by punching her out, but I admired her courage.

Jassa, meanwhile, stretched out her palm and lifted Regina up by the throat with an invisible hand, which stretched forth from her body. I could see the energy forming from her aura. On her right hand, I saw a white gold ring, which I'd given her in lieu of a wedding band. She'd turned that into a backup object of power.

Stretching out, I felt all of the dark power buried into the masonry around me. Eldritch runes and blood sacrifices had been woven into each of Everfrost's stones. The power flowed into me and with it as my object of power, I unleashed a shadowy wave of darkness which I hoped would drive her away, but it only seemed to enrage her.

"Do you think you can drive back the light with the dark? The smallest candle can hold back all the darkness in the universe!" Jassa said, sounding genuinely *pissed* now. She started firing another blast of light at me, dropping Regina on the ground. My companion started wheezing, having been almost strangled to death.

"I know little of light and dark, only choice and consequence," I said, concentrating the shadowy power of this place into a blackened shield of living night. This device held back her terrible rays, albeit barely. Pressing forward, I came closer and closer to her. "Humans are made of light and dark, good and evil. If your perfection requires everything flawed in this world to be destroyed then I say you have exchanged a living world for a tomb!"

Jassa snarled and the shield shattered before I felt my connection to the Tower of Everforst shatter. "I see, now, what you represent, Kurag Shadowweaver. You are my final temptation, the sacrifice I must make to purify my soul and prove I am worthy to lead this world to salvation. Begone, foul spirit, and trouble the world no more."

The words she spoke next caused the entire tower to shake. She was speaking in the divine tongue, but calling upon magic I was unfamiliar with, a pure form of light magic which rivaled or surpassed true name magic.

Chill's Fury cracked as the power of the weapon leaked out in black wisps. Destroying the blade of Kurag on the battlefields of Winterholme allowed me to kill the Dark Lord and this spell was far greater than my own meager efforts. I had struck the sword with a spell powered by my love for Jassa. It was only fitting now she would strike me down with her love for the Lawgiver. Yet, as her hands were outstretched, she was vulnerable. I could pierce her heart with Chill's Fury and kill her. The power which flowed into me was almost gone but I had enough strength for one final act. It would end her life, save mine, and probably save the world.

But I still regretted it had come to this.

"Do not make me do this," I said, stepping forward.

Each movement was agonizing.

Like walking over glass on fire.

Yet I did not stop.

Jassa continued her spell, nearing the end of it by the loud shattering words which threatened to bring down the tower around me. Indeed, given the power of her spell, it was very likely she was about to destroy the whole of Everfrost. I lifted my blade up above her breast and then struck down.

Only for a barrier spell to knock away the attack.

Jassamine's look of betrayal was solely in her eyes.

But it was there.

And she continued her spell.

Nothing could stop her now.

That was when the entire room filled with darkness, causing Jassa to scream. Despite the room being pitch black, I could see as if it was noon. During all this, Serah, Curse, and Payne had gone for the Crown of Weeping Gods. With its curse weakened, the power of the Crown was now available to Serah and she channeled it through the room.

The crown smothered the light in the room, drowning it in an inky tenebrosity which was less an absence of light than some sort of opposite to it. It was the last remnant of the King Below's power in this world and while Regina was a messenger of the Lawgiver, the crown was a symbol of evil's triumph.

Or perhaps the freedom to choose.

Or both? The Trickster said.

"I, too, have been called deviant my entire life, *Saint!*" Serah spit out the last words. "Righteous men have spit upon me and priestesses have said I was damned for the way I was born. So be it, I want no part of your heaven! I would rather be part of a kingdom which wants me for who I am!" Serah said, focusing her vast skills through the Crown to oppose Jassamine.

They would not be enough.

It belonged to only one master.

Regina got up, though, ready to fight again despite it being hopeless. Curse and Payne were there to avenge their father while Serah stood ready to challenge the heavens. Each of them was willing to fight despite there being no hope, despite their foe being the God of Good who would consign them to the darkest pits for their crime. A place which I now imagined much better due to the quality of people the Lawgiver was turning away.

I would protect them.

I would protect them all.

Watching Jassa gather her strength to drive back the darkness, I could see murder in her eyes. "I shall cook the flesh from your bones and feed them to the hungry dead!"

"No, you shall not," I said, stretching out my hand and pulling the Crown of Weeping Shadows to my hands with a tentacle made of shadow.

I placed the crown upon my head.

"Arcus Maeharl "

It is done, the Trickster whispered. *At last.*

The dead god vanished as the King Below's ghost merged with

me and was obliterated, the two of us becoming one. In a single instant, I was connected to all of the people who had died in the King Below's service over the past ten ages. They were a strange mix of people to say the least. In addition to the killers, thieves, rapists, and monsters I expected to see, there were many others. I felt kinship to doubters, disbelievers, so-called deviants, those who followed different interpretations of the Lawgiver or other gods at all, the driven by desperation, the despairing, the ignorant, the questioning, and the weak. Anyone who could not follow the Path or simply did not want to was cast from the Lawgiver's bosom.

I accepted them all.

The World Below was remade.

Soon the World Between would be as well.

With the crown upon my head, my armor became a solid suit of rune-covered plate mail and the cloak around it was made of living shadows. I felt like a giant, my body now more solid and substantial than it had ever been while alive. Chill's Fury changed, too, becoming a curved long sword covered in true names for Darkness, Ice, Hope, and Redemption. The Crown of Weeping Gods changed into a simple, but intimidating helmet. All of the magical knowledge of the past two hundred years in the King Below's service was available to me.

I was the King Below.

I was Jacob Rivers.

I was everyone who would not kneel.

Jassa stopped in her next attack, a spell which would destroy the entire region with a volcano. "Jacob, *what have you done?*"

My next words were spoken with all the power I had behind me. I no longer feared fading away nor needed to vampirize the living to feed my strength, though I still hungered for the life-force in the living around me. "I have chosen to act. It is a better thing to do rather than predicate, even if the choice be momentous." I lifted Chill's Fury in the air and focused every bit of my power onto her, casting a geas with the few words of the Great Magic I knew. "*I command you to leave this place, harming none of my people, and to never return to the Eyes of the World. Begone, Jessamine False-Friend and know I am coming for your Nine. I choose the living over the dead, which includes our love.*"

I had chosen to set myself against the Lawgiver, the God of Good, and there was no indication I had any chance of success. I could spite his plan and mar his works, but the possibility of actually defeating him seemed remote, if not nonexistent.

So be it.

I could have killed her now, but visions of the future were now open to me. By striking her dead here, I would only make her a martyr. This was more than a warrior against Jassamine, profane and horrific as she'd made the Path. I would need to destroy her far more completely than striking her dead could. I needed to destroy what she believed in. Hearing her retreat before the new King Below would also weaken the confidence of the Seven remaining Usurpers. They had killed a previous King Below and I would need to defeat their spirits if I was to prevent an encore performance.

Besides, I knew Jassamine would flee before the killing blow.

She was not stupid.

How had I ever loved her? Or had I only been loving a shadow the entire time?

"You will regret this decision when you and all you love burn in a lake of fire," Jassa said, looking between us all. I could see her struggling against the compulsion which bound both the spirit and mortal within her frame.

"If I loved one being at the expense of..." I decided this conversation wasn't worth it and focused the remainder of my power. "*Leave!*"

The spell broke through Jassamine's defenses and bound her to obey. The Great Wizard might send an army to lay siege unto Everfrost, but she would never be able to step foot here herself. Swirling around her robes, they shifted and merged into her body. A snow-white owl appeared where she once stood and flew past Serah to the doors. Curse and Payne fired arrows while she departed, hoping to finish her.

They missed.

I took a deep breath, the air filling with the cold from my frozen lungs. I was now the Lord of Winter as well as Master of Evil. I had no idea if the original King Below was down in the depths of the World Below or if I was, somehow, him but the place of this world's tyrant king had been fully assumed by me. I was the leader of the Dark Lords, Shadow Races, heretics, traitors, and demons on this world.

I needed to get used to it.

I fell backwards, wishing for the first time I could have a throne to lounge in. Despite all of the immense power I wielded, it had barely been enough. That was the real trap of power in a way. No matter how much you wielded, it was never really enough. A man could spend his whole life accumulating power to change the world but would die before he ever achieved enough to accomplish half his dreams.

Or worse, gained it, and discovered not everyone shared his vision.

I wondered if that was what it was like to be a god.

I was about to find out.

Regina and Serah both came to my side while the daughters of Creature went to their father's remains. I could feel Creature inside me now, as if the old Formor had joined with a far greater being which I was but merely the first of. I hoped the World Below was not a terrible place for it seemed like many-many people were going there.

Regina removed my helmet and placed her hand to my face. "Are you—"

"I believe alright is a stupid question," Serah interrupted.

Regina stared at her. "*Must* you say such things?"

"Yes," Serah said. "I must."

"I am the new King Below," I said, staring at them. "I understand if this is a shock."

Serah laughed, uproariously. "After that? I think not. That is the first time one of my tormentors was ever sent fleeing. It seems I am a witch and friend of the dark after all but only after the light has turned to madness."

"I am at your side forever." Regina placed her hand on the side of my face. "I would make you my consort and be your queen. Whether that makes me the bride of the God of Evil or not, I care little."

Serah gave Regina a look then nodded. I couldn't read the subtleties of her expression, though.

"Let us speak of this more, but not now." I would love them both, if Gods of Evil could feel such an emotion, but now was not the time for our companions had lost their family.

Walking over to Curse and Payne, I looked between them. "I am sorry for your father."

Curse spoke first. "He died as a Formor warrior should, in defiance of the light."

Payne glanced up and down. "You are the King Below?"

"Yes."

Payne stared up at me. "We will take up the rulership of Frostiron tribe. If you stand against the Lawgiver and his works, you will have our weapons and blood. We are weakened by the war, though, and it will be many years before we are full strength again. You will need to do many great deeds and show your strength often to convince the others to join."

"I would have you teach me your ways so I can aid you best and rule justly. Just understand we're all going to be changing the ensuing months."

"So be it," Curse said. "I am yours."

"My master," Payne said, bowing her head.

"Payne, Curse, take care of your father's remains in the manner of your people."

They muttered something in Demonspeak and carried his remains away. It was a private ceremony, the Formor rites of the dead, or I

would have joined them. I had not known Creature long but he had proven himself a worthy being.

But it left me time to make a decision of how I would live my life from this moment. I walked over to Regina's side and placed a kiss upon her lips, my ice-cold lips warm against hers. The King Below's magic protected her against the darkness within me and made it a pleasant sensation for her.

"I would have you with me," I said, no matter the cost. I did not know if I loved Regina, but she had shown me a flame in the night and I wanted to hold onto it for as long as possible. "As my bride, lover, companion, consort, and equal."

Serah looked stricken, but accepted it with a nod of her head.

She didn't need to.

"I know not where the Path will lead us but it seems it takes us against the one who laid its brickwork. If so, then so be it," Regina said, smiling. "You are a true knight and king. Even if it of the lost and forsaken."

"I wish you the best," Serah said. "I—"

I could feel her heartbreak.

Which would not stand.

I turned to her, holding Regina's hands in mine. I prayed I had read her correctly or this would turn from the beginnings of a new day to a horribly embarrassing fiasco. "Whatever *we* become, I am ever yours too. You are a beautiful red rose in a sea of thorny whites."

Serah blinked. "And you, Regina?"

Regina smiled, unsurprised by my choice. "I pledged my heart to Gewain, but I am not so burdened by the past I cannot look beyond convention to see I have two wonderful paramours awaiting me. Accept my love and I will accept yours, from here until eternity."

"A demon god and a witch," Serah said, smiling.

"No one is perfect," Regina said.

"Whatever we do, from this day forward, it will be together,"

I said, offering my hand to Serah.

"I agree," Regina said, offering hers as well.

Serah took them both. "I would be honored."

"Be our moon," I said. "I would not have you as my subordinates but as my equals. My power is yours as my love."

Serah's next words were smooth like silk. "I would be a fool to turn down such a lucrative offer."

"Good. There is much to be done. We have a world to conquer."

ABOUT THE AUTHOR

C.T. Phipps is a lifelong student of horror, science fiction, and fantasy. An avid tabletop gamer, he discovered this passion led him to write and turned him into a lifelong geek. He is the author of The Supervillainy Saga and Red Room series. C.T. lives in Ashland, KY with his wife and their four dogs.

You can find out more about him and his work by reading his blog, The United Federation of Charles: unitedfederationofcharles.blogspot.com